CHRONICLES OF THE HUMAN SPHERE

AIRAGHARDT

JOHN LEIBEE

**INFINITY
UNIVERSE**

Airaghardt by John Leibee
Cover courtesy of Florian Stitz
Line drawings by Tommaso Dall'Osto
For more on Tommaso, see TommasoDall'Osto@tdosto
Scottish Gaelic translation by https://www.akerbeltz.com

This edition published in 2023
Airaghardt is published under license with Corvus Belli SL

Winged Hussar is an imprint of
Winged Hussar Publishing, LLC
1525 Hulse Rd, Unit 1
Point Pleasant, NJ 08742

Copyright Corvus Belli SL
ISBN 978-1-958872-376
ISBN 978-1-958872-383
LCN 2023949835

Bibliographical References and Index
1. Science Fiction, 2 Infinity, 3. Space Opera

Winged Hussar Publishing, LLC All rights reserved
For more information, visit us at
www.wingedhussarpublishing.com
Twitter: WingHusPubLLC
Facebook: Winged Hussar Publishing LLC

To Ben and Selina, who graciously shared their time and experience in the armed service to give my prose verisimilitude.

For Shellie, and Ben, and Madason, who had the gall to believe in me so much I started believing in myself.

To all my family in Arizona Infinity, for kicking my ass enough to write a story about what happens to the models who survive getting tabled.

For every player anywhere who's needed a 19 to throw smoke, and rolled two 20s back-to-back—
This one's for us.

GLOSSARY

3rd Highlander Grey Rifles – A Scottish infantry unit that traces its history back to Waterloo. Specialists in assault operations.

AKNovy – The most common firearm brand on Ariadna. Reliable under severe conditions.

ALEPH – Benevolent AI that controls all facets of PanOceanian culture.

Acheron Blockade – A naval blockade guarding the Acheron Gate, a wormhole that leads to Combined Army-controlled space.

Aquila – A continent on Neoterra, home to the Aquila Officer's Academy that produces Aquila Guards.

AR – Augmented Reality

Arachne – The Nomads' answer to Maya. Pirate internet independent of ALEPH.

Ariadna – The coalition of nations made up of the Ariadna's crew left stranded on Dawn: Caledonia (UK), Tartary (Russia), Merovingia (France), and the United States of Ariadna (USA).

Ariadna Exclusion Zone – Sections of Dawn closed to non-natives. Wild, dangerous frontiers.

Aristeia! – The premier bloodsport of the Human Sphere. A modern-day gladiatorial arena.

Atek – an a-technological person who exists outside the system, often in poverty.

AUV – Ariadnan Utility Vehicle

Baba/Yaga – A long-lasting fever-inducing euphoric blended with a fungal entheogen.

Balena – A luxury-class low-orbit transport.

Bio-Technical Shielding – CBRN (chemical, biological, radiological, or nuclear) shielding; reinforced by neomaterial armor, medical technology, or Voodoo-Tech.

Biografting – Body-part replacement, i.e., organs or limbs. Common and inexpensive, cloned specifically for the recipient.

Blackjack – 10th Heavy Rangers Battalion, infamous for their calling card (a literal Ace of Spades) and for their extremely heavy Buffalo servopowered armor.

Bourak – The central planet of the nation of Haqqislam. Where Silk is produced.

Breaker – Nanotechnological ammunition.

Bulleteer – A PanOceanian remote, often found equipped with a shotgun or Spitfire.

Bureau Gaea – O-12 Bureau in charge of planetary development and biological research.

Bureau Ganesh – O-12 Bureau overseeing international trade.

Cailleach – A fortress city topped with a lighthouse. Known for its cattle and military presence.

Caledonian Gaelic – A pidgin of Gaelic, Irish, Welsh, Dutch and English spoken by the Caledonian Highlanders.

Capa Blanca – A PanOceanian holding in the archipelagos east of Ariadna.

Carbonite – *Hacking*. A program that locks servos and shuts down mobility in remotes and armored infantry.

CasEvac – Casualty Evacuation

CHA – Caledonian Highlander Army

Chain-colt – A compact, pistol-sized chain rifle.

Chain Rifle – A firearm that superheats and detonates a length of chain as its primary ammunition. Devastating at short range.

Charlie Mike – 'Continue Mission' in NATO Alphabet slang.

CineticS – The firearm brand of choice for the PanOceanian military-industrial complex.

Cú Chulainn – Folklore. The legendary hero of the Ulster Cycle.

Cù-sìth – Folklore. A fairy dog. Any who hear their bark three times dies of terror.

Circular – Massive, train-like ships that enable casual and accessible interstellar travel.

Combi Rifle – Lightweight, ubiquitous firearm found in every corner of the Human Sphere.

Commercial Conflicts – A years-long proxy war fought on Dawn between corporate mercenaries and the locals.

Concilium Convention – Rules of engagement officially upheld by O-12 and unofficially ignored by almost every faction.

Concilium Prima – The planet at the center of the Human Sphere. The seat of O-12's power.

Corregidor – One of the three Nomad motherships. Originally a cryogenic prison ship. Now the inmates run the asylum.

CrazyKoala – A small remote in the shape of a cute koala that hugs its victim before exploding.

Cuando Me Muera – *Spanish*. 'When I'm dead.'

Cube – A small device placed at the base of the spine. Records every detail of a person's life, including their DNA, enabling their resurrection after death.

Datasphere – A shared network of coordinated data and user experiences.

DFAC – Dining Facility (pronounced 'dee-fack')

Dog-Bowl – Football with Dog-Warriors.

Twice as violent, twice as popular.

Dog-Warrior – Human/Antipode hybrid. Transforms into a bloodthirsty werewolf if you piss them off.

Dog Whensday – The mythical day when Dogfaces rise up and take equality by force.

Domotic – Automated processes in the environment, such as automatically vacuuming carpets, self-washing dishes, or objects that announce their location when queried.

Dozer – The Ariadnan Corps of Engineers.

DRC – Dawn Research Commission (pronounced 'dark').

Druze – Usually referring to the Shock Team, a particularly bloodthirsty mercenary company.

Dullahan – Folklore. The headless horseman. An omen of death.

Dumb Mode – Without a network connection, the vast majority of any equipment's features cannot be accessed. What can be is referred to as 'dumb mode' and highly disadvantageous.

EC – Einstein Chronometer. An AI-mitigated timekeeping standard designed for interstellar civilization. Nicknamed 'easy time.'

E/M – Electromagnetic Ammunition

Evolved Intelligence – The ruthless AI that commands the Combined Army.

Feuerbach – A quick-loading heavy support anti-tank weapon. Means 'river of fire' in German.

Foreign Company – A private security consultancy company famous for their Soldiers of Fortune team comprised of Aristeia! stars.

Full Moon's Dead – Quantronic trash-metal.

G-5 – The five major powers given seats on the O-12 security council: PanOceania, Yu Jing, Haqqislam, the Nomad Nation, and Ariadna.

Hassassin – A branch of Haqqislamite military intelligence. Rumored to harbor an order of assassins.

Haqqislam – A faction characterized by the

neo-Muslim renaissance.

Helios – The central star in the planetary system that Dawn belongs to.

Human Edge – The edge of human-inhabited space.

Human Sphere – The totality of human-inhabited space.

IFF – Identification Friend or Foe

Ikari Company – An immoral but pragmatic mercenary company of JSA and Yu-jingyu expats known for suppressing worker strikes.

International Standard Code – A universal list of callsigns and nicknames for each branch or unit of the military.

Karnapur – A PanOceanian city on Paradiso threatened by the Second Offensive and overrun by the Third.

Ken – *Scottish English.* "To know, have knowledge about, or be acquainted with a person or thing."

Kinematika – Tactical combat relocation techniques characterized by bursts of movement.

Kosmoflot – A branch of the Ariadnan Army that primarily deals with interstellar conflict.

Krug – The celebratory occasion when all three Nomad motherships meet at the same place and time.

Kuang-Shi – A political prisoner brainwashed by the StateEmpire and strapped with explosives.

Kurage Crisis – The conflict resulting from the Uprising on Novyy Cimmeria, fought between PanOceania and Yu Jing.

Lens – Technological contact lenses that allow interaction with the local datasphere and AR.

LAI – Limited Artificial Intelligence. A non-self aware artificial intelligence used for daily tasks. All AI must be limited due to the Sole AI Law passed after ALEPH's creation.

Lhost – Living Host. An improved clone body used for resurrection or to prolong life.

MULTI – A prefix indicating that a firearm is technologically capable of housing and firing a variety of special ammunition fabricated on trigger pull. Expensive and difficult to maintain.

Machinist – A PanOceanian engineer.

MagnaObra – PanOceania's largest mining company

Mariannebourg – The capital of Merovingia

Maya – The internet, maintained and curated by ALEPH. Ubiquitous and inescapable.

MediKit – A handgun-sized medical device capable of nano-injection. Less modern versions deliver treatment via hypospray.

Military Orders – PanOceanian heavy infantry styled in the trappings of an old-world Christian religious society of knights.

Mimesis – Passive camouflage, whether through movement technique or natural mimicry.

Miyamoto Musashi – *Recreation.* Legendary swordsman and Aristeia! fighter.

Molotok – Russian for 'hammer.' A light machine gun of compact design used for urban warfare.

Moto.tronica – The tech company responsible for PanOceania's remotes, TAGs, and transportation.

MSV – Multispectral Visor

Myrmidon Wars – A children's cartoon glorifying ALEPH's Assault Sub-Section's battles on Paradiso.

NC – New Calendar. Designed for ease of use when moving between planets with different day-night cycles or yearly cycles.

NCA – Neoterran Capitaline Army

NeoVatican – The seat of power for the Catholic Church on Neoterra.

Neoterra – The Jewel of the Human Sphere, home to PanOceania's capital city.

Nitrocaine – An illegal Silk derivative

that bonds with the user's synapses, creating a high that can be controlled via geist interface. Addictive.

Nomad Nations – A conglomeration of the citizens of the three largest Nomad ships: The *Corregidor*, the *Bakunin*, and the *Tunguska*.

Novyy Cimmeria – An island off the coast of Ariadna in hot contention between Yu Jing, PanOceania, and the Combined Army. The location of the Kurage Crisis in the aftermath of the Uprising.

O-12 – An international representational governing body evolved from the UN.

Oblivion – *Hacking*. A program that forces all of its victims equipment into 'dumb mode.'

Oceana – PanOceanian currency.

ODD – Optical Disruption Device

PanOceania – The Hyperpower. The largest faction in the G-5 nations.

Paradiso – An embattled planet riddled with conflict between the G-5 and the Combined Army.

Posthuman – Human consciousnesses in cyberspace that can download into artificial bodies. The next evolutionary stage of humanity.

Pound – Caledonian currency.

Quantronic Revolution – The discovery of neomaterials (such as Teseum) that enabled the creation of nanobots, ushering in a post-scarcity economy.

Recreation – A modern approximation of a historical figure created by ALEPH, i.e., Joan of Arc.

Red Fury – A standard team rifle designed to withstand rapid, sustained fire.

Repeater – A military-grade device that expands the signal of hacking devices.

Resurrection – The placement of a Cube into an artificial Lhost body. Prohibitively expensive.

Rodina – The Russian nation of Ariadna. Home to the original seed ship *Ariad-*

na and its capitol, Матр.

San Pietro di Neoterra – The political center of Neoterra and seat of the NeoVatican.

Scáthach – Folklore. Legendary warrior and teacher of Cú Chulainn.

Scots Guards – A unit of Caledonian soldiers unaffiliated by clan whose origins stretch to 1642.

SecDet – Security Detachment

Second Resurrection – The events revolving around Joan of Arc's death defending the fortress of Strelsau on Paradiso, and her subsequent return.

Sensaseries – Serialized entertainment experienced in first-person via Augmented Reality.

Separatist Wars – The short-lived attempt by the Ariadnan Nations to secede from under Rodina's control.

Serum – Medical fluid flush with reconstructive surgical nanobots.

Shona Carano – An Aristeia! Bahadur famous for her swordwork.

Sierra Hotel – NATO Alphabet slang. 'Shit hot,' or impressive. The inverse, Hotel Sierra, indicates the opposite.

Silk – A miracle substance that enables interaction with human cells on an individual, microscopic level, enabling the technologies of cloning and resurrection.

Sin Eater – A male member of the Observance of Saint Mary of the Knife, Our Lady of Mercy. Historically not treated well.

Skara Brae – A city on the border between Rodina and Caledonia where the brunt of the Third Antipode Offensive was fought.

Snake Eaters – A nickname for members of the Varuna Immediate Reaction Division.

Spawn-embryo – An egg carried by most Shasvastii on the battlefield containing their own clone, created through parthenogenesis.

Spitfire – A light machine gun.

Spotlight – Hacking. A program that broadcasts location and assists incoming fire on its unfortunate victim.

SSS – ALEPH's Special Situations Section. Dedicated to stomping out illegal nascent artificial intelligences.

StarCo – The Free Company of the Star. An altruistic mercenary company (or so they say).

StateEmpire – The central governmental body of Yu Jing, so inseparable as to be synonymous.

Stavka – The Ariadnan Intelligence Department, working closely with all four Ariadnan nations.

Steindrage – A draconic megabeast that occupies Teseum-rich Khurland.

Submondo – 'Underworld' in Esperanto. A catch-all term for the pervasive criminal element of the Human Sphere.

Sukeul – A type of Tohaa commando.

Svalarheima – A perpetually snowed-over ice planet, controlled in parts by PanOceania and the StateEmpire.

SymbioMate – An empathic alien parasite, most often used as a bullet sponge by the Tohaa.

T2 – Ammunition jacketed in reinforced Teseum that splinters into monomolecular fragments on impact. Infamously lethal.

TAG – Tactical Armored Gear

Tanit – The primary moon of Dawn. A mining colony. Not a safe place for solo travelers.

Techno-favela – Where Ateks live, cut off from AR and Mayanet. The poorest of the poor districts.

Teseum – Monomolecular neomaterial that enabled the Quantronic Revolution.

TO Camo – Thermo-Optical Camouflage

Tohaa – A secretive alien race opposed to the Combined Army.

Tubarão – Spanish for Shark. A light assault transport used by the PanOceanian military on Paradiso.

Überfallkommando – A Nomad undercover Sport Crimes field unit that undergoes radical body alterations to infiltrate illegal Aristeia! circuits.

Ulveslør – The Svalarheima location of a secret PanOceanian research and development laboratory.

Umbra Samaritan – An extremely dangerous, classified alien operative serving in the Combined Army.

Universal Teseum Cradle – Universal assemblers. Capable of printing objects and materials wholesale from nothing via nanotechnology.

Uprising – The tumultuous events that led to the Japanese Sectorial Alliance separating from the StateEmpire, becoming the Japanese Secessionist Army.

USARF – United States of Ariadna Ranger Force

Viral – Ammunition coated with viral agents or biodesigned nanodevices. Particularly effective against Dogfaces.

William Wallace – *Recreation*. Defected from ALEPH to join Ariadna.

WarCor – War Correspondent. A war journalist.

Wardriver – A mercenary hacker.

Woobie – A poncho liner, nicknamed after a baby's security blanket.

Wotan – The events surrounding a failed Shasvastii infiltration through the Wotan Jump Gate connecting Paradiso with Svalarheima.

Xanadu Station – A Nomad space station kept in orbit around Dawn.

Yuan Yuans – Space pirates often found in the employ of various unscrupulous mercenary companies.

JOHN LEIBEE

CHRONICLES OF THE HUMAN SPHERE

AIRAGHARDT

**INFINITY
UNIVERSE**

Noise. Pain. Heat.

Harness straps vised Wilhelm Gotzinger's powered combat armor's joints. Debris washed across his faceplate. Gauntleted fingers squeezed divots into both armrests, deforming the steel like clay. Information read-outs flickered across his heads-up display, projected on quantronic lenses: 195 km/h. 15-degree angle of descent. 3,650 meter elevation and falling fast.

A missile—they'd been struck by a missile.

Smoke clawed into the Balena through the gaping hole in its side. The multispectral visor he wore cut past the billow, painting the transport's interior in burning golden lines. Across the cabin interior, Rajan tangled in his seat straps. Limbs awkwardly folded by the centrifugal force, he jostled without resistance. Unconscious.

Beside him, an empty chair. The diplomatic aide, Rajan's assistant, had vanished. Wind screamed against the blown cabin doors, and her unfastened seat-belt flapped between the armrests. No trace of her presence remained.

Wil wedged himself into his seat and tensed his legs until his bones bowed. Anything to keep blood in his brain where it belonged.

The alarms blaring from the cockpit and the desperate grinding in the port nacelle died at the same time. Total silence, save for wind cut with the doppler chop of loose maglev and his own pitched breathing against the inside of his helmet. Shards of polysteel and glass hissed along the floor as the Balena's nose pitched down, pattering against his boots.

Shadows careened past. Daylight flickered in the windows, erratic. Branches scraped the hull. The winglet of the Balena bashed into something and rebounded, juddering his ribs, his neck, his collar. Another collision. Something splashed across his chest. Not water. Needles, from a fir tree, or whatever passed for a fir on this godforsaken—

The Balena struck ground.

Skipped.

His seat danced wild. Bolts came loose. Another shock, and the harness snapped.

Wil speared into the ceiling head-first. Ribs crushed. Head torqued. A jerk, a snap, and an urgent cold followed after—numbing agents, auto-injected from his armor. Artificial muscle ripped along the surface of his neck. No chance to flinch, to embrace the hurt. Shards of the overhead light coated the sleeves of his duster.

Going back down wasn't half as pleasant. Neither was the second time up.

On the third drop, a thrum raced along the soles of his feet. Red flicked to green in the corner of his HUD, and on next impact, his boots clamped down on the flooring and fixed him in place. Magnetic anchors, intended for zero-g conflict in deep-space Circulars. Before he could consider thanking the Knights of Santiago for making them standard-issue on an ORC, a loose chair rebounded off his face and sucked out the open cabin doors.

The transport skidded, jumped. The sky spun. His stomach sucked into his throat, then vice-versa. Polysteel fuselage crunched and tore overhead, underfoot, all around him. Sunlight lanced past the holes in the Balena's exterior, darkened, lit again.

The roll slowed.

Stopped.

Arms dangling, Wil hung from the floor. His duster's hem brushed the other contents of the churned Balena interior puddled two meters beyond his fingertips. Steel. Plastic. Glass. Everything sharpened to daggers save for some oxygen masks.

Pain. Lots of pain, along his jaw, his shoulders, behind his ears. Freezing anti-kinetic fluid oozed along his collar, dripping into the mess below. If the reserve in his gorget had burst, it meant he'd only narrowly avoided breaking his neck.

The cabin doors were long gone, lost far behind where the transport had turned into a crayon on the rocks. Outside, boreal wilderness stretched out in all directions, surrounding the dry, rocky riverbed they'd landed in, like something out of a holo-ad for scented candles. A carpet of vibrant moss coated bark and stone alike, and it was very quiet.

Too quiet. Loose wiring sparked silently in his peripheral vision. Debris shifted without sound. Wil tapped his breastplate. Nothing. His sensors must've short-circuited, lost audio outside his armor. Examining his helmet by feel, he found both of his radial antennae wrenched out of shape, the right dangling by a single stubborn bolt.

Wil queried his geist to open his faceplate. Servos whirred loud above his cheekbones, and it didn't move. That they made sound at all meant they'd been compromised. Desperate to listen and fearing fire, he reached for his helmet's manual release. Something too blurred to read in his HUD switched color, and the thrum in his boots went quiet.

The ceiling rushed up to meet him. The cushioning of his armor's interior wasn't enough to soften its full weight crushing atop him. His shoulder bore the brunt, folding inward. More pain. Immediate. Severe. Sprawled atop the debris pile, Wil weathered the sprain until his armor recognized the injury and replaced it with fresh, cold numbness.

Painkillers made his head spin. He coughed. "Fuck."

Breathing through the fresh pain, he took firm hold of his helmet's release and pulled. As the bodysleeve of artificial muscle around his throat slacked, the world came alive. Above him, the mangled engine chattered. The cabin roof groaned, struggling to bear the weight of its floor. Inside the paneling, electronics sizzled and popped. A low wind rattled the pines, whistling the myriad wounds in the Balena's hull.

The smell came next, the sickening tang of metal-on-metal churning inside an earthy stench he hadn't breathed since their withdrawal from Karnapur. Nothing like Maya sensaseries, or the chlorine-washed alleys of King's Den, or the proving grounds in the Aquilan outback flush with greasewood and pittosporum.

Wet. Alive. Untamed.

Dawn.

Wil fumbled his duster off his face and rolled to his knees. He tried to stand, but the servos in his greaves whined, impotent. Blown. Any amount of movement meant deadlifting a hundred kilos of ORC Combat Armor. Wasn't as if he had a choice. He groped above for a handhold to haul him to his feet and touched something soft.

Rajan. Blank-faced and swaying. Unconscious, but breathing. His vitals blipped in the lens of Wil's left eye, edging toward critical. Brushing the young commercial attaché's suit jacket aside, Wil saw why. A small hole punched into Rajan's charcoal-matte designer vest, no larger than his thumb. Blood dripped along the embroidery, riding the threads to soak in his beard.

His geist scanned the injury: a long, tapered piece of the transport's hull had pierced Rajan's ribs and stuck snarled in his diaphragm. Move the injury by centimeters, and it would've grazed through the meat of his flank. The other way, center mass, instant death.

Unlucky.

He shoved aside the insults from the heliport and worked to untangle Rajan. The job outweighed his personal feelings. He just hoped that when someone reviewed his lens footage later, they'd consider his hesitation shock and not deliberation.

The partition window to the cockpit had cracked but hadn't left its frame. In the midst of undoing a buckle, Wil craned his neck to see through the shatter to the other side. The pilot's seat was missing. Through the empty windshield, beyond the Balena's nose, a smear of red terminated in an upended chair. Tilted onto its face upon the rocks, two legs stuck out from beneath it—or what was left of them.

Beside the gap, Keyes swayed upside-down in the co-pilot's seat, his chest a pincushion for all the shrapnel Rajan hadn't caught. Blood drooled up his face without a heartbeat to propel it, mouth gaped in a perpetual scream.

The metal-on-metal stench intensified. Fire. Getting away from the explosion hazard seemed a smart first step. The second was finding a place to hide.

Whoever had put a missile into their transport didn't do it because they'd wanted to take prisoners.

Harness undone, Wil drew Rajan across his aching shoulders like a sand-bag. No time to favor a side or keep a gentle hand. Limp by limp, Wil distanced himself from the dying Balena, wobbling on the uneven riverbed stones.

Wil spun up his comlog dial from his wrist-mounted unit, feed painting across his contact lenses with his helmet disconnected. He scanned for secure channels. Nothing but snow. A distress call sent direct to the comms array back at the DRC-9 failed, and again a second time. Jammed? Hacked? No way to tell, but—

Ten meters from the crash, Wil fell. He struggled up and made it another three before he hit the dirt again. Branches slithered overhead, blurred leaves soaking up the rays of Dawn's alien sun. The way they moved put the taste of paper on his tongue.

A concussion. The anti-kinetic gel hadn't soaked the full impact.

Soft staccato beeps signaled the arrival of undesignated targets. Hostiles? Friends of their ambusher, no doubt. No clue how they'd closed on them so fast across the mountain terrain or what they were armed with. Red lines on his lenses traced movement vectors through the overgrowth. Shifting, blinking. Focusing on the visual feed churned Wil's stomach and threatened to bring up the morning's sour coffee.

He struggled to his full height and groped for his MULTI Marksman Rifle. Gone.

With a weak double-tap, Wil queried his geist for it, expecting its outline to highlight within his lens's field of view. Nothing. Some small hope urged him to scan the crash site, praying to find it lying atop a rock under a sunbeam or something.

He didn't. It wasn't.

Maybe he should've joined the Military Orders, after all. At least then he'd have a goddamn sword.

Wil drew back his trench coat and unlimbered his pistol. Sixteen rounds of more than enough for anything he'd ever seen on the battlefield, save for that time with the Kriza Borac—or the two Sù-Jiàn—or that gaggle of fucking Yuan Yuans—

Metal scraped metal. A massive lupine shape ambled atop the crumpled Balena. White fur. Bared fangs, broad and sharp. In its curled claws, a primitive knife, wide and long as a human leg. Its silvery sheen caught the light as it drew to a two-legged stand and growled.

An Antipode.

Beneath the multiplying alerts of incoming hostiles, a notification flashed in Wil's peripheral vision. It was one he'd only seen once, back when he'd first requisitioned his armor, before he'd been taught how to plug tertiary systems into the ORC's onboard battery. Something his instructor on Aquila had promised that the Hyperpower's bottomless war chest would never let them see.

Low Power.
In the corner of his vision, movement.
A blitz from the side.
Just before his visor died, Wil raised his pistol and opened fire blind.

1

ONE DAY AGO…

Joan of Arc extended her gauntleted hand, smiling like the Mona Lisa.

Wil dismissed the advertisement.

The hologram froze and flickered away, receding into the display underneath. There, clad in power armor, Joan sheltered a trio of children in her fortified embrace. A beatific halo shined from behind her braided blonde hair, and a sword weighted her hip. Knights of the PanOceanian Military Orders always carried swords, and their de facto leader was no exception.

Text scrawled below, floating in mid-air: SUPPORT THE NEOTERRAN INTEGRATION FUND! THE HYPERPOWER UPLIFTS ALL CITIZENS EQUALLY! And below the loglines: TRUST ALEPH. ALEPH IS YOUR FRIEND.

The jury was still out on that one.

On a more civilized planet where MayaNet was abundant, skipping an advert might've triggered any number of competing ads to take up the free space on his lens instead. But the MayaNet signal at the DRC-9 was unusable at its best, and one loading wheel spun into another before his geist dropped signal and dimmed.

The expansive hallway windows gave a vantage point over the Dawn Research Commission, and he scanned it from above. Personal dormitories and scientific research labs lined the forested mountainside, interconnected by a network of narrow switchbacks and elevated walkways that overlooked the still, dark expanse of Loch Eil trailing over the horizon far below. Sparse, boreal wilderness crawled along the loch's rocky shores and blanketed the bordering mountains in resilient greenery. Above, where the clouds met stone—snow.

And if not for Wil's multispectral visor, that incredible panorama would've ended a meter from the glass in an impenetrable wall of fog. Myriad feeds on multiple spectrums supplied the foundation for his geist to make a digital best-guess, compositing shared photographs, surveillance data, and algorithmic assumption into something more poignant than flat gray.

Not quite real, but real enough.

The peripheral of his visor indicated incoming movement, ten o'clock. Wil scanned the lobby, his geist already estimating the height and weight of the two unknowns ascending the staircase from the third floor. Male. Large. The Dawn Research Commission insignia glowed atop their security vests, projected in AR. Not soldiers, or SWORDFOR Kappa, but corporate security. CSUs.

Their social clouds were open and easily skimmable: The tall one was Fontaine; the shorter, Ghent. Both wore mirrored shades, sported crew cuts, and followed military-adjacent meme-tags chock full of guns, glitz, and glory.

And if they were allowed to carry anything but stun pistols and telescoping batons, they would've been half as threatening as they thought they were.

Fontaine squared with him like the armor was an open invitation for posturing. "Hey, big guy. You the new secretary? Where's Melantha?"

Wil nodded to the door to the executive suite behind him. "She's inside, with Counselor Odune," he said, voice turned deeper by his helmet's vox. "If you've got an appointment, you'll have to wait."

Ghent hooked his fat thumbs in the armpits of his security vest. Unlike his friend, he seemed worried, almost reticent. "About how long?"

"Didn't ask."

"Be a good lad and knock for us," Fontaine said. "Won't be a minute."

"Take a seat," Wil said. He dropped his hands to his side, closer to where his pistol magnetized to his hip. "Wait your turn."

Fontaine's smile wavered. "Real helpful."

"I aim to please."

Ghent pulled on Fontaine's shoulder, and they made for the seats across the lobby, shooting glances over their uniformed shoulders. Halfway there and five meters away, words clicked into place along the bottom of Wil's field of vision.

[FONTAINE, PETER]: WHERE DOES HE THINK HE IS, THE Öberhaus? WHAT A PRICK.

Odune's fourth-story admin building lobby wasn't the seat of the G-5 on Concilium, true, and maybe full arms and armor was a bit much. But it hadn't been his choice—Wil had dressed to Rajan's expectation, no more, no less.

The vacuum-tight suit of artificial muscle and fiberweave underlaid beneath the plating of his ORC Combat Armor bulked his silhouette from six-foot-four to Not to Be Fucked With, and the calf-length duster he wore over it bore battle scars from six different systems—particulate ammo, explosive rounds, plasma bursts, worse.

The MULTI Marksman Rifle he carried was a SG-A2 Schärfe II, top of the line, interlinked to his visor and armor via his geist. With his multispectral visor overlaid on his four-eyed helmet, its gaze sharpened into something predatory, like the eagle of his old unit's namesake: The Aquila Guard.

The crème de la crème of PanOceanian officers, masters of tactical acumen and wartime strategy. Leaders. Warriors. Their motto: *In Omnibus Princeps*. First in All Things. When an Aquila Guard put boots on the ground, it was usually the first sign the tide was about to turn in PanOceania's favor.

He'd been one, once. Not anymore.

In truth, the visor was on loan; the duster, a keepsake; his MSV, privately acquired. Probably shouldn't have put it on, but Rajan insisted—apparently, being escorted by an Aquila Guard was better optics and 'venned with his halo' more than the Orc Trooper Wil officially was, and for a man like Rajan, aesthetics always trumped practicality.

The two CSUs fell into the minimalist square couches, gesturing to their geists on their private haloes. With two flicks of their wrists, their ruddy, mirror-shaded faces blurred, words replaced by unintelligible electronic scratching. Their clouds derezzed, leaving only a few scant legally required identification codes visible in the empty nothingness of their social media.

They'd blacklisted him.

But the closed captions on the bottom of Wil's vision kept translating their conversation. [GHENT, HESSEL]: I WAS HOPING WE WOULDN'T HAVE TO SEE THAT COWARD HERE.

Though Wil was blocked, his multispectral array wasn't. Its onboard geist read the breath cadence and movement of the lips and larynx of those within his field of vision, supplying his comlog with enough data to extrapolate the faintest whispers into intelligible subtitles.

He could've raised a privacy screen. Been discreet. But while on security detail, Wil didn't have the luxury to drop his guard for privacy's sake, and he'd just been informed he was a cowardly prick otherwise.

Face artifacted into a pixelated mask, Fontaine sighed. "Don't tell me that's him."

"In all the disappointing person," Ghent said. "Wilhelm Gotzinger III, worst Guardsman in the history of the unit."

"I thought Aquila were s'posed to be good," Fontaine said.

Ghent chortled. "Not this one."

"Then what's he still doing in uniform? Didn't he get court-martialed or something?"

"Should count his lucky stars, then. Back in the old days, deserters got executed, mark my words."

Fontaine's heart rate must've jumped; Wil's geist pinged the pistol on his hip. "You saw the footage, right? Fourteen effing people."

"Fourteen effin' people," Ghent echoed. "Doesn't matter how many Shasvastii he's killed, get me alone in a room with him and I'll make him wish he died back on Svalarheima."

Fontaine pounded his fist on the table, posturing. Ghent escalated to casual death-threats. Wil comfortably tuned them out.

The Shasvastii Expeditionary Army. Tall, gangly slug-skinned aliens infamous for their guerilla fighters and nightmarish saboteurs, dead-set on clearing a path for the Combined Army and its leader, the Evolved Intelligence, to put an end to free will in the galaxy.

Despite Fontaine's assumptions, Wil hadn't ever killed a Shas. Just two of their Q-Drones. Never even seen a live one, at least not close enough to look them in the eyes. All he remembered of that day was plasma flares, frost smoke, and fleeting shadows.

Ads for Eco Cars, reruns of the Myrmidon Wars, and The Go-Go Marlene! Show, ONLY ON OXYD! played in sequential order on the holo-ad's surface until Joan returned, arm pleadingly outstretched. "The Shield of Skovorodino safeguards—"

"Sure," Wil said and dismissed her for the fiftieth time.

The office door sighed open, and Rajan and Counselor Odune sauntered out, followed by their respective assistants. Their social media halos floated after, bombarding Wil's datasphere with high-res images of space-station charity galas, crystal-clear Varuna beachfronts, and eccentric Concilium fashion shows.

Wil jumped to attention, returning to the SecDet routine ingrained in him on Aquila. He scanned for hostiles on three different spectrums, squaring his body to shield his charge, painstakingly aware of every minute notification that skimmed past his lens.

Rajan snapped his fingers twice. "Oi, Gotzinger! Stop spacing out. Come over here and say hi."

Despite Wil's suggestion to come prepared for the rugged terrain, Rajan had insisted on dress shoes and a suit. After ten minutes planetside, both were tinged brown at the fringes from mud. A domotic shimmered the embroidered orchids on his undershirt with pink and blue light, and his eyes swam with technicolor mandalas, garish even for cosmopolitan Neoterra. Not real. Geist-assisted programs, only visible in AR. But Rajan enjoyed those kinds of things—they distracted from his medium height, the one thing he couldn't biosculpt without spending a fortune for a custom Lhost.

Standing beside him was Administrative Counselor Xandros Odune, the official liaison to O-12 for the DRC-9 Dun Scaith. He was bigger than the photographs suggested, as tall as Wil in his armor but much, much thinner. His nose was blunt, and a snowy pallor lined the edges of his dark, clean-cut hair and beard. Compared to Rajan, the simple ivory-white three-piece suit he wore nearly glowed, woven with self-cleaning fabric that kept the color bright.

Odune flashed a hollow smile, and the two of them traded double-taps on their extended forearms. "Captain Gotzinger, my word."

"Only for a moment, sir," Wil said. "Lieutenant now, I'm afraid."

"*Mea culpa*," Odune said. "A pleasure."

Something itched in the back of Wil's head, a kind of déjà vu. Intrusive. He dismissed it along with Odune's granted level-two social access—a quick glance confirmed it was mostly PR shots and blurb biographies, puff pieces about Odune's spearheaded efforts to secure funding, settlers, and scientists. How he R&D'd the prefabricated housing pod's mountainside stabilizers on his own dime.

Wil had read it all already on the Circular to Dawn. After Kurage, building an outpost in the wildlands of Planet Dawn had been unpalatable to most investors, and Odune had graciously taken advantage of that.

"I must admit, Rajan," Odune said, "I was expecting Yearwood's replacement from Neoterra to be another stodgy, boring old mathematician. Instead, this conversation has been the highlight of my year."

"You must be glad I showed up a few weeks before your coronation, then," Rajan said. "A whole delegation of donors from Neoterra flying straight to your doorstep—and one hell of an honor, if I read the release correctly?"

Odune scoffed. "Oh, spare me. Honor? Only another useless accolade from Bureau Gaea and the Dawn Research Commission, soon to join the others collecting dust on my mantel. Like you said before, it's all bullshit."

"The check it comes with better not be," Rajan said and fell into a competent impression of human laughter.

Wil trailed back to surveying the adjacent rooftops, glad that neither of them could clock his twinged patience through his helmet's faceplate.

Wrists clasped behind his back, Odune approached the fogged-out windows. "A new frontier. Scientific discovery. Cultural exchange. Those are the true rewards. And while a soirée is welcome, in the end it's but another frivolous ribbon." Suddenly, he broke out in a wide grin. "You know, you should attend. Liven things up."

Rajan cast a sidelong glance at Joan on the holo-ad and grinned wolfishly. "I heard you were expecting a surprise guest."

Odune cracked a single, thundering laugh. "Oh, please! As much as I wish that were true, I can't imagine the Maid of Orleans would take time from her busy schedule after the Second Resurrection to deliver a simple Exceptional Civilian Service medal. *Absit omen, dei gratia*, hm?"

"Yeah, gratya," Rajan mumbled, bemused. "Agreed."

Joan of Arc was a Recreation—ALEPH's approximation of the historical figure from the 15th century, downloaded into a Lhost body and trained in the Order of the Hospital at Skovorodino on Svalarheima. The greatest tactical mind in the PanOceanian army, a military leader whose presence on the battlefield always signaled imminent victory. She was as much the real patron saint of France as Achilles of the Steel Phalanx was the real conqueror of Troy, but there was something Wil found inspiriting about her rise from the lowest rung of the Knights Hospitaller to her place as the figurehead of their nation's military—even if that was what she'd been made for.

Judging by Rajan's momentary leer at her literal breastplate, he didn't share the same admiration. While his religious affiliation hadn't been registered in his file, what *was* present confirmed the cover matched the contents: rich father; multiple arrests before adulthood; purchased Ivy-League degree; nepotism hire. The rest hid beneath redactions on redactions, expunged records, and settlements.

The last guy had somehow been worse. After a full year of ghosted negotiations, Yearwood dropped off the grid rather than return to Neoterra and face his superiors or the media.

Honestly, Wil didn't blame him. He'd rather get shipped back to Paradiso naked than face another wall of WarCors and their camera drones.

"If time allows," Odune said, "you should consider spending a few nights in Mariannebourg once the clan introductions play out. No modern city in the Human Sphere compares."

Rajan fiddled with his cufflinks. "If we have the time."

His assistant—a thin, artificially pretty woman who'd introduced herself to Wil as *hmph*—brightened. For the first time since he'd met her aboard the Circular to Dawn, she pulled away from AR. "I've heard the diaspora culture in urban Merovingia is mad lindy. Cravats, scarves, berets. So cute."

"The French are a fascinating bunch," Odune said. "Intellectual, spiritual, fashionable. Much more interesting than our rainy neighbors here at DRC-9, and much less *plaid*."

Everyone laughed again. None of it sounded real.

A dark-haired bodysculpted beauty scowled her way out of Odune's office and over toward Fontaine and Ghent. His secretary, Melantha—another *hmph* if not for a courteous double-tap. Beyond the open door she'd left, Wil caught a glance of four highball glasses surrounding a half-empty bottle of Caledonian whisky and a marble chessboard. White was playing a perfect game; black, not so much.

Odune must've smelled blood in the water. He traced Wil's gaze and grinned. "Not too shabby, hm? Rajan gave me a run for my money, but I can always tell when someone's geist is playing for them. You dabble?"

"No, sir," Wil said. "Had a CO back in the day who made everything a chess metaphor. Pawn this, en passant that, castling this. Called everything a gambit, or a mate. Kind of ruined it for me."

"Alas," Odune said. He clicked his tongue as the hallmarks of a quantronic distraction ran across his face, and changed gears abruptly. "Rajan. Captain Gotzinger. I apologize, but something came up. Let's take an adjournment, and after you return to Dun Scaith, you can tell me how the meeting went?"

"If you keep the champagne ready," Rajan said. It sounded painfully forced.

†††

Outside, the administrative building loomed over the scattered prefabs and Ariadnan pines, shock white and brutally angular as Odune himself.

The drizzled beginnings of another freezing downpour spurred Wil's assets across the muddy road to their waiting AUV—Ariadnan Utility Vehicle, an unholy union of armored personnel carrier, lunar rover, and racing REM. Uncomfortable, but better than a one-way ticket to the bottom of a ravine.

Rajan climbed into the back seat, salesman's grin replaced with a glare. "I'm pissed at you, Gotzinger. Know why?"

"Sorry," Wil said. "Just a checkers kind of guy."

"Not that," Rajan snapped. "I'm the one chugging this shit raw while you sip on recycled air from that filtered helmet. I can feel the mold setting root in my lungs. It's disgusting, puts me off my game."

"Can't be that bad," Wil said. "The Ariadnans seem to love it."

"The Scots, the frogs, the yee-haws, or the Ruskies?" Rajan said and slammed the door.

Wil went around to the other side, opening the door for Hmph. She hummed noncommittally and climbed inside, engrossed in her invisible fantasy. With her halo set to private, it turned what could've been very specific motions in her AR game into strange, purposeless groping.

Back in King's Den, they called people like Hmph zoners, so addicted to AR that they forgot the real world existed beneath it. Turns out that when you're the grandniece of a Moto.tronica sub-executive, being a zoner was just another kind of profession.

When Wil slipped into the AUV's passenger seat, Rajan started again. "You know, they got this motto here: *Dawn is Ours*. What an assumption. Who ever said I wanted it? Spare me the planet and leave us the Teseum, am I right?"

Teseum—the vital neomaterial that started the Quantronic Revolution, first discovered in the atmosphere of Jupiter. Difficult to find and expensive; the surface of Dawn was unusually rich in it. While the great minds of the Human Sphere harnessed the secrets of Teseum to fuel their dreams of ending scarcity via the Universal Teseum Cradles, or unraveled the mysteries of death itself to bring about the first Recreations and normalize resurrection, the Ariadnan Army used it to make especially sharp knives and bulletproof helmets.

Most folks back home considered it a waste. After the rediscovery of Dawn twenty years back, two-hundred-years after the the *Ariadna's* landing, the colonists weren't too keen on sharing—so everybody started taking instead. 'Dawn is Ours' was usually the last thing a Teseum smuggler heard before some bastard in a kilt gave him a lethal dose of it.

The limited-AI driving program carefully navigated the inclines back toward their accommodation. Muted prefab strip lighting cut through the fog along with a smattering of pedestrian shapes. Several times they banked into gray nothingness, floating on solid clouds until the mist faded and the ground reasserted its existence.

Rajan snapped his tawny fingers in Hmph's face. "I'll need a toxicology screening the moment we're offworld and another antibiotic booster. I'm not taking a fungus back to my penthouse in San Saba, no way. Oh, and next time you want to share your shitty opinion? Don't."

She blinked several times. "I didn't—"

"Mariannebourg, *so cute*," Rajan sneered. "Are you a child?"

"Sorry, sir."

"I bet you are. And if you marked down Odune's god-awful party in three weeks, cancel it. If I'm still here by then, just shoot me."

Shrank against the window, she returned to gesturing aimlessly, lips tucked in a pout. Her seatbelt remained unbuckled, and she made no motion to change that.

"Hey," Wil said, low and kind. Waved. But beyond a brief flicker of annoyance, she didn't register his presence.

Wasn't worth the energy. Didn't want her to feel like he was ganging up on her, too.

Rajan kicked back and fiddled with his cufflinks. They were different from this morning, pearl squares replaced by silvery Teseum studs. "You ready for the no-show showcase tomorrow, Gotzinger?"

"Ready as anyone can be," Wil said.

"The MacCallums, the O'Brien, the Campbells, the Munro, and the MacArthurs. Five minor Caledonian clans in four-hundred kilometers, all squatting on Teseum deposits they can't tap, all refusing to cooperate. You know what this place would be if the local yokels worked with us, instead of against us?"

Wil shrugged. "Loch-front resort?"

"Lake-front fucking resort."

"They call it a loch up here, I think."

"Tomato, tamaatar," Rajan said. "The point is, it's all bullshit. At the end of the day, the world runs on money, Gotzinger. Money! If only the locals weren't too blind and backward to see it. It's a goddamn travesty, is all I'm saying."

"Maybe they just want to be left alone."

"One drop of freedom isn't worth getting eaten by wolves or dying of cancer, no matter how much tartan you dress it in. Ateks, man. Almost too stupid to live."

A specific spot in Wil's neck throbbed, embedded in his neck below his ear. Memories of cardboard, halogen lights, and wet black plastic sheets gave way to the rational desire to keep from a second court martial.

He cracked his knuckles. "Sure."

"Well, strap in for the long haul," Rajan said. "If my boss has his way, you and me are stuck on this godforsaken rock under Odune's thumb until the day they run out of Silk on Bourak."

Wil furrowed his brow. Forever wasn't the assignment. Six months, they'd said. Diplomatic negotiations. Corporate elbow-greasing. Protection detail. A handful of quick forays westward for a cultural exchange with Caledonian clan chieftains, negotiating joint ventures regarding the Teseum mines, and then they were out of here.

"What you're thinking right now," Rajan said. "That's *our* plan. Their plan—PanOceania's plan—is to keep us here until I get at least two of these five chump chieftains to agree to let in a drill team." He licked his teeth and straightened his suit jacket. "AKA, never."

Now, this whole scenario was starting to make more sense. This is where high command had sent them to disappear, the long-overdue coup de grâce on his career as an Aquila Guard in the Neoterran Capitaline Army.

Wil could've danced.

He'd expected his long-due retribution from the NCA to be a permanent assignment to a space station on the Human Edge, or an arctic research station punched into a glacier, or some doomed bulwark on Paradiso. But on Dawn, there were actual trees instead of ones biomodified for aesthetics, and the air tasted crisp instead of refurbished. So it rained three-hundred days out of the year? So there was more mud than solid ground? Cold, wet, and permanently tinged with mildew was more than he deserved.

It was getting off easy.

But this wasn't for him, was it? It was Rajan's protection detail he'd been assigned to, and it was Rajan who would be stuck organizing meetings with disappearing Highlanders in perpetuity, glued to Odune's side playing lapdog in a holding pattern. No nanoweave bed sheets; no sensorium pornography; no nitrocaine or nightclub bathrooms to bump it in.

He really must've pissed someone off. Likely the same guy who put all those redactions in his file.

Rajan stared into the fog, brows pinched with uncharacteristic gravitas. "Tomorrow, after we go through the motions at Fort Resolute, I want to alter the flight plan and do a flyover of the southwest shore."

"That's restricted airspace, sir. Don't think we can do that."

Quantronic mandalas reflected in the AUV's squat, dirt-flecked window. "Their plan. Your plan. Odune's plan," Rajan said. "I've got a plan of my own."

2

On Paradiso, Wil discovered his secret talent: sleeping.

He'd done eight in his combat armor, stuffed beside a disconnected heating unit in the middle of a blizzard; dozed twelve hours in a mud-pit, gut packed with his own beret; taken a power nap under active fire on Flamia Island; slept while standing during graduation at the Aquila Officer's Academy. He always woke up prepared, refreshed, invigorated.

Today, he woke up tired.

Not quite morning yet, though his comlog's clock read 1700EC—still synced to Neoterran time, electronically and biologically. Interstellar jet lag, worsened by Dawn's twenty-five-hour cycle compared to Neoterra's twenty-two. At least it wasn't Paradiso's twenty-eight, with its eight-month long seasons and one-point-two times Earth gravity.

His geist intruded on his groggy reverie, replacing the interior of the cramped domicile with a live feed of his apartment on Neoterra. Didn't work. Outside the window, cars juddered back and forth in mid-air, projected display buffering, buffering, please wait. And the smell was entirely different. The old domotics kept his apartment flush with the smell of hot metal, but it was garlicky here, almost like stale food. Must be the heaters coming online—it hadn't been there last night when he'd turned in.

But the heat didn't come, and the cold got colder.

Wil dismissed the sensorium and rolled out of bed. Right leg, left leg. Belt, breastplate, biceps, gauntlets. Pauldrons went on second to last, before the helmet. Cables connected. Artificial muscle tensed beneath the fiberweave, sucking to his skin. Peripheral lights ignited, servos hissing loudly once before dropping to a whisper. Diagnostics green; all clear.

No more morning chill. The weird air turned scentless as it recycled through his helmet's filter. Affixing his duster and his Schärfe, Wil caught sight of a shadow over the bathroom sink—his hulking reflection, looming in the mirror.

He hooked the door shut.

Outside, a fresh layer of rain dripped off every prefabricated surface. Fog swirled underfoot, obscuring the mud and the potholes. DRC personnel lingered at his domicile wall, engrossed in an open hatch. Judging by their quiet surprise, he wondered if they'd known it'd been occupied.

At the northern end of the DRC, red dots blinked lazily atop the communications array tower, and along the tall perimeter fencing, automated F-13 defensive turrets pointed outward. Warning signs declared the location an O-12 outpost and urged caution in English, Esperanto, and Caledonian.

Caledonia. One of the four factions from the abandoned seed ship *Ariadna*, originally comprised of Welsh, English, Danish, and Scottish settlers sent north to defend the Teseum mines during the First Antipode Offensive. Over the last century, the cultural diaspora merged into a distinctive singularity: an isolationist, xenophobic warrior culture, something between doomsday preppers and a renaissance faire.

He'd heard the Caledonians held grudges like nobody else. That they made up for the gulf in their tech with sheer bravado and nothing more. He'd heard that if you killed a Highlander, their corpses got back up and kept fighting.

So he'd shoot twice, then.

While the Ariadnan government held off-worlders at bay thanks to O-12's backing, they'd allowed non-militaristic scientific research stations to set up shop along the edge of what they called the Ariadna Exclusion Zone. As long as the settlements stayed far from Ariadna proper, the powers that be could pop up some prefabs and scan the trees.

DRC Dun Scaith was one of those stations, a joint operation between the PanOceanian Dawn Research Commission, and O-12's Bureaus Gaea and Ganesha. According to his intelligence briefing, the majority of the prefabs here housed PanOceanian research personnel who organized expeditions along the fringes of the AEZ to gather data; analysts who interpreted that data; and escorts, drivers, and pathfinders who brought them back alive. Their military presence was utterly nil, in accordance with the treaties—O-12 oversaw all procedures, all actions, with incredible scrutiny.

In reality, Wil knew that O-12's protectorate over Dawn had dwindled over the last decade, stretched so thin that the offices in most major cities only employed a single rep. He'd seen the official staff list for the DRC-9. No rep. Odune had total, irradicable control. As usual, the rich made the rules with no expectation of actually following them.

One of the terms and conditions with setting roots on the planet was a blanket heavy arms ban: nothing punchier than a pistol, though the local clans were gracious enough to donate a pittance of archaic pump-action AKNovy light shotguns in case of Antipode attack. It'd taken some convincing for Wil to keep his Schärfe and his armor, and Rajan had been the one to grease the necessary palms. If the Ariadnan MPs spotted him, it might've caused a fuss, but it wasn't like the natives came within a hundred klicks of Dun Scaith. Caledonians were infamous for keeping to themselves.

Two sour coffees in the empty commissary later, Rajan's geist pinged him a wake-up notification and his order: Blended iced Americano decaf, half almond milk, half nonfat. One cup blended ice, stirred. Then add 1/2 cup zero-cal hazelnut flavor, add ice, shake. No straw.

Good thing the machine knew what an Americano was, because Wil sure as hell didn't.

Minutes of SecDet routine preceded hours of boredom. Rajan's meet-and-greet with the researchers zipped by, nothing but smiles, nothing of substance. Medical sign-off was cursory at best and included an antibacterial booster shot and a liability waver.

Needles. *Mierda.* Wil glanced over the digital form's lip at the medical tech, already slipping on latex gloves. "Booster shot's a no-go. Sorry."

"Mandatory," the tech said.

"I've received the Dawn cocktail before, back in the Fusilier Corps. Should still be active in the Silk in my blood. No worries."

"Mandatory," the tech said, but slower.

"Armor stays on," Wil said, and he swiped the form back into the tech's sensorium. "Check the box."

The medtech tightened his jaw. "Do I need to contact the counselor over this, Lieutenant Gotzinger? Mandatory—"

"—means you get to answer the call from my boss and explain the reason my geist is screaming distress signals is 'cause I was forced to take off my armor in the middle of SecDet duty. And when the Bolt fireteam shows up from Capa Blanca and gets sloshed in the DFAC, then what? You gonna clean up the mess?"

A bluff. Maybe true for actual high-prio assets, but Wil's armor had no such alarms, zero safeties, no outside comms. He just didn't want another god-damn needle in him. Not like it mattered—he wouldn't be breathing Ariadnan air anytime soon if he had any say in it.

The medtech grimaced. He considered the form for a long moment and sent it back checked. "Have it your way."

"Appreciate it," Wil said. Flipping the page, he paused hard at a red-out-lined confirmation requiring him to divulge his pregnancy status.

"Antipodes can smell it," the medtech explained. "You gonna call your boss over that one, too?"

Antipodes. The original inhabitants of Dawn. Massive lupine beasts, sla-vering monstrosities hell-bent on evicting the Ariadnans from their homeworld. They killed for sport, for territory, and for the hell of it, but also to feed the roots of their primal god, something they called the Blood Tree.

Once an Antipode fell into a triune with at least two others of their kind, they started getting smarter. The more of them, the worse it got, until they were capable of just enough civilization for cruelty.

Made sense. Bad things always happened in threes.

Among the known extraterrestrial races, the Antipodes possessed a unique evolutionary mechanism: the cuckoo virus. A single bite applied to a pregnant victim would graft the Antipode's genetic material to their unborn child, creating a human-alien hybrid—the fearsome Dog-Warriors of Dawn.

Now, those were the werewolves from old movies: hulking, atavistic brutes that transmogrified from men into berserking monstrosities when the trumpets roared and the bloodlust hit. Tough as hell, Dog-Warriors were the sole living creatures in the Human Sphere that could weather a monofilament mine payload and come back for more.

By the time they'd made it to the heliport, the morning light from Helios barely pierced the thickening fog. Golden haze choked the staircase that wound the heliport's support pillar, killing vision beyond arm's reach. Wil changed spectrums on his visor to best accommodate the no-vis zone and cranked up the glow of his periphery to serve as a beacon for the others. "Hand on the railing, eyes peeled. One-hundred twenty-six steps, same as when we came in. Slow and steady."

Rajan scuffed his fancy shoes on the first step and growled a string of curses. "Some warning would be nice, pal. The hell did I buy you that visor for?"

Ninety-six steps later, they crested the final flight to the heliport proper. Red and green beacon lights pulsed on its corners, their glows skimming the hard planes of a luxury-class VTOL aircraft. Wil recognized the make and model—a Balena V7, armored as a Paradiso Tubarão with all the trimmings of a sports car. Likely Odune's personal craft, given the excessive polish and matte-cream finish. Personnel jogged around her among towers of topographic drones and cargo containers, deep in the midst of final preparations.

The three of them waited. Politely. Then, impolitely. Rajan scrolled the news. Every time Maya dropped signal, he chirped a new uninspired spiel of vulgarities, pushing Wil to relocate over to a place with better overwatch and less colorful acoustics.

A prompt loaded in Wil's HUD and was killed by his geist. Curious, he opened his incoming/outgoing to find a connection attempt from Arachne, the pirate internet network used by the Nomad Nation. He'd heard the locals vastly preferred it to ALEPH's MayaNet, even with its Swiss cheese firewalls and crumbling security protocols. But then again, after the Commercial Conflicts, anything even remotely PanOceanian-adjacent on Dawn might as well have been synonymous with poison.

The signal had to be strong to graze him this far from their holdings. Passing satellite, maybe. Tempting. But as much as he wanted to get a glimpse of the other side of the looking glass, Wil's datasphere was content-restricted by his military codec, and so he was stuck with the dripfeed of bandwidth transmit from a smattering of unreliable satellites up in low orbit.

A man in a flight suit with an enclosed helmet traipsed over, Balena system checks fluttering within his shared sensorium. "Good morning, sir. I'll be the co-pilot for your trip today. Looking forward to meeting the locals?"

"Only 'sir' if you're a CSU," Wil said, and they traded a double-tap.

In the culture of the Human Sphere, double-taps had long replaced handshakes. A quick two-fingered tap on your new acquaintance's palm queued the geist, traded details, enabled comlog-to-comlog connection. The co-pilot's digital halo unfolded as Wil's access permissions went one level deeper: identification, certifications, license dates, employment records, test scores. KEYES, ROGER; 26 years old; Unmarried; Privately contracted. No need for introductions when the convenience of modern civilization would suffice.

The Balena's engine roared. Wil's implanted aural filters cut sound, reducing the deafening growl to a muffle.

Keyes continued the conversation digitally via private connection: "Everything alright today, sir? Feeling good?"

He cocked his head. "Should I not be?"

"Altitude sickness is no joke," Keyes said. "And correct me if I'm wrong, but you're the Aquila Guard, right? Your halo's pretty sparse."

Wil chuckled. "You sure I'm not an Orc, or a Knight of Justice?"

"The duster gave you away. That, and everybody's talking about you and your boss."

The vox in his helmet turned his sigh into an electronic crackle. "What'd he do this time?"

"Heard he got into a screaming match with the kitchen staff. Something about no egg whites in his Caesar salad? He put in a complaint with the consulate."

"I'll keep him on a shorter leash," Wil said. "He barks, bring him to me, alright? Getting yelled at is my job, not yours."

Keyes' voice sounded like he was smiling. "Thank you, Lieutenant."

The arrival of the pilot preceded a second double tap and another quick introduction. Business concluded, they approached Rajan to go over the plan from top to bottom. Parameters, schedule, weather. Everything looked above-board from Wil's experience.

When the rundown finished, Rajan pulled the pilot aside. Their conversation stalled. The pilot tensed. Disagreed. Rajan pressed and offered something. The handout melted away the pilot's protests, and with a quick double-tap, they became best friends.

The Oceanas practically jingled as they left Rajan's account. More than enough to change this backwater pilot's life forever; so small, Rajan's daddy would never notice the transaction.

Once the flight crew stepped away, Wil sidled over. "I don't like this, sir."

"I didn't ask," Rajan answered.

"Going off flight-plan, in this weather, without warning? Won't look good."

"And I don't care."

Exasperation lent an edge to Wil's voice. "I'll give it to you straight: My job's to keep you safe. What you plan on doing is illegal on multiple levels. If you think the DRC-9 is bad, you do *not* want to give Rodina an excuse to make an example out of you, put you in a cell where the sun never—"

"Shut up," Rajan said. "You do what I say. Got it?"

"I do what PanOceania tells me."

Rajan leaned in, eyes raging with vermilion chakra. "And how'd that end up last time?"

Wil's neck twinged. More anger, strangled for the sake of professionalism. He kept silent to avoid saying something he'd regret.

"It's just sightseeing," Rajan said. "And if we find that missing attaché, all crashed on the lakeside? That's our ticket home. Caledonia presumes they can stonewall PanOceania. Let's see 'em stonewall *me*."

The dots connected, admittedly late. "Wait. You think Yearwood's transport was shot down?"

"My intel puts him and his entourage on a shuttle from Mariannebourg the day our boy vanished. They planned to come back, so why didn't they?"

"And the only logical explanation is death?"

"Exactly! Logic. Love logic. Sad for them, good for us. We find their corpses, I leak proof he got fragged, and non-essential personnel withdraw off-world. AKA, we get the hell out of here."

"That could start a war."

Rajan sized him up for a moment and deflated with a bitter, halfhearted snicker. "Man. I forget, sometimes, you know? How you are. Could've hired a guide here. Should've. Definitely regret taking the recommendation for you. A local would've known the place better. Wouldn't shake when he shoots, or bitch so much, either."

Wil hadn't known he'd come recommended, but it didn't change his opinion. "Mr. Brizuela, sir, with all due respect, we cannot—"

"Mr. Brizuela," Rajan echoed in falsetto and straightened his nanoweave shirt. "You know, I used to live in 'cannots,' too. Can't stand out, can't get the girl, can't can't can't. Used to believe that there was an intangible quality, an nth factor that divided the good and the great. You know what that is?"

Wil clenched his teeth. "What?"

"Luck," Rajan continued. "Inscrutable, ephemeral luck. Some people are born lucky, some unlucky, and the rest of us take what we can get. But the older and wiser I got, Gotzinger, the more I realized that luck isn't inscrutable, isn't ephemeral. You can change it if you want. Choose your luck. Make it, break it, steal it. For good, or—in your case—for bad."

"Excuse me?"

"I know you think I'm the unlucky one, getting assigned to a place like this. But that's just once, you know? You, you're unlucky always. Unlucky in war. Unlucky in life. Unlucky in *thinking*. And once I realized that, I knew I should've left you behind. And I bet all those Fusiliers you killed on Svalarheima felt the same."

The hard edges of his gauntlet cut against his grip through its polyfiber padding. "They had names."

"Shhh," Rajan snapped. "I don't pay you to talk. If I want your opinion, I'll slip you an Oceana. 'Kay?"

Deep breath. Forceful settling. Wil closed his eyes to compose himself, and in the eigengrau saw enamel shards decorating the gaps in his ORC's armored fist. Rajan floundered on his back, palms clamped hemorrhaging lips, pleas wet and sloppy with a mouthful of broken teeth.

But when he opened his eyes, nothing had changed.

The Balena engines flexed and flared. Blue light burned away the fog. A crewman waved them over, and Rajan whistled a vapid L-Ease synth bop as he swaggered toward the open Balena doors.

⇑⇑

Boarding was comfortable and fast. Four plush seats surrounded a state-of-the-art center console. The broad one-way privacy windows provided ample opportunity for sightseeing from behind centimeters of blast shielding, impenetrable to small arms fire and most large ordnance.

Rajan strapped in, waist and shoulders secured. Across the transport, Hmph sat on her knees and zoned. The emergency kit laid fastened beneath her seat, a shotgun case secure beside it. A useful tool for managing the inevitable Antipode meet-and-greet if they lingered too long in the woods.

Wil squeezed past her with a gruff, "Seatbelt."

She locked eyes with him, eyebrows creased, and continued unbuckled.

"It might be a little bumpy," Keyes added cheerfully from the co-pilot's seat. "Minimal rain today! Might even see some sunshine, if we're lucky. Wouldn't that be nice?"

She didn't hear him. Or didn't care. A minute later, they took off.

Their destination, Fort Resolute, nestled along the shore of Loch Eil between the DRC-9 and the local clan holdings. Not in the AEZ, but not restricted airspace, either. Originally, the frontier fortress had served in a secondary capacity as a trading post for loggers and miners, but the Second Antipode Offensive left it abandoned. A hundred years after the massacre, the Ariadnan Army repurposed the ruins into a training center for real-world combat simulation. After twenty more, the *stanitsa* caretakers were executed by mercs and their barracks burned to the ground during the Commercial Conflicts. Since then, it lay abandoned, infrastructure swallowed by the encroaching wildlands.

The perfect neutral ground for a meeting.

Or a shootout.

Wil leaned his MULTI Marksman barrel-first atop the carpeted floor, exhaustion weighing every joint. Leaning back against the padded interior of his ORC Combat Armor, he followed Hmph's lead and did some zoning of his own. Shapes rose and disappeared on the mist-soaked countryside, boulders and trees, until they became like faces, like arms and legs, like men and women plowing through snowbanks with their shins, scrambling for cover as spirals of lightning burned through the blizzard winds all around him.

He slept. Probably about an hour.

Outside the window, the day had finally mustered enough heat to drive the fog beneath the boreal treetops below. The highland plateaus and valleys reminded him of dim-lit advertisements all throughout King's Den of untouched planetoid paradises waiting in the mythical off-world that everyone always talked about but no one could afford to grasp.

Rajan craned against the safety partition between cabin and cockpit, digital halo on private. A couple hundred Oceanas drained from a visible bank account notification along his wrist before he dismissed it and slipped back to his seat. He leaned against the window, scanning the countryside, and the Balena banked left.

So they were really doing this.

Rajan directed his assistant to the starboard side and ordered her to keep her eyes sharp. Colors rushed past the windows in a comfortable blur. Wil glanced out, looking, but not really. He wasn't paid to look.

Words shook out of the aerodyne drone to either side. The pilots, conversing via comlog connection. He almost interrupted to say hello when he realized it wasn't on purpose—he was still on the private call with Keyes, and now the pilot had joined their cluster. He moved to dismiss it but figured he wasn't paid to do that, either.

"This isn't right," Keyes said. "There are others at Fort Resolute waiting for us."

"You heard the boss-man," the pilot said. "Minimal activity from their holdings, and no AUVs on M-828 means this's all a waste of time. Instead, we both get to make some money."

"We need to set down at Resolute. It's in the flight plan."

"We hit some turbulence, remember? Doubled back. Do I got to spell this out for you?"

Keyes made a strange sound deep in his throat. "It's illegal."

"Best things in life always are," the pilot said and smoothed out his bank.

Wil understood the nerves. Folklore spoke of the legendary Highlander Caterans, invisible in the trees, able to scale any structure with preternatural ease. One shot from a Teseum-coated T2 sniper round would hollow out powered combat armor, and two could stop a colossal Tactical Armored Gear dead in its tracks. God help you if they bothered to aim and put one in your head.

But the Balena's hide should be tough enough to soak at least a few rounds, and the limited AI in the vessel would activate evasive maneuvers before the pilot knew they were taking fire. Out in the middle of nowhere along the edge of the AEZ, they ran the risk of running into a routine patrol, but at best that'd be Caledonian Volunteers—similar to the lowly Fusilier, subtracting the smart gear and targeting assistance. At this height, a chain rifle may well have been a bow and arrow for all the harm it'd do.

The core of Wil's body iced, cold as the Ariadnan air that rushed over the winglets. His fingers quickened along with his pulse. The dips and rises of their flight must've reminded him of something, put him back on Paradiso. A momentary glitch in his instincts, still not quite up to par after two years of torpor. They were safe, so why did he feel like this?

His visor pinged. A thousand meters away, a crouched figure illuminated atop a granite outcrop.

Wil craned his neck to reestablish visual, but the Balena turned, slowing to ascend over a ridge. From the cabin, a pressured beeping grew louder, faster. A hiss, then rapid fire pops. The aft of the vessel clouded with chaff, and Keyes sucked in a breath.

The engines jumped, slamming Rajan back into his seat. He shouted for the pilot to slow down, that he was crazy, fought hard to buckle his harness and only barely succeeded. His assistant scrabbled for the armrests and slid half to the floor, cries inaudible over the engine's growing burn. The transport listed sideways, and then, from the starboard corner—

A streak. A flash. Heat.

His ears popped.

And then they were falling.

3

... Now

Wil braced, blind, anticipating jaws and the nothing after.

The Antipode rammed him head-on, yanking him off his feet and carrying him at least five meters before his back struck stone. It fell atop him, armor groaning beneath its ridiculous bulk. Limbs straightened like ramrods, convulsed, and went limp.

Its lifeless eyes were a perfect shade of blue.

The howling in the trees transformed to yelping and receded.

With an unhelpful splash screen, Wil's multispectral visor kicked back on, sprinting through startup diagnostics. Lines of naked code obscured the blank-eyed gaze of the lupine monstrosity dead on his chest, skull punched by a single lucky shot. The overpowering stench of loosed bowels pried past the gaps in his helmet, chased by the metallic tang of blood and dried saliva.

Servos groaning, Wil squeezed breathless from beneath it. His shoulder joint squeaked like metal on glass in its socket, gouging his muscle with every twist and pull. Kicks propelled him until he could lift its arm and wrestle free. Shoulders burning, he staggered to his feet and searched for the knife-wielding albino he'd seen gloating over the Balena's smoldering corpse.

But they were gone. Run off, maybe. He'd heard trinary intelligence made losing a member of their ménage à trois something like a mental breakdown. Wil naively hoped he'd convinced them to retreat but knew they'd return with friends—and soon. He hefted Rajan again and made it another eight feet before his HUD flashed.

Error Reporting has suffered a critical error. Close program?

His vision went black again.

Blindfolded and huffing, Wil smacked the visor's side. "Come *on*," he growled, and the sound of his own unprocessed voice startled him.

Behind him, the Balena detonated.

The shockwave flattened him again. In his feeble attempt to keep Rajan from eating shit, he cracked his faceplate on a rock, and his teeth snapped together hard enough to feel the echo in his tailbone.

Pressure grew on the inside of his skull and bulged against the back of his eyes, throbbing in his temples. Wil lay flat and worked through the pain. He leaned into it, let it inhabit him. Head, neck, teeth, shoulder, legs. A lot of places, sure, but none as bad as surgery, nothing like back then.

Pain wasn't pain, he told himself. Pain wasn't pain.

Ready for more, Wil crawled to his knees and tore off his helmet. Freezing air bit into his skin, his neck, his sweat-soaked hair, at war with the heat raging from the burning carcass of the Balena. Almost relief. Too far to choke on the smoke, but not far enough to avoid the heady, noxious stench.

His helmet looked like it'd been stepped on by a Squalo. The bottom-left oculus had shattered, and feeble light sparked within. No use, now, and dangerous to wear. He let it fall by the wayside and ran an armored palm up his face to search for injury. Ropes of grimy anti-kinetic gel slimed from his burst gorget, sticky on his face and neck. Many small cuts, more bruises, but nothing gushing.

Beyond the brush, shapes moved, indeterminate and strange. Their colors shifted in tandem with the landscape. Not photoreactive—mimesis. More Antipodes. Not three, but an entire pack, impossible to count by eye as they faded in and out of vision.

Heavy panting grew louder, drowning out the growing inferno in the Balena's gut. A howl split the morning air, source invisible within the terrain.

Time to move.

Seizing Rajan by the wrist, Wil dragged him away, desperate for advantageous ground. Nothing but cracked boulders and looming trees that juddered and swam in waves of vertigo, limbs swaying like ribbons on the wind. A granite slab hunched over a small hummock of muddy ground, not far away. Enough to guard his back. Wil staggered to its base and left Rajan at his feet.

This would have to do. Back to a wall, better than in the open. Wil checked his pistol—without the interface in his helmet, he wasn't sure if he'd fired three times or four. Didn't matter. He nursed the crick in his neck, licked the sweat from his lips, and listened.

Silence, undercut by the sigh of leaves. The gentle reverberation of flames inside the Balena's cockpit.

Claws on stone. A small, dark Antipode darted from the treeline and reversed course, cutting back into the green. Wil took a shot, and it sliced into the brush. No yelp. He'd missed. Another maneuver in front of him, a sprint and fall back. When he didn't fire, they tried again, testing boundaries, his reflexes, his patience.

Or providing a distraction.

Wil spun and cracked a blind shot over the boulder's edge. A furry blur flinched back out of sight, Teseum-coated claws scraping the rock in its retreat.

They were setting up flanks. Surrounding him.

Quiet, now. Only his breath. His vision narrowed. The ground tilted, and he almost lost balance. If he fell down again, he knew he'd stay there. He needed to scare them. Kill a few. Open a path and take it. Every other path led to death, and like hell PanOceania would waste a resurrection on his sorry ass.

The white Antipode loped through a tendril of smoke into the open just meters away, fur pale as the granite underfoot. This close, the pink of his albino eyes glinted with something like conceit. It raised its knife, teeth bared in a challenging snarl.

Wil took the free shot.

It recoiled. Not hit. A dodge. Wil trained his aim and opened fire. The pale bastard skirted through the barrage, transferred the primitive blade to its teeth, and charged.

The brush behind him cracked. Another surprise attack—no, a distraction. The white Antipode was almost atop him. He turned and put one in its chest.

Its fur stained red. But the shot didn't pierce.

The knife flashed. The steel of his breastplate carved open without resistance, burning a line across him from armpit to armpit. He recoiled into the stone. Leathery claws stretched down from above. One skirted his gorget, and the other engulfed his gauntlet.

And pulled.

Wil managed the release command before the artificial muscle tore. He narrowed his hand, but the unfolding internal mechanism snagged his skin and pulled. The momentum whipped him away from the Antipodes. He kept his footing but lost the pistol.

Blood spattered against the scree. Instant shivers, cold sweat, even before the razor-wire slice of degloved skin took root. The skin of his forearm had unzipped from the bed of his elbow to the webbing of his thumb. The vacuum-tight suit beneath his armor hissed and sagged, no longer sealed, and numbness flushed his arm from the bicep down—more anesthetic, delivered by his dying suit's autoinjectors.

An instant's hesitation, and he'd have lost the limb. Out here, alien bacteria rampant, he still might.

Antipodes crowded out from the brush, tails high, ears perked, eyes wide. Twelve in all. Their teeth shined in the morning light, umber lips wet and glistening. His ambusher circled around to join its packmates, stolen gauntlet held high as it traded deep snuffs of its bloody interior with its friends.

One of the Antipodes trotted up beside Rajan. It pawed at his wound, claws dipped red, and licked up the wet. Tentatively, it pinched his sleeve between its teeth and dragged him toward the pack.

A new Antipode took point, mouth frothing. The albino yanked it back. It growled and chuffed, tongue undulating as two small, dark allies joined in. Language. He'd heard it called 'Snarl,' and that description was apt. The albino was claiming its kill.

Or making his case for feeding the Blood Tree.

With quaking fingers, Wil drew his knife. The thunder in his pulse rattled the cracks below his ear. "Kill me," he gasped. "I fucking dare you."

The white Antipode perked and straightened. Its alien gaze locked on his, flush with understanding, and it shoved its subordinate aside. Brandishing the Teseum knife, it loped forward.

A small, dark shape bounced among the rocks and exploded.

Wil jolted back, covering his face with his arm. A second and a third crack followed, dousing him in a cascade of stones. Grenades. Gunfire raged over the ridge behind him, aimed at the Antipodes' feet. Dust jumped from the river rocks. Bark spilled from the trees in errant gouges. No impacts, no kills. But the pack broke and made for the trees.

The white Antipode hesitated. Revenge or retreat—it made its choice and lunged. Wil saw its arc, knew how he needed to move, but his legs were too heavy and it was too fast.

A green blur launched over his shoulder. A woman: tall, built, hair red as a Paradiso sunset and dressed in muddy forest-colored fatigues. She held an enormous sword in one hand. A claymore. The blade matched her height, and she carried it as if it weighed nothing at all.

Steel flashed. Met. Both weapons rang out, and it was done. Blood splashed the rocks in a crescent. Clutching the gurgling chop in its shoulder, the white Antipode disengaged and fled for the trees.

Its small, dark friends trailed after, tails tucked between their legs. One of them dragged Rajan in its jaws. Wil launched his knife at its back. His toss flew wide, but the clink of steel on the stone was threat enough for it to abandon its prize, and in seconds there were no Antipodes left in the clearing.

Safe. Finally, safe, and with it, the storm inside died. Unbalanced by its loss, Wil sank to his knees.

The pressure in his skull doubled, and thinking became very difficult. Wil's geist populated his lens with safety warnings. Minor breaks. Numerous cuts. Probable concussion. It automatically attempted to arrange transport to a local hospital and lagged through a loading wheel before playing a downrezzed ad for Eco Cars in his peripheral vision.

A soldier stepped into the sunshaft above him.

Vision blurred, Wil focused on keeping grip on the gurgling tear in his arm. "Thank you," he said. "Almost—almost got me. Thanks."

The soldier leveled their weapon at him and shouted, "Get tae fuck, PanO bastard! Hands down, now!"

Not a CSU. Not a PanOceanian, or a SWORDFOR Kappa. A young blond man in a dirt-brown field jacket and a green and gold kilt. The chain rifle in his arms looked like it'd come from a museum, rust and dust and all.

The growl of engines preceded the arrival of three weathered AUVs burgeoning with armed frontiersmen in kilts. And though a herd of monstrosities had just beat a tentative retreat, all eyes and iron sights in the clearing trained on Wil.

"Princess," the soldier called. "Tin man here's pure fuckered. Might be done for. 'Pode gave him a Teseum kiss."

The woman who'd saved him sheathed her weapon and wiped her lips with the back of her gauntlet. A furrowed, vertical scar dashed up her right cheek from jaw to hairline, disappearing into a shoulder-length tangle of crimson hair. Tartan matching the soldier's colors hung across her hip, and her face was strange, though he couldn't focus enough to know why.

"Don't look too lethal," she said. "Just bag 'em, Neil. I'll carry. Quick, now."

Wil opened his mouth to rattle off his name and identification number, but before he stumbled over lieutenant, Neil cracked him in the forehead with the butt of his chain rifle.

4

They pried the quantronic lenses off his eyes and stuck a bag over his head.

The AUV motor chugged beneath him. Sharp jolts echoed from his bashed shoulder into his lungs with every random bump. Blood swamped the sleeve of his bodysuit, bicep vised in a tourniquet. Black fabric smothered him when he inhaled, sickening exhaust muddled with the campfire scent of the AKNovy barrel level with his temple.

His escort spoke English until someone snapped, "Whisht!" and every voice, male or female, changed to a roomy, rolling language. Caledonian, a pidgin of Scots Gaelic and the other languages used by the original frontiersman sent to colonize the highlands two-hundred years ago.

Back in Aquila, they'd done three weeks of SERE school—Survival, Evasion, Resistance, and Extraction. Simulations, but educational. Those memories urged him to summon up whatever strength remained to make a break for it, but an icepick stirred his temple with every heartbeat now. His legs burned instead of bending. All he'd manage by resisting now was suicide by Ariadnan.

Wil counted the seconds between stops. Between turns. Tracked their bearing by what scant sunlight penetrated the bag.

The vehicle ground to a halt. Two soldiers took him by the arms and hauled him into a concrete tunnel. His boots scraped against descending stairs. Another steel door. More stairs. A new woman's voice joined the chorus, shouting orders. Bright light. He slammed into a chair.

Someone snipped the zip-tie around Wil's wrists and unfolded his arms from behind his back. He clenched his teeth, but his shoulder ground in its socket and he couldn't hold back the grunt.

They ripped the hood from his head, and a spotlight focused on his face. An older woman in scrubs assessed his arm. Beyond the door, Rajan raced by on a stretcher surrounded with people.

Princess shadowed the exit. "Crash landed on the border of Achadh nan Darach, near got ate by 'Podes," she said. "If he didna have a concussion afore, he's got one now courtesy of Neil. Care—he's got a comlog in his arm, and a

Cube."

The doctor stood back, hands on her hips, and stared at Wil's combat armor. "Bloody hell. Anyone got a can opener?"

Beside him, knives glinted on a surgical tray.

Wil snatched up the sharpest one. Lunged out. The shadow to his left flinched clear. The doctor backpedaled out of his reach, back against the countertops. Wil stood, listing wildly, blade outstretched, until what had to be a battering ram smashed the breath out of him and left him puking on the floor.

Princess stood above him, sunfire hair curled wild over her eyes.

Not a battering ram. Just her.

Barrels swiveled toward him. Voices ordered submission. Wil refused. Fighting to a crawl, anger surged in him again—a fifth wind, a shout, a burst of desperate—

Cold steel bit into the meat of his neck and hissed. He swatted it away. An autoinjector dart rattled across the linoleum, blue liquid within drained into him in a second. Serum. Medical fluid, flush with nanobots. And something else. The ceiling spun.

Across the room, the doctor holstered her MediKit gun with a twirl, and her next words were inaudible. The assembled soldiers laughed, and their cacophony drawled into a low roar. His vision smeared like the lagging Neoterran skyline back in his prefab, shimmering and shaking as the colors sharpened to a miserable edge.

The tile softened, the pain faded, and then, so did Wil.

⚔

No, he shouldn't sleep. Not now. Wil jerked awake, fumbling for the knife.

Not the examination room. Somewhere darker. No longer in his own clothes, or his armor. He'd been reduced to a plain white shirt gone grubby from sweat and baggy beige elastic-band shorts. No shoes. No skivvies.

Prisoner wear.

The examination room had been replaced with a dingy concrete cell. Mildew and old earth clouded in the air, and rain dripped past the glass of a barred window on the wall. Electric light glowed from underneath a tall steel door along the far wall, brightest near the eye-level slat. A grimy bucket occupied the opposite corner.

Mierda, it was cold. He pinched the edge of the blanket and pulled.

The moment he tensed, fireworks erupted behind his eyes, and an all-encompassing hurt stomped him into the coarse fabric of his cot. His ribs ached, all twenty-four bones throbbing out of time with his head, his shoulder, his spine. A cluster of neat black stitches plucked along the olive length of his forearm, and a similar squeeze graced his chest and his scalp.

They'd taken his lenses and his earpiece. The lingering threads of half-remembered urban legends drew his hand to his neck, brushing the old scars there.

No stitches. At least they hadn't cut out his Cube.

Something weighed his wrist. A silvery shackle. Thick. Two green diodes on the band blinked at random intervals. Loose enough to slide the length of his arm, but not enough to remove without taking his hand or his fingers.

He'd seen devices like this before, on patrol after Karnapur. The onboard computer overloaded implanted comlog's quantronic processors to prevent them from sending automatic distress calls—like a never-ending flash pulse. But unlike the slapdash version the Ikari Company had left on the corpses of their Yujingyu victims, this version was Teseum-alloyed. Nigh unbreakable.

Footsteps thudded outside the cell door, receding as fast as they came. A patrol.

He hoped Rajan was alright. Would be a shame to carry his dead weight that far to have him die anyways.

When Wil woke again, night had fallen and the storm outside had grown. Rain rattled the glass. A flash of lightning glinted across the rims of a thin tray lying by the door; thunder jostled its contents.

Wil reached for it, but his arms felt hollow. A lukewarm puddle swamped his cot, and all his clothes had gone sticky with sweat. Bit by bit, he unraveled his frail lethargy and drummed up the strength to hook the tray with his thumb.

What awaited him hardly felt worth the effort. A spoonful of porridge, vegetable medley, four neat cubes of white meat, a paper cup of water, and a plastic cup of pills. After briefly considering the consequences of eating food he hadn't seen prepared, hunger won. He fingered the scant meal from the compartmented tray to his mouth and choked the water down. He didn't realize how much he needed more until it'd run out.

His chest itched madly, deep and unabating. Where the Antipode's knife had grazed him, his skin puffed taut and radiated uncomfortable heat. Damp crust piled between the stitches. The bandage had gone askew, interior padding stained more yellow than red.

Wil's reservation about the pills ended, and he swallowed them dry.

Muted thunder lulled him back to sleep.

⇈

He startled awake, mired in the comfort of a clean white bed. Nice and dry. Bright. The air smelled like bleach and linen instead of stagnant water and sweat.

The line across his chest. The infection. Layers of fresh gauze prevented his clumsy probe. Where his shoulder once ground inside the joint, the pain had dulled considerably, and he could move all his fingers and toes. He might even be able to walk.

All pretense that he might have returned to the DRC faded when he glanced to his right and saw the bedside stand of obsolete diagnostics machinery. The ceiling was brickwork; the walls, water-stained plaster. An electric fan wobbled on the ceiling, just above the privacy screen.

Behind it, the soft beep of a machine. A second patient.

An indignant huff to his left stole his attention. A pretty strawberry-blonde in a field jacket and plaid slacks sat at his bedside, blue eyes locked on his exploring hand. Same uniform as the kid in the clearing.

As his fingers grazed the bandages, she reached out and slapped his knuckles. "Stop touchin' it, numpty-muppet."

Wil coughed. "My mistake."

"Oh, hell!" she yelped and wobbled in her chair. "You're awake! Here, here."

The blonde fetched a paper cup from the bedside table and tilted it against his lips, thin hands rough as any soldier's. Water. Lukewarm. It spilled down his chin to his neck, and she wiped it up with a cloth.

An archaic dial flickered to life above her clunky wristlet comlog—holographic projection, the kind of tech that was bargain-bin before Wil learned to walk. She swiped the touchscreen instead of in midair and smiled. "You're in the infirmary. My name's Nora. How you feeling?"

He coughed. "What'd you do?"

"No worries," she said and did it again. The bed beneath him whirred, headboard lifting until he was sitting. "You had a hell of an infection. Almost died in your cell. Been out of commission three days, loaded up with steroids from offworld, antibiotics from... somewhere. Comfy?"

Cell. So he was still in Caledonia.

Wil cracked his back and stretched his limbs. The stitches down his left strained halfway and stung. He tried to go farther, and it started to really hurt until Nora grabbed his forearm and folded it back onto his chest.

"You tear those again and I won't hear the end of it," she said.

Wil laid back. "Sorry."

She wore a nametag that read McDERMOTT, and Wil wasn't sure why it gave him déjà vu. A patch of the staff of Asclepius on her shoulder confirmed his suspicion: paramedic, not a doctor. Still, better bedside manner than most Trauma-Docs he'd met, but he had yet to see if she'd mix up her MediKit gun with her pistol.

Someone on the other side of the privacy screen got Nora's attention with a whisper. She lifted a rifle from its prop beside her chair and flit over, mumbling a quick, "Sorry, one minute! Hang tight."

Hushed conversation filtered through the gaps in the screen. Wil slowed his breathing and strained to listen.

"Don't think he took a booster," a woman said. Doctor Quickdraw, from earlier. "Immune system's basically nuked. Infection may well still kill him yet."

What a perfect ending to a wonderful weekend, dying of easily avoidable sepsis all to avoid an autoinjector and a pinch. What an utter genius he was, making so many good decisions.

"That scar, below his ear," Nora whispered. "We didn't—"

"Not us," the doctor said. "I'd never extract a Cube. Too risky, too cruel. My bet's he got one put in, back alley-like, ken?"

"I thought all PanOs were born with one," Nora said. A response, unintelligible, and then, "Is Eideard gonna hurt him?"

Fantastic. Should've played dead. He'd survived something—an infection, anemia, or maybe he was a Dog-Warrior now, too—and now that he was hale and hearty, these bastards would show him the hospitality Ariadna was famous for.

Ten seconds later, the infirmary door burst open, and Wil hadn't gotten two words out before they'd shoved another goddamn bag over his head and dragged him out into the hall.

"Be gentle," Nora called after them, soft and ever so futile.

† †

The infirmary's laundry-fresh scent fell away, replaced by motor oil, then lacquer, then dust. Stone, tile, then wood. Stairs, several times—some narrow, most wide. The rattle of a kitchen in full swing on his left. The chug of washing machines, his right. A door clicked twice—double doors?—and the ground went from hardwood to carpet.

The bag ripped free, and Wil hurtled into an armchair. A wide, stately room filled with tables and mismatched carpets stretched out around him. Shelves loomed up to the ceiling on every wall, lined with rolling ladders and packed to bursting with weathered hardback books. Two chipped teacups on two chipped saucers sat atop a tea table in front of him. Something in the air smelled like burning potpourri.

A paper library. He'd never seen one before.

An old man stood beside the hearth, minding a kettle hung above its flames. He had a nice turtleneck sweater on. Slacks. Thin, with receding white hair barely a fingertip long. The boss, but not clan chieftain. Wil didn't know why, but he was sure the chieftain would've had a sword.

A portrait twice the size of any other hung above the mantel, depicting a healthy brunette sitting on a drystack wall. She held an M-16 against her woolen sweater and wore a crucifix around her neck, defiant eyes the color of Loch Eil. By the fade of the acrylic, the painting had to be a hundred years old.

Wrists zip-tied in his lap, Wil took stock of his new escort: four soldiers in kilts with pistols on their belts. The guy who'd cracked him in the forehead was among them. Neil. A checker-strapped Glengarry bonnet cocked atop his head, failing to hide his mess of blond curls, and his name badge read MCDERMOTT— same as the paramedic, Nora. No wonder he'd recognized her. With the familial resemblance, he guessed they were siblings, if not fraternal twins.

Wil wormed in place, trying to find a position where the ache in his bones didn't worsen.

One of the soldiers unlimbered his pistol. "Eyes forward."

"Gentlemen," the old man called. "That's enough."

The escort grimaced and holstered their weapon.

When the kettle whistled, he brought it over and filled both their tea cups. "You'll have to forgive the lads. They've never met a PanOceanian before, and especially none who'd put our doctor at knife point. Understandably, they're none too chuffed about it."

Protocol said to spit out the chicken feed—his name, rank, identification number, and birth date—and hope it was enough to delay an execution. But Wil got the feeling that when the Caledonians weighed the consequences of owning up to black-bagging an Aquila Guard and a Neoterran diplomat, or dropping their corpses off at the local Antipode den and claiming they'd died on impact, they'd choose simplicity over sympathy.

So, he chose silence, instead.

"My name is Eideard Carr," the old man said, and sat. "Do you ken where you are?"

Wil missed his geist and his lens already. If the local datasphere didn't get a hit on that name, a quick rewind to when he'd been reading the files on the Circular to Dawn would've sufficed. Instead, he was without auto-search for the first time in two decades.

Eideard unfolded a sheet of paper from his pocket. A readout, likely pried from his armor's wrecked onboard systems. "Can you tell me how you got here? The names of your compatriots?"

With the right equipment and a hacker, they'd have had access to his com-log by now. Without, the numbers were very pretty on the page, and Wil had the feeling they were exactly as Atek as a paper printout suggested.

Atek, short for 'a-technological,' meaning none. An Atek's sensorium was limited to only their five senses plus what their obsolete comlogs could process in 'dumb mode,' and they generally lacked the hardware to interface with most digital systems such as halos, domotics, AR.

In the wider Human Sphere, being Atek was considered a disability. To doggedly resist the technology that defined the 22nd Century was the realm of the mentally unwell, conspiracy theorists, and Ariadnans.

Eideard's reedy eyes flit across the page, and then to Wil. "We stand on MacArthur land, in Castle MacArthur itself. Your transport crashed within our clan territory three days ago. Care to explain what you were doing flying a hundred klicks outside your airspace?"

MacArthurs. Rajan had mentioned them, so Wil had done his due diligence. Their clan holding was the closest to the DRC-9, and the border of their claim ran parallel along the frontier, sectioning off Odune's little corporate kingdom. He wasn't that far from home after all—400km, at the farthest. So they'd been flying for an hour while he was asleep....

Interesting wording, too. Crashed.

"The Antipode you killed, Indigo River? He was chieftain of the Winter Dancer Tribe. You've unbalanced a tenuous peace, and worse, elected Pale Shadow their leader."

Indigo River—the dead blue-eyed monstrosity. Pale Shadow must've been the albino.

Unspoken threats of literally being thrown to the wolves aside, Wil focused on the room. Needed to find bearings. Landmarks. Four massive windows stood guard along the far end, three flags hung beside them: an Ariadnan bullseye, a crimson lion rampant at the center of a white saltire on a blue field, and three crowns laid across a blue shield.

Outside, an Ariadnan holding stretched out beneath them, crammed into the hollow between two gray peaks. Old-world brick and mortar buildings muddled amongst concrete fortifications haphazardly strewn down the hills. A sliver of Loch Eil shined from between inclines, but the rest of the landscape was lost in the trees.

Paired anti-air batteries reclined along the ridges closest to a large, dark facility. A Teseum mine.

Across the library, a woman sat alone, dark, cloudy hair tied high and tight behind an azure bandanna. A camouflage-patterned poncho hung over the armrest beside her, and on her lap, an old Tartary Army Corps Molotok. From where Wil was sitting, the rifle looked patchwork. Custom. Old. The gunmetal of its stock almost perfectly matched her obsidian skin.

She caught his look and curtly waved, pistol in hand.

Funny—he'd heard most of the Scots Guard had left Dawn with the Kosmoflot.

"Admiring our library, I see," Eideard said. "You ever read a paper book before? Some of our collection came to Dawn aboard the Ariadna, shuttled to this place in an old motor with Ceilidh MacArthur herself."

Honestly, this was a softer approach than Wil had expected. He'd nursed a little fear that the Caledonians had been the ones to shoot down the Balena, but if that were true, they wouldn't have tried so damn hard to be cordial.

Eideard reclined in his chair, fingers latticed on his knee. His untouched teacup had stopped steaming. "We haven't had PanO armor touch ground in Kildalton since the Commercial Conflicts. Your presence here violates a hundred small treaties, and more than a few big ones. Not to mention the contraband your friend had decorating his sleeves."

Rajan's gift from Odune. The brand-new Teseum cufflinks. Should've known that it wasn't above-board. All things said, if Rajan was alive, Wil owed him an apology: his theory about the missing attaché seemed less ridiculous by the minute.

"We've attempted to contact your compatriots at the DRC-9, but they're not answering. Given the fact that you were engaged in the air in a ship meant to carry six, I assume you, your friend, and the pilot weren't alone. Are there more in the wilderness we need to concern ourselves with? Allies, perhaps? Someone who might need help?"

Damned if he did or didn't. Tell the truth, and it became easier to declare total casualties with no fault. Lie that backup was waiting in the trees, and Eideard would grab a rag and a pitcher to find out where.

You, your friend, and the pilot, he'd said...

That was more than enough information to make a decision. It'd been three days minimum since the crash. If PanOceania or O-12 hadn't come asking by now, it meant they either didn't know they'd crashed or weren't certain they'd survived. If Rajan's missing attaché theory was true, the former was more likely than the latter.

No use pretending that words would solve this, or that someone was coming to find him. He had to leave, and soon. To make the opportunity he needed, he only had to get back to his cell. And while he didn't like the most obvious route, it was quicker than the alternative.

Wil reached forward and took the teacup.

The four soldiers' boots creaked as they shifted weight. Like he was dangerous without his armor, without all of his gadgets and his MULTI Rifle and his multispectral visor that knew down to the second the last time his target brushed their teeth.

He was. But he needed them to think he wasn't.

Wil gave Eideard his best King's Den face. "You the chief around here?"

"The MacArthur isn't available right now," Eideard said. "But you already knew that, didn't you?"

No clue what that meant. "The other guy. How's he?"

"Your friend? Alive. Answering a few of my questions may extend that. Make things easier for you, for me. For everyone."

Wil sniffed the hot leaf water. He took a sip. "What blend is this?"

"Ours," Eideard said. "We grow the tea shrub here, in the township. Can't find it anywhere else in the Human Sphere."

"It sucks," Wil said and poured it on the rug.

5

Wil opened the door of his cell with his face. The burlap sack ripped away, and Neil propelled him into the wall. The impact jostled a grunt loose and woke all the old hurt from the crash.

Neil closed on him, kicking the empty cot out of his path. "Start talking, galactic. Where is he?"

Wil grit his teeth. "I don't know who—"

"Liar," Neil shouted. "Tell me, now!"

"I said, I don't—"

Neil hooked his fist up into Wil's gut. His stitches bulged, and he caved to the urge to double over.

Keeled against his knees, Wil caught his bearings. The other escorts from the library crowded the cell, outnumbering him four-to-one. The skinny runt playing lookout wore BELL, the well-fed lad in the back SHAW, and the patchy-bearded bastard sneering from behind Neil was TALBOT.

No patches or identifying marks. Line troopers. Low ranks. Volunteers, non-commissioned. Not the best situation, but he'd make do.

"Gentle, bruv," Shaw said. "ALEPH spent a lotta money refurbishin' this one."

Bell snickered. "Should call in the warranty, aye? Looks broke."

"Like a Sin Eater's cock after Krug," Shaw chirped.

"Was gonna say a Pupnik's."

"Or a Riot Grrl's."

"Enough patter," Talbot barked, and the two morons deflated. He turned to Neil. "No clue where your sister's gone. Make it quick."

Neil cocked his fist again. "Last chance, galactic. Where's my cousin, and what'd ye do tae him?"

Wil coughed. "Please."

"I didn't say *beg*, bawbag. Where is he?"

"Please, no more talking," Wil groaned. "If it's all the same, I'd rather have my ass kicked quiet—"

Neil's fist blurred. Wil rocked back, the taste of iron muddled in his spit, and barely held down the urge to strike back.

"Y'think that's funny?" Neil said. "Huh?"

Needles of pain sucked through Wil's teeth. "No. But your skirts are."

Blond hair jerked into a headbutt. Stars erupted behind Wil's eyes, and he dropped to the floor on both knees.

Neil followed him down, fists stretching the fabric of Wil's collar. "Dawn is Ours, galactic. Not yours, never yours. PanOceania was a mistake."

"How original," Wil groaned, and slipped his hand into Neil's jacket pocket. Dull fingers glanced the rough edge of a bottlecap. A frayed combat patch. Then, hard plastic. A card. Bingo. Wil snaked his prize free and hid it under his body.

Neil didn't notice, too focused on yanking the dagger from his boot. The blade was very short, about thumb-length, but serrated. "Ten count, yeah? Then I let some sunshine in. Talk."

Back at SERE, the instructors prided themselves on disassembling the soldiers in their 'care.' Deep in that abyss, at the mercy of men without light in their eyes, Wil had things done to him that he never allowed himself to remember, things that tested the boundaries of what was legal. He'd not given in, never gave them the satisfaction of a scream. They might've killed him trying to extract one if they hadn't conducted the program in AR.

One knife was nothing compared to what someone could do with an alligator clip and some imagination. "Do your—"

A whistle echoed like a gunshot into the cell. Shadowing the door was the same tall redhead from before, the one who'd saved him from the Antipode. Princess. Tall, pale, and lithe like a mountain lion. Tattoos ran rampant across her skin, adorning her arms in slapdash sleeves—unit sigils, briar knots, butterflies. On her right shoulder, roses bloomed from the hollows of a skull. Behind the shreds of her neon-splattered crop top, spots of dark bandeau were visible in the tears.

She had an apple in one hand and the scruff of Bell's neck in the other. "What're ye morons doing?"

Bell made a noise, hands wrung around her wrist but wholly unsuccessful in dislodging himself. He kicked. She ignored him.

"The galactic kens somethin'," Neil said, presenting the knife with pride. "He's done something to Alastair, him and the other bastard, aye? I'll make him tell."

Her lip curled, revealing a long, broad canine. "Could ye fucking not?"

"Mind your business, hen," Talbot said. "This don't concern you."

Princess cocked a brow and shoved Bell at him. Together, the two Volunteers upended onto the cell cot. Talbot pushed Bell to the floor and swaggered back up, fists balled like he had a plan. But Princess didn't flinch, and he didn't dare take a second step forward.

"Saoirse," Neil said. "Please."

Her lip curled. "C'mon, Neil. D'ye really think some allmharach na galla could take our Alastair in a fight? Really, truly? Might be the storm kept 'em at Odhran's Ford, or they got a flat, or maybe they're bloody suntanning. So set the knife down before I feed it to ye. Respectfully."

The Volunteers watched Neil, waiting for his rebuttal. None came. Instead, he sheathed his blade and released Wil, rising to his full height—more than a few centimeters beneath hers.

"Remember how you got that sword," Neil said, chagrin writ large on his square face. "If somethin' happens to Al, I'll never forgive you."

Princess grinned, teeth just slightly too large. "Aye right, Feartie. Fuck off before I fetch yer mother."

Neil lingered, glaring, then left. The Volunteers followed after, dragging their feet and casting glares at both of them with equal furor. "Boot," Bell muttered, and scuttled away when Princess turned on him.

The scant light from the window above caught her face. Both eyes, milk-white and terrifying. Ears, pointed. Teeth, too large to completely hide behind her lips. Wil hadn't noticed when she'd saved him. If he had, he might've mustered the stamina to get up and keep running.

Saoirse held out her hand, fingers tipped with thick, dark claws instead of human nails. "Up ye go."

Wil flattened himself against the wall. "You're a Dog-Warrior."

Amusement became indignation, and she retracted her hand. "Ahm a Wulver, ye bloody wanker. Want your nose broke?"

Wulver. He'd never heard that one. "Sorry, I didn't think—"

"That's right," she snapped. "Ye didn't."

First, Pale Shadow, and now, the Volunteers. This woman was making a habit of pulling his ass out of the fire, and she deserved better. "Sorry."

"Dinnae scrap again," she said. "Next time yer about to lose, yer on yer own."

He sat up. "Duly noted."

"Saoirse Clarke," she said and held out the apple.

Wil stayed silent. Stayed still. Good cop, bad cop—he shouldn't be speaking to any cops. Even so, he was hungry, and she didn't seem like an answer was contingent on being fed. He reached for it.

Saoirse withdrew the apple last-second and bit a hunk from its side. The gouged remainder landed in his lap. "Sorry, mate," she said, cheek bulged and chewing. "The skirt shite was too far."

"Funny though, right?"

She smirked. "Fuck off."

The door slammed shut, and the Atek keypad outside clicked when she swiped her card. Five numbers, mechanical entry. The lock buzzed, and her footsteps receded. Brief conversation muffled in the hall and faded. Someone sat against the door—presumably, his guard.

Wil listened for a long time, cradling the gouged apple. When he was certain he wouldn't have another visitor, he extracted the prize he'd nicked out of Neil's jacket pocket from the inside of his shorts.

A keycard. He'd have preferred an officer's, but this would do fine.

"You can take the carterista out of King's Den," Wil said, and studied its simple surface. Despite a torn arm and a fading infection, he still had it, even if it cost him a split lip and a dent in his forehead. That Neil kid had one hell of an arm.

Eideard had put on a good show, but in his desperation to get a reaction, any reaction, he didn't realize he'd told Wil too much. Rajan was alive, sure, but more than that. He'd said, *I assume you, your friend, and the pilot weren't alone....*

Nothing about Keyes, or Hmph.

Without his lenses, and with the Teseum shackle disrupting his implant's signal, Wil was disconnected. Even if he ambushed a local and got his hands on a wrist-mounted box model, like the one Nora wore, they wouldn't have the codec to connect to Maya and, by proxy, PanOceanian command. But living or dead, Keyes or Hmph would have a link bracelet, and an unsuppressed comlog. With that, a priority SOS direct to the DRC-9 was an ocular gesture away.

A cold weight settled in his stomach. Hmph. The pithy nickname had run its course now that she'd died. No matter how much he hoped, it didn't make surviving a thousand meter drop any more possible, and he needed to show her the respect she deserved.

Keyes, on the other hand...if he had survived, the real question was *how*. Wil had seen his vitals—but then again, it wasn't long after his visor had gone haywire. Had that been blood, or something else? Fluid from the engine, perhaps. Keyes' jacket could've been too thick for his visor to pick up his heart rate, and he'd not understood that a lack of data didn't indicate an absence of it....

Seven minutes off-road, if Wil's count was correct. That meant six klicks— six kilometers. Could he untangle the vague memories of travel enough to make it back to the crash site? And if so, was it worth tempting death by Antipode a second time?

No use worrying. He'd work with what he knew and hope Eideard hadn't misspoken. Maybe his goons had counted both shredded pilots as one after the explosion, or a million other more reasonable explanations. But in the end, lost in the woods without a prayer sounded a helluva lot better than awaiting his execution.

While Wil considered how he'd slip the guard, what this keycard might unlock, and if his Teseum shackle had an embedded tracker or not, his stomach squeezed out a lengthy growl. With no other option, he took a bite of Saoirse's apple.

Sour, with a hint of honey lip balm.

Not bad.

⇞⇞

By his calculations, the cell he occupied was deep in the complex. The window had to lead to a barred pit, the way the sun hit it. Judging by the distance Neil and his boys had taken him back versus the initial trek up to the library, the infirmary couldn't be too far.

Rajan. Had he been there all along on the other side of that privacy curtain? Wil considered searching for him, dragging him with, but it was too risky. Seven kilometers of wilderness barefoot in the dark was already enough without adding ninety-five kg of acerbic dead weight to the mix.

Get help, get guns, come back. And if Rajan didn't make it....

Unlucky.

Time was the limiting factor of his escape: how long it took Neil to notice the keycard missing, how long it took Eideard to realize who he was, and if Wil could wriggle free before both came calling. By his estimation, only a few brief hours to formulate a plan. Memorize the sound of footsteps past the door at the end of the corridor. Time the routes in his head.

He'd have to go tonight.

The sole wildcard was Saoirse. If he ran into her in the hall, well, that was it. If she had a nose like a Dog-Warrior, she'd smell the sweat and antiseptic off his skin long before they made visual contact. And even if he nicked a gun, would it stop her? If Dog-Warriors were tough enough to eat a missile and come out smiling, the hell could a Wulver do?

Soon, the light outside the cell window died. The intervals between hallway patrols stretched. A shallow yawn and receding footsteps announced the departure of his guard. Both faded, and Wil crept to the door.

The slat pushed aside with ease. Left unlocked. Past the narrow aperture, a hallway: brick and mortar, damp, dark. The keypad hung on the wall outside, mechanical and obsolete—exactly like he'd hoped. And no evidence of posted sentries.

Voice low, Wil called out, but no one answered. Strange decision by his captors, leaving him on his own, but he didn't have the luxury of mulling it over. Testing the slat's width with his good hand, Wil slipped his arm through the opening. Wide enough to fit his elbow, but hard to see past. He groped until he located the keypad, felt for the reader on its side, and ran Neil's card through the machine.

It snagged on the rubber and pulled from his grip.

Wil jolted to catch it. Slapped the door to stop its fall. And though the card pinned to its surface under his palm, his strike drummed the steel like a cymbal, and the crash echoed down both sides of the tight hallway beyond.

He held his breath.

No alarm. No approaching footsteps.

Safe.

One careful centimeter at a time, Wil nudged the keycard back into his grip. "First in all fucking things," he mumbled and swiped the card again.

This time, no catch. The keypad light changed from red to green, and he flipped the card to use its corner to tap in the number he'd heard Saoirse enter:

High, mid, same high, low, low. 2-3-2-8. The pound sign had more wear in its grooves than the others, so he hit it last.

The keypad flashed red. A single beep.

It'd been five clicks, right? First and third were the same number, both on top. Fourth was on the bottom row, same as fifth. She'd had to hunt for four, but five had been second nature—pound.

Another swipe, another try. He'd boosted dumb-mode lockers in San Pietro subway stations all throughout his childhood, mapping tactile clicks to exact locations by ear. Compared to their nine-digit codes, four was nothing.

3-5-3-7-#.

Red again. Two beeps. Last chance.

5-7-5-8-#.

The lock clicked and turned in its chamber.

Outside, eight similar doorways ran the length of the hall spaced at wide intervals. Ropes of bulbs ran high along the corridor walls, shining the damp spots on the masonry—LED lights, long replaced by fiber-optic laser diodes in most civilized systems.

A bulky, conspicuous surveillance camera perched high on the corridor's end, staring down an adjoining hallway. Vintage tech. Antiquated. Kind of sad, actually, that they didn't have—

It rotated toward him.

Wil hit the brickwork beneath the camera's perch in seconds, choking on the air.

He kicked himself. Obsolete, sure. Did that matter? Make it any less able to put him back in that cell? Unless he wanted to wake up in the NeoVatican sometime in the year 3000, he needed to stop acting the condescending PanOceanian and start respecting how deadly simplicity could be.

The gurgle in his heart deepened, and he thumped his chest twice. Nothing dislodged, only hurt. Heat burdened his knees, his shoulder, his spine. Still not over the infection and crash. If he wanted to survive tonight, he'd need to be soon.

Wil ducked the camera to the stairwell door, punched in Saoirse's winning numbers, and pushed inside. His goal: the kitchen, which would have an exit to the outside for deliveries and plenty of knives that no one would know had gone missing.

Stairs led to halls led to doors led to halls led to stairs. On the fourth landing, he paused to assess the adjoining hall. Familiar. Ten meters down, white light flooded past the cracks in a simple steel door.

The infirmary.

Despite what Wil had decided about Rajan, the sickening warmth pooling in his joints won out. Painkillers were reason enough, and if he was lucky, a scalpel. No. If he was lucky, he'd scrounge up a D.E.P. and a check for a million Oceanas. The way things were, he'd be grateful for half an aspirin and a pair of sandals.

Wil opened the door, and the scent of disinfectant hit him. He scanned the open rooms. No nurses; no soldiers; no Nora. Behind the closed privacy screen lay Rajan, swaddled in blankets, wrists leashed to the bedside railing. A hundred plastic tubes dripped solution into him from an IV stand weighed with bags—21st century medicine.

Grim and invasive, especially when nanosurgery and biografting made most practices redundant. He'd hate to see what the Caledonians had relied on before the Human Sphere rediscovered them—leeches, essential oils? He'd heard that people still died of cancer up in the hills, that cigarettes weren't illegal there, and he didn't understand why.

An errant hope spurred Wil to check Rajan for a link bracelet. No dice—a Teseum manacle hung on his wrist, too. So much for snagging his comlog and calling in the cavalry from a broom closet.

Wil dredged the drawers and desk compartments, scanning labels and bottles until he recognized a few familiar names and pill shapes. A handful of painkillers. A fresh dose of overdue antibiotics. No equipment—at least, nothing that'd kill someone in a pinch—so he called it a wash and scurried back into the maze.

Stairs led to a hall he didn't remember and the sounds of approaching boots. He doubled back and turned left. Dead end. A short ramp led him to a locked hatch, clouded with the lingering scent of bleach. Laundry room. An adjoining hall led to a junction of bricked doors. He circled right and stumbled into a dry Roman bath stacked with dusty Christmas decorations and about nine million fucking folding chairs.

Right when it'd become reasonable to worry that the Caledonians might find his dessicate corpse wedged in the corner of a long-forgotten storeroom a few years from now, he scented motor oil. A new landmark. Wil waited until the bootsteps faded and followed his nose.

Around the corner, a chain-link gate stretched over the entry to a massive concrete garage. Workbenches ran in rows along the lockers on one side, and on the other, disassembled and Frankensteined AUVs propped on greasy metal car lifts. An emerald EXIT sign illuminated a steel door on the far corner, and as far as Wil could tell, there weren't any cameras here.

Past the fence, four red optics lit the surface of a workbench. A PanOceanian multispectral visor.

If he'd had any reservation about cutting through their garage before, he didn't now. Wil swiped the keycard, and the gate buzzed open.

Dented, beaten, but indelibly his. They'd peeled the visual array from his helmet and affixed it to an adjustable brace for ease of wear. Its power supply had been rigged to recharge from an AUV battery, and a pair of rubber cables connected the two. They'd replaced the broken lens, but the biometrics and datasphere-mapping relied on geist-assisted programs. Without his shoulder-mounted sensor unit, radar and sonar were impossible.

So much for eavesdropping through walls and in hurricanes.

Wil thumbed the analog reset. It booted without incident, four oculi burning with an accusatory red glow. Worth bringing, or dead weight? Disconnected from Wil's comlog and geist, the visor's functionality plummeted. Still, it'd give him night vision in a forest full of monstrosities, and if he killed the glow on the oculi, then—

A loud, metallic thump echoed through the garage. A relay switch. Blinding light flooded the far end of the chamber. Another thump, a new line of lights, and then again. Illumination closed in fast on his position. Just before the spotlight hit him, Wil threw himself prone behind the workbench, dragging the repaired visor and its AUV battery down too.

The click of a steel door shutting, followed by muffled voices. They grew louder, until a woman's raised among the rest: "Excuse me, stop it! I need to get back, please."

Quieting his breathing, Wil leaned out and confirmed his suspicions. It was Nora McDermott, the petite blonde from the infirmary. Neil's sister, the Volunteer paramedic. A silver tray lined with a meager plate and a pill cup occupied her hands, and by her closed-off stance, she was annoyed—annoyed, and genuinely worried.

Three of the four idiots from earlier walked alongside her, guiding her like lions might a lamb. Talbot, Bell, and Shaw. Her brother wasn't with them. And while none carried their rifles, only Nora's hip holster was empty.

Encumbered, weakened, and weaponless. Great. He'd have no choice but to hunker smack dab in the center of the room and pray they'd pass quickly.

Shaw drew the sliding gate shut, and reached up and dragged the security shutter down over it. No going back now. Bell checked the garage office, and when Nora wasn't looking, sidled a chair under the door handle.

Nora wrenched her arm from Talbot's grip, and the contents of the tray shifted dangerously. "That hurts, Chris. What's wrong with you?"

"What's wrong with us?" Bell called, bustling back. "Are you kiddin' me?"

She made some distance. "This isn't funny."

"You're right." Talbot glared, cutting her off. "It's not."

"We were 'bout tae play slap the galactic when Saoirse Clarke burst in," Shaw said, crossing the room to glare in her face. "Barked about feedin' us our knives, *respectfully*."

"Issat what she was up your arse about," Nora said, vocabulary code-switched from upmarket to farmer's market in the blink of an eye. "Oft, sorry lads. Cannae do with her, ken like? Sorry."

Talbot chuckled wryly. "Oh, aye?"

The blonde held her ground. Didn't flinch. Tried hard to not betray her obvious, pathetic lies. "Prob'ly woulda liked to get some one-on-one time with him myself. Payback 'n' all. Dawn is Ours! Yep. Sorry though, that's rubbish, with Saoirse? Real shame."

"Hackit bitch thinks she's better than us," Talbot said. "Bitch might be blood to the MacArthur, but she's still a Dogface, aye?"

Nora's brows pinched together. She seemed on the verge of saying something but bit her tongue instead. "Aye."

Sensing his moment, Wil crawled out from behind the bench. It was a straight shot to the exit door from here with only one complication: His multispectral visor's eyes still glowed crimson. Unsure of how to turn it off without his geist, Wil tucked the oculi against his stomach and began to crawl.

Bell clicked his tongue and muttered something under his breath.

Nora cocked her head. "What?"

"Vern says he saw *you* get Saoirse, hen."

She went very still. "Vern's a liar."

"No, but you are," Talbot said. "Scared of how far your brother would go to get Alastair back, you made the choice to pull his leash. You're a good sister, but a shit soldier, Eleanor."

"Saoirse's expecting me," Nora blurted.

Shaw barred her path. "No, she en't. She's with Eideard, gettin' lectured fer roughin' up Bell."

"Coulda took my arm off." Bell rolled his shoulder. "Half-breeds just dinnae ken their strength, eh? May never wank again."

Nora bit back another flash of anger. "Neil, I meant Neil—"

"Naw," Shaw said. "He's on wall tonight."

Wil sidled to the exit door. The keypad only had two buttons: LOCK, and ALARM. No code required, only a card swipe, and a sign on the wall read USE KEYPAD OUTWITH NORMAL OPERATING HOURS—whatever that meant.

A row of switches lined the wall beside it, marked 1 to 8.

Porridge slopped to the floor, and the tray clattered after. Disarmed, Nora backed into the armory lockers surrounded by the three thick-necked Volunteers.

"Neil said he'd lost his keycard," Talbot said. "I ken you took it."

"Didn't," she said. "Promise."

"I'm askin' nicely, hen. When my granda was in the service, he would've just come up on you in the barracks with his keys in a sock. You wanting that instead?"

Nora shook her head. "I've just got my own."

"That'll do," Talbot said. "And when they run ID to find who splattered the galactic, you'll stay quiet. Right, love?"

She blinked, wide-eyed. "You can't be serious."

"Deadly," Talbot said.

Nora stammered. "I—I amn't letting you—"

"No more jawing," Bell said. "Gie it over."

Talbot jut his hand forward. "*Now*."

Wil slowed, fingertips resting on the keypad's edge. This was not his problem. This was a convenient distraction. This was his gimme after two years of gotchas, a shining opportunity he'd be a fool to let slip through his fingers. He slid Neil's card through the reader and watched the light turn green.

Nora lunged for her jacket pocket. The three Volunteers descended on her. She squealed. Fought to open her comlog. It lit, but Shaw clamped his palm over the holoprojector. Bell pried open her grip, and Talbot snapped up the keycard.

It'd been bent in half. Cracks lanced down the stripe.

Wil placed his fingers on the button marked OPEN.

Bell and Shaw laughed, nervous and brief, close to cracking another joke until Talbot roared and upended an entire workbench onto the floor. Its contents scattered wild, coating the floor in loose bolts and the mixed contents of a toolbox.

The two idiots jerked back, but Nora held her ground. "Do no harm," she said, and her voice shook only slightly. "I swore an oath, do no—"

Talbot whirled on her. Slammed her against the locker doors, forearm crushing her throat. She croaked. Slapped. He didn't care. Fist pounding the steel, Talbot breathed a string of words point-blank into her face, coarse and dark and ugly, the kind of things no decent person would ever speak aloud.

And then he called her a cunt.

Wil forced on his visor and turned off the lights.

6

Talbot recoiled and let Nora hit the floor. "Bloody hell, now?"

"Cor," Shaw gasped. "Power's out."

"Power out, with the exit lights on? Certain genius, you are—"

Bell didn't finish his barb before the AUV battery cracked him across the scalp and the cara de pija crumpled. Hefting his weapon, Wil went to brain Shaw next, but the cables snagged on the corner of a workbench. The battery slipped free, clapped against the ground, and burst open. The smell of acid kicked up behind his eyes. Bitter as vinegar. Cables unclipped, his HUD pixelated, then froze.

With his comlog blocked and no geist to drive it, the CPU choked. Bold, golden outlines of the world smeared into motion.

NEW USER DETECTED. OFFLINE MODE: ACTIVATED. DO YOU REQUIRE CONTROL INSTRUCTIONS?

Talbot's eyes shined in the visor's glowing oculi. "It's the PanO!"

Shaw belted a "Shite!" and spun up his comlog dial.

Wil caught him mid-motion, hand over the holoprojector, same as Shaw had done to Nora. But in the rush, he stepped wrong. A loose bolt from Talbot's tantrum stabbed up into the bed of his foot, forced him to step short. His follow-up swing lost momentum. Missed.

Shaw caught him by the shirt. His fist flickered, and the iron taste of blood shocked across Wil's tongue. Two more impacts rattled his jaw, his ribs. A shove sent him reeling onto his back, and the steel leg of an automobile lift intercepted his fall. His skull bounced against the strut, edge blunted by the visor straps.

This was going great.

Footsteps rushed past, paired with gasping. Feminine. Nora, retreating. Louder ones from the left, deeper, scarcely audible over Shaw's litany of curses. Wil flinched back, and the air cut beside his ear. The ratchet head of a bolt wrench rang the strut where his head had left a dent.

Talbot braced his wrist and cursed, shaking off the aftershock. "Grab 'em!"

"Got it!" Shaw barked and closed the gap with a left straight. Wil ducked, putting the leg of the lift between him and Shaw's extended fist, and hooked his wrist with both hands. He hurled himself backward. Caught against the strut, Shaw's elbow inverted with a loud, wet pop.

Wil let him go. Shaw stumbled back, jaw dropped. Only after he groped at his elbow did he realize what'd happened—and then he started screaming.

Of the three, now only Talbot remained. Skirting another near-miss with the bolt wrench, Wil wrapped an arm around Shaw's neck and braced the mewling Volunteer between him and Talbot like a riot shield. Not fair, but fuck fair. They should've considered fair back when they brought Nora in here alone.

Shaw sobbed, pliant. The pistol on his belt highlighted in gold, but the clip held taut to its holster, unhelpfully left dim by his visor's chugging CPU.

TRUST ALEPH, his visor output. ALEPH IS YOUR FRIEND.

Talbot didn't hesitate. Hostage or not, friend or not, he swung hard. The initial arc went wide, but the backswing knocked the visor. Nose tweaked, Wil stumbled back. Shaw dragged with him. Together, they collided with a workbench, collective weight sliding it across the concrete.

Talbot went two-handed. Screamed.

Wil ducked, but Shaw didn't. The poor bastard hit the ground a second later, pained whimpers silenced by the friendly fire.

Wil made space fast, distancing himself from Talbot, but he'd gone stock-still staring at his crumpled friend. No reason that should've missed, not with his eyes glowing like Breaker rounds in the dark. Standing, Wil tested his nose with his knuckle to check if it was broken and saw his forearm didn't change color under the ocular glow. The impact had shorted them out.

He wouldn't get that lucky again.

Talbot shook Shaw once, then harder. No response. Face contorted in rage, Talbot wheeled back to Wil. "Bastard! You killed him, you bloody killed him!"

No. Stunned, sure, but not dead. No fencing response, so no concussion. Groaning—just stunned. Might need to blenderize his meals for a bit, but nothing worse. Lucky, given the weight behind the swing. Could've put his eye out. But before Wil could articulate any of that, Talbot went for his pistol.

Wil tackled him head-on. Grappled. Fingers crushed against fingers. The wrench lashed across his back, but the motion conceded enough leverage to jerk the firearm free. When it fell, Wil kicked it beneath the lockers and hugged him from behind, pinning his biceps to his ribs.

Wrench neutralized.

No plan after this.

Talbot bellowed and charged backward. Wil lost his balance just before he crushed against cold steel, air knocked from his lungs.

The lockers. Talbot was ramming him into the lockers.

Recovering, Talbot strained against Wil's arms. Fingers interlocked, he refused, and they went for a second go.

Midway, Wil pitched all his weight to the right. Forced a pivot. Talbot's heels squeaked, and he impacted the locker wrist-first. The bolt wrench clattered from his smashed hand and bounced away into the dark.

Talbot hunched over, gripping his bent fingers. Veins popped to the surface of his forehead. Under the night vision, the sweat sheeting down his face shimmered red and spectral white.

Wil shoved free, but it was just posturing. Couldn't muster the energy to finish things. Couldn't do much other than pant. Adrenaline fumes and waning desperation were enough to stay standing, but weren't enough to lay Talbot low. Beaten, exhausted, underfed—that he'd gotten this far was a miracle. No farther. Once he recovered, Talbot was going to kill him. Only a matter of time until he found another weapon, and at that point—

Talbot turned and spat in Wil's face.

In the span of one second, years of practical training with some of Pan-Oceania's highest paid hand-to-hand instructors in officers' academies, VR simulations, and training camps across the Human Sphere evaporated and all that was left was the starving boy from King's Den, venting his rage into his hands.

Elbow to jaw. Visor met forehead. Left jab, duck, right hook, shove. Wil sidestepped a desperate straight, repaid it in kind. The lockers rattled. Up under the ribs, one side then the other until Talbot's arms sagged and the next swing torqued his jaw. Burst lip drooling dark lines onto the concrete, the defenseless idiot caught two more against the teeth before he fully hit the ground.

Across the garage, golden lines silhouetted Bell. Long licks of red cascaded from his hair. He wobbled to one knee, fingering his holster.

A tape measure glinted from a locker, its door jarred open by their scuffle. Wil snapped it up and pitched. Silver glinted into the dark, followed by a crunch. He rushed over, bloody knuckles clenched, but Bell was... done. The measure had hit him square in the nose and flipped its bridge like abstract art. All the kid could do was writhe and beg for his mother.

Couldn't blame him. A bloodless break was bad news.

"Like a Blackjack on the Fifth of July," Wil muttered and stole Bell's pistol from its holster. Even if he hoped he didn't need it, it was better than nothing at all.

Light returned with a quartet of metallic claps, whiting out his night vision. Wil yanked his visor up, fearing reinforcements. But instead of soldiers, it was only little Nora standing beside the exit with her palm flat on the switches.

Wil panted. His hands throbbed, middle knuckles thinned to pink fibers over the bone, and loosening his fist took work. The stitches in his left arm had ripped, smearing him palm to elbow with fresh, glistening red.

"Sorry," he said, and stuck the pistol under his waist band. "I know, shouldn't touch—"

She shrieked and speared at him.

"Wait!" he shouted. "Wait, I was helping!"

Nora didn't slow. Didn't hold back. Neon pink fingernails gouged lines up his arms. Steel-toed boots battered his feet and shins till she used his jewels like a step to reach for his face and a thumbnail dug under his visor to scrape across his eyelids.

Nope.

The open locker loomed behind her, inviting. Big enough. Wil charged it and planted Nora inside the empty compartment full-force. Before she could recover, he slammed the door shut. The hinges rattled, stainless steel muffling the unholy chorus within. Padlock secure, numbers spun for good measure.

Wil tried to catch his breath. No good deeds, he thought, and resisted the urge to double over when the nausea bled up into his gut from the boot she'd delivered. A twinge of regret struck him—wasn't this what he'd meant to stop in the first place?—but it ebbed along with the last of the adrenaline. Those boys would've done worse. They had it coming.

Pain wasn't pain. Wil limped for the door without making a sound.

A low shelf stood near the door, nigh-invisible before in the dark. Waiting there were a pair of standard-issue Caledonian stompers, size thirteen and everything.

Some good deeds.

⇡⇡

Out on the lawn, the smell of grass and night rain whorled amidst the Ariadnan pines. In the distance, dark clouds blotted out the stars. A bigger storm, chasing the smaller one away. The freezing mountain air bit into his exposed skin and dug into wounds both new and old. Had to be in the negatives. Nothing like Svalarheima—his eyelashes didn't flash-freeze on exposure, for one—but too close to be comfortable.

Wil hooked the boots on and started sprinting.

Only a few low stone walls topped with crushed glass and barbed wire separated the castle's grounds and the township beyond. Wil mantled them in ten seconds and dug the glass dust from his palms on the run down the hill. Past the slanted anti-air batteries, across a landing strip, he left the ghostly crown of floodlights that glared from the highest parapets of Castle MacArthur and slid into a ditch.

His jaw throbbed where Shaw had grazed him. The fingers on his left hand had already swollen up, and the cold had them shaking already. Tying the laces on his new boots was an exercise in frustration, but at least his HUD held stable. The Atek repairman had done a good job after all, even if modes beyond night vision were inaccessible. At least Talbot's percussive maintenance had killed the ocular glow.

He checked Bell's pistol. An AKNovy Kremen. Dirty didn't cover it. AK-Novys were infamous for their reliability, but the CO in Wil cringed at the muddy fingerprints left all over the slide.

Seventeen in the magazine. One more bullet than his lost TauruSW Ferro.

Wil checked for pursuers. None. Yet.

He picked up the pace.

Small, single-story dwellings of mottled brick huddled together along the winding roads and bridges up the hillside. Wil cut downhill through the narrow spaces: alleys, irrigation ditches, the playground of an apartment building. The farther Wil descended, the more the buildings multiplied, the more the infrastructure crumbled until he was speeding down alleys and over brick walls.

A clothesline stretched across a narrow garden, hung heavy with forgotten laundry. He stole a wool sweater off the line and donned it, careful of Bell's pistol tucked into his waistband. The itching in his forearm started again, and fresh red blotted along the sleeve from inside. No time to stop and address. No pants on the line, either. Legs numbing, he nicked the thickest coat he could see—better to cover razor wire—and carried on, careful to stay away from the streets.

At the terminus of the township, a massive patchwork palisade stood between civilization and pitch-black Caledonian wilderness. Corrugated steel sheets layered in a shield wall along its frame. Faded graffiti doused its base, and spotlights haloed the ramshackle walkways, aimed in all directions. Only one entry, one exit: a chain-link sally port lined with armed guards and tank-treaded Traktor Muls.

Triangular rocket tubes meant Uragan. One centimeter too close, and their Total Reaction matrices wouldn't leave his shoes behind in the crater.

So much for shadowing an AUV through the checkpoint.

A broad stretch of open dirt roadway separated the township buildings from the palisade, lined with sandbags and concrete blocks. Rails cut along the concrete, winding toward a shadowed installation huddled on the darkened hillside. The Teseum mine. Probably the first place they'd look—any exit from there would prematurely put him one step behind.

Spotlights swung along the wall's base, splashing across AUV hoods and graffiti-splattered concrete bollards. Light played along the undefended rungs of a ladder. That was his ticket. Straight through, no time wasted. Up, then down. The palisade itself was only a paltry ten meters tall. A few cheeky handholds and the drop would cut to five, easy. That was survivable. Maybe not enjoyable, but did he have a choice?

Alarms flared to life atop two of the four watchtowers, shattering the silence. Soldiers rushed from the shadow of the wall, comlog dials burning like watchmen's lanterns. Both Traktor Muls locked in place, battery turning on a swivel. AUV engines growled in the parking lot. Headlights cut lines in the dark, turning northward toward Castle MacArthur.

He was so stupid. This is what stopping to help had earned him. He shouldn't have bothered—not like she'd ever have the opportunity to say thank you. Worse, if he was going, he had to go now. No time left for reconnsaiance or hesitation, not when they were still catching up. Heart pounding, he timed the spotlight's lazy sway, stayed as low as his knees allowed, and charged.

The road was behind him inside ten seconds, and he slid flat behind a cluster of sandbags at the foot of the palisade. With his pistol at the ready, he scanned the distant troopers for a sign that he'd been spotted. Nothing. Silence. Scot-free, literally and metaphorically. Standing, he reached for the ladder above when a door in the wall creaked open.

Nowhere to hide. Wil surged against the palisade wall, just behind the opening door, and held his breath.

A flashlight beam cut over the sandbags, illuminating where he'd just been. A patrol. Two men. One rushed left toward the AUVs, rifle in hand, and the other stomped out into the cold, furiously spinning the holoprojected dial of his comlog.

It was Neil.

"C'mon," Neil muttered. "C'mon, damn it. C'mon."

A tinny jingle interrupted Neil's cursing. A comlog call.

He accepted it. "Hey, you all right? Cluster's gone mental—wait, you're where? He *what*?"

No room to maneuver. The slightest motion, the smallest sound would be enough to alert him. No choice but to wait. No other option. Finger on the Kremen's trigger, Wil prayed the kid didn't turn around.

"Bell? Talbot?" Neil said. "Slow down, Nora, slow down."

One step to the left, and their elbows would be touching. A glance too far, it'd be impossible for Neil to not catch Wil in his peripheral vision.

Neil reached back for the door and paused. "Bolt cutters? No, we en't got bolt cutters here. But I know where," he said, and started toward the AUVs. "Hang tight. I'll be right there!"

As the crunch of Neil's boots on the pavement faded, Wil removed his finger from the trigger and started breathing again.

Without ado, he slipped up the ladder, covered the razor wire with the surplus coat, and dropped onto the other side. His landing sucked and he twisted his knee, but sixty seconds of hasty limping later, he'd lost sight of the MacArthur palisade and all the Atek psychopaths who lived there.

Good riddance.

⚔

Roots gnarled up from beneath leaning trees and turned the flat ground hostile. Glacial boulders scattered amongst rotting logs, saturated by carpets of moss. Shallow ponds of rainwater dotted the uneven forest floor, reflecting the scant moonshine from Tanit far, far above.

Seven kilometers took more than an hour. Visions of Pale Shadow haunted him the whole way, mingled with the mournful song of Antipode howls. No matter how many times Wil scanned the misty treeline with his night vision and saw nothing, he didn't shake the eyes on his back, or the fear.

Just when he was ready to declare himself utterly lost, his visor highlighted tire marks along the damp black trail and extrapolated a path straight to the crash site.

Didn't know it had that without a geist.

The metallic carcass heaped in the center of the clearing was nearly unrecognizable. What remained of the Balena after the explosion had been ravaged by scavengers: steel plates skinned to iron bones, panels disfigured, circuitry gutted. The surviving aerodyne had been amputated, and what the explosion hadn't melted had been stripped. Claw marks across the scorched chassis became drag marks on the rocks, winding away into the forest.

What the Antipodes wanted with paneling or tail rotors or circuit boards, Wil didn't want to know.

He circled the Balena, gave his lost MULTI Marksmanship Rifle one last chance to show itself, and climbed the escarpments to the wood's edge. Amidst the sea of Antipode tracks, a human shoeprint. It aimed away from the crash, the pattern of its sole notably different from an Ariadnan boot. He scanned for more, unearthing a jagged trail into the western woods. By their gait, they'd been limping.

Wil's mind raced, searching for an explanation, but the how didn't matter. Keyes had survived, and Wil had his bearing.

But the clawed tracks suggested he'd gone in the same unfortunate direction as the Antipodes' retreat. Alone and injured, Keyes' chances were slim. If the Antipodes were kind, they'd leave his corpse impaled on a branch for ease of discovery. At least then his comlog would still be intact. Might even be warm still, depending on the timing.

Mierda. Wil couldn't believe he was considering this, but what other option did he have? After manhandling the Volunteers, he'd made his choice, and the MacArthurs would shoot on sight. The only way out was through.

A hundred meters beyond the crash site, he found the survival kit from the transport cracked open and emptied of both its MREs. The shotgun case laid nearby, along with two hollow shells and a swathe of dark earth.

Blood.

A few meters farther, Keyes' trail broke up. He'd started hiding his tracks. Pawprints in the dirt from some indeterminate small game highlighted on the path, like a marten or a rabbit. Not unreasonable, considering the amount of transplanted Sol wildlife that'd escaped captivity over the years.

The gentle sigh of water lilted amidst the midnight stillness. A creek lay ahead, slowly twisting through the green. The storms had fed the flow, and what must've been a shallow trickle two days ago had swollen to a thick, deceptive current.

On the other side, a small, square hut of stacked stones huddled in a clearing, its base choked with tall, flowering weeds.

A bothy—a communal hunter's cabin left unlocked for whoever needed it. Dirt floor, simple, no furnishings. Light pulsed through the empty windowsill, slow and dim as fire.

Keyes.

Wil snaked along the shore to a shallow crossing of piled rocks. Moss slicked their tops, but his boots kept traction, and soon the rocky embankment gave way to the crunch of fallen leaves.

He tightened his hands around the grip of Bell's pistol. It'd gone sticky from his burst stitches, and the lines that Nora had clawed into him still stung. God, he hoped that Keyes didn't see him first, soaked in his own blood and half-naked besides. Might confuse him for a cannibal come down the mountain to search for a dinner guest. Palm on the windowsill, he stepped into the light.

The orange-red periphery of a Nomad closed-channel hacking device doused the bothy in fiery color. Keyes crouched beside it on the dirt floor, helmet absent. He had brown hair. Dirt marred his cheeks in heavy stripes. A loose, gray survival mantle hung over his shoulders, and he held something to his mouth, like a rag or a cloth.

Something furry, and wet.

A rabbit.

Keyes startled. Turned. Eyes a putrid white, his face was slit open from above the nose to below the chin. Four bony mandibles protruded from within, dripping with steaming viscera.

7

Keyes jerked back. His hands jumped.

Wet, stinking fur slapped Wil in the face. Red stained his vision, covering his oculi right as he startled the Kremen up and fired twice.

Footsteps rushed away. Two misses. He spun from the window, back against the uneven stone wall and cleared the blood from his visor's face in a panic.

No dead monstrosities greeted him from the dirt-floored bothy interior. Keyes was gone, and with him, the light of the Nomad hacking device. On the other side of the shelter, a ramshackle door creaked in the growing breeze.

That'd been a Shasvastii. No question about it. He'd caught an alien eating a rabbit. Keyes hadn't been human. Maybe ever. Or if he had been once, it'd been before he'd been quietly murdered, before his Cube and his memories and everything that was Keyes had been absorbed by the split-faced thing that'd just hauled ass into the woods.

Fifteen rounds remained in the Kremen.

Wil strained to listen over the drumbeat of his heart. He wasn't ready for this. Exhaustion had taken its toll on him from the infection, from his escape. Steady pangs in his abdomen bled through the rising adrenaline. His mouth was dry. Tongue, sandpaper on his teeth. Keeping the pistol level seemed an impossible challenge with the persistent shake from the cold and the twinge in his knuckles.

He stepped back. Dead leaves crunched underfoot.

The empty air around the corner of the bothy glimmered.

A shotgun blast shattered the silence. The stone wall beside him exploded, and Wil scrambled for cover, plunging behind the bothy corner and into a pile of spiny, flowering vines. The planks of a disintegrating planter box obscured beneath the green dented his ribs.

A second shot scoured the eaves from the overhang and showered him in splinters. For an instant, Wil had eyes on Keyes' silhouette, and then he was gone again, ducked behind the cabin.

Camouflage. Not thermo-optical. Bioquantronic. A Shrouded—a guerilla surveillance unit dedicated to spearheading sabotage efforts. But Shrouded didn't wear human faces, so then this was what, a Speculo Agent? The hell could they do?

Wil's exhaustion evaporated, replaced by a rush of sickening electricity. His breath quickened, heaving in the crushed flower pile's acidic tang. He refused the urge to make space, to flee for the forest. Gaining range would've been smart if Keyes wasn't better armed. A geist-assisted shotgun's smart ammunition could detonate at long or short range, making its threat variable and impossible to predict. Worse, he was surrounded by a field of dead leaves, and only one of their footsteps made sound.

There had to be an angle Wil could press for an advantage. Something nearby.

The Kremen? No—low caliber, no stopping power. Dive into the bothy? Close-quarters with zero cover versus a weapon optimally utilized in a choke—yeah, great idea. The animal corpse, twitching beside his leg—what he'd be in ten seconds if he didn't do *something*.

A swathe of small, dark shrapnel pocked the wall. Flechettes.

He paused. Looked again. Low-tech, low-yield. No evidence of armor-piercing coating. Closer to nails than razors. Nothing like the shot he'd seen on Paradiso, buried in the walls of their checkpoint after the Dāturazi's failed charge.

It was human-make. Light, 20-gauge tops. The shotgun from the Balena. Purpose-made to dissuade an Antipode, not for warfare. Ariadnan. Outdated. It'd only load three shells at a time.

If he provoked a salvo, he could close the gap before Keyes managed a reload. Jumpy as he was, cornered without a proper firearm, he'd probably mag dump anything that moved. Just needed a poke in the right direction and reflexes faster than his reload.

Wil stifled the steam in his breath as he edged to the corner. Careful, like threading a needle, he popped two shots around the bend and flinched back.

The stone clustered with nails. Grit scattered into his face, and then again. Two shots. No third. Bait untaken. He snatched up the dead rabbit, hedged his bet, and tossed it into the clearing.

Mid-flight, it vaporized into pink mist.

All pretense of subtlety abandoned, Wil ripped around the corner and stormed Keyes' cover. A single line etched in his HUD there indicating a possible camouflage silhouette, and he filled the space with bullets.

Gore spattered the bothy wall. Leaves crushed and scattered without sound. Atop them, bioquantronic camouflage crackled and died, revealing Keyes' sagged semi-human shape. His mandibles squeezed together like smashed spider legs and went limp, ejecting a sloppy wad of chewed rabbit. Violet oozed from the hole in his throat down across the shotgun, alien blood steaming in the cold.

It didn't have a smell.

One downside of relying on targeting programs and aim-assisted smart fire was the human element. His geist painted targets, read IFFs, and adjusted aim, but it didn't discriminate and didn't pull the trigger. Keyes hadn't seen a rabbit, but a red dot, and now he was dead.

Wil picked the shotgun from Keyes' limp hands and tossed it aside. Nothing worthwhile in his pockets. The Nomad hacking device dimmed on his wrist, periphery shattered by two deflected shots from his Kremen. No way it'd call out now.

An itch drew his attention, along his left arm. Wet, dead leaves coated his elbow from where he'd lay. He brushed them away, but the itch remained. A trickle of something darker oozed past his fingers.

Blood. He'd been hit. One unlucky flechette nail stuck up at an angle from his shoulder. Red welled up its length onto the surface of the sweater, dashing down the stitching of his sleeve.

In that moment, it wasn't the pain that frustrated him. It was that he couldn't remember the last time he'd had all his blood inside his body.

Somewhere way too close, an Antipode howled.

Wil surveyed the forest's edge, each individual hair on his arms and neck needle-straight. When he turned back, Keyes was gone.

He shocked to his feet, scanning the clearing past the Kremen's iron sights. Burning gold outlines highlighted every errant blade of grass, every twig, every weed and flower and tuft of moss until it clocked a camouflage shadow speeding silently over the field of dead leaves. Keyes. He absorbed the discarded shotgun and broke for the trees.

Easy shot. Clean. But the instant Wil squeezed the trigger, the visor decided the Kremen was more interesting than his target—and the feed fractured. Data overflow cascaded past his vision, blinding him. The bullet cut into the underbrush, and Keyes' silhouette disappeared into the night. Another miss.

As soon as it'd appeared, the error message cycled and returned to first boot: NEW USER DETECTED. OFFLINE MODE: ACTIVATED. DO YOU REQUIRE CONTROL INSTRUCTIONS?

Wil hammered the side of his visor until the message closed and his vision cleared. The purplish bloodstain in the grass was full and deep. No way in hell was that acting. He'd seen enough fresh corpses to know death when he saw it. So then, what? Regeneration? If so, it wasn't Haqq-make, wasn't medicine—but alien genetic woo-woo, science like magic from beyond the Human Edge.

And after all his bravado about taking two shots.

Wil eyed the dark forest beyond the clearing, skin pricking with electric tension. Adrenaline failed to wash the fatigue from his tired feet, the dull ache from his burst stitches, the fresh sting from the nail dug into his shoulder. And judging by how much lighter the Kremen had gotten after he'd blown half the mag, he had about five rounds left.

Regeneration alone made waiting the wrong choice. If Keyes lost him now, he'd heal and wait until morning to come back with a vengeance; and without the darkness, Wil would lose the advantage of his visor. He could turtle up in the bothy, but humans had to sleep. Did Shasvastii? Keyes still had camo, had shells. Hell, a sharp rock and some patience would be more than enough.

No other choice. Had to finish things now, before exhaustion took him under. Pulse quickening his blood through his fingers, Wil followed Keyes' into the woods.

Thin strands of moonlight penetrated the boughs above, streaking through his multispectral vision like frozen tracer rounds. Tree trunks faded in and out of the night, crags of bark outlined in bold, bright gold, and he went cover to cover between them.

Low POWER blinked in the corner of his eye again. Last time, that'd meant two seconds. This time, Wil prayed for sixty.

The wind shifted. Less than five meters away, a puddle of pine needles compressed without sound.

Wil jerked back behind the tree. The bark beside his face punched away, and sawdust bombed his visual feed. Arm against the trunk, he fired back. Two bullets whistled into the dark. Nothing screamed, nothing fell.

Three rounds remained.

Slow and steady, Wil left cover. No visual alerts. No motion. Just trees, shifting in and out of focus in the perfect dark of the Caledonian wildlands.

Up ahead, the swollen creek slithered on, pale light reflected on its rippling face. Loud enough to drown out his heartbeat. Wider than where he'd crossed, far from the flat stone bridge. Its earthy shore was empty, wide-open, free of any obstacles. The perfect place for an intergalactic quickdraw competition.

The wind blew, carrying the smell of oncoming rain. Adrenaline tremors wracked his hands, so he deepened his breathing to compensate. A blade of grass by the creek's edge danced, then pivoted in the wrong direction.

Two shots, parallel to the forest floor.

Nothing hit.

Motion from behind. An ambush. Wil spun, and two strikes to the jaw sent him toppling to the muck. His pistol ripped from his hands and broke the creek's surface with a plunk. Shoving himself to his knees, he found the dark cylinder of a shotgun barrel and Keyes' alien gaze drawn level with his face.

Wil sucked in his last breath. Stared up the smoothbore tunnel. Waited for the flash, the heat. Hoped it didn't hurt, but knew it probably would.

Keyes' eyes creased. His mandibles clicked together, rapid-fire clicking. A brux. Had to be their version of a laugh. "Unlucky," he said, and a tree branch snapped behind them.

Leaves crunched. Keratin clicked against stone. A ghostly shape ambled out onto the moonlit shore, gripping the hilt of a wicked knife.

The white Antipode. Pale Shadow.

Keyes followed Wil's gaze. His mandibles clenched. "Shit."

The brush shifted, unnatural. Red lines traced paths through the dark.

He'd seen this before. Knew what came next. In the woods, he wouldn't stand a chance. The creek was his only option. He hoped the swell was too wide to jump, the water too cold to chance. In the scant second of distraction, Wil shoved Keyes toward the forest and dove into the current.

Keyes stumbled. The shotgun roared. For a brief instant, a second Anti-pode illuminated in the muzzle flare, jaws collaring his unprotected neck.

The freezing creek water swallowed Wil whole, soaking through his clothes in an instant. It punched the air from his lungs, stabbed up inside his nose, into the back of his head. Burning knives gouged his shoulder. His lungs spasmed—and as fast as the shock had upended him, his entire body numbed.

Toes, deadened. Fingers, locked. Heart pounding. Breath short. Every limb felt disconnected, distant. He needed to go back. This was a mistake. Hypothermia would kill him if the shock didn't drown him first.

Wil turned back to catch Pale Shadow opening Keyes from neck to navel with his knife. Intestines burst from beneath clothing, beneath yellow fat. A third Antipode joined the frenzy, tail a blur. Human screams twisted into inhuman trill-ing, and the triune buried their snouts into the mess.

The creek deepened. Its current towed Wil's foot from beneath him. He slipped under.

Back up. Ears stung. Eyes.

Other side. No choice.

Closer.

Thought, difficult. Cold.

The rocks. He dragged himself. Up. Out of the river.

Onto the shore. Shaking.

Blood leaked from his sleeve. It drew a trail in the dirt. Four fresh nails needled his arm, dashing from bicep to shoulder like a constellation. A graze, but still deadly. Heavy breaths contained the pain when it threatened to overflow until a shiver twisted the embedded spikes and left him writhing on the shore.

Across the creek, Pale Shadow stared, amber eyes glinting from their hol-lows. It loped from Keyes to the water's edge and tested it with one claw. Snout wrinkled, it paced the shore in tight circles, considering the distance. Tested the water again, paw-deep, and shook away the drip, hackles rising and falling like tall grass in the wind.

It snarled. The jump was too far and not worth the hypothermia.

Wil gave it the middle finger.

Pale Shadow narrowed his eyes. It flipped the knife in its paw, arm cocked back, and its swing cut the air.

Wil recoiled, iced-over limbs hardly capable of motion. But nothing struck him. The knife glinted in its grip, unthrown.

A feint.

The expression on its face—

Just enough civilization to be capable of cruelty.

The Antipodes' tails fluffed out, tucked in. Alarm. With a chuff and a yip, they swiveled and sped away, dragging the gurgling Keyes behind them. His fin-gers raked the turf until he disappeared into the dark.

Wil knew better than to assume he'd won. Soaked to the bone in this cold, he'd be dead in minutes. The Antipodes knew that. Hadn't shown mercy. The bleed wasn't slowing. Too many nails. Feeling wasn't returning to his hands or feet.

He had to stand. Couldn't die here.

A sharp, sudden light whited out his night vision. When it returned, a Caledonian Highlander stared at him down the barrel of a chain rifle.

8

Branches scraped by against his shins. Rocks, his shoes. Ahead, the wilderness drowned in the headlights of a trio of AUVs surrounded by the shadows of men. Ten steps from the lead vehicle, his escort dropped him onto the damp black earth and kept their distance.

Wil struggled to stand. Didn't have much luck. Dull pain radiated from every flechette nailed up his arm, and his Teseum shackle dripped with creek water and blood. He'd been right about the tracker. Arrogant, really, to think he'd outrun them in their own backyard.

Eideard exited the vehicle in the lead, wrapped tight in a long, dark coat. He held a snub-nosed revolver far from his torso, like it might wriggle free and bite back.

"Found him by the water, menaced by Antipodes and shivering." His escort held out Wil's waterlogged multispectral visor for inspection. "Gunfight, sir. Private Bell's pistol isn't on him, but McDermott's card was."

Eideard glanced at the visor and tossed it aside. "A gunfight with whom?"

"Another galactic," the other said. "Couldnae see who, not with 'Podes on site. Hounds hauled the sorry bastard off into the hills in three pieces, weapon and all."

"Hopefully that settles their blood debt." Eideard glared at Wil. "Did your agreement with the Hexahedron sour on their part, or yours? How much did they promise you? What's the name of your commanding officer? Are you an agent of the Foreign Company?"

Wil straightened himself out. "ForCo couldn't afford me."

"You brutalized a trio of young men tonight, and I'm not wont to keep a wild beast caged where it can sneak loose and wreak havoc," Eideard said. "I urge you to become useful before I put you down."

There was no point in hiding a Shasvastii infestation from these men. Honesty might even save his life. "It was an alien," Wil said. "Caught it eating a rabbit, wearing the skin of the co-pilot from the crash. Shasvastii."

"More lies. Who sent you?"

"I'm not fucking around, man."

The revolver barrel went level with Wil's forehead. "Last chance, galactic."

Halogen lights. Cardboard and black plastic.

Wil set his jaw. "William goddamn Wallace."

Eideard's finger curled atop the trigger as a voice echoed up the trail.

Eideard froze. The soldiers tensed, weapons raised. But the voice called out again, closer, and surprised relief washed away the uncertainty in their eyes. Clustering in the road, the soldiers whispered madly and craned their necks to see around the bend.

At first, the headlight beams caught the bottoms of legs, large and dark and shining. Horses, complete with saddles and everything. A trio of riders galloped toward them on the trail, slowing as they neared the gathering. One rider shouted a greeting, waved his arm—and then must've spotted Wil, knelt and held at gunpoint, because their enthusiasm instantly died.

Eideard fumbled his revolver into its holster. "Guns down," he said, and snapped his fingers several times. "Gag the galactic. Quick, now!"

The men traded glances. One of them checked their pockets, but they came up empty. Surprisingly, none of these gentlemen had a ball gag on their belts beside their sidearms.

The moment Eideard lost his nerve, the urge to run surged in Wil's legs. To break for the brush and make back for the bothy. To try for a gun. Any gun. But he was tired, and his arm was riddled with nails, and everything hurt too much. Only anger remained, and not enough to give him wings.

The riders drew from a canter to a walk as they closed in on Eideard's convoy. The lead rider was enormous, hairier than what he rode on and bulked with corded muscle. A wildman mop of dark hair tangled into the bushel of his beard, and his scowl seemed natural on his windburned face. He wasn't dressed for the rain and the cold with bare arms and no coat, but he showed no sign of discomfort. Wrapped in tarpaulin on his saddle lay a two-handed weapon. Not a claymore. Bigger.

The second in line was an old man in a gray tam-o'-shanter, silver-black beard well-kept and trim beneath a hawkish nose. He wore a length of plaid from shoulder to hip, the same green and gold as the MacArthurs. A claymore lay sheathed on his left side; on his right, a single armored pauldron flecked with azure paint. Only when he rode closer did Wil realize that the armor was defaced on purpose, scratched with so many tallies that the original color was all but erased.

The final rider was the youngest, only a year or two past twenty, dressed in an anorak and insulated pants. Handsome and pale, his eyes were a piercing blue beneath the casual mess of his auburn hair, shoulders sturdy as a Hellenic statue. Capping the pack bundled at the end of his saddle hung a meter-long ballistic shield of refined Teseum, adorned with a Caledonian cross and a unicorn's head in profile. Beneath it, a long rifle tested the limits of a wet-weather bag.

A Mormaer. More armor than an Orc, and the best gear in all Caledonia. Second to none in the Highlands, and what passed for aristocracy among the CHA.

The boy seemed the greenest, so it surprised Wil when he took point past the other two. "Uncle! What's going on?"

Eideard approached with open arms. "Alastair, thank God you're alright! We feared the worst, lad."

So, this kid was the one Neil was so worried about. They looked about the same age. Probably served in their mandatory service in the Ariadnan Army at the same time.

"Feared the worst of what? I told you we'd be gone three days," Alastair said. "Who's this man?"

Eideard dropped his hands. "It's been four."

The old timer in the tam-o'-shanter cleared his throat. "Answer his questions, Ed."

"After a few of my own, thank you," Eideard said. "Where've you been? Why didn't you ring, what happened? And where'd these bloody horses come from?"

Alastair didn't answer. Just dismounted, eyes fixed on Wil. His anorak shifted enough that the headlights glinted off the Americolt chain-colt holstered on his hip.

The giant lurched out of his saddle to the whickering protest of his mount. "Care," he said. "Blood smells funny. Too clean. *Galactic.*"

"Noted," Alastair said. "Cailean, do you mind?"

"Not at all," the old man said and trotted his horse forward. "Reached Fort Resolute after a day, no galactics in sight. Kicked about the ruins till wen saw a fancy transport flit by. Got good and ready. But nothin' came of it. After another hour, we heard a thunderclap and a boom. Trouble. So we went radio silent, started our way back. And that's when Gordon sniffed out some poor dead lass, crooked on a pine branch twenty yards overhead."

A pang of remorse jumped through Wil. He imagined Rajan's assistant in her final moments—terrified, falling, atmosphere too thin to suck oxygen for a scream. He could've done more. Should've done more.

The kid handed his horse's reins to one of Eideard's goons. Cautiously, he approached, appraising the pincushion of Wil's shoulder. "He's been shot."

"Grazed." Wil clenched his teeth until it hurt. Anything to keep from giving in to another shudder. "Not—not by yours."

"Then by who?"

Wil nodded at Eideard. "Ask him."

Closer now, the kid reached out his hand. "Can you stand?"

Legs quaking, Wil managed without his help. The soldiers all straightened out at once, hands hovering over their weapons, but with a gesture from Alastair, their alarm dulled away.

"Sam," Alastair said, "grab your kit. Crawford will need to tend those wounds, but let's ensure he doesn't bleed out in the meantime. And Logan, trade him your shirt or he's liable to freeze to death. Can you tie off his arm?"

"Aye, cousin," Logan said, and without question, stripped off his coat and undershirt. The other man, Sam, rushed to unhook a red box from the AUV trunk. Strange that they didn't spare a glance to Eideard for permission, seemed to jump right to it—

And then it clicked. The kid wasn't just a Mormaer. The guy gladly holding his horse's reins; how everyone carried out his orders without question; how Eideard couldn't compel his attention, or his answer. Only one explanation made sense.

The friend Neil had been worried about and the leader Eideard feared dead were one and the same. Alastair was the MacArthur. This kid was clan chieftain.

Peeling the ruined fabric away from his cuts and bruises hurt worse than getting them in the first place. Wil held his flechette-riddled arm out, and Logan inspected it for only a moment before tying his arm off with a makeshift tourniquet of paracord. Hurt like a son of a bitch, but dry—dry was good.

"Works till we get back," Sam said, and stripped the tab off a small plastic pouch before pressing it into Wil's hand. A disposable warmer. It didn't distract him from the following hypospray, coating every square centimeter of the wreck of his upper arm in stinging liquid bandage, or the lingering realization of what exactly *get back* meant.

"Burying the poor lass took longer than we'd planned," Cailean said, huddled over the horn of his saddle. "Storm came, quick. Chose to weather it out when the Antipodes got frisky. Shredded our AUV tires, the right bastards."

Eideard glanced between Wil and Alastair, frown deepening. "Bloody hell."

"Hiked the ten klicks on foot to Odhran's Ford tae find their Arachne relay tipped by the storm. Of course, Bleedin'-Heart MacArthur here couldnae leave the poor homesteaders disconnected. That stole a whole day on its own, but at least they lent us horses. Sent a message and rode up right after. Unwise to push this far so late, but we had a worry. Right when Gordon smelled 'Pode, we heard the hullabaloo."

The giant—Gordon—soothed his nervous horse. "Thought it was a search party. Thought you ran across the Winter Dancers."

"Aye, you're not far off," Eideard said. "We were hunting this man, here. PanOceanian. He crash-landed into our territory on a secret mission and killed Indigo River."

Cailean's eyebrows hitched. "No surprise the 'Podes were narked."

"And he wouldn't tell us who he was, or who he works for," Eideard continued, gaining steam. "Then, he broke free from the basement, and walloped a trio of our lads. Tweaked Sebastian Bell's nose sideways, beat Christopher Talbot to a pulp, and gave Joseph Shaw a concussion."

Despite the shiver, Wil couldn't hold himself back. "Talbot did that."

Eideard wheeled on him. "So you don't deny it?"

Alastair stared at his uncle, incredulous. "Broke free," he said, voice strained. "You imprisoned him. The first offworlder to visit Kildalton in years... and you imprisoned him?"

"He's a trespasser," Eideard said. "And besides, we suspected he'd—he'd done something to you, lad. Taken you from us."

"How many times have I told you we need to encourage diplomatic relations, not squander them," Alastair said, closing on him. "Do you know how much of a benefit this could have been? Rescuing a crash victim would've improved our esteem with the Dawn Research Commission, with Bureau Ganesh, given us opportunities. But no, as always, you kent better."

Cailean's weathered, wind-burnt face set in a grimace. "Kipped out to tea fer five minutes an' we come back tae this? Jaysis, Ed."

Eideard's glare deepened. "He's dangerous," he said. "He's an *assassin*."

Alastair leaned in close, but his furious whisper carried far. "I don't care if he's the devil himself, Uncle Eideard. I decide who we shoot by the roadside. Not you. Are we clear?"

He kept Eideard's gaze until the old man faltered and shrank away.

The black sky above shuddered and broke open. Rain fell, first slow, then fast. Thunder. Cailean whistled, and the men jumped into action. In two minutes flat, they set out back up the road toward the township with Wil riding shotgun in the lead.

Out of the fire, and into the frying pan.

9

Rain drummed the Traktor Muls' chassis like tin techno-favela rooftops and drained off the palisade crenelations in rivers. Every floodlight focused on their convoy, casting long shadows off the abandoned pillboxes lining their approach.

"Welcome tae Kildalton, off-worlder," Cailean shouted over the growing storm. "I pray yer stay's a short one."

It was as if his first arrival had been a bad dream or a failed rehearsal, and the entire town came together to do a second run. Lots of folk watched the procession from their doorsteps, expressions muddled with relief and fear. Some braved the rain to call out, and Alastair echoed back, "Good evening, all's well, no cause for alarm!"

At the castle doors, Neil dashed into the rain from under the portico. Alastair dismounted to embrace him. The blond volunteer's hasty Caledonian slowed to a crawl when he laid eyes on Wil bleeding in the AUV's passenger seat.

"Cousin," Neil said. "The galactic's still alive?"

Alastair led him aside. "Let's talk."

Wil's second visit with the doctor—Lilah Crawford, now that she had a chance to introduce herself without him leaping for a knife—was much more congenial. A heavy dose of painkillers made him only tangentially aware of the flechette nails she plucked from his meat, though the ones she had to dig for with pliers kept him white-knuckled on the armrests.

All in all, fourteen nails. Not so bad, considering a boarding shotgun would've amputated his limb at the elbow. He'd take a handful of holes and a bruise like a sleeve any day over having to biograft a replacement limb.

Crawford produced a foamy blue vial and loaded it into her MediKit gun: Serum, a cocktail of medical nanobots and synthetic hormones suspended in nutrient fluid, drained via autoinjection directly into the core of Wil's ass cheek despite his feeble protestations. A minute later, the purple of the bruises had already begun to recede, and his bleeds slowed from a trickle to a drip.

The Caledonians brought cutters for the Teseum shackle, but Wil insisted it stay on. Couldn't chance a connection after what he'd just seen, and while the DRC couldn't ping his vitals or his location without his consent, keeping it jammed simplified the matter.

Where there was one Shasvastii, there had to be more.

Above the basement levels, the castle stretched out like something from a MayaNet historical. Tall ceilings, wide corridors, walls and floors of mortared granite supported by a network of wooden crossbeams. The most interesting bits were where the ancient world and the contemporary clashed: wrought-iron chandeliers wrapped in strings of cheap filament lights; steel folding chairs lined up beside elaborate, hand-carved tables; SA80 assault rifles crossed like display sabers, mounted proudly on the wall.

This time, he wasn't thrust into the library armchair with a bag over his head, but led to his seat. Fresh fire licked at the kindling in the hearth, bathing him in soothing heat. Wil tested the range of motion of his new bandages, basked in the comforting simplicity of the fresh sweater he'd received, and finally allowed himself to process what had happened.

He'd killed an alien pretending to be a human being.

Not enough payback for Svalarheima. Not nearly enough.

The curtains over the towering windows glowed ethereal, bathed by the hearth light. Rain clashed against the panes, distorting the village below in sheets and waves. Far below, a hundred Caledonian dwellings stained an inviting arc-sodium orange along with the mist that rolled down the mountains.

The grandfather clock struck midnight. Seventeen days until the delegation arrived at DRC-9 Dun Scaith.

That had to be the reason the Shasvastii were here. This ugly, forgotten backwater littered with Highlander holdings and archaic fortresses was of military value solely for its Teseum, but did the Combined Army care? His gut said no. Odune's kingdom had been compromised, and it'd been compromised for the approaching PanOceanian vessel.

He racked his brain, inventing worse and worse fates. Spawn embryos smuggled to the core of the Human Sphere. Speculo, naturally integrating into every walk of life. And for the Neoterran socialites, assassination, abduction. Or sepsitorization—the Combined Army's VoodooTech weapon that corrupted a Cube and twisted its bearer into a willing thrall of the almighty Evolved Intelligence.

Someone had to warn Xandros Odune. Someone needed to save those people. And here Wil was, too terrified to remove his Teseum manacle and give himself away to whatever sleeper agents waited out of sight.

That missile had been intended for Rajan. But why?

Alastair doffed his anorak and hung it on a hook near the fire. He fetched the kettle from the hearth, poured two cups of hot flower water, and sat in Eideard's seat. The fireplace crackled, and shadows darted between the bookshelves.

"Here." Alastair pushed a teacup toward Wil. "Drink. It's warm."

Wil glanced over his shoulder for permission from his handlers, but none remained. Somewhere in his preoccupation, the rest of the circus must've excused themselves. Only Wil and the boy chieftain remained.

"Chamomile's good for your blood pressure," Alastair continued. "Or do you prefer Earl Gray? We have a black tea we grow here in Kildalton that's somewhat similar."

"Not a tea person," Wil said. "Sorry."

He sipped. Slowly. "Alright."

"If I may, what do I call you? Your Majesty? Sir?"

"Alastair will do," he said. "Alastair Lucas MacArthur. And you?"

With no more cards worth playing, he had nothing else to lose. "Lieutenant Wilhelm Gotzinger III. 3508-9469. 27/1/44NC."

A slow smile spread across Alastair's boyish face. "For his sanity, I'm going to tell Eideard it took me half an hour and a cattle prod to get you to start talking."

"Eideard planned to shoot me, so with all due respect, he can fuck himself."

The young chieftain mulled it over without disagreeing. "The girl in the tree. Who was she?"

"Rajan's assistant. Diplomatic aide."

"I'd like a name to put on her cairn."

Wil slumped against the armrests. "She never told me."

Blue eyes narrowed. If Alastair wasn't judging him before, he sure as hell was now. "Is there someone we can try to contact for you, Lieutenant? The sooner I can send you home, the better. And the less you mention our inhospitality, the more indebted to you I'll be."

"Like PanO's gonna go scorched earth for a grunt like me."

"An Aquila Guard isn't a grunt. I've seen that visual array before on a Nisse, and on a Kamau. Yours is nothing like theirs. Yours is the kind that reads lips through walls and senses virginity out to a hundred meters."

"And you're a Mormaer," Wil said. "Though, I read Mormaers were supposed to be second and third sons. Weird tradition to break. Had to have it all?"

"Clan chieftain isn't a hereditary title, nor passed on via primogeniture. This isn't the medieval ages, Lieutenant. We elect our leaders."

"So if you lost, you'd give your castle to the other guy, or...?"

Alastair smiled patiently. "There's a gentleman downstairs in our adjunct infirmary. He's Xandros Odune's new hire, the one who begged the clan leads meet him at Fort Resolute. Rajan Brizuela. The executive's son who wants to steal our Teseum. Correct?"

Wil had to hand it to him: the kid could've tricked him into thinking he was the soft-handed high-value-target type with his big vocabulary and straight back. But with that came his own special brand of gentle ruthlessness. He'd hate to see him on the battlefield, apologizing to all the dumb bastards hollowed out by his Teseum-coated 7.62mm.

"His message would've gone much farther if he'd sent it via Arachne," Alastair said. "Most of us don't get Maya in the hills. The Campbells didn't even know he'd asked to set a meeting."

Wil took the teacup by the edges, frustrated at the tremble of his wrist. He smelled the water and drank it, choking it down like he'd choked down coffee all his life. The heat it lent him was worth holding his nose. "Anybody else show?"

"We were the only ones. Been the only ones, all six times we've gone."

He failed to stifle a bitter laugh. "Figures."

"What? Were you under the assumption your people were popular here, after the last twenty years? You're lucky I'm willing to entertain diplomacy at all."

"If it's the same with you, let's put a kibosh on PanO-bashing for now?"

The young chieftain placed his empty cup back on its saucer, stiff-lipped. He rotated it with his finger, aligning the handle and the table edge. "Who did you kill in the woods?"

"Wouldn't believe me if I told you."

"Try me."

"A Shasvastii."

Alastair scoffed. "You're right. I don't. De Hell Group flattened the beach-head on Novyy Cimmeria years ago, and Kurage finished the job. Whatever Combined Army remain on Dawn are clumped in the south—tightly controlled, outmaneuvered, and very far away."

Wil bit his tongue to hold back an acerbic laugh. Maybe what the kid was saying was true, but only in propaganda pushed by Stavka channels. As of two years ago, the official belief was that the Kurage Conflict had only displaced the Combined, infighting between the factions opening inroads to the unpopulated corners of the planet, and that Dawn was ground zero for the next alien incursion. Or, maybe that was just Hexahedron propaganda in turn.

Either way, Wil couldn't hold himself back long. "That's where you've gone from wrong to *fucking* wrong," he said. "The Combined are pushing everywhere. Paradiso. Concilium. And tonight, I caught one eating a rabbit in your backyard."

Alastair's ice-blue eyes narrowed. "A rabbit?"

"Wouldn't need to cook it. Shasvastii are the ultimate survivors. Had a camouflage cloak, sound dampening, the whole nine. No gun, though. He'd salvaged the one in the survival kit. Think I took him by surprise."

"And you killed him?"

Fury surged within him, remembering the double-feed. "No. Antipodes did that."

"And the Winter Dancers let you live?"

"Your boys scared them away."

"I heard you shot their leader, Indigo River," Alastair said. "Are you sure they didn't recognize you?"

Wil remembered the feint and the smirk. "Nah. They knew me."

"Antipodes are as smart or smarter than people, depending on their number. They're not animals."

"As far as provocation goes, I figure that Pale Shadow guy's got me to thank for his upgrade to pack alpha. If he didn't, he would've killed me when he had the chance. So I'm guessing there's no hard feelings."

"Guessing."

"Best I've got."

Alastair folded his hands atop his knee and didn't break eye contact. "Crying self-defense is a convenient way to avoid a death sentence, Lieutenant. Lucky for you that there's no body."

"Lucky, yeah. We can call it that."

"This is how I see it," Alastair said. "Your friend—proudly wearing contraband Teseum cufflinks, I might add—called me and the other clans to a meeting on an unreliable channel as an alibi. Afterward, while on mission, you were shot down by a third party far, far away from Fort Resolute. When given the chance to escape, you rushed back to your transport, crash-landed in Antipode territory. So whatever you were returning for was worth your life and abandoning your comrade."

"Not quite," Wil said. "I'm an Orc on security detail, ex-Aquila Guard. And Rajan? He's the asset, the new commercial attaché for Xandros Odune. We were en route to the negotiations when Rajan bribed the pilot to go off plan. Then, some asshole shot us with a missile."

His auburn brows raised. "Is this Rajan a Shasvastii, too?"

That piqued Wil's interest. Not everyone in the Human Sphere was allowed to know that Shasvastii could replace people, that Speculo Killers and Agents even existed. Wil himself had only been briefed by necessity an hour before putting boots to snow at Ulveslør, and honestly, he wished he hadn't. The hours he'd spent accusing every person involved in the events of that day of being Shasvastii almost forced an indefinite psychiatric hold when his stint in solitary ended.

That Alastair knew meant he'd either faced them in battle or met someone who did. Wil hid his surprise inside a long, shallow breath. "No. He's not."

Alastair edged forward on his seat. "Why run?"

"At first, I thought your people might've been the ones who tagged us," Wil said. "That changed once I met Eideard. Too scared, gave up his hand easy. Blamed me for your disappearance. Things got rough, and I got going."

"Saoirse told me she looked out for you."

"A bit," he said, and regretted how fast he undersold her.

"So, why risk going back? Why not go elsewhere and hide."

Wil tried to gesture out his point on his fingers, but his hands didn't cooperate. "Your folks said three in the Balena, when I knew it was four. Survivor or not, I figured that extra had a comms device I could use to call a rescue. Then he turned out to be an alien."

Alastair hesitated. "The Speculo was impersonating one of yours?"

"That's what I've been trying to tell you," Wil said. "Listen. Get me a secure channel to someone, anyone outside this planet. I need to warn the Hexahedron before something especially fucked-up happens."

"You're talking about the delegation to the DRC-9 Dun Scaith," Alastair said, pronouncing it differently—'dune sky,' instead of the 'done scathe' Wil had heard from Odune. "You think they're planning an attack on the *Sword of St. Catherine*."

"I don't know the ship name. But, yeah, sure. That."

"Well, I have the advantage of having received an invitation, same as every chieftain with territory on the loch. It's caused some… consternation, let's say. Our home isn't a tourist destination."

"I'll take 'galactic' over 'tourist' any day, thanks."

Alastair unfolded his hands, fists laid over the armrests. "Would their target be the donors or the vessel?"

"Doesn't matter," Wil said. "I'm concerned for the personnel—scientists, researchers, civilians. The *Sword of St. Catherine* is run by naval grunts, starship technicians, janitors. Those are the guys the Shas will gut to get at the one-percent. Those are the guys in *actual* danger. Everyone else important on that boat will wake up on Concilium Prima in a fresh Lhost, loaded from their backup before they came aboard. For everyone else, it's True Death."

Though Alastair tried to disguise his surprise, it was still visible in the subtle twitch of his wrist. "And Odune is aware you're on the planet?"

"We met him in person. Talked about chess. But there's no telling who might be part of this, alright? Anyone could be replaced, even him. We need outside assistance."

"I'll just go right ahead and try not to confirm your story with anyone," Alastair said. "What an incredible idea."

Lightning flashed outside, origin lost in the haze of the storm. Thunder reverberated in the old library, low as the devil's breath. Books clattered on shelves; teacups clinked in their saucers. The kindling in the hearth cracked and toppled onto the grate. Uneven shadows ran across the painting of the woman above the mantel, turning her expression from pensive to pissed.

"Please," Wil said. "If you query the DRC, all you're doing is giving their sleeper agents advance warning. So, bypass them. Contact off-world. Concilium Prima. Neoterra. Kosmoflot. Hell, call in the Corregidor for all I care. Just tell someone, anyone, who'll warn the delegation."

Alastair stood. Paced. He drew the curtains back over the windows and surveyed the township below past the trickles on the glass. Kildalton glowed like the dying coil in a portable heater, every surface gone reflective in the rain.

"With this storm, I can guarantee another relay's gone down," he said. "And since you riled the Winter Dancers, I can't send out men to repair it without providing an armed escort."

"Then send troops to the DRC and check things out in person. Strap a camera to my chest and send me if you gotta. Don't stand by and let innocent people get hurt because our governments don't see eye-to-eye."

"And if you're lying, that's military action that will result in sanction." Alastair tugged the drapes shut. "We'll see what the DRC-9 says when I get in contact with them."

"Come on, man, are you not listening? If Odune's one of them, dropping in without an announcement guarantees you catch him on the back foot. If he isn't, nothing changes. I just—if there's one, there's more. We can't trust anyone."

Alastair returned from the windowsill. "Good point."

Wil sputtered. "I didn't mean *me*."

"Who else have you told about this?"

"Eideard," he said. "He didn't give a shit."

"And no one else?"

"No one."

"Good," Alastair said. "Keep it that way."

"What's that mean?"

Pacing in front of the hearth, Alastair spoke into the fire. "If you're right, inaction is worse than action, even with the possible fallout. With Brizuela alive due to our intervention, exchanging him might provide the goodwill we need to smooth diplomatic relations over if you're—what'd you say—wrong, or *fucking wrong?*"

Wil shut his mouth. It wasn't precisely what he wanted, but it was close enough. This was Alastair MacArthur's castle, not his, and he wasn't about to test if they had a deeper dungeon to throw him into.

"If Odune asks, I'll tell him you died in the crash," Alastair added. "How's that for compromise?"

The urgent, helpless fire inside doused. Wil loosened his grip and un-clenched his jaw, and all across his body, every little wound accumulated in the past night all stung and burned at once, like nothing more than stubbornness was keeping them closed. "Works for me."

The far library door cracked open. Saoirse Clarke stood in the shadow, toothy and hard-bodied with her face full of worry. Gordon the Giant lingered behind her, blotting out the hallway beyond.

Alastair regarded Wil with momentary regret. "While you're here with us, I'll make sure you have more comfortable accommodations than a holding cell last used during the Separatist Wars. Have patience. Heal. I'll resolve this as soon as I can, and with the appropriate amount of care."

Separatist Wars—as in, decades ago. That explained some things. A proper brig would've had more locks, better security, tighter checkpoints. "Am I still your prisoner?"

"You're still my guest," Alastair corrected. "I intend to treat you well during your stay—though, it goes without saying you're not free to leave."

Wil loosed a dry chuckle. "You could've said 'yes.'"

Alastair paused. "Yes."

It didn't make him feel better.

Saoirse studied Wil for a long, silent moment, Antipode eyes crimson under the firelight. As Alastair left, she followed him down the hall. Gordon plodded in after they'd gone, regarding Wil like a hound that'd come in muddy and laid on the couch.

Wil cocked a brow. "You my new warden?"

He grunted.

"Name's Wil. And you?"

No grunt this time. Just glared, dark eyes burning.

"Huh. Very insightful."

Gordon hooked thumbs on his belt loops. Chain rifles hung there, heavy-duty Yungang Xíng Type 9.0s that would put a grown man on their back if they didn't lean into the recoil. Their stocks were filed and refitted with pistol grips. Nestled in a forest of chest hair, his dog tags glinted a brighter silver than the aluminum kind Wil had seen in old war museums. Teseum.

He was a Dog-Warrior. No other explanation.

"This oughta be fun," Wil said. "You seem like a real barrel of laughs."

"Good," Gordon replied. "You seem like a joke."

10

The door kicked open, and Wil jumped for his gun.

But this wasn't his bunk, there wasn't a pistol under his pillow, and the intruders were two gangly teenage cleaning girls leaving behind a basket of folded clothing. They startled back into the hall, giggling and chancing glances at the scar across his chest until the door shut tight behind them.

Gordon showed up next, and that was way less fun.

Redressing his wounds at the infirmary—the real one, not one in the basement—took about thirty minutes. No matter how many times he limped off a battlefield with a gunshot wound, Serum always surprised him with the speed at which it knitted the meat back together. Wounds that would've taken months to patch took days, instead. A marvel of modern medicine.

Left the meat tender, though.

After, it was off to a spacious, historic dining room with vaulted ceilings. It seemed like every single person in the castle was inside, stuffed elbow-to-elbow at long, hand-carved wooden tables. Tin silverware clicked against tin plates. Mugs steamed from atop coasters. Warm grease tinged the frosty morning air, promising bacon, potatoes, and cheese.

Grim trophies stared down from mounts along the walls. Helmets, mostly. Wu-Ming, Myrmidon, Azra'il—and many more. On the far side, a collection of close-combat weapons from all across the Human Sphere hung below the colossal broadsword of a Seraph TAG and a half-burned flag of the PanOceanian Military Orders.

He'd seen more expensive DFACs—dining facilities—but never one like this. It looked like a sensorium fantasy hotel, or something from a fairy tale. The MO flag was decades old, since it still maintained symbology from the excommunicated Knights Templar—

Smack dab in the middle of his first step down the landing, Gordon yanked him by the arm around to the kitchen and shoved him toward a dusty corner barrel.

Wil scanned the sweltering stovetops and glowing oven windows, the pile in the sinks, the spacious walk-in refrigerator. The kitchen staff inspected him right back, none happy, and returned to the morning rush.

Gordon plonked a plate of breakfast dregs atop the barrel. Eggs with broken yolk, well-done toast, and black shreds of wet oats that smelled like old scabs. The fork didn't seem cleaned all the way. "Eat."

"Chef's table, not bad," Wil said, and sat down on a milk crate. "There a reason I can't chow in the ballroom with everyone else?"

Gordon grunted. "They hate you."

Fair enough.

Wil put the official story of last night together from whispers in the kitchen. Bell had to have his nose reset with special forceps; Talbot's face had swollen into a sphere; Shaw had escaped with 'only' a dislocated shoulder and a mild concussion. Worse, Nora McDermott hadn't told anyone about what the three had been doing with her alone in the garage, so according to the sous chefs, she was Wil's victim, too.

And to pile on the misery, Cailean had apparently handed all the other Volunteers their lunch over the whole thing. Not his escape, so much, but that they'd lost a three-on-one fistfight versus a PanOceanian of all things. So that's why every garrison troop they passed in the halls carried bruised knuckles, blindfolds, and daggers in their eyes.

Three lads' lads, the local sweetheart, and corporal punishment.

Already off to a great start.

Beside the inexplicably soft mattress and a threadbare reclining chair, his quarters didn't have much else to offer other than pointless worrying and a window. The rain came frequently, often light. In the morning, a beaten lorry shipped Volunteers to and from the township, and then once more at twelve-hundred and sundown. AUVs ran the switchback up to the castle gates on a frequent basis, racing the traffic lights with a growl.

The idea of a civilian behind the wheel of any vehicle without a limited-AI pilot put a chill in his bones.

As far as Wil could tell, Castle MacArthur was a fully stocked military installation moonlighting as a hotel and community center. Difficult but not impossible to assault from the air, but that was what the Tartary SAMs dotted along the edge of the castle grounds were for. Besides soldiers, civilians from the township meandered up at a reasonable trickle, and more than once he saw Alastair personally attending to their questions—and just once, joining some old timers for croquet.

Out near the trees, the horses grazed, undisturbed.

He'd never seen one in real life until last night.

While Wil ate, Gordon stood watch from the pantry. When he slept, Gordon snored in an armchair outside the door. All other times, he lingered a few steps away, blessed with a permanent scowl.

Gordon wedged the lavatory door open with his boot. "Stays open."

The dearth of sharp objects in his quarters said 'risk factor,' but the total absence of belts meant suicide watch. Wil could get used to loose trousers and having to ask permission to have a razor to shave with, but a Dog-Warrior playing audience to all his bowel movements would take more adjusting than he was capable of.

He made the mistake of asking to walk the grounds exactly once. Without missing a beat, Gordon produced a pair of handcuffs, locked the two of them together, and dragged Wil on a brisk jaunt around the lawn that felt more like torture than he'd expected.

"So you don't run," Gordon said. "Alastair's orders."

For all his size and menace, the big guy stayed glued to his comlog, texting someone and watching Myrmidon Wars reruns. Gordon's holoprojector was implanted in his forearm, controlled by linked pads inside his fingertips, same as Wil's. Made sense—when he bulked during his transformation, any link bracelets tighter than a hula hoop would snap right off.

Requests were all equaly answered with grunts and glares. Conversation was stilted and sparse. The most animated he got was when Alastair called them over for a daily status update, usually at the market green smack dab in the middle of Kildalton.

Alastair paced across the broad, flat field, past a line of Caledonian children bristling with wooden swords. He demonstrated the proper grip for each of them on the claymore he held, hefting the weapon in both hands. No teenagers, just kids—the young adults were apparently already working one-on-one with their fathers using real blades instead.

The sheathes on their backs caught his eye. Long blades were impractical, but the Caledonians had worked a sheathe that was little more than two hooks for the crossguard, leather backing, and an endpoint capped in reinforced steel to cradle the point of the blade.

The claymore in Alastair's hands was Saoirse Clarke's, the one that made Pale Shadow flee when a gunshot hadn't done the trick. The edge had the telltale pallor of Teseum, monomolecularly sharp. Nothing in the Human Sphere was tough enough to blunt its edge. The raw material alone would've been worth nearly a million Oceanas.

"I was right," Alastair said, staking the priceless weapon into the mud.

Wil tugged on the handcuff, forcing Gordon to keep pace. "About what?"

"A relay lost signal near Outpost 16 during the storm. Branch on the line. Repairs will take a few days, minimum, thanks to the Antipode presence. Until then, we're offline—unless you'd like to try HF radio. There are old towers aplenty in the Highlands if the DRC keeps an open channel."

Wonderful news. VHF and HF radio had long gone the way of headphones, car keys, and vacuum cleaners, replaced by Li-Fi broadcast via quantronic tech. That it still survived on backward Planet Dawn didn't surprise him at all. "How long?"

"A few days," Alastair repeated and hefted the claymore. He gave the kids a slow example swing. Left to right, from the hip to eye-height, smooth. "Don't chew your paw off."

A few younger children crouched in the grass, crowded around a fuse-box—a tutor tablet, long obsolete in the wider Human Sphere. Caledonian words flashed on the screen, and when the English equivalent replaced it, the children stumbled over the pronunciation.

A faint smack against his thigh drew him back. One of the younger boys had taken the opportunity to give Wil one right in the leg, cheeks puffed in anger. Eye contact was enough to make the kid back a step and freeze.

Wil chuckled. "You can do better than that," he said and stuck out his leg. "Let's go. Round two. Put your back in it."

Gordon cocked a brow. He said something in Caledonian to the boy, and the little terror gave Wil a second whack barely harder than the first.

Even so, he faked a wince and sucked air through his teeth. "Not that hard, damn! You tryna kill me?"

A giggle ran through the children. Good sound. Better than the one the adults made when they saw him in the castle halls.

On cue, Saoirse Clarke hurried over from the corner shop, arms filled by a paper bag filled to bursting with fried food. She knelt by the boy, presumably to admonish him, and corrected his hold instead.

"Och, Ethan," she said. "Not tellin' ye again. Right over left, up high. There y'are. See? Hit 'em again."

Third time glanced Wil's kneecap, and the wince was much more genuine.

"Better, right?" she said and flashed a sharp-toothed grin.

Cheeky, and the kids seemed to enjoy it. But before Wil could try his hand at flirting back, Gordon yanked him along. He faked a limp for his first few steps, and when the children started whispering, he heard 'clara' and 'galactic' more than once.

Saoirse grinned until they left the market green, refusing to look away before he did.

Wil guessed they were entangled, Saoirse and Alastair. Lovers, maybe, though by the way they stuck together perhaps she was his bodyguard. And while she seemed a whole different kind of violent and crude than what he was used to, at least she spoke. Better than being stuck handcuffed to the monosyllabic missing link. And he still needed to thank her. If he did anything before he left this place, he'd do that, assuming she didn't tell him to fuck off a second time.

After three mornings and two chasers of imported Haqqislamite steroids, his left arm knit back together clean. With the stitches removed, the angry red lines across his chest and up his arm remained—permanent reminders of his scrap with Pale Shadow and the Winter Dancers. And while the holes in his shoulder would need a few more days before they stopped sweating blood, he felt right as rain.

By Wil's reckoning, it'd been a week since the crash. No grand cavalry charge had arrived via dropship; no show of force; no rescue team. Unable to reign in his overactive imagination, Wil spent his time alone inventing and reinventing scenarios and possibilities, playing out the consequences of one disaster after another. Was Rajan a Shasvastii? His assistant? Was Odune? Had high command known they'd be shot down, and if so, did they know he'd survive? Who could he trust, and why had no one come looking for them yet?

Keyes had been awaiting extraction. But to where?

At night, laid alone in a castle bedroom larger than his Neoterran apartment, Wil was struck by the encapsulating silence. No sirens, no arguments, no footsteps. No MayaNet to scroll or sensorium channels to doze to. No geist to micromanage the temperature, to suggest an AR change of scenery, to interrupt his rest with reminders of tomorrow's schedule or push notifications from subscribed sources.

Just the darkness, and on occasion, the rain.

It kept him awake.

Wil didn't know how to feel. No domotics meant he had to get used to flushing the toilet, buttoning his slacks, and flipping light switches, sure. But not being able to access the halo of every passerby who grazed his social cloud felt... nostalgic. Asking people's names instead of double-tapping and reading their profile reminded him of his childhood, before the Cube. And no one had mentioned Svalarheima yet, at least not to his face.

The possibility of a second disaster had crossed his mind. If this went sideways, he didn't have a Plan B for his life. He'd spent his entire adult life in the military. Owed them everything. Even disgraced as he was, the NCA lent stability he wouldn't have found otherwise; and above all else, he couldn't stand disappointing his nation a second time.

But if he succeeded in saving Rajan, if he was right about the DRC, if he could save those people and spare the delegation from Neoterra... what would happen then? His command had placed him on this duty to get rid of him, but what if this was his chance to prove them wrong?

The more he considered it, the more he liked the sound. Captain Wilhelm Gotzinger, once more. Then everything that'd happened would be worth it. All the misery would've been for a reason.

On the fourth morning since his return, Wil's door banged open. Instead of Gordon, or the two giggling maids—Neil McDermott stomped in with his eyebrows knit and his rifle on his back.

"'Mon," Neil said. "Your friend's woke up."

Wil hadn't expected an apology anyways.

† †

Rajan squinted from his fluffy nest in the infirmary bedding, both groggy and haughty at once. He stared at Wil through the infirmary door window, first dazed, then smirking. Doc Crawford crooked his attention back to her spiel on aftercare and prompted him for any drug or material allergies.

He licked his lips and said, "Atek bitches asking questions."

Before Wil could barge in to play damage control, Alastair and Eideard marched up with Saoirse Clarke in tow and cut into the infirmary in front of him.

"We'll soften him up for you," Alastair said. "Wait here."

Wil didn't like it, but it made sense. He was the boss, and they needed to confirm their stories independently. It wasn't mistrust, just common sense. Or, at least, he hoped.

While Saoirse posted up beside the stairs, Crawford excused herself. As she stomped her way upstairs, Wil tried his best hand at an apology, but she either didn't hear him or didn't care.

Eideard shut the door behind them. He glared at Wil through the tiny window, and twisted the blinds closed.

Prick.

Saoirse had her red hair loose this morning, unruly curls hiding the long scar up the side of her face. Her broad torso was wrapped in a bleach-spotted crop top plastered with complaining skulls, short enough to show off a strip of her tautly muscled abdomen, bare arms splashed with freckles and battle scars. Silvery Teseum-laced dog tags glinted from the curve of her cleavage.

From this angle, another tattoo caught his eye on her forearm—a crescent moon missing a notch, gap struck by a sword. Suspicious. He wondered if it meant something different here and chanced another glance at her Antipode eyes. Saoirse was already staring back, waiting for him to realize he'd been caught.

This time, he didn't look away. He kept her gaze, trying to see the humanity behind her missing irises, no longer content to play prey to her predator.

She broke contact first, smiling like she'd won a prize. "Hey, Neil. Weren't ye gonna say somethin'?"

Neil shuffled beside the dusty sub-basement brickwork and kept his eyes averted. "Nah. Nothin' to say. Not fer no keycard thieves, at least."

Saoirse twisted her lip until one sharp tooth snaggled over it, and frowned. She stood with a groan and a stretch. "Oft, ugh. Skippin' breakfast was a mistake. Anyone wanting somethin' from the mess?"

Grumbling, Neil shook his head.

"If you're headed up there," Wil said, "I could—"

"God gave ye legs," Saoirse said and shouldered past him.

A bit brusque. She could've easily gone around. Wil couldn't place it—maybe bullying, maybe flirting. He'd prefer the latter, but women had never been his forte. Though, why he was expending his few surviving brain cells on psychoanalyzing an inconsequential nudge, he had no idea.

Anything rather than planning what he'd say to Rajan.

And he'd missed his chance to thank her. *Again.*

Rajan's voice carried through the door, hoarse but brimming with condescension. "This illegal detainment violates four different statutes of three interstellar peace treaties, bitch! Ganesh and Rodina are gonna spit roast you over this. You're so screwed and you don't even know it!"

The resulting shouting match, though unintelligible, was likely audible in low orbit.

Wil's sigh jumped into a breathy laugh. "Should've let me go in first."

Neil clicked his tongue. "Prob'ly."

"Gordon busy this morning, or?"

"Ask him," Neil said, and chanced a glare from the soggy spot on the floor. "And fair warning, mate—stay far from Saoirse Clarke."

So Wil's gawking wasn't as hidden as he'd hoped. "Or she'll what, feed me my knife respectfully?"

"For you? Disrespectfully. Y'see, Saoirse don't take nothing from no one. It's why she's back in Kildalton instead of with the 9th Grenadiers in Cailleach. Ignored the wrong orders, broke the wrong nose. Some say she's got a bit o' the devil in her."

Her and Wil both.

Neil whisked the Glengarry from his head, blond curls dropping over his eyes. "Ta muchly—I mean, thanks. For Nora, in the garage. Truly."

Ever since his comment on the lawn, Wil had nursed a little worry Neil would come try to find him again. Now he knew why he didn't—his sister had told him the truth. Funny enough, now that the bruises had faded, he didn't hold a grudge against Neil for what he did, or Nora for defending herself. Maybe a little resentment for the headbutt, but now wasn't the time.

"You know, in retrospect?" Wil said. "She probably could've taken 'em."

"And if ye dinnae fight dirty, you couldn't."

"Well, that's rule number one, kid. Always fight dirty."

Neil huffed. "And you're still a galactic, *kid*. Watch your mouth."

Yeah. That was a bit much.

A minute later, Eideard stomped from the infirmary, cloaked in exasperation. "The nerve," he muttered, storming up the stairs. "Saved his life, and not even a goddamn thank-you!"

As he passed, Alastair apologized with a grimace. "Good luck."

Wish as he might, Wil already knew the outcome. Rajan would switch from insufferable to apoplectic, throw a tantrum, demand groveling despite being at his lowest point. Wil would still try to bring across the severity of the danger and insist on a course of action that would no doubt fall on deaf ears. But despite how pointless it felt, he held out hope that Rajan might actually listen.

He wouldn't. But Wil hoped.

11

A cloud of sterile solution fogged the infirmary air. The lighting hummed in tandem with the old-world hospital machinery, BPM and blood pressure displayed in blacks and greens on an antique display. The amount of bags hung on the stand had thinned, but plastic tubes still harpooned Rajan down by the thigh, the collar, the neck—enough needles and stents to give any reasonable person nightmares.

Rajan glared up from the bed. Sans lenses and AR connection, the polychromatic mandalas had disappeared, leaving a limp brown behind. "Now," he said, "who the hell are you?"

Wil faltered mid-greeting, mouth agape.

Rajan urged with his eyes, increasingly patronizing, then clicked his tongue. "Alright, *mate*, be like that, *mate*. Can I get another pillow over here? Unless that's another part of your *bloody* Ariadnan torture program, Pommie motherfucker. Limey fucking bitch."

He couldn't believe it. Rajan didn't recognize him.

"No comprende?" Rajan said. "Aap angrezi bolte ho kyaa? Och aye the noo?"

One thought shook out of the jumble. Wil said, "Your assistant."

"Jings crivens, he speaks. What?"

"She died."

Rajan's lips pulled in a mawkish frown. "Yeah, I know. They told me already."

"What was her name?"

His eyes widened. "Her name?"

"Yeah," Wil said. "Her name. For her headstone."

"Callista," Rajan answered, and rolled his lips. "Or Camilla. Catalina? Caroline."

"You don't know?"

Rajan looked askance and exhaled a nervous laugh. "You know, I, uh… She was brand new. Yeah. No clue. Met her right before we took off, damn shame.

Try asking the other guy? My useless-ass bodyguard, if he hasn't ditched me for the third time."

"She worked with you for *two years*. I knew her for *six days*."

"How'd you—I didn't—wait," he said, and startled straight. "Gotzinger? Shit, Gotzinger! Wait, are you for real? I always thought you were white, is that you?"

Fire kindled in his chest. "El único e inigualable."

"Sure, cool, yeah. Grab a scalpel, cut me free?" Rajan rattled his restraint, sending the tubes swaying on the pole. "You see this, man? We gotta get outta here. These Atek hillbillies are gonna harvest all my organs, bro."

"Calm down. Listen—the people back at DRC-9 and the Neoterran delegation are in danger. I saw something in the woods, and the MacArthurs are trying to—"

The spikes on Rajan's heart monitor squeezed closer together. "Do I look like I give a single, solitary fuck about the DRC-9? They'll be fine without us, believe me. Don't Svalarheima me on this."

The fire inside doused, replaced by something hotter. "Don't… what?"

"Leave me to fuckin' die? I'm actually important, unlike your bullshit Fusi—"

Palm against stubble. Rajan's bloodshot eyes widened until the whites surrounded the dark.

Wil had Rajan's throat in his hand. He didn't remember moving.

Buried in the bedding, Rajan grinned. "When we get back to Concilium, you're done, Gotzinger. Forever. Assaulting an asset—"

"Whitehead. McCombs. Nicholls. Sankaran. Kovac. Not 'Fusilier.' Not a joke. Real people."

"You're shaking," Rajan croaked.

His grip tightened. "Shut up."

"This isn't the real you."

Wil cocked his fist. "You wanna meet him?"

Behind him, the door clicked shut. Neil stood there, concern writ large on his pale face along with something else: complicity. His back eclipsed the window. "Oi, galactic. Saoirse's due back soon, aye? Give the corpo one fer my da, and I winnae say a word."

All of the fight washed out of Wil on a sickening tide. What was he doing? Acting like Neil, like Talbot, beating a defenseless civilian for the crime of, what, being an asshole? Rajan was right—this *wasn't* him. Fists against his forehead, blood roaring in his ears, he blew past Neil out the infirmary door.

Laughter chased them into the hall. "Highly recommended, this guy, right here! Watch him go! Worst Aquila Guard there's ever been!"

This time, it was hard to disagree.

A whole day passed of pacing the confines of his room and failing to imagine a life outside the PanOceanian military.

Several times, he held the doorknob, beta-testing the script for his apology to Rajan before he steeled himself and refused to give the shitstain the satisfaction. Twice, he mentally played out the court martial for abandoning his asset behind enemy lines—neither went well. This time, public relations wouldn't bother with a holding pattern; he'd eat a dishonorable discharge, a prison sentence, and go right back to the gutter where he'd always belonged.

Another godforsaken rain washed in with the sunset, and Wil perched on his chair waiting for the distant crash and another milquetoast excuse from Alastair. When it didn't come, his thoughts turned darker—of the last time he'd seen his mother, and what advice she might've given now. God knows he'd gotten the *cuando me muera* speech enough times while she was alive, and now here he was, running it through its paces a decade after she'd passed.

Someone had recommended him for this. Someone had faith in him. The only question was who, and if it was a sick joke or not. Jury was still out on the latter.

The rain redoubled. No thunder, this time.

Someone knocked at his door. Wil ignored it until it became insistent and the hinges juddered against the jamb. Outside stood Saoirse Clarke, Teseum claymore strapped high between her shoulders.

He glanced out into the hall. "Where's Gordon?"

Saoirse brushed past him into the room. "On break," she said. "He says you're on hunger strike, and I've permission to stick a tube up yer nose if it's true."

Wil closed the door but kept the doorknob in hand. "It's not."

She scanned the room. Sized him up. "How's the arm?"

"Why do you care?"

"Alastair told me tae look after you, so I'm doin' just that."

"Well, I'm tired," he said. "Can you—"

Saoirse planted her feet. "Show us yer hands."

The interruption chafed him, but Wil did as he was told. The pink scar line from the Antipode's yank faded up beneath the frayed cuff of his sweater. "There. Happy?"

"And the shoulder?"

He pried the wool up and over his head to present his bare arm. Only a few stubborn bruises remained from where the nanobots had glued the lasagna of his shoulder back together.

Saoirse gave it a quick inspect and a thumbs-up. In the midst of reclothing, she took his left hand with both of hers, holding his fingers apart.

Ladies' hands were always cold, but her mitts seemed the exception. Callus and clawed, wrists strapped with dueling bracers, they radiated heat like she stored them in a furnace. No matter how strong or indignant Wil might've been, she was stronger, and she pried open his fist until she was happy with its spread.

Close now, her hair carried the scent of pine needles, gun smoke, and sweat. He'd never been next to her standing up before, and it surprised him that they were of roughly equal height. Most women only came up to his chest.

The lens of her eye caught the bedroom light, glinting a strange and primordial red. Wil couldn't look away.

"Knuckles healed good," she said and released him. "Haqq drugs, aye? Offworld-make, sure, but better than rubbin' dirt on it."

He massaged his freed fingers. "Thought your people hated off-worlders."

"We make exceptions fer trade. Arachne's got all the non-shite television, and Sol sheep roast the best. Snack cakes, always good. Double-Action ammo, Myrmidon Wars, display fabrics." She jiggled her crop top, and the design changed from clustered neon-tone skulls to three wolves howling at a moon. "Pure dead brilliant, aye?"

"But the people, we're garbage."

Saoirse ignored his challenge and sauntered away. She kicked a little pile of clothes beside his bed and shot him a look. "Should fold yer laundry for the girls. Make it easy on 'em."

"Next you'll have me stamping license plates."

Her eyebrows bobbed. "More than a few potholes need fillin' down the township if yer offering."

Wil bit down the next barb and doused his petty anger. "It's fine. I'll fold them."

"Issat so? Big difference 'tween now and the skirt shite. Crawford sedating you, or did yer nighttime frolic in Achadh nan Darach scare you straight?"

"Still think it's funny," he said. "But... sorry, if it isn't."

"Ye should be. Breaking out like that. Stealing clothes. Getting everyone in Kildalton riled. And ye spooked Alastair so bad these last few days, he won't even tell me how." Her pale eyes narrowed. "And what ye did tae Nora in the garage."

Cheek tingling, Wil clenched his teeth and anticipated the slap.

But it didn't come.

"I talked tae her," Saoirse said, softer now. "Heard what you did. That ye fought all three at once in your skivvies tae spare her a thrashing. Woulda told everyone if she hadn't asked me keep hush. Woulda sung it off the palisade: the one good man in all of PanOceania, crash-landed right in our garden."

Somehow, admiration was more uncomfortable than antipathy. "It's no big deal."

Her lips twisted into a toothy snarl. "Neil disagrees. Nora disagrees. And when I told Gordon, he disagreed, too."

"Good enough."

"Good enough's not good enough," she pressed. "If I were Alastair, I'd be narked, aye? Finally got a dyed-in-the-wool galactic in the township, and every livin' soul here has a different reason to despise 'em."

"So, what, I'm supposed to play ambassador for PanOceania? I didn't sign up for that."

"Aye, well, the actual one's indisposed and unkind. Yer the next best thing."

Her audacity spurred a laugh through his teeth. "Don't pin all your expectations on me just yet, okay? My hidden talent is disappointing people."

"The eighth circle a' Hell is reserved fer pessimists, Wilhelm."

"And optimism is something they give you a medical discharge for in the Fusilier Corps. I'm a realist. As in, I'd really like to be left alone, if that's okay?"

Saoirse swept a loose strand of sunfire hair behind her pointed ear and said, "Your accent. Where ye from?"

"I have an accent?"

"Everyone's got an accent."

He crossed his arms. "You sure?"

"Well, yer friend Odune most certainly does."

Control became impossible. Wil seized her by the shoulders. "You should've led with that! What happened, what'd he say?"

The velvet tension of her muscle surprised him. More in common with armored lattice than bare skin. And when she twisted his fingers back, he let go—but she didn't. Maybe deciding whether or not to break them, or bite one off.

"Hands," she snapped, and released him.

He took a step back, shaking out the twinge. "Damn, sorry. Won't happen again."

"Good," she said. "Was only about an hour ago that Al got through. First ring, some hen picked up and put him on the line. Big man, narrow? Looks like he could trick a Hollow Man tae vote for an E/M grenade."

"And then?"

Saoirse searched his expression, pale eyes glinting. "He said he dinnae kent ye."

12

Display cases lined the fourth-story landing, brightly lit under the morning light: M16s, AK-12s, Kevlar vests. Hundred-year-old trophies and memento mori, some dating back to weeks after the *Ariadna*'s landfall. Flickering holopanes displayed the name and rank of a hundred men and women who'd died to protect the Clan MacArthur.

One memorial held the rifle he'd seen the woman carrying in the library portrait. Another displayed a pre-Uprising Japanese Sectorial Alliance katana, embedded lengthwise down the fuller of a Teseum claymore.

At the end of the memorial hall waited a meeting room, its wide space dominated by a broad circular table that had to be as old as the township itself. Alastair sat on the far end, straight-backed, reading a paper file. He glanced up to see Wil and greeted him with a silent nod.

Eideard Carr took his left side, eyes lethal as they were on the trailhead. On Alastair's right sat Cailean, etching lines into a bulky Holland-12 cartridge with his knife. He'd exchanged his armor for a wool sweater and his stiff-boned gauntlets for fingerless gloves as weathered as he was, but kept the pauldron decorated over with tally marks.

Gordon pulled a chair out for Wil. May as well have been the Siege Perilous by how much he dreaded sitting in it.

"Thank you for joining us, Lieutenant," Alastair said. "Some introductions may be in order: This is Cailean Rutledge, my uncle and advisor. Cailean, Wilhelm."

"Aye," Cailean said and didn't look up. "We met enough."

"And you know my other uncle, Eideard Carr," he said. "So, let's—"

Wil talked over him. "You spoke to Odune, and he said he didn't know me."

Cailean startled, pleasantly surprised; Eideard blinked, nose wrinkled in disgust. Alastair hardly reacted, his face a diplomat's mask save for the subtle tension in his eyes.

"What'd he say when you mentioned the crashed Balena?" Wil asked.

"Anything about Rajan, or me? Did he seem nonplussed, or was he calm?"

Eideard grimaced and cursed under his breath. "Clarke," he muttered. "Of course she told you. Why wouldn't she? What use is subtlety or intelligence when that bloody girl has neither?"

Cailean scoffed. "Leave her alone, Ed. I've other business today than tea-time gossip. So his sister gabbed to the galactic? Great. Less time wasted, get on wi' it."

Wil didn't envy Alastair for having a subordinate who mistakenly considered himself the superior officer. Worse that they were family. He couldn't imagine having to share a roof with—

Wait. Sister?

He inspected Alastair's face, searching for the familial resemblance he must've missed. Nothing in their skin tone, earlobes, facial features. Freckles were a dominant trait, weren't they? Saoirse was dripping with them, and Alastair's windburned cheeks were completely unmarked. Though, then again, if her eyes and teeth had come from an Antipode, maybe the freckles did too. He had no clue.

And why was he suddenly relieved?

Alastair laid out the papers on the table and folded his hands over them. "Odune told me he'd lent his ship to a visiting friend flying up from Marianne-bourg. He expressed grief and asked how many died. I answered, everyone. He apologized and told us he could send a team to retrieve their Cubes. I declined, as most had been lost in the explosion. He said he'd pay for the removal of the wreckage, and I declined again."

"No space invader sets foot on MacArthur land and lives tell tale." Cailean paused and cocked a brow. "Present company excluded, of course."

No way he really meant that, but Wil didn't press.

"When I told him there was evidence of damage to the craft in-flight," Alastair continued, "he seemed distracted. Asked after Submondo activity records and pivoted to the possibility of Caterans. When I assured him neither were active in Achadh nan Darach, he abruptly requested an 'adjournment' and ended the call."

"Sounds like him," Wil said. "Where's that leave us now?"

Alastair studied Wil's face for a long moment, auburn brow knit. "I think I believe you."

Eideard grumbled, shoulders hunched. Over by the door, Gordon crossed his arms. The three compelling arguments Wil had spent hours painstakingly preparing last night evaporated in a single bewildered, "What?"

"What you said to me in the library didn't make any sense," Alastair said. "The *Sword of St. Catherine* will be tightly surveilled and bear an accompaniment of soldiers besides. Any direct action would be immediately crushed. Discovery of their assailant's true nature would not only see their sleeper cell wiped out, but betray their further presence here on Dawn."

"And that makes you believe me... how?"

"Because if it seems like such a terrible idea from this distance, it means the Shasvastii know something we don't. They have VoodooTech weapons, secret intelligence—or, it may not be the Expeditionary Army at all. Not to say you're a liar, but you'd barely survived a fever less than a day before your escape, and we've had numerous encounters with local smugglers using AEZ regulations as a smokescreen to ship Teseum offworld."

Wil was getting real sick of being told that he was seeing things, but he let it roll off his back. No use arguing a victory. "Possibly."

"What outsiders do on our land or off it is not our personal responsibility," Eideard said. "Now is the time to keep our heads down, avoid notice from the Cossacks, try to retain what little independence we have."

Alastair regarded his uncle with cold intelligence. "Innocent people will die without our intervention."

"Innocent Caledonians?" Eideard asked. "And if not, why should I care?"

"If we have the ability to render aid, it's our moral imperative. Only a coward would say otherwise, and we are not cowards."

Cailean glanced up from his work. "Now yer soundin' like yer da."

"Not as colorful as he would've put it," Alastair said.

"Color, aye," he snickered. "They make crayons wae *fuck* and *cunt* on 'em now?"

Eideard thumped the table. "This is no laughing matter! Aggressive action against O-12 holdings could start a war, lad, and the history of Clan MacArthur is written in enough blood as-is."

"And if it's Shas, then?" Cailean asked. "They take control of that ship, they'll turn their guns on Kildalton tae ferret out the junior diplomat they didnae kill. What then?"

"If," Eideard spat, and returned to Alastair. "Lad, consider what Alexander—"

Cailean rapped his knife on the tabletop. "Christ, mate, come off it! Ye talk like ye've got a dial tae the grave, but the lad kens his da best. Plus, if we're mistaken, the blueberry'll do the explaining."

Eideard crossed his arms. "This about the Díreach again, isn't it?"

Cailean scowled. "Hardly."

"So you'll put the whole township in danger to hunt a ghost story, hm? Is that what we do now? Throw caution to the wind, and muck about with uninvited galactics?"

"Uncle," Alastair said firmly, and the argument abruptly ended.

Judging by Cailean's glare, he had more to say but not so little respect for Alastair that he'd say it. Muttering, he returned to carving his bullet.

Wil cleared his throat. Eideard sneered at him, but Alastair seemed glad for the distraction. "I assume I'm the blueberry?"

"Oh, aye," Alastair said. "Officially, we'll be patrolling the AEZ border for Submondo activity near Fort Resolute. Unofficially, I'm selecting a task force of MacArthur soldiers to investigate the perimeter of the DRC-9. Ten, give or take— and you'll be one of them."

"Did the Corregidor hang up on you, or...."

"Arachne signal's dead for a hundred klicks around," Eideard said. "Bloody relay dropped out again, shredded by the Antipodes *you* exacerbated. This time, the damage is severe enough it'll take months to repair. I'm of a mind your kith should pay for it."

"Our Dozers'll do it in four days," Cailean said. "Months? Christ, Ed."

Wil wasn't sure if it was his Stockholm syndrome talking, but he didn't mind Cailean so much now. "Alright, old-timer. You running this shindig?"

"No, but I am," Alastair said. "After all, my participation is effectively mandatory. If you're wrong, Lieutenant Gotzinger, we'll be able to claim confusion: misunderstood directions for erstwhile negotiations. Then, we trade you back to the PanOceanians as a gesture of goodwill, arrange the return of their wounded commercial attaché, and everyone forgets this ever happened."

Wil glanced from eye to eye around the table. "And if I'm right?"

Cailean tapped his knuckles on his marked-up pauldron and smiled like only an old soldier could. "I add some notches tae my plate."

† †

Two full arguments over whether the 'proportional response' should include heavy machine guns and a missile launcher later, the meeting ended with a grumble and another invocation of the spirit of Alexander MacArthur. When Alastair fell to Caledonian, Gordon walked Wil out ahead of the others.

Outside in the hall, Saoirse paced, milky eyes inspecting the interlocked katana and claymore. She turned to them, expectant, but Gordon whispered, "Eideard's raging, Sersh," and she made herself scarce with a quickness.

"His… sister, huh," Wil asked, memorizing the sway of her hips. He still couldn't wrap his brain around it. As in, her relation to Alastair, not her rear, though wrapping his hands around *that* didn't seem like such a bad—

"Don't," Gordon grunted. "She'll rip your cock off."

Wil stammered, hopelessly derailed. Before he could recover, Cailean sauntered out of the meeting room and gripped him by the shoulder. "Got a gift fer ye, blueberry. Hand?"

Curious, Wil did as he was told, and Cailean slapped cold metal into Wil's palm. The H-12 bullet. He rolled it in his hand until WILHELM glinted back at him, carved into the brass of the jacket.

His stomach buoyed into his lungs.

The old man's carefree smile darkened with murderous fire. "Fer the next time ye lay hands on one o' my Volunteers," Cailean said and snatched it back. "Tread lightly."

Wil wiped the sweat from his palm and mumbled an agreement. He didn't dare challenge him. Alastair might've stopped Eideard from burying him in the woods, but that mercy didn't extend to the rest of his family, or for the rest of all time.

Alastair sped down the hall ahead of Eideard's slow departure, patience obviously thinned by the meeting. He paused. "Uncle?"

Cailean pushed Wil aside. "Aye, lad?"

"Lieutenant Gotzinger will need a rifle and a sidearm for the trip, and I need to inform Mr. Brizuela of the situation. Can you take him to the range, talk to Sharlene? She'll ken what can be spared."

"Depends," Cailean replied, and turned back. "Can ye shoot without Wi-Fi, PanO? Or does the ALEPH do that for ye while ye browse the girlie sites out in cyberspace?"

"It's just ALEPH, no 'the' required," Wil said, still feeling the weight of the bullet in his palm. "And no one uses Wi-Fi anymore. Or calls it cyberspace, either."

Gordon arched a brow. "He didn't say no."

⸱ ⇈

The silver-haired old man led the way downstairs, insistent on 'shortcuts' that felt entirely like the opposite. He stopped to chat with passersby several times about the weather, about the mountain, about what someone named their new baby, stretching the journey from a jaunt to a meander. The entire time, Gordon loomed over Wil with a strange sharpness in his eyes. Still his jailer, and Wil was still a prisoner. Getting to sit in on big-shot meetings didn't change that.

A strange realization came upon him while Cailean jawed with some kitchen staff. "Hey," Wil said. "Alastair's what, twenty? So if the old guys are his uncles, why aren't they leading the clan?"

Gordon regarded him the way an adult would a bothersome child. "Not blood. His dad's war buddies."

That explained it, if only a little. And then Gordon surprised him and kept talking. "When chieftain went up for grabs, nobody ran but Al. No one wanted the risk. Not like the old fuckers aren't tough—Carr was SAS, and Rutledge a 3rd Highlander Grey Rifle. They fought in the Commercial Conflicts, start to finish. Against your people."

Twenty years ago, the re-discovery of Dawn by the Human Sphere pre-ceded a mass landgrab. PanOceania and the StateEmpire went head-to-head in a proxy war with the Ariadnan nations trampled in the middle. Mercenary compa-nies, political assassinations, a cold war between ALEPH and the Nomad Nations that nearly turned hot. After six years, the Commercial Conflicts ended when O-12 stepped in, and not long after, Ariadna joined the G-4 to make the G-5.

That explained Eideard's hostility and Cailean's distaste. He'd read that occupation had been harsh and only a few cities won their freedom before the war's end. Wil hadn't been involved—seeing as he was eight years old—but knew they'd hold him responsible, nonetheless.

Not the first time he'd been blamed for someone else's mistake.

Definitely not the last.

"Funny," Wil said. "If Eideard wants to lead so bad, why didn't he run?"

"Can't. He's sept, same as Cailean—from another clan. Carr's an O'Brien, and Rutledge is a Sinclair. Their kids could be chieftain, if they had any after they swore in. But not them."

Talkative, today. Wil wondered if Saoirse's gift for gab had anything to do with that. "You said 'the risk.' Mormaers are supposed to be second and third sons, right?"

Gordon glared. "He is."

"So, if he's got a brother, then why—"

"Plural," he said. "Two. Same as me."

"Defect, die, or disown?"

Gordon grunted. "First warning."

"Alright, apologies. The hell's a Díreach?"

"Second warning," he said, and unfolded his arms.

Not that talkative, apparently.

Outside was nice. Wet, freezing, and a bit windy as always, but not raining. Helios muted behind the cloud cover, turning midday to an early evening. The grass squelched beneath his shoes, turning the edges of the sole green by the time they'd cleared the lawn.

The gun range lay along the western side of Castle MacArthur, not far from the lot beside the garages. Wil recognized landmarks he'd passed on his ill-fated attempt at freedom: the glass-topped fence, the ditch, the anti-air batteries bunkered over the hill. A small crowd surrounded the stalls, running the gamut from Volunteers running drills to parents with children. As they came closer, the crack of gunfire paradoxically grew quieter, and Wil was glad for the aural filters implanted in his inner ears. But they didn't stop there, continuing on until they'd left the green and entered a copse of trees.

There, deep into the grounds waited a second range much older than the first. Moss striped the aging structure's exterior, and mold, the interior. Inside, bucket-shaped dugouts lined the lanes, giving away the installation's purpose: live-testing explosive ordnance. Here, the evening wind buffeted away on the bullet traps, and someone had already staked in a handful of paper targets twenty meters out.

That someone was Sharlene, a middle-aged bottle-blonde who managed the gun forge and the armory besides. She was suntanned and top heavy, with a laugh like a witch from a sensorium fantasy, and a neighborly politeness that took Wil off guard. He'd gotten so familiar with translating the Kildalton brogue that her Great Lakes dialect was almost painful in its clarity.

"Used to be a Dozer for the USARF before she married into the clan," Gordon said. "She knows her shit."

Bombshells defusing bombshells. Sometimes, the world just made sense.

Once he'd put in his earplugs, Sharlene passed him a rifle with a glint in her eye—an AKNovy Strela 7.62x39mm. Ridiculously light. Wil suspected the magazine hadn't been loaded, and a cursory check proved him right.

"Ope," Sharlene giggled. "Golly, and without a spare? Geeze Louise, gonna have to load it yourself, sweetheart. Can I show you how?"

"I got it," Wil said. "But, thank you."

Somewhere between the castle and now, Cailean had slipped on mirrored sunglasses, lenses impenetrable as his glare. From his seat on an old folding chair beside a shelf, he held up a dusty paper box and tossed it at Wil.

He caught it against his chest with his forearm. Its contents jingled loudly. Rifle bullets.

"Hear that? Brass," Cailean said. "And mind the mag goes in the right way, aye? Our guns make sense on this planet."

"Acknowledged," Wil said, and went to sit beside the dugout. Gordon didn't. The handcuff snapped taut, and Wil's arm jerked up, splashing a handful of rounds into the dirt.

"Och," Gordon said. "Sorry."

"No problem," Wil muttered, but when he bent to pick up the first round, Gordon refused to slack. He tugged, but the big hairy bastard didn't move, so he really leaned into it—fingers brushing a case—just in time for Gordon crack a yawn and stretch both arms over his head. The motion reeled Wil off the chair and back to his feet.

Sharlene hid a smile. "Boys. No rough-housing in the gun range."

Gordon grinned. "Sorry, Shar. Long night."

Wil blew out a frustrated breath. This was just razzing. The worst thing he could do was lose his cool now and jeopardize either his freedom or the DRC. All he wanted was to go back to a place with air conditioning, discount takeout, and self-cleaning carpets instead of pouring rain, kitchen scraps, and fuzzy sons-of-bitches who scrutinized him on the toilet.

Shit. Rajan really *had* gotten to him.

Ammo box balanced on his left hand, Wil held out the magazine with his right. "Good idea, man. You load, and I'll hold 'er steady."

Gordon made a weird sound, almost coughing—laughter. Just once, like he'd never done it before. He fished the handcuff keys from his pocket. "Pass."

A minute later, the rounds were gathered in their box. Breeze cooling his wrist, Wil considered the task—loading a foreign weapon by hand—but saw the trick inside a quick glance. Thirty-round mag, so he thumbed in twenty-eight before seating it and pulling the bolt.

Cailean arched a silver brow above his equally silver lens. "Two short."

"Better two short than forcing a misfire by putting too much tension on the spring," Wil said. "Or was that what you were hoping for?"

Sharlene shot a glance to Cailean, grease-stained fist perched on the hip of her overalls. "Not bad, galactic. What'd you say your name was?"

"Don't encourage 'em," Cailean said. "He don't need the ego trip, believe you me."

The remainder of their idle conversation washed out in a hail of downrange gunfire. A go with the AKNovy Strela cemented his preference, though iron sights would take getting used to over having his geist suggest shots. Twenty rounds later when he asked for a swap, Sharlene presented a pistol with an almost reverent pomp: a beaten FGA PD-7 Detour.

"ALEPH's choice," Sharlene said. "Belonged to anybody you know?"

Minimalistic. Deadly. Configurable projectiles, with a smart-targeting interface. She wasn't wrong—this pistol was standard-issue for the Special Situations Section's Tactical Assault Team, located square on every Yadu Trooper's post-human hip from Concilium Prima to Paradiso. It'd been refitted with a beavertail safety grip in lieu of its geist-linked safety systems, and the reservoir of binary propellant and particle ammunition had been removed to make space for a magazine of eight .44 rounds.

Wil racked the slide to admire the dull shine of the interior. "Where'd you get this? Did you do the repairs? This is amazing."

Whatever reaction Sharlene expected to her jab, it wasn't this. The older woman flustered. "Well, no titanium on-hand to repair the chamber, so I figured—"

"Teseum alloy," he said. "Real goddamn smart. Balanced, too. I know some Snake Eaters on Varuna who'd kill for this."

Cailean whistled sharply. "Oi, bawbag. She's married, aye? And you aren't impressin' anyone wae made-up planetoids, either."

"Varuna's a real place, man. Beaches. Sunshine. Total opposite of here." Wil took his place behind the barrier at the edge of the range. "You wanna tell me about the last planet you visited? Dawn doesn't count."

"I thought ye were an Aquila," Cailean said. "Ye gossip like a Tech Bee."

He lifted the Detour and let the barrel tilt, searching for the intersection of control and alignment. "I've seen eight sunrises in six systems. You ever leave this mountain?"

The humor bled from the old man's face. "If yer gonna have a wank before ye shoot, have the decency to not involve the lady, aye? And furthermore—"

Wil squeezed the trigger: One, two, three, four. Each paper target fluttered, center mass punched one after the other. Sharlene's Teseum additions added just enough weight to tame the recoil, smoothing each shot, every trigger bringing the sights back to the target with minimal adjustment. He didn't want to call it perfect, but it was real goddamn close.

Four rounds left, so he went back and hit them again, shots grouped so tightly they were touching.

The smoke cleared, and Sharlene let loose a low, impressed whistle. "Never seen a Tech Bee shoot like that."

Cailean's thin-lipped grimace resolved into a begrudging smirk. "We get it," he said. "Yer PanO. Congratulations on bein' minimally competent."

Wil unseated the magazine and presented Sharlene the Detour in two pieces. "If you don't mind, ALEPH wants to know if it can try a shotgun now."

Gordon actually laughed.

↑↑

Thirty minutes later, he'd had a go with an Armadyne, an Obrez, and an Americolt. The verdict: While he missed his Schärfe MULTI Marksman, he missed his geist more. Bringing his own spotter who gauged effective range, barometric pressure, wind speed, velocity angles, and elevation was convenient, not to mention the minute adjustments to posture and timing it'd achieve when linked to his combat armor.

A multispectral visor was a distant runner-up, but it wasn't like he was about to go scrounge on the trail to find where they'd left it behind.

As far as the weapons went, his favorite was the Yungang Xíng Type 9.0 chain rifle. Its simple, brutal design inspired reverence. How it loaded. Its frenetic rate of fire. The crackle of the flash-forging chain inside the chamber before the shrapnel belched from its muzzle like dragon's breath. It was the only gun Sharlene let him try that he loved.

Cailean stubbed his third cigarette out on his gauntlet's weathered knuckles. "Ye act like ye've ne'er seen a chain rifle before."

"Not from this end," Wil said and gave it another rip.

With its iron sights, the AKNovy Strela was closest to his Schärfe, and the Detour would provide a competent backup in a pinch. Being outgunned wasn't something he'd gotten used to after years of lugging HMGs and MULTI Rifles, but he'd manage. And if he was lucky, they might even let him throw a smoke grenade.

The sky bled orange, then purple, until the automatic lights flicked on with a persistent electric hum. Range run officially over, Sharlene hiked out to collect the paper targets. Both men offered to help, but she insisted she had it and picked along the bullet traps in her blue jeans, stacking the obliterated targets under one arm and humming to herself.

Gordon stood beside the far dugout, arms crossed. He considered the shadows in the deep forest all around them with unusual disquiet. "Hey, PanO," he said, casting Wil a dark look. "You really see an alien?"

Wil's first instinct was sarcasm, but it didn't seem right to rake him over the coals when the big guy had finally started talking in whole sentences. "MacArthur believes me. You don't?"

"Unsure," Gordon said. "He's been calling the other clans. Asking if they've seen anything weird. If anyone's acting strange. Then he asked Cailean how you can tell if someone's been replaced."

"Ye can't," Cailean answered.

So that explained how Alastair knew that Speculo existed in the first place. Cailean. Judging by the old man's steady expression, Wil knew he'd tallied some of those 'space invader' kills on his pauldron in a more literal sense than he'd let on.

"The other clans," Wil said. "What'd they say?"

Cailean licked his teeth. "Six variations of, 'sounds like a PanO problem tae me.' I've come tae believe that if the whole Human Sphere lit aflame at once, ye'd have the border clans waitin' hear tell PanO and the StateEmpire burned away before they'd put themselves out."

"Everyone thinks he's stupid," Gordon said. "Alastair. For trusting you. Is he?"

Alastair had asked Wil to tell no one. But he'd saved him in the forest, stuck up for an unwelcome outsider, and antagonized his own uncle to protect him. He and his family had suffered during the Commercial Conflicts and had all the justification to treat him like an enemy. But he'd chosen otherwise. Wil owed him. If not materially, at least in the reassurance of his men.

"He's not," Wil said. "It was a Shrouded, or a Speculo Agent, I guess. He had this noise-canceling photoquantronic cloak over his flight suit. Fought me off with the light shotgun from the Balena's survival kit."

Cailean raked his beard with his fingertips and shared a glance with Gordon. "Can't stand the stench of their blood. Howlin' bad. Nothin' like it, aye?"

Wil shrugged. "Didn't smell like anything to me."

The old man's eyes grew wide. He stood swiftly, voice dropped to a hiss. "Mary and Joseph. Yer telling the truth?"

"Have been since the start," Wil said, patience tweaked.

Gordon joined their conspiracy circle. "I'm lost."

"Shas twist their DNA to suit each mission," Cailean explained. "Goin' in on Dawn, they'd prep fer 'Podes and Dogfaces. The smell of blood's a liability, ken, and in the wildlands, it'll get 'em nothin' but hunted. So they take their devil machines and fry the stench out of it, long before landfall."

Not entirely correct, but close. Shasvastii possessed a special kind of RNA, codenamed RNAsh. Where normal RNA copied information from DNA to ribosomes to build a being from a blueprint, RNAsh linked to the macro-chromatin fiber network laced through their body—like naturally occurring Silk. This fiber network encoded millions more times information than human DNA, allowing the Shasvastii to provoke natural, rapid evolution from a library of eidetic blueprints in their blood.

Ruined your lungs? Grow new ones, and while you're at it, might as well develop an organ to synthesize the toxin-laced atmosphere that took them to begin with. Too much gravity? Denser bones and ligaments like steel cable couldn't hurt.

Planet swarmed by hostile life-forms with incredible olfactory senses? Now that Wil thought it out, their scentless blood made sense.

"Christ on the cross," Gordon said. "Good thing you stole your visor back, eh PanO?"

"It was broken," Wil said.

Gordon tilted his head. Strands of dark hair fell across his brow. "What?"

"Just night vision, nothing else," Wil said. "Couldn't swap spectrums without my lens. Lagged so hard it didn't nullify his mimetism."

Cailean pulled his sunglasses aside, dark eyes skeptic. "Yer sayin' ye hunted a Speculo alone, at night in a forest, with no MSV, and not only survived—but led it tae ambush?"

"We can lie and say the Antipodes were on purpose, sure."

In an instant, their glares changed. Still an outsider, still PanOceanian, but amongst that vitriol glimmered a measure of respect.

It kind of pissed him off.

13

Gordon didn't look away from spinning his holographic comlog dial. "Saoirse?"

Wil squinted over his plate of breakfast scraps. "I'm just trying to get a read, man. Nothing to do until Alastair says jump, and that might take days. You know her well?"

Gordon shrugged. "Sure. She's family."

"You're related?"

"No," he said, and shielded his comlog screen with his arm. "Shut up."

Morning rush raged through the kitchen, pans and ladles and plates all clattering like a one-man band down a staircase. The squat side-door lay stoppered open, letting the morning chill dull the stifling heat clouding the stovetops. A small argument broke out between the staff over a miscommunication, and it all it took to make things worse was someone blasting a song on their comlog nobody liked.

Wouldn't have been a problem back home. Personal soundtracks auto-generated via event-centric algorithms had replaced playlists, inaudible to anyone but the user. Even their little misunderstanding could've been smoothed by their geists well before either party was aware of the mistake. Hell, washing dishes was something they didn't even do in King's Den, not with how prevalent simple domotics were.

One day, the people in this country would get lenses, Cubes, and geists, and they'd get to see how the Human Sphere really was. How life's simple pleasures were only enhanced via interconnection, how infinite information made personalized reality a possibility. How *necessary* it was to exist inside the system.

Or maybe none of that was actually a good thing. Maybe 24/7 interconnection turned life into a zero-sum game, twisted every waking second into a new frontier of real estate to be bought and sold without consent. Maybe it subtracted the humanity from humankind and left them malicious and hungry, chasing the ghost of perfection, unable to see the enemy battering down the Acheron Blockade for their own perfect faces in their personal funhouse mirrors.

Yeah, something was definitely wrong with him. He hadn't been like this since solitary.

Desperate for any distraction, Wil jabbed his spoon at Gordon's dial. "Hot date?"

"Job," he grunted.

"Money's always good."

Gordon swiped the air, and the holoprojector dimmed. "Be better if you stopped talking."

Sixty seconds later, Saoirse Clarke came in like a redheaded landslide. She swiped a strip of bacon from a passing tray, barked her good-mornings to the staff, and loomed over the head chef's shoulder until she gave the poor woman a scare. A few playful smacks with a wooden spoon later, she giggled her way over, bright and sunshiny and beautiful.

Gordon hunkered over him and said, "Right. Off."

Wil choked on his water.

Saoirse greeted Gordon with a quick, "Madainn mhath," and the two fell into a lightning-fast Caledonian conversation Wil could never hope to follow. Saoirse chewed her bacon, stole from another plate, scavenged up a thick slice of toast—eating, eating, eating. She talked with her mouth full, shooting Wil amused glances all the while.

Gordon jut a thumb at him, and Saoirse snorted when she laughed. "Sure, sure," she said. "Na gabh dragh."

"Mòran taing," Gordon said, and with a genuine bow, left the kitchen.

Wil fumbled halfway to a stand. "Hey, where's he going? I'm not done eating."

Saoirse picked a slice of toast from Wil's plate and flashed her pronounced fangs. "Dinna worry, PanO. Finish yer breakfast, I'm yer minder now."

"I was saving that."

"Shoulda been quicker," she snickered and pointed at the untouched handful of crisp, black dregs. "Ye've got pudding. Eat up. Unless?"

He sank back down and pushed her the plate. "Help yourself."

She did. Messily, tearing the bread into pieces and cleaning up the egg yolk. When only sausage remained, she slapped the barrel like a drum, rattling the silverware on the plate. "So! I heard Cailean likes ye now?"

"I'm certain it's still the opposite."

"Bitter's just how he is, aye? Cross as two sticks and don't get along wae no one, ever since Novyy Cimmeria. But I ken how, so, no skin off my teeth. Not like I'm any kinder."

"And the reason is…?"

"Not tellin'," she said. "Don't do your head in about it."

He exhaled a thin laugh. "Gordon's not coming back today, is he?"

"Tired of me already?"

"Nah," Wil said. "You talk. Breath of fresh air."

Her smirk faded into a genuine smile, but only for a moment. "Am I?"

"You gonna do all the same stuff he did? Watch me bathe, watch me—"

"Oh, aye, especially that," she said, pale eyes bright and round. "Say, wanna help me win a bet? Llowry says that all galactics got a gene mod in vitro, vaccines and Silk and such. Says it swells yer todgers from pistols to Feuerbachs."

"Improved Human Baseline," he said. "Don't think it works that way."

"If it'll win me ten pound, I'll fetch a measure right now. Unzip?"

Wil laughed, but Saoirse didn't. Her lips held tight in an expectant line. The longer the silence lasted, the more his amusement dissolved until her deadpan finally cracked.

"Fuck's sake, PanO, your face!" she crowed and broke into nasal giggles. "Almost believed me, aye? Christ, mate, I said not to do your head in."

"Sorry," he said. "Head's out, promise."

Then her gaze sharpened. "At least buy me dinner first."

Gordon's words echoed in his head: *Right. Off.*

Her clawed and callused fingers tore his sausage link in two.

⸸

The day with Saoirse wasn't any different than with Gordon, and time went slow as it always did. However, Saoirse liked to talk—about anything, nothing, all the time. While they did laps in the halls, she spun him the story of Ceilidh MacArthur, the founding mother of their clan, and how she and her brother built the castle stone by stone during the First Antipode Offensive and defended it during the Bloody Race. She jawed about the electric lights: how they were powered, the surprising cost, and the controversy involved that persisted fifty years to today.

Saoirse dragged her claws fondly along the mottled stone wall. "Defiling history, they said. Not what Ceilidh intended, they said. And then they had to defend her from dropships by torchlight, and suddenly all those complaints...."

Wil pieced together Saoirse's deal from fragments of casual conversation. As far as he could tell, she was a ranger who patrolled the border from the end of autumn until the beginning of spring. She lived out in the woods during that time, going from tower to tower something like the fire watch of old American national parks. But instead of watching for smoke, she kept eyes on the sky, making sure all aircraft that flew over the AEZ were scanned, tagged, and logged in the Stavka database. Illegal mining operations were rampant, and she helped hold the line.

At a checkpoint near the central foyer, the Volunteer on duty was in the midst of being lectured by an old woman wrapped in plaid—maybe his grandma by the way she wagged her finger. When she caught sight of Saoirse, she froze until she passed.

"God's blood," the grandma whispered and drew a cross over her breast. "Out in the day without an ounce of shame."

"Gran, please," the Volunteer said. "We've been through this."

"It's just we had a different door for *those people* back in Scone," she continued, and the Volunteer hurried to quiet her.

Wil slowed. His blood boiled. Fists clenched. He'd heard Dog-Warriors were second-class citizens in the south, that their existence was both a threat and a reminder of weakness, proof that their males were unable to protect their females from assault. Sexist, puerile, and stupid—but biopurists rarely held PhDs.

Judging by the reaction Saoirse had got from the old bat, he guessed Wulvers were a distant relation. Or a crossbreed. Her Antipode eyes, fangs, and clawed fingernails were evidence enough to support that theory.

But he had no place to speak, no right to lash out. So he kept step and didn't look back.

Once they'd rounded the corner, Saoirse leaned in close. "Relax, eh? Just someone's gran, nae bother. Been called worse by people who meant it more."

The tacit acceptance in her voice gave it away; for her, this wasn't new.

On their next lap around the grounds, Wil hung back and paid attention. An hour later, he'd come to the conclusion that not every glare and curse in the halls over the last few days had been intended for him. When Saoirse sashayed by, more people drew crosses into their shirts than the San Pietro faithful on Ash Wednesday.

Which meant Gordon likely earned the same, and like Saoirse, never mentioned it.

Ascending a narrow spiral staircase, they emerged onto the south rampart and into the frigid Caledonia air. Moss and spats of mold carpeted the centuries-old stones, winding around puddles of rainwater. Saoirse showed him the gap in the rampart where he could see the entirety of sleepy Kildalton nestled in the crook of the mountains; the riot of cottages; the council housing topped with so many solar panels; the bustling farmer's market nearest the gate.

But his mind was somewhere else.

Before long, Alastair sent a message apologizing for not touching base and promised they'd speak tomorrow. Lunch was brief—a quick stop at a vending machine—and the tour continued. Wil learned the little bag worn in front of the kilt was called a *sporran*, and their boot knife, a *sgian-dubh*; Saoirse learned *boludo* meant the same as 'mate,' with all the situational baggage included.

Dinner was louder than normal. A good loud. After, Saoirse dropped Wil back at his quarters. Undressed, he laid on his bed, and wondered if he'd lost his mind.

He liked Saoirse Clarke.

It was a strange feeling. Unexpected. The girls he'd been into before were tough, sure, but they hadn't clocked double his bench press, and they sure as hell weren't sloppy eaters with a hundred dick jokes locked and loaded. They'd all been petite, clean-cut in uniform and fixed up nicely outside it.

Beyond eyeliner and lip balm, Wil wasn't certain that Saoirse knew what makeup was. And her facial scar—most people on Concilium Prima weren't allowed to be that ugly, imperfections masked by the ever-present digital patina of modern civilization.

But something about her made him irrational. Her insolent, lopsided smirk. Those freckles. The claymore she treated better than herself, apologizing to the hilt after she banged it on door jambs and corners. How eager her laughter, and how easy it was to earn it. The pleasant curve to her, from forearm to thigh.

Growing up on ultra-progressive Neoterra might've colored his perspective, but he didn't care if she was stronger, or taller. All he cared about was how gorgeous she was in motion and how much she surprised him every time she spoke.

Even her sweat smelled good.

Yeah. No. This was bad, and he was desperate. One week from now, Saoirse would be a distant memory, and then he would cringe at his brief infatuation with the scar-faced ladette who talked at a yell and stole food off his plate. Instead of some girl, he should've been focused on the Shasvastii, or his eventual return to Concilium Prima. More important things.

Things that actually mattered, unlike Saoirse Clarke.

A pounding rattled the door.

The clock on his wall read 24:28. Hours had slipped by the blink of an eye. A hundred worst-case scenarios flashed through his groggy mind as Wil flicked on the lights and struggled into a shirt.

Outside stood Saoirse. She'd traded her grenadier's vest for a short-cropped leather jacket, her dueling bracers for hairbands, and her combat boots for grungy sneakers. In the tears of her ragged denim jeans, the broad, pale expanse of her legs nearly glowed. All her clothes were sized slightly too small for her broad-shouldered six-foot-two warrior's frame—everything but her frazzled black beanie, struggling to contain the wavy totality of her sunfire hair. It looked hand-made and well-loved.

When she saw him, she shared a crooked smile and shoved a ratty sweatshirt into his hands. "We're goin' out."

The hooded sweater was violently blue, old fabric spattered with fading oil stains. A deteriorating Omnia Research & Creation Corporation logo spread dead-center across the chest. "Seriously?"

"Should make ye feel right at home, aye? Blue enough?"

"No, seriously, am I allowed to leave the castle this late? It's almost tomorrow."

"Och, aye, right, o'course, *rules*," she said. "Want me to ring yer mummy, ask if ye can play? Yer a long time dead, ken like."

He laughed. "You can try."

Saoirse's pale eyes trailed down his chest and halted below the belt. Wil followed her gaze: his bare legs were only a few shades darker than hers, standing there in only a shirt and boxer briefs.

Wil bunched the hoodie over himself. "Need a minute."

She cocked her head, grin unrestrained. "Downstairs in five or I'm ditchin' ye," she said and traipsed off along the hall.

Despite the heat climbing his neck into his ears, Wil couldn't look away. Fascinating at rest, arresting in motion... was this level of fixation normal, or was the concussion to blame?

All the fiberweave asses and synthetic breasts and biosculpted muscula-ture back on Neoterra hadn't prepared him for the weapon of mass destruction named Saoirse Clarke. Gordon had warned him, Neil had warned him—hell, his own instincts warned him.

He slipped on the hoodie and a fresh pair of pants and went after her any-ways.

⸸

A small, gravel-strewn footpath wound its way down the hillside, away from the castle and toward the city streets. Alien insects chirped unfamiliar songs from the grass. Stars swam through the sparse holes in the sleeping rainclouds above, tinted by the city lights, and it was very, very cold.

Halfway across the green, Saoirse slowed to a halt. She pointed out a trio of large, dark shadows grazing out by the fence.

The horses. Wil had completely forgotten about them.

"Don't worry, so did Al," she said. "Busy as, last few nights. Gorgeous, though. Right?"

"You're an," Wil began, and the words 'animal-lover?' died on his tongue. No telling what negative connotation he'd almost stumbled into. "Yeah. Gorgeous. Right."

Saoirse didn't notice the stumble, transfixed. Slowly, almost painfully, she pried herself away. "There'll be time enough for starin' later. Follow me."

Within minutes, they were crossing through the township proper. Rain set-tled across Kildalton in potholes and pavement cracks, reflecting up the scattered orange streetlights that ran the length of the winding hillside roads.

Steam curled from Saoirse's lips, intermingling with his own. As they crossed a bridge, she pressed close and took his arm in hers. Bold, but not unwel-come.

Cold steel clicked around his wrist. Gordon's handcuffs. The matching restraint glinted on Saoirse's sleeve as she stepped away, letting his leashed arm dangle. "Problem?"

He jingled the chain. Tugged. Her arm barely budged. "You really think I'd run?"

"It'd be a bad idea," Saoirse said.

"Because you're faster."

"Aye."

"And stronger."

"That, too."

"Smarter?"

She narrowed her eyes. "Chess don't kill Antipodes."

"Might bore 'em to death."

Saoirse sized him up and undid the cuff. "Not me."

"I always preferred checkers," Wil said, and offered his arm again, but she didn't take it.

At the hill's end, Kildalton once again transformed from a sleepy, anachronistic township into a mountainside boondock. Cozy cabins gave way to apartment buildings, grass to gravel, gardens to parking lots. Concrete bollards and derelict anti-tank hedgehogs clustered on the wider thoroughfares, spit-shined by neon lights and laser-projected Mk3 holo-ads in dire need of repair.

Under a floodlight-strewn back lot, a trio of brawny teenagers practiced Dog-Bowl passes while their partners crowded a decades-old brick-style comlog, listening to Candy Double flirt with a handsome Circular conductor in 2½D.

Their path curved parallel to a long stretch of chain link lining a canal near the center of town. At first, Wil assumed the papers anchored in the concatenation were scraps from a holiday event or trash caught in the linkage. But the farther they walked, the more clean and crisp the papers became, until young men and women were staring back at him from print-outs scrawled with personal details and contact information. HAVE YOU SEEN THIS MAN; LAST KNOWN WHEREABOUTS: OUTPOST 16; IF YOU HAVE ANY INFORMATION, PLEASE....

Wil slowed and scanned the fence. "Damn. That's a lot of missing persons."

"Four-thousand-plus people in the city limits, and a thousand more scattered up 'n' down the highlands," Saoirse said. "Lot of empty outwith the gates. Antipodes, bad weather, sickness. Some up and leave, uninterested in northern baggage and searchin' fer a better life. Some slip away, and it takes weeks tae find their grave. Some get taken. Frontier's a dangerous place."

"Taken," he repeated and scanned over the still image of a smiling grandmother, crowded baking sheet held proudly in her polka-dot oven mitts. "By who?"

"Submondo, meat traders, Yuan-Yuans," Saoirse listed. "Heard every brothel and mine on Tanit is chock full of folk from backwoods like Kildalton."

Wil had no words. That he'd spent his childhood in the gutter of the most prosperous nation in the Human Sphere was one thing, but he'd never worried a day in his life about being trafficked to the moon and enslaved in a mine, much less worse. And he understood now why Alastair's absence had been felt so keenly—the shadow of a possibility that their own clan chieftain had been taken and sold would've lit a fire in him, too.

Wil hustled to catch up, trying not to think about how old some of the papers on the chain link were.

14

At the far end of the no-man's-land near the palisade hunkered a fat, ugly drum of a building. Spray paint layered the foundation and first story walls: DEAD END, DOG WHENSDAY?, and FREE CALEDONIA! fought for space atop a jumble of block letters and saltires, and it got more complicated from there.

Above the doors, mismatched neon lettering: THE CROATOAN. OPEN 25/7. DOGFACES WELCOME.

Judging by the concrete exterior and the blast door entryway, it'd been a bunker once upon a time. A few people lingered outside, beer bottles in hand, night air clouded with the bittersweet stench of menthol and ash. Trash-metal wailed from within, guttural vocals drowned out by the roar of a crowd.

Wil turned to her, incredulous. "A dive bar?"

"Best in town," Saoirse said. "Ever drink Coca-Cola?"

Defunct 21st-century excesses like that were embargoed on Concilium Prima due to adverse health effects, same as nicotine-laden tobacco products. It hadn't stopped his friends in King's Den from partaking, but Wil had never joined in.

"Guessed not," she said. "It's *class*, Wil. Ye've got tae try some."

His laugh was sharper than intended. "We walked all the way here for fizzy syrup water? For real?"

A tall, brutal slab of a man glanced over, the cherry of his cigarette illuminating his face. His ears were sharp, like Saoirse's, and his eyes reflected gold in the light. His shirt read BOUNCER in white block text, and he definitely looked the part.

"Not entirely," she said, and pushed him inside.

The Croatoan's interior was donut-shaped and multilevel, chock-full of tables covered in empty bottles and crumpled garbage. In the center—a ring. Heavily reinforced chain-link fencing separated the patrons from the bloodsport on every level. About a thousand ancient photographs wallpapered the first floor, and all the light in the bar came from either the myriad neon signs advertising beer or the flood lights hung above the arena. More than thirty people clustered against the links, voices raised, fists high.

The chain jingled, taut, and a massive, hulking Antipode easily twice the size of Pale Shadow scaled the interior fencing. Where the mane on his body thinned, tattoos of Celtic crosses and scissoring rockabilly girls intersected. And he was wearing athletic shorts.

Not an Antipode. A Dog-Warrior.

Holy shit. How were they bigger?

As the crowd gathered in to shout point-blank, the monstrosity climbed to the top, took aim below, and caught the eye of a chesty woman in the front row. The Dog-Warrior winked awkwardly, and hurtled out of sight, elbow-first.

A dull crunch echoed up, and the screams of the crowd joined the machine-gun peals of a bell.

Saoirse placed her hand on the small of Wil's back. "Runnin' already?"

Wil froze. "What'd you say?"

"We're over in the splash zone," she said. "Gawk any more, and we'll miss Gordon."

The chesty woman twisted around, cackling in dismay. A splat of gore had arced up from below to bullseye her deep, deep cleavage, and she pried both sides of her blouse wide open for her friends to sop up the mess.

Wil gawked, stalled. "Gordon's here?"

Saoirse caught his eye with a disapproving smirk. "Who d'ye think we're about to watch fight," she said, and helped him along with her elbow.

Two flights of bare concrete steps later and they'd reached the bottom floor, and a far better view of the aftermath. The gray Dog-Warrior had changed into human form, overstretched shorts winched up in one hand, the other arced in triumph. All of the veins on his body had shocked to the surface, prominent and throbbing, and his roar cracked and broke in celebration.

His opponent lay with his back to the chain link, swollen features wreathed in blood. With a medic's help, their stray hip joint wormed back into position with a loud, wet pop.

Everyone pretended not to notice the man in the nice suit and sunglasses seated by the cage, folded fingers swathed in gaudy tattoos. He held an Askari AS Thueban pistol loaded with glowing Viral rounds—the Dog-Warrior's singular, fatal weakness—and met Wil's gaze with a muted, professional nod.

Russian. Submondo. Dangerous.

An old photograph hung on the wall above a dingy jukebox: a crimson-furred Dog-Warrior with a crew cut and a metal arm, sitting across a table from a petite redhead with a waist-length braid. About thirty empty pint glasses separated them, and neither looked about to give up. Sloppy handwriting dashed along the white space beneath the photograph: CHERRY & DEARG.

Couldn't be.

Wil caught up with Saoirse at the bar, talking to a small, heavily tattooed man in a floral shirt. "This is Joe," she said, and handed Wil a whisky bottle. "Joe, this is Wil."

Joe dipped under the counter and produced a bulky, lensed device. He aimed it at them. It clicked, flashed, and a glossy paper square squealed out of a narrow opening beneath the eye.

While Wil shook off the spots in his vision, Joe leaned out from behind his device. "Sersh," he said. "When you said he was a bootlicking capitalist galactic, you didn't say he was *hot*."

"That was Joe," Saoirse said and stole the square from his machine. She swept up two glasses and made for the tables. "See ya, Joe!"

Saoirse led him around the other side of the arena, away enough from the crowd but with a good vantage point on the action to come. She called the table there her 'usual seat,' and by its conspicuous vacancy, Wil had a feeling her dibs held at least some weight. Glossy square laid face-down on the stained tabletop, Saoirse slid over his glass.

A quick comparison to the wall confirmed his suspicion. "That's a photo."

"Yep," she said.

"Of us?"

Saoirse poured a finger of whisky for both of them. "Yep."

"Is that really how they used to make them? Can I see?"

"Still needs cooking," she said and tapped her glass atop his. "Slàinte."

He reluctantly followed her lead. "Salud."

The liquor was bitter as medical mouthwash and clouded up into his sinuses along with the aftertaste of rubber bands, like swallowing bile without having to spit it up first. Wil gagged it down in a vain effort to seem tough. When he finished wincing, Saoirse's glass had emptied, and she was struggling not to laugh.

"Don't, often," he croaked and cleared his throat in the crook of his elbow. "Helluva lot stronger than what we got back home."

"Then ye shouldna balked at sugar water. Another?"

He waved her off. "Still recovering."

"More for me," she said and made herself a second drink.

"So, uh, the Croatoan," Wil said. "Weird name for a bar. Looks more like a bomb shelter to me. Or a prison. There a story there?"

"There is, and I could tell ye. Fair warning though, I've been told it's a boring one."

A lifetime of fixation on International Standard Code, arms manufacturer lore, and military apocrypha made that statement so much more alluring than she could ever know. "Bore me."

She threw back the second drink and jumped straight into it. "So! Commercial Conflicts. Seventeen years ago. Kildalton's occupied. Three years in, there's this skirmish outwith the holding near Odhran's Ford. PanO mercs versus StateEmpire mercs, fightin' over who'd keep our Teseum mine. When no-one's lookin', the whole town packs into the bunker where they stored the explosives fer excavation. Here."

Wil glanced around. Yeah, made sense. With these walls, anything short of an orbital bombardment would leave a few scorch marks at best. If the explosives in here went up, the townies in the village wouldn't have felt more than a soft whump. No windows, which meant it had its own independent air filtration system. No exits but the one. Optimal for a bunker, but a hazard for a bar.

"Before they hid, we tossed our homes like we'd left," Saoirse said. "Dinner on the stove, telly on, dogs loose. Ditched the cars but took the campin' equipment. Strapped an entire town's worth of comlogs tae a horse, slapped its arse and let it ride. When the PanO mercs returned triumphant, we were vanished. Their only hint was 'Croatoan,' splattered in red on the side of their commander's prefab."

He perked up. "Same as the missing colony, on Earth?"

She tapped his nose with her finger. "So, so clever."

His cheeks burned, and he tried not to feel patronized. "How'd the mercs take it?"

"Fell right for it, of course! We waited till the wankers had gave chase, and stormed the fuck-all security left behind. Took the palisade, the Traktor Muls, the anti-air, and that was that. Kildalton was ours again."

"Damn. They didn't try to shoot their way back in?"

"Nope—well, not as if they had a chance. Conflict ended about three weeks later, and the mine ran dry by year after. So it's not like our 'victory' mattered, but—I was eleven, ken? Men from beyond the stars stole our home from us, and I didnae feel like we'd survive them till that day."

"It's a good story," he said. "Not boring at all."

She flashed a cheeky grin. "Fuck off."

A few shouts in the crowd smothered his protests, and Saoirse backed away as if she'd won. He attempted another sip of the whisky. Still didn't like it, but at least now he was ready. Noisy patrons passed by, singing. Stale water mixed among the stench of sour beer and sweat in the air. The longer he sat here, the more the humidity clung to his skin under his shirt.

The Dog-Warrior from the ring swaggered by, chesty woman on his arm. They necked all the way to the stairs and disappeared just as her hand snaked into his shorts.

Wil cleared his throat. "Nice place you got here."

Saoirse applied a fresh coat of lip balm, unbothered. "Aye, Wilhelm, sure."

"My friends call me Wil," he said. "One L."

She snorted. "Aye, Wilhelm. Sure."

He laughed, though he wished he held it in. Whisky must've been taking hold already. Saoirse took that as permission to pour him another and made this one a double. He put another dent into it, if only to quiet his thoughts, and muffled another cough she found deadly amusing.

Saoirse peeled back the corner of the photo, approved, and flipped it over. On it: him, bewildered; her, beautiful. She produced a bent pen from her pocket and signed it 'WIL & SAOIRSE.'

He quickly pivoted from what he wanted to ask—how do you get 'Sersha' from *that*—and back to, "So, of all the places in Kildalton, why here?"

"Well, ye've been locked in the MayaNet historical set at Castle MacArthur so long, I was worried y'were about to start believin' the daydream. Had tae make sure ye saw the real Caledonia, at least once."

"I mean, I've been in worse bars," he said. "None with blood sport. Usually folks just watch Aristeia! on AR simulcast instead, you know? Don't got to mop up after, no teeth on the floor."

She narrowed her eyes. "If I asked ye to show me PanOceania, would it be a penthouse apartment in Neoterra, a make-believe amusement park, or somewhere actual people live?"

Wil breathed out a shallow, bitter laugh. "King's Den."

"Sounds posh."

"It's not," he said. "It's where I grew up."

Her white eyes brightened. "And here I heard they farmed you in pods! Tell me more."

"It's boring," he said.

She smiled. "So, bore me."

Gladly suffering her turnabout, Wil hesitated. But when he took in the grime, the oversexed groupies, and the jukebox blaring Pinewalker and Full Moon's Dead, he knew she'd understand.

"Guarida del Rey," he said, thumb tracing the rim of his glass. "219th to 221st Street, center of the worst part of San Pietro. Everyone else called it 'override your car's LAI so it doesn't stop on reds,' but we called it home."

Saoirse cocked her head. "Worst places always got the best names, huh?"

"Guess the first guy who put up street signs had a flair for the dramatic. No signage without AR, so we had to make our own, y'know?"

"None at all?" she asked, ears perked. "Everything's AR?"

"Yeah, just about. Even public transportation's jacked-in on Neoterra—buses won't stop if they don't detect a quantronic presence, so if you're Atek, they rip right on by. Got to hire someone to stand with you or get good at jumping on. Knew a kid who died doing that."

"Jesus. What's it like now?"

"The same."

Saoirse blinked. "Nothing changed?"

"Why would it? Nobody cares about you in San Pietro if you're poor."

"Wait, now. I thought PanOs got money for nothing. You're on the demo… thing. Universal basic income. Always sounded too good to be true, ask me."

"The demogrant," Wil said. "Not if you're an Atek. No Maya address to send the Oceanas, so if you wanna eat, you gotta work. Or steal."

Her pale eyes widened slightly. She'd gotten what he'd been putting down—who he was, and where he was from. That he'd been Atek once, same as she was now.

The bar quieted for a moment as the jukebox switched from one ancient, grimy track to another. The lighting changed hues from a bright orange-red to a deep, dim violet, obscuring the paramedics dipping backstage with the loser of the last match.

She leaned closer. "You miss it?"

"Sometimes," Wil admitted. "I miss the food trucks outside church, doling out the day's excess. The tías trading chisme in the market aisles. The tíos shooting the shit while hanging asado. I miss Good Friday and how everyone would get together and do one big fish fry for the whole bloc."

"Sounds nice, honestly."

"I don't miss finding dead people behind the shops," he said. "Or the gangs. Or the Jackboots, either."

"Where d'your parents fall on that spectrum?"

His mood flattened. "Let's not."

"Ooh, bullseye," she said, and wiggled in her seat. "Gie 'em a call when you get back to civilization, aye? Tell yer mum ye miss her, say hi to yer da for me."

"No can do."

"How no, too guilty? This'll prob'ly make a helluva story for tea." Saoirse stuck out her pinkie and thumb in a strange gesture, and held it to her head. "Mum, ye'll never guess! I was kidnapped by Caledonians, and they shoved me intae plaid and force fed me a whisky—"

"They're dead," he said.

Saoirse's face fell. She shrank back, studying the tabletop. "That was fucked," she managed. "Sorry. No, really—sorry."

"It's fine."

She lingered for a moment and then touched his arm, briefly and sincerely. "Seriously."

"I'm not cut up about it, don't worry. It's no big deal."

Saoirse withdrew, dark claws tapping the tabletop. She scrunched her lips, resisting the awkward momentum. "So, uh. Aquila Guard, aye?"

"That I'm not one anymore, or how unlikely it is I was one?"

"… If I keep diggin', d'ye think I'll dig myself intae another pub?"

"Shout if you hit Teseum."

A pause. "You mad at me?"

"Not at all," he said. "It's just… my story's basic. Yours is probably better."

She licked her lips. "Deserve this, don't I?"

"A little," Wil said.

"Alright, fine. After my mandatory year of diggin' holes and runnin' laps, I came home and realized there's nawt for jobs in Kildalton for a Wulver, much less a woman one. Could've gone logging, spent blood in the arena, or gone tae bootleg wae the Caterans, but the army suited me. Only ever been good with my hands."

"Well, you did fight back that Antipode like it was nothing. Talent's talent."

Saoirse laughed, short and sardonic, and hooked up the sleeves of her jacket. He'd noticed her ink before, numerous and varied in style, but now without her gauntlets on, the extensive work on her arms was both visible and impressive.

"Talent, aye, and seven years in the Caledonian Highlander Army."

Dominating the center of her left forearm was an archaic grenadier's sigil—a pot overflowing with flames—flanked by a ring of laurels and surrounded by a belt tied in a knot. The words FIDE ET OPERA rocked across the bottom, same as the MacArthur crest.

A litany of smaller images peppered her right, locations slapdash: the crescent moon struck by a claymore; an arrow piercing a serpent, footnoted 1924M; the nine of diamonds playing card; a lion rampant with lightning bolts for feet; a crossed pair of hatchets, ringed in simple blue; and many, many more.

"Gotta tip the needle in Teseum, or I heal it away in a day or two. Hurts like hell, but can't deny the results." She ran her eyes up his arms. "Show me yours?"

"Don't got none," Wil said. "Never stayed in an assignment long enough or drank that much in one night." He gave the crossed hatchets a gentle touch. "You were an assault pioneer?"

"Someone's got to play minesweeper when the Traktor Muls are out. Who better than the Dogfaces no one wants around?"

Wil furrowed his brow. "Okay, can I ask—is that a slur, or—it's just the way I keep hearing it. I can't place it. I don't want to offend."

"Depends on how ye use it," she said and withdrew her arm. "Simple as, ken like?"

He twisted his lips inward. "Not helpful."

"It's like, literally too easy, you know?" she translated, brogue smashed flat into a PanOceanian inflection. "Better?"

"No. Hell no. Is that what I sound like?"

"Not at all," she said, but her grin gave her away.

"So, if I said… I'd heard it was difficult for Dogfaces in places like Rodina or Merovingia, that's okay?"

Saoirse glanced at the crowd and nodded. "But not so loud."

"Acknowledged," he said, and leaned in. "Honestly, up here, with how interconnected everyone is, I thought it'd be different."

"Well, that's partly my problem, innit? Everyone kens my family line—that's how my callsign's Princess."

"Your brother. Right."

"Ooh! Gordon gossips, does he?"

"Don't blame him," Wil said. "I'm persistent. And very clever."

"You're very something, alright. And if we're bein' specific, Alastair's my half-brother."

That explained the lack of family resemblance. Wil wanted to ask more, but he wasn't sure how much she wanted to share, how far would be too far.

Saoirse must've read him like a geist. "His da, my mum. Any questions?"

"One," he said, and chanced it. "I'm totally lost on this whole Wulver thing."

"Wulvers are about the midpoint of a human and Dog-Warrior, though we don't transform," she said. "Not as tough, but tough all the time. What ye get when a Dogface and a human intermarry. Dog-Warriors breed true, but us, we're the halfbreeds."

"With how important family is 'round here, must be a lot of you in Caledonia."

"Nah," Saoirse said. "Thirty in Kildalton, tops. Wulvers are sterile."

The arena bell pealed three times, cutting their conversation short. The crowd thickened back toward the chain link and away from the bar.

A giant in ragged green and gold boxing trunks padded out from the staging area, thick beard carved into a burly mutton chop style, scalp coated in vicious stubble. His arms were thicker than Wil's legs. Hairier, too. Scars climbed his body from shin to scalp, the largest and most prominent diagonal across his belly. It looked someone had shoved the big bastard into a wood chipper and he'd come out the other side swinging.

Wil blinked. It was Gordon.

He didn't clean up half-bad.

His opponent was smaller, dressed similarly scant in red and blue. Their pink skin was decorated the same shade of tacky as the Russian in the suit: grinning Antipode skulls, thieves' stars, and the Virgin Mary with a blunt in a gentry grip. He desperately peacocked at the crowd, swaggering from turnbuckle to turnbuckle to flex and animal scream.

Gordon waited in his corner, eyes closed, still and cold as Teseum.

"Quick," Saoirse said and bounced off her stool. "Before it gets goin'," want another? My treat."

Wil drained his glass, and the burn muddled in his stomach and intensified. "More of that and I'll be sick."

"Then what, water?" she said. "Milk? Apple juice? Somethin' with MULTI in the name?"

"MULTI Fruit, please. With a little umbrella in it."

Her jaw dropped. "A shìorraidh—issat a real thing?"

Wil laughed, to her instant chagrin. "No."

"Cheeky—" she gasped and stripped her jacket. The crop-top underneath was sleeveless and scant, revealing the elastic edges of a sports bra. Her pale, shallow cleavage and skull-rose tattoo both seemed bolder in the dark light. "That's it. Yer gettin' a coke, and yer likin' it."

Whatever protests he had evaporated versus the hypnotic flick of her hips as she jogged to the bar. Beneath the strands of crimson hair that'd fought free from under her beanie, a tattoo stretched across her back from one shoulder to the other. A single word.

AIRAGHARDT.

"Well, well, well," someone clucked behind him. "Look what the Dogface dragged in."

Wil turned to find Talbot's swollen face leering from the shadow of a baseball cap, flanked by Bell and Shaw.

15

The three idiot Volunteers surrounded a nearby table and sat down. Beer bottles filled their hands, stances just askew enough to suggest their first round was long behind them. They were all in casual clothes, kilts and dog tags ditched for athleisure and gold—chains, watches, comlogs.

"Hey, friend," Wil said. "How's the face?"

Talbot glared past two black eyes and a ladder of bandage strips. "When you take the dog out, it's not s'posed to walk you, aye?"

"Still got time tae tuck n' run, lad," Shaw said. The side of his head where Talbot had teed off was still purple, and his torqued arm hung in a sling. "Saoirse's right famous for rippin' specific appendages."

"I wouldna ride her into battle," Bell added, voice squeezed nasal through his resculpted nose.

Shaw snickered. "Bet she'd be doin' the ridin', mate."

"Her dick's prob'ly bigger'n his."

"More like Saoirse Cock, aye?"

"Out on the lash?" Bell chortled. "More like out on the leash."

A pointy-eared bloke at another table glared over his shoulder at them, and they shut up real quick.

Back in King's Den, Wil would've already asked them to go outside and made them eat crow—off the pavement, if necessary. But judging by the fire in his eyes, Cailean hadn't been bluffing. One wrong move, and Wil would get that H-12 cartridge back, no matter how righteous the beating administered. So he smothered his anger and said, "Thanks, great. Y'all can shut up now. And Bell, do me a favor and clean your gun sometime, alright?"

Bell's eyes bulged. "Heavy fucking thief, you are. Piss off."

"Can't believe Neil blocked us over a galactic," Shaw mumbled. "It's mental, right?"

"Does my head in," Bell chirped.

Shaw checked for the point-eared guy and got louder. "Should do *his* head in."

"Now now, lads," Talbot said and held out a biding hand. "Galactic here's had a tough life, same as us. No reason to play right-hook diplomacy with our poor PanOceanian ambassador, eh?"

Shaw paused, mid-drink. "Play what? Not playing, me."

Talbot pointed at the scarred knot below Wil's ear. "See that? Real PanOs, they've got Cubes put in at birth. By professionals, yeah?"

"Them scars don't look professional to me," Bell said.

"Zactly," Talbot said. "Too poor to afford a Cube, too poor to afford a doctor. Worse than garbage, PanO treats their least fortunate. Barely considers 'em human. Calls 'em Ateks instead."

Shaw whistled. "Jaysis. And he's on *their* side?"

This wasn't just annoying anymore. As enticing as it might've been to see Talbot try to swallow the bottle he was holding, Wil didn't want to chance ruining Saoirse's mood, or the night, or anything else. He stood, considering the whisky bottle and its neck like a handle, but had to leave it behind. How he was now, he couldn't trust himself picking it up.

Talbot rolled his shoulders, teeth bared. "Couldn't beat 'em, so you joined 'em, eh? And they kicked you right back to the gutter. Kinda sad, innit?"

Wil stepped away. "Have a nice night, fellas."

"Your dead mum," Talbot said. "Think she'd be proud?"

He paused. Turned back. "What'd you say?"

"I said," Talbot growled, "how many y'think yer PanO mum gargled to get that Cube up in you?"

Cailean's cartridge evaporated. Words failed. His blood ignited; he raised his fist and took two heavy steps forward, digging in with his toe to commit to the twist—

And his punch stalled. Fell short. Someone had him by the bicep with both arms, anchoring his charge. Wil spun ready to go to blows and found Nora McDermott holding him back with all of her featherlight weight.

Blue eyes wide, she kept Wil's gaze. "Don't."

"Oi, clearin' barrel!" Bell clucked. "Piss off, fud, men're talkin'."

Nora ignored him. "They're not worth it. Please."

"Puss," Shaw called. "One more step an' I'll burst ye."

"Don't," she said.

Wil set his jaw. Breathed deeply. Let her lead him away.

Bell and Shaw howled after them, but Talbot only grinned.

By the time they'd crossed the bar away from the Volunteers, Wil had enough of being touched. He pried his arm from her grip, gentle yet firm. "Alright, enough. Please stop."

Arms straight at her sides, Nora squared with him. "The hell's wrong with you? Are you mental, starting a fight here of all places?"

Wil breathed deeply but failed to cage his anger. "I didn't start that."

"You really are a muppet," she said and started pointing out sharp-eared giants in the crowd. "One, three, seven, eight—ten Dogfaces I can see. More I can't. Bar's hoaching with lethal ones, and they might not be Talbot's friends, but you aren't either, ken? Any reason's good enough."

The overhead lights faded from a sultry purple to a radioactive green, and Wil realized that Nora was out of uniform. Under the neon, her blonde hair glowed a lime-white, unleashed from its bun to drape over her shoulders. Fishnet stockings clung to her snowy thighs, hips obscured by a short, dark skirt. A long-sleeved sweater failed to hide her curves, and the riot of studs up her ears matched the one in her lower lip.

Saoirse's leather jacket bunched in Nora's grip. He'd left it behind. He scanned the surroundings, searching for red hair, but couldn't make out a thing in the neon shitshow.

"Fantastic," Wil griped. "Super fantastic. So glad I got to see the real Caledonia. Very cool, very fun."

Nora's lips thinned. "I thought you were supposed to be nice."

Regret and guilt twinged together like a hook in the gut. She didn't deserve this from him. Excuses came to mind… but they were just that. "Sorry," he said. "Listen, I'm—"

The speakers shrieked to life, feedback unbearable for one sharp second before the announcer's voice penetrated the growing clamor. Patrons condensed along the arena fence, thickening until Talbot and the Volunteers disappeared behind the crowd.

"I heard Cailean carved your name on a bullet," Nora said. "That you've got an audience in the loo. That you're eatin' spit in your eggs every day, crammed into the pantry apart from everyone else. Used to think you didn't deserve that."

His stomach turned. "Eating what?"

"And I still do," she hurried. "I'm so sorry, Wil. I thought you'd tell Cailean about Talbot, tell Alastair, make a stink, but you just… took it. Why?"

"Had worse," he said, tempering his disgust. "I'm just passing through, you know? And as you said, this is your home. You're keeping what happened secret for a reason. It's not my place to make that choice for you."

"I go to church with Bell's mum," Nora said. "Shaw's sister, Kelsie, is on my fireteam. Talbot—well, his dad's rich, ken like? Everyone loves him. He's been mates with Neil since primary."

"Believe me, I get it," Wil said. "Running away is easy."

Her brow pinched. "I didn't say that."

The confused disappointment in her eyes said everything. Not just taken aback at his words, but perhaps larger expectations.

He scanned the Croatoan for Saoirse again and once more found her absent. Now he knew why. This was the real reason he'd been brought here—not to flirt and trade life stories, not to see 'the real Caledonia,' but to be ambushed by Nora, suffer her apology, and see what happened next: if she'd tell the truth about Talbot and the others or keep it hidden to save face.

Manipulative, and it meant Saoirse really *was* smarter than him.

Nora wanted him to agree, wanted him to say her meek acceptance of the status quo was the right call. Saoirse, perhaps the opposite. He didn't really know. Just a feeling.

So he centered himself in the past, stepped into the officer's shoes he'd left empty for so long, and said what he would've said then. "If you don't tell Alastair now, what'll you say when this happens to someone else?"

Her eyes stretched wide, but no answer came.

"Tell Saoirse I'll be back," he said. "Gotta hit the head without an audience while I can."

Nora strangled Saoirse's jacket, lips pursed, until he rounded the corner.

↑↑

Wil propped himself over the sink and focused on the mirrorless, graffiti-laden spot on the men's room wall. The grimy light hummed above; disinfectant and human waste churned in his inhale. Outside, the crowd burst into muffled cheers as height, weight, and win/loss ratio warbled unintelligibly through the door.

This was good. No mirrors to avoid. Just him and the anger he needed to kill before he made an ass of himself a third time tonight.

There was no way that Talbot had heard him tell Saoirse about his mom. The jabs about running away, Saoirse's comment—they were starting to add up. He'd given Alastair his full name, and someone had plugged it into Arachne and shared the top results with the Kildalton cluster. Or Talbot listened well, or threw insults until one stuck, or, or, or.

The moment he left the men's room, he'd leave this fear behind. Enjoy the night. See what happened with Saoirse, and if nothing did, at least try to have fun. Releasing his grip from the sink, he opened the bathroom door and someone on the other side punched him in the face.

Wil impacted the grubby tile hard. His nose clogged, overflowed. Blood. The doorway shadowed with three men who had to duck under the door jamb, leaving a fourth to play lookout. No two had the same traits—a tusked overbite, peach-fuzz fur from the neck down, hands like clawed catcher's mitts—but they all shared the same strange primeval lens in their eye, the same atavistic hulk.

Wulvers.

A big son of a bitch with an ugly mustache towered above him. "Not so tough wi'out your armor, eh?"

"S'uptae," the fuzzy one said. He took rough hold of Wil's collar. "Let's chat."

Years ago, he'd seen a hacked Gūijiǎ close its colossal hand around a Kuang-Shi's head and squeeze until the bomb inside went off. Wil hadn't ever truly understood how that poor bastard must've felt until the fuzzy Wulver lifted him off his feet and pinned him against the wall.

"I'm Stuart," said ugly mustache, sauntering close until Wil could taste the beer on his breath. He nodded to fuzzy and overbite. "That's Dante, and this is

Wagner."

"Dawn is Ours," Wagner giggled.

Dante leered close, peach-fuzzed features creasing. "Talbot says you're the prick who locked li'l Nora McDermott in a locker last week. Says you played wi' her first. Says you're the dirty PanOceanian everyone been gabbin' about."

"Talbot's a liar," Wil gasped, "He's the one who—"

Stuart hauled back his snow-shovel-sized palm. Slap. Crack. The men's room pitched to one side, and Wil's teeth rattled like pool balls after the break.

"Language, mate," Stuart said. "Talbot's a good cunt, simple as. Be kind."

The Wulvers' words became noise. Fuzz, on the fringes of hearing. Halogen lights, cardboard, and black plastic raged in the peripheral of his dimming vision, but his memories afforded him nothing.

Dante pinched Wil's nose and gave it a twist. "No sleepin' in class!"

The yell Wil swallowed nearly dislocated a rib. Heart restarted, fuzz fading, he wheeled his feet and gurgled.

"Sounds like a PanO, right," Stuart said. "Not as whingey as a Yujingyu, but twice as loud."

Dante shrugged. "Wanna feed him the sink?"

Wagner's face split in an overfull grin.

Wil kicked. Swung. No use. Porcelain knocked his chin; wet spots soaked into the knees of his jeans. Dante held his arms, and Stuart took a fistful of Wil's hair, measuring out his strike. Wagner watched, eyes trained through the holographic dial of his wrist-mounted comlog, recording.

Wil shouted for help, but the arena bell rang twice, and the roaring crowd overpowered his cries.

"Mouth shut, quiet down," Dante instructed, and knocked Wil's front teeth against the sink.

Panic jolted up the ligaments in his legs, turning his bowels into water. Dull, vicious hurt clouded up inside of his gums, reverberating along the bones of his face until it exhaled out his broken nose with a wet, red snort.

Both teeth stayed planted. For now.

"And plug yer gullet, mate," Stuart added. "Dinnae swallow, aye? Goes in sharp, comes out sharp. Not pleasant. Trust me on this. Ready?"

Wil wormed a wrist free, but Dante wrestled it back effortlessly. "Ready."

"On three."

The door kicked open, and the lookout flopped into the men's room and onto his back. His shirt was caked with brownish froth, jaw lolling dislocated, the circular shape of a pop-tab can indented in his ruddy forehead.

Saoirse stood over him, bloody soda can in hand. "Hey, boys."

Relief, chased by fear. Her eyes were different, now. They'd always been close to an Antipode's, but the light in them remained indelibly human. Now that light had dimmed, replaced with something else. Something dark.

Something primal.

Wagner spun, fists raised. Saoirse ducked his flail, shoved him aside. Stuart groped for her shirt, and his head put a dent in the hand dryer by the door.

Dante snapped from his shock and hauled back to hammer Wil into the sink. Before he could complete the motion, Saoirse spiked the coke can into his face and her sneaker into his groin, and the three of them sprawled to the floor.

Wil fought to his elbows. Weathered a graze to the back. Took grip of the urinal trough and leveraged it to stand. The instant he was upright, Saoirse rammed Stuart past him into the wall. The Wulver elbowed her in the ear, and in one swift pitch Saoirse took him by the arm and whipped him skull-first through the porcelain basin.

Cold water sprayed from the open pipes into Wil's eyes. He jerked away, sputtering, when a wild haymaker skimmed past his ear to crack the concrete beside his head. Wagner. The toothy idiot roared in pain, middle knuckles flattened, and fell back cradling his wrist.

Wil took the opening. Planted a hook into Wagner's undefended jaw, and then again. He put everything into the third swing, but the Wulver barely stumbled, and Wil's days-mended knuckles reopened on the rough surface of his cheek.

How he'd hurt himself worse than the person he'd hit three times, Wil had no idea. As he stemmed the bleed in his shirt, Wagner folded his broken hand shut, grunted "Dawn is Ours," and came barreling back in.

Wil ducked back. The wall stalled his escape. No room to maneuver. He sidestepped a right, shielded a left with his bicep. Regretted it. Worse than being shot, and the sheer force upended him onto the floor again.

Centimeters from his face, the smashed sink's lead S-trap pipe tilted loose against the tile. He yanked the pipe free, gagging on the rotten mist that followed, and about-faced in time to bunt Wagner's next straight with the bar.

The noise his knuckles made, breaking all at once—indescribable.

Choking out sobs, Wagner keeled at the hips and strangled his twice-broken hand, but not for long. With more fight than before he'd ruined his hand, Wagner surged forward, tore the dented pipe from Wil's grip, and shouted, "Dawn is—!"

Saoirse interrupted his cry with a knee to the spine from behind. Wagner faltered, and she hurled him into the corner beside the spewing sink. Fast as hell she bounced into a stomp, sneaker buried in his belly, then again. And again. And again, and again and again.

"Wait, wait," Wil sputtered and grabbed at her. "Stop! Saoirse, stop!"

Saoirse wheeled on him, eyes wild. Teeth bared. Her claws rushed toward his face. Dante intercepted and yanked her into a right cross. Fury redirected, she barreled into the new target, claws flashing, fists flying. He lifted her by the belt and crashed into the handicapped stall, collapsing the framework down around them.

Gordon. He needed Gordon.

Outside, the crowd had split, half jockeying for an angle on the spectacle through the dislocated bathroom doorway, half cheering as a gigantic, bestial wolfman pummeled a limp human being into the arena floor hand over fist. Blood smeared the mat.

But the wolfman wore red and blue, not green and gold. Gordon was the bloody ragdoll.

Alastair. Cailean. He needed—

Balance. A sharp strike from behind sent Wil stumbling. Saoirse, but not on purpose. Dante had her cinched her under the arms, and they ricocheted out of the restroom, into the tables, the walls, wrestling madly for dominance. Saoirse snarled, raking his scalp with her claws.

Not a snarl. She was grinning.

Her beanie thwumped to the concrete and soaked up a puddle of beer.

Wagner burst from the men's room door, face dripping with urinal residue. He snapped a bottle off a table into a truncheon grip, and its owner caught his wrist. Foam arced from its open neck into the face of a nearby brunette. She shrieked, and her boyfriend stood, and the men at the bar. Shouts redoubled when the first punches flew. The crowd didn't pull away, magnetized by the fresh violence.

Glass shattered on the wall beside Wil's head. His lips flecked with sour mist. Track pants and gaudy sneakers raced up the stairs, aiming for the entrance above.

Talbot and the Volunteers.

For an instant, Wil considered following, far enough removed from the scrap to escape. Without a shotgun he barely stood a chance, and with one, his odds were only 50/50. But his fingers quickened, and his pulse, and he couldn't leave Saoirse alone with—

Lightning bolts of red and white. A sound like metal on grapefruit. Wil didn't remember falling, or how to stand up. The Croatoan kicked on its axis and swiveled. His palms stuck to the residue on the floor. Neon lights burned holes in his eyes. Amazing that the liquor hadn't come back up yet, he thought, then it did.

Stuart sauntered away, lead S-trap pipe cocked over his shoulder. "Don't go nowhere, galactic," he ordered. "Stay down."

Wet, feral growls interrupted Wil's burgeoning anger. A meter away, Saoirse struggled in Dante's grip, arms pinned to her sides from behind. No matter how hard she thrashed, he refused to let go.

Stuart leveled the end with her mouth and gave it a practice swing. Its dented edge cut the air just centimeters from her chin. "Nice smile, hen. Let's fix that. Hope ye don't mind purée."

No. No, that wasn't happening. Not if Wil was conscious. Not if he wasn't bled out, limbless, eviscerated. Even if there was nothing left of him but a puddle of red, raw meat.

He stood. A piece of Talbot's shattered bottle scraped against his shoe. The jagged neck fit Wil's hand. Stuart rared back the pipe, and Wil leapt onto his shoulders and scribbled the glass shard across his big, ugly face until it snagged somewhere soft and sunk in.

Stuart choked on a scream. Hands slip-sliding on the bottleneck jut from his eye socket, he dropped to his knees and the pipe followed after.

Saoirse cracked her skull against Dante's fangs and blunted his nose with her palm. Freed, but exhausted. She wobbled. Collapsed. Wil lunged to cushion her fall, and the dead weight of her torso smashed the last embers of fight out of him.

Panting, Saoirse curled atop him. Her top had come askew, and most of her body dripped with blood—hers, or someone else's. She tried to stand, but her balance didn't keep, and she began to laugh.

Beautiful.

Across the bar, two gunshots. The Russian, Viral pistol held high. Indoors, the sound was deafening, and it startled the crowd into a stampede. Clocking the Viral, the bouncers went with them. By the time he'd gotten close enough to shout, the crowd had clogged through the exit, leaving behind only a terrified, huddling few.

"Блядь! On the ground, both of you! Now, ку́рва, now!" the Russian shouted, and a massive, snarling black shape rushed from the arena to pummel him into the jukebox.

A Dog-Warrior.

Gordon.

As a man, he was tall. Transmuted, Gordon scraped the ceiling. Save for the stretched mess of scars across his new anatomy and the glint of disdain deep within his haunted eyes, no hint of his previous form remained. Bloody gouges glistened in his midnight-black fur, smeared across the straining green-and-gold boxing trunks he wore.

A growl radiated from his core that pulped the marrow in Wil's bones.

The music died.

Dante roared. Charged. Gordon stomped him out of his rush, snapping his ribs like stiff wicker. Wagner burst from the fleeing crowd. Swung. Hit once, twice, until Gordon caught him mid-flurry and painted the wall with his face.

Nora darted from the evaporating crowd, tearing her fishnets as she slid to Wil's side. "Wil! Wil, look at me. Let me see."

He did. The blur didn't lessen, no matter how wide he pried his eyelids.

"Birthday," she said. "In reverse."

"44, 1, 27?"

A flicker of a smile. "Saoirse! You alright, hen?"

Saoirse coughed, flecking the concrete with red. "I'm well. Still mad. But well."

"Gordon, lovey," Nora called. "Calm down, and help Saoirse."

Sharp black ears perked and folded, chastised. Gordon lumbered off Dante's writhing torso and flung the limp Wagner aside. Both Wulvers squirmed, agonized—but alive. Seated in the machinery of the jukebox, the Russian loosed a long, hollow groan and fingered his rings.

"Chill," Gordon said, deep voice monstrously low, and yanked the jewelry free. Rolled between his paws, the rings' frames shattered like eggshells to reveal hidden nanopulsers kept within. Licking his chops, he chucked the smashed remainder over his shoulder. The shards sailed into the ring through the tear in the chain-link and bounced off the limp back of the peacocking idiot unconscious in the arena center.

Joe sprang up from behind the bar, shotgun stocked to his shoulder. When he surveyed the amount of writhing, bleeding Wulvers, he let the barrel drop. "Sersh! Bizzies are a minute out. Get going, darling, now!"

Fifty-three seconds later, the four of them broke from the Croatoan back into the freezing night, barely ahead of the blue-white flash of the approaching police.

16

Stuffed with blankets and antique lamps, plush toys and family portraits, Nora's apartment was the picture of lower-class comfort. But on the balcony, that comfort waned in favor of the relentless Caledonian cold. Freezing without Saoirse's gifted sweatshirt. But outside was better than bleeding all over the carpet.

Potted plants dangled from the balcony overhead, mostly overgrown, somewhat dead. Past the fourth-story balcony railing, blue police lights flashed from the street around the Croatoan. Despite his urge to rubberneck, Wil focused on keeping the overflow from his nose running into a ceramic bowl decorated with cartoon Aristeia! fighters.

"Didn't know they let enlisted have private quarters in Ariadna," Wil said.

"It's my mum's," Nora replied. She picked a cylindrical capsule from her paramedic's bag and held it to the light. Blue liquid sloshed within. Serum, just about a quarter dose. "But she's away now, visiting my aunt in Scone for her birthday. That's her bowl you keep drippin' in."

"I'll buy another. Promise."

At the bottom of the bowl, a big-headed cartoon of Miyamoto Musashi glared up from beneath Wil's blood splatter, flanking Wild Bill with... a blot. He thumbed the dark mark to make sure it wasn't something that'd dripped out of him, but the smudge stayed surprisingly resilient.

"Mum burns off the Shona Caranos," Nora said, loading her MediKit gun. "She stole a sword from someone, or something. We don't remember whose, but that en't the point."

And here he thought their grudges were exaggerated.

Nora swabbed his arm and snubbed the injector there. "Dogface dosage, but this'll help. Ready?"

"As I'll ever be."

A pinch and a sting later, liquid apathy buzzed him better than Joe's disgusting whisky. His dribbling nose squeezed to a trickle, and all his bruises stopped aching at once. But instead of total relief, it was like a focusing lens—the worst pains were evident now, separated from the noise of little hurts.

"MediKit supplies aren't cheap, either," she said, wiping the mess from his upper lip with a wet wipe. "Just... next time, leave the fist-fighting to Saoirse?"

His head swam, and his limbs felt very far away. "Gladly."

Nora set the bowl aside and tested his ribs with two fingers. The hurt was like a shout through a closed door. "Bad?"

"Yeah," he said. "Kind of bad."

She pressed harder. "Worse?"

"Getting there."

"Lovely! If it was broke, you'd be crying, eh? Nanobots can fix bruised no problem—broken's another story. Better than most get, honestly, after a scrap with a Wulver."

Wil considered his skinned knuckles, already glistening with a thin film of protein fibrin. "You warned me, and I didn't listen."

"Because you're an idiot," she prompted.

"Because I'm an idiot," he agreed.

Nora let a little giggle slip through her stern nurse demeanor. "Shocked Saoirse didn't wring your neck, acting the absolute weapon in there. But then again, no lack of targets for the blood fury."

"Blood fury," Wil repeated, chewing on the words. "Wulvers are kinda badass."

"Unreal. Is that really your takeaway?"

"And they scare the bejesus out of me," he said. "But don't tell her I said that."

"Hey, hey," Nora snickered. "I won't."

Inside, voices rose. Saoirse and Gordon, arguing. Damp hair tied back in a tight bun, barefoot, Saoirse had traded her bloodied ensemble for one of Neil's shirts and athletic shorts, and her previous congeniality for a big-sister frown. Their conversation was audible but incomprehensible through the glass. Serious enough that he shouldn't listen in, but not so much he didn't wish he could.

"Kind of bullshit," Wil said, meaning their healing factor, meaning Saoirse's lecture despite Gordon's rescue, but also... "Is he seriously not getting paid?"

Nora shrugged. "Doesn't need the money, so much. Alastair takes care of most things, same as he does for everyone else around here. Rodina pays Kildalton to keep the mine safe from the galactics, and we all split the dividends."

"So if he doesn't get paid, what's he do it for? The pain?"

Fear and resignation conjoined miserably on Nora's pretty face. "That'd make him a bigger idiot than you."

She could've said that nicer, but he was the one over here ruining her mom's favorite bowl. "Hey, Nora, you know what?"

"What," she said, and dabbed his nose with antiseptic cream. He hesitated. No, not flirtation. Medicine. She really dolloped it on, and under his eyes, and on his ear and his jaw....

"You should be a doctor," Wil said. "It'd suit you."

She crooked a thin blonde eyebrow. "Not a nurse?"

"I would've said Helen of Troy, but they've already Recreated that one."

"Flattery will get you *everywhere*," she accused and smiled wide. "112's the plan once I'm done in the Volunteers this summer. Head to Scone. Get my own flat. Do the whole uni thing with what I've saved up playing soldier, and then come back to 'prentice under Crawford."

"112?"

"Ariadna Emergency Services. Doctors, firemen, first responders. Out here, they mostly do rescue work: lost hikers, stranded travelers. Lotta that in the winter."

"Oh, dude. And then you get a fireaxe?"

"Ayup," Nora said and closed her kit. When she turned back, her blue eyes were awash with concerned curiosity. "Those Wulvers. What happened to make them jump you? They say why?"

Dazed by the Serum, it took Wil a moment to piece together a lie. "Talbot told them I was a PanO," he said, certain that honesty here would come across as sanctimony. "They said they'd teach me a lesson, take revenge for their dads or something? I dunno. I was too busy kissing a sink."

Nora seemed disappointed but not surprised. "Talbot."

"Yeah."

"I hear PanOceania was a mistake."

"Jury's still out on that one."

She smiled. "Well, now that I've met you, I think it's more of a happy accident."

The sliding door yawned open, and Saoirse came through, a box of bandage strips in her hands. Of all her wounds, a faded blemish was all that remained—no bruises, no cuts. It made him wonder what the hell left the trench in her face, but he managed to keep his thoughts to himself.

"Hey," she said. "What're you hens gossipin' about?"

"You," Wil said, and enjoyed her little glare. "How's the… everything?"

Saoirse snubbed her freckled nose. "I'm pure done in. You?"

"Likewise," he said. "Think I broke my hand."

Nora frowned. "You didn't break your hand."

"Nora said she's gotta cut it off."

"No, I did not," she said, and her sigh was half-amused, half-murderous. "Sersh, wanna trade? I figured that much tranquilizer would totally send him."

Saoirse stole a packet of antiseptic wipes from Nora's lap and dragged up the other chair. "Get on, gorgeous. Our Gordon needs his angel tonight."

Nora passed her a hug and fluttered into the apartment, calling out to Gordon. "Alright, lovey—you wanting some food? I could fry some sausage, a few eggs?"

Gordon shrank back into the couch corner, frozen food against his forehead. "No. I'm fine. Don't—well, alry, aye. Good. Yes, please. Thank you."

Another painful laugh, but this one was worth it. How the hell did such a little lady put a guy big as him on the back foot? A Dog-Warrior, intimidated by—

Wil gasped aloud. "Oh, shit."

Saoirse narrowed her eyes. "What?"

He shook his head. "I didn't say anything."

"Realized it, huh?" she said. "They're cute, even if they're keepin' it secret from most."

"Does Neil know?"

She took his hand and dug in with a wet wipe. "Why's that matter?"

"He's like, thirty," Wil said, wincing. "And she's, what, nineteen? It's skeevy."

"Spot on fer Nora, but Gordon's the same age as Alastair if ye believe it."

"Twelve?"

"Twenty-two," she insisted, and flicked his wrist. "Dogfaces like us age quicker 'n normal. I was loomin' over my foster-mum by age *eight*."

With Gordon's size, beard, and surly, grunt-centric method of communication, he'd always assumed they had their late-twenties in common. A little doubt wriggled in his heart as he stared, searching her sharp features for laugh lines. "… How old are you?"

The corner of her lips pinched in a reluctant smile. "Fuck off."

"I'm twenty-eight. Higher or lower?"

"Fuck off," she repeated and kept working.

"What? I'm just… you just…"

"Keep yer worries to yerself, aye? Not our fault we grow up faster, and hairy. Been shaving my elbows since I was a wean."

"Damn. You too?"

Good feeling, making a woman laugh. Helped him forget that she was cleaning the men's room floor from cuts in his hand, or how useless he'd been in that fight, or how close he'd come to having to shop for a new pair of front teeth.

Saoirse affixed the bandage strips to his knuckles with as much care as she could muster, prodding his bloody knuckles more than once with clumsy claws. Wil didn't mind a little hurt, not if it meant he got to take a second look at her decorated forearm.

"That crescent, with the sword," he asked. "Is that…?"

"Hassassin Fiday," she said, tongue stuck in the corner of her mouth.

"Didn't know they were real."

"Said the same thing after I ran 'em through. I'd show ye the mark he left, but then we'd have tae get married."

Wil examined the trench in her face. Her scar. Back in the bar, he'd decided a Húláng Shocktrooper was what'd done it. Hassassin Fiday would fit that bill, too, but he had the strangest feeling both guesses were wrong. The line was so impeccably straight.

She tilted her head to meet his eyeline, brow cocked. "Need somethin'?"

He unstitched his eyes from her face, unable to tell when she'd noticed. "So, uh. You and Nora are pretty tight. That's cool."

"Uh huh," Saoirse said, sharp teeth sharper up close.

"Gordon said you're family. Big family."

"Aye, he's sept, same as Neil and Nora and Cailean, and me, technically," she said, and answered his question before he asked. "Sept's sworn clan who didnae take the surname. Vassals, in layman's terms. Can tell who's sworn by the Teseum dog tags, old tradition datin' back to—are you sleeping?"

He blinked. Might've laid back and drifted too far. "Wide awake."

"What'd I say, then."

Wil scrunched up his face. "Och, aye. *Vassals*."

Saoirse gasped and drew back her hand for a playful smack, but a flash of guilt and shame in her eyes killed the motion midway. Crestfallen, she straightened his shirt collar instead. "Told ye I was boring."

So, she remembered turning on him in the men's room.

Wil hurried the conversation, intent on distracting her. "Gordon's a Dogface, you're a Dogface. He your half-brother too?"

"Not by blood," she said. "Dated his brother Malcolm back in secondary school. Even after our amicable split, we were thicker 'n thieves. Ate at their house more often than my own."

Wil took note of the past tense. Addled as he was, he clearly remembered Gordon's aversion to answering questions about his brothers, and chose not to press. "And Neil, you called him Feartie. That some nickname from when you were kids?"

"He's still a kid," Saoirse insisted and then relented. "They lived in the castle for a time after their da passed, until his mum got on her feet. Ten years old, and he'd startle at every little thing. Carried a torch on him always, deathly scared of ghosts. Fer good reason, but."

"Why's he care about how you got your sword?"

She smiled. "Why ye ask so many bloody questions?"

"Thought you said to ask anything," he mumbled and let her finish her work.

Plastic strips aligned, Saoirse drew near to smooth out the edges. She squinted just enough for him to make out the faint blue-white imprint of a vestigial iris in her eye, and for the first time, didn't notice him watching. So he just... appreciated her. The sharp cowl of her ear. The way she stuck her tongue out when she focused. The curve of her neck into the cut of her shirt, and how her pale skin went paler the farther in he looked. He considered leaning over to kiss her, but when he tensed to try the motion, he snorted a blood clot into his mouth.

Romanticism flattened, he slumped back against the cold plastic of the lawn chair and onto a bump in his jeans. He retrieved Saoirse's beanie from his pocket and held it out. "Found this."

"No way," Saoirse whispered, and hugged it to her chest. "My favorite shitty hat."

"Thank you," he blurted. "For everything. Jumping into the Antipode's path, saving me from getting jumped—twice, now—and being cool, and—"

Her brow pinched. "Ye havin' a stroke, or givin' one?"

"You're awesome, okay?"

An amused sigh sifted past her fangs. Saoirse slipped on the rescued beanie, red curls curtaining her eyes. "From where I'm standin', yer not so bad either. Stupid as it was, and brave. But, next time, mind that I've a healin' factor, and you… well, you've got whatever the opposite of that is."

"I stabbed that Stuart guy," Wil said. His elbows weighed to the armrests, torso taking on the wicker shape of the chair beneath him.

"Yep."

"In the eye."

"Aye, nae danger."

Wil laughed, albeit shallow. "And I don't feel bad, at all."

"I wouldnae either," she whispered. "Can't believe I had tae carry yer arse outta the fire again. When are you gonna stop bein' a pain tae look after?"

"Never."

Saoirse clicked the kit shut and set it aside. "Dogface dosage's a lot, even fer an Aquila Guard first-class or wha'ever. Sure yer feelin' alry?"

"I only ever made captain," he said. "Demoted on my first go."

"That's a shame," she whispered, head against his shoulder.

"Not really. And to be honest, also no. I kind of hate 'em."

She looked up at him, confused. "Aquila Guards, or Dogfaces?"

"No—well, Aquila Guards? Kind of. I meant painkillers. Alcohol, too. Messes with my head, y'know, take me somewhere I don't want to be. So I try to avoid them when I can, and now this's the third or fifth time in nine days, and…"

She ran her fingers across his chest. "Where's it take you?"

Halogen lights.

She cocked her head. "Wil?"

Cardboard, and black plastic.

"Nowhere," he said, and kept his stupid mouth shut.

17

When the painkillers wore off in the morning, Wil regretted surviving the Balena crash.

Nose only slightly broken, no teeth knocked loose. Wil's face was an absolute mess of bruises, and he woke several times in the night to a dull, persistent ache where a new swell had risen on his skin. Every time, he curled into himself, counted backward from one-hundred, and hoped his ribs would float back toward where they were meant to be.

The teenage maids flounced into his room at midmorning, all giggles as usual, when Gordon lumbered in from behind and scared them away with a growl and a curse. They scattered into the hall, shooting glances over their shoulders at Wil's black eye. And whispering.

"Jig's up," Gordon muttered. "Got a good excuse for your face, yet?"

Wil squinted up from his fully clothed curl atop the comforter. "Do you?"

Gordon actually laughed.

Limping, exhausted, Wil set out to put his ear to the ground. A fistfight like that couldn't have gone unnoticed, and consequences couldn't be far off. In the castle halls, tension hung thick as the fog outside. The whispers remained stable, the glares the same as before. When Eideard saw them in the hall, he still made a face like he'd stepped in dog shit. Results inconclusive, but leaning toward bad.

Gordon flashed Wil his comlog screen. "Al wants us upstairs. Memorial hall."

A nice, private place for the evisceration. Made sense.

The farther upstairs they climbed, the less sunlight pierced the windows. In the hall, the only illumination was the dim glow of the holoprojected displays. Portraits of old soldiers and panorama shots of battlefields past ran the full length of the wall, depicting Antipode assaults, crushed rebellions, and a scant few victories.

Alastair lingered near the entrance, hands clasped behind his back. He glanced up, first concerned, then amused. "Rough night?"

"You should see the other guy," Wil said. "Bruised his knuckles up a storm."

Gordon and Alastair traded some brief words in Caledonian, and whatever it was must've been big. Gordon's eyes widened, and he loosed a spate of low, incredulous laughs before dropping to a whisper. Wil didn't glean much—just a name. Stuart. The mention injected ice into his veins, canceling out the heat from all the swelling in his face.

"Guma math a thèid leat," Gordon told him and lumbered away.

Just the two of them, now. Or at least, he thought. Alastair had already wandered away, inspecting the lines of memorials. Planning his apology, Wil followed after.

They slowed in front of the JSA katana embedded lengthwise into the Teseum claymore. For a long moment, Alastair said nothing. Just stood there. So did Wil, and then his curiosity finally won out.

Whereas the claymore was about the same as Saoirse's, all business with little frill, the katana was a work of art. Red and white cloth knotted into diamonds along the handle, blade guard wrought in the shape of a crescent moon. The blade was unnaturally thin, and its edge had an ethereal tinge to it—monofilament. Ephemerally thin monowire, capable of cutting all known material on a molecular level. A single, well-placed strike spelled instant death for most anything save for ALEPH's Hoplites and the Dog-Warriors of Dawn.

But the monument confused him, now. Monowire would cleave Teseum like paper, so why hadn't it? The display hadn't been posed, and it wasn't as if Teseum alloy was impenetrable, despite the neomaterial's legendary resilience. Nothing along the cut suggested a chemical reaction. Had the Teseum disrupted—

Alastair gestured to the katana's hilt. "While Teseum is known to disrupt electromagnetic radiation, the field maintaining the monomolecular edge was stable for two years after the event."

A nervous laugh shook out of him. "Gotta say if you're telepathic, man."

"It's everyone's first guess, is all."

"Everyone, as in…?"

Alastair smiled. "Something about the mystery invites the imagination, let's say. We've had scientists, journalists, all types come to inspect it. A witch from Cailleach, once, though all she did was burn Sol sage and pray."

Wil edged closer to the blades. "Wanna walk me through it?"

Though his brow creased and he hesitated, Alastair acquiesced, gesturing to each weapon in turn. "For starters, the claymore is Teseum alloy, manufactured in Skara Brae. Sharp—but standard-issue, in all fairness. But the shinobigatana, on the other hand? It's a technological marvel. Custom-made. Monofilament, lightweight, its own onboard combat geist. The blade functions as a support structure for the monowire lacing the edge, but look at the craftsmanship. Meteoric iron. Handmade."

"Never been a swords guy. NCA, remember?"

If he'd heard him, Alastair didn't let it show. His explanation picked up speed. "The parry, the blow. Both delivered expertly. So why did the monofilament arrest? Was it a lack of care on either side? Or the angle of the strike, or the speed, the force, the subtle application of technique? Barometric pressure could've played a part. Shentang is zero-point-zero-four-five gees lighter than Dawn, does the fault lie there? Or is it something else, something invisible, something we won't understand for another hundred years?"

"Don't call it a miracle."

"Perhaps," Alastair said. "All I know is that nine years ago, a Highlander parried a sword that could cut anything."

The admiration in the kid's voice woke something in Wil. Grim as it was, he couldn't help but tinder a spark of jealousy. To be remembered like this, as a mystery, as a hero? When Wil died, he wouldn't mind going out like this, in a way no one would ever figure out. Go big, go loud, burn bright. Defy the laws of reality long enough to become a legend and earn a memorial of his own.

Wil glanced at the holo-epitaph, searching for a clue.

ALEXANDER NATHANIEL MACARTHUR, 6/8/23NC–25/12/63NC
LLOYD MCDERMOTT, 19/11/32NC–25/12/63NC.
"THERE IS NOTHING IMPOSSIBLE TO HIM WHO WILL TRY."

And the jealousy in him fell away, replaced by castigation. Alastair's father, and McDermott—judging by the age, Nora and Neil's father. Two dads for four people he knew, and here he was, salivating over fantasies of sharing their glory in death.

What the hell was wrong with him?

Alastair folded his hands behind his back, let the silence rest a moment before continuing. "You should be aware that Nora McDermott came to my quarters this morning and told me about what happened in the garage. About Christopher Talbot and the keycard. About what you did."

Relieved and a bit proud, Wil said, "Good for her."

"Then, she kept talking. About what happened at the bar."

And let out a sigh. "Good for her."

"I'm not angry," Alastair said. "The Croatoan's not a savory place to begin with, and according to Nora, you were the victim. It's not my right to be judgmental, and I've already requested Saoirse have better discretion for locale in the future."

"Hey, man, she did the best with what she had."

"Perhaps. She also came close to killing two people."

It felt important to defend her. "Well, I'm the one who poked that guy's eye out. If you're blaming someone, blame me."

Alastair paused, lips pursed. "Stuart Walker, I know. Recordings weren't hard to find, but I wouldn't feel bad. Stuart's a wanted man, you see—we'd been searching for him for eight months before the trail dried up. Eideard assumed he'd fled to Merovingia."

"That mustache is bad, but I didn't think it was *illegal* bad."

"He and his half-brothers are traffickers," Alastair said. "Drugs, weapons, Teseum. Women. *Young* women."

Wil bit down the bile and the sudden fire in his veins. Focused on the middle distance. Teseum kindled a memory of the cufflinks Rajan got from Odune, and the wall of posters along the chain link. Traffickers, the trafficked, and the DRC-9—he didn't need all the pieces to know they had to be connected.

"And as for the wayward Volunteers," Alastair continued, "Talbot's receiving a discharge. I don't need or want soldiers at my side whose first instinct is violence, no matter how well-connected their parents are. His father sent me a sternly worded message, but after hearing my side, he thanked me for my discretion and remanded his son to the family business in Dal Riada. You won't be seeing him again."

Wil whiplashed from silent anger to unabashed shock. On Neoterra, a discharge would've taken a tribunal, a court, time. That one elected official held unilateral decision-making power over their local military, untethered by the necessities of bureaucracy—it felt positively medieval.

He liked it.

"For Bell and Shaw, I offered some choices," Alastair said. "Shaw apologized to Nora, for what it's worth. The Ariadnan Army will make fine use of him for the next nine months, and when he comes back, he'll never make a mistake like this again."

"And Bell?"

"Not so apologetic. Raised his voice. Spoke unkindly of my sister, had some choice names. Unlucky for him, Kosmoflot is taking volunteers—and in his case, literally. But before that, I need a driver, so he'll be accompanying us to Dun Scaith."

"No problems here. He acts up, I'll fix his nose for 'em."

Alastair gave him a long, silent sidelong glance.

Wil cleared his throat. "And, uh, speaking of the DRC: What's the holdup? It's been three days since you got to Odune. I figured we'd be outside the wire by now."

"About that," Alastair said and spun up his comlog. "I was going to ask your opinion later, but now is a fine time."

A holographic photo gallery fanned out over his wrist. Images expanded and sharpened as Alastair turned the dial, cycling the reel. Fallen leaves. Gouged tree bark. Muddy pawprints. Bullet casings. Feces. The dismembered torso of a rotting human being impaled atop a fencepost.

The flesh had darkened and hardened in its decay, ribs white stripes against the leather of its skin. Nothing he hadn't seen before, but something about it was wrong. The skull had mandibles. Multiple. Its blood was like wine.

Not human.

"A homesteader from Odhran's Ford found this impaled on the perimeter fence yesterday morning," Alastair said. "A warning from Pale Shadow, no doubt."

A creeping fear slicked up behind Wil's ears, and he looked closer. The clothing scraps, the build, the wounds—nothing about it felt right. With Alastair's permission, he swiped the reel. Closer shots, of withered eyes and strange teeth, of broad hips and black hair—

"Keyes had brown hair," Wil said. "That's not the Shas I saw."

The young chieftain's eyes darkened. "I hoped you weren't going to say that."

"Might just be the recovery team looking for his body?"

Alastair remained stone-faced. "There was evidence of tampering on the node, here and here," he said, flipping pictures of cut chain-link and exposed wires. "Some of it matched methods we'd attributed to the Antipodes as far back as last year."

A cold weight settled in Wil's gut. "Think I know why the relays keep going down, MacArthur."

"Perhaps it's in someone's best interest we not call for help until a certain date has arrived?" Alastair said. "Meanwhile, Eideard says that's all conjecture, and the corpse is clearly human."

"With all due respect," Wil said, "your uncle's a moron."

Alastair didn't disagree and closed out his comlog. "I'm increasing our patrol from limited insertion to a full fifteen. Sergeant Muriel Dunne and her four-man mercenary outfit will accompany us. They've been safeguarding the workers at Outpost 16 while they reinforce the node there, but you're right. We've wasted enough time."

Wil knew better than to ask why they didn't bring the whole Kildalton garrison. Nevermind the logistics, the legality of amassing an army and marching it on a PanOceanian settlement might spark another Conflict. No, fifteen was good. Close-knit, structured, disavowable. "Rajan might be able to help us out, provide some comms codes or—"

Alastair blinked. "Pardon me, Lieutenant. Did I meet the wrong Rajan?"

Wil fumbled to a stop. "Could try asking nicely."

"Nicely or not, I'm afraid Mr. Brizuela refuses to speak. Hardly moves. He's ambulatory, but non-verbal since I explained the situation at hand. I'm not sure why, but he sure seems smug about the whole thing."

Of course he did. That Rajan would obstinately enjoy putting others' lives in danger—Wil didn't know why he was surprised. "No, you're right. ETA?"

"Tomorrow," Alastair said.

Ten days until the *Sword of St. Catherine* arrived at the DRC-9 Dun Scaith. With a day's flight, that left them nine days to stroll into town, call in the cavalry, and burn out the Shasvastii. It felt… doable. Attainable. Optimistic. "Dunne. Should I know who that is?"

"I believe you've already met. Eideard asked her to sit in on your conversation, in case something went wrong?"

"Conversation, sure," he said, recalling the female Scots Guard with the custom Kazak Molotok. "What's our travel time? By air, it'll be, what—an hour?"

Alastair crooked a brow. "I'm afraid I have to inform you that only two four-person helicopters are hangared in Kildalton, and one belongs to the 112."

"But you've got a whole tarmac."

"And did you see any planes on it?"

Wil pursed his lips. Thought hard. "No."

"The space is reserved for bi-monthly supply drops from Scone, search-and-rescue helos, and the occasional visitor from the south. We wouldn't want to go by air, anyways, not after what happened to your transport. And Dogfaces are deathly afraid of flying, besides. Gordon and my sister wouldn't make it thirty meters without jumping or berserking, much less a hundred kilometers."

Lots of reasons. All of them good.

Alastair's clunky link bracelet blinked blue along his wrist, and he excused himself.

Wil lingered at the display a moment longer, inspecting the monument. The way it begged for an explanation for its impossible results intrigued him. He pictured the Highlander, stance low, their rush to jab the claymore up under their defenses. The ninja, katana high, and the Kendo slice that bisected the claymore lengthwise....

Both warriors had bet their lives on a deathblow.

18

Outside. Fresh air. In, out.

Alone. No handcuffs. No Gordon.

Wil tensed his hands, testing how healed his knuckles were, and meandered his way across the green. Couldn't enjoy it, watching the perimeter over his shoulder as if he'd spot thermo-optical camouflaged assassins before they'd put two between his eyes, but he needed to shake his nervous energy somehow.

Something about the bar fight yesterday had changed things. When Wil had mentioned swinging by the garage to beg Sharlene for another few plinks at the range or taking in some fresh air, he hadn't expected Gordon to agree.

"Think I'll stay behind," Gordon said, comlog display scrolling with texts from a familiar blonde Volunteer. "Catch an early dinner. Rest. You go it alone."

"I'll miss you," Wil said. "Tell Nora I said hi."

Gordon glowered. "I won't. And I won't."

Muddy puddles pockmarked the emerald lawn. Above, the persistent clouds strangled the evening's last rays, casting their edges with a fiery orange hue. The snow-capped peaks above shined an inviting, celebratory white, and the chill that descended the slopes left Wil wishing for a jacket.

Gunshots rang out near the range. Percussive bursts, paired with the familiar rattle of brass. Before he knew it, he'd been drawn all the way to the range.

Empty stalls. No one around save for Cailean, who occupied the far lane. He manned the trigger of a heavy machine gun, tam-o'-shanter's toorie wriggling with every kick of the black-iron beast in his arms. Each shot launched a report through the Highlands that rivaled Varuna's loudest thunderclaps.

Intoxicating.

Belt depleted, the old man hefted the giant weapon over one shoulder and peeled off his ear protection. He pawed for the switch, but Wil clicked it for him, and the target whirred closer in silence.

Cailean's lips curled beneath his silver beard. "Cannae uncarve the casing."

"Wouldn't ask you to."

"Still on thin ice."

Wil indicated the heavy machine gun. "That a Molot, or a Hischnik?"

"*Molot*, he says. *Hischnik*, he says." Cailean scoffed. "In the 3rd Rifles, we use real guns, lad. Nothing like those overdesigned, temperamental CineticS you blueberries piss about wae."

"So, a KGR—a Kilgour? Armor piercing rounds on a paper target must be expensive."

The old Grey whistled condescendingly. "He kens guns."

"I'm PanO, remember?" Wil said. "Minimal competence comes in handy every once in a while."

Cailean chuckled before he caught himself and glared instead. "Wait, now. Where's Gordon? Ye aren't tryna escape again, are ye? And fer the love of God, what happened tae yer face?"

He shrugged. "Met some locals, hashed out some disagreements."

"Not a good thing, ken, havin' too much in common with Job."

"You say that, but I've been feeling more like Jonah for about eleven days now—"

Without warning, Cailean plunked the HMG into Wil's unprepared arms. Heat radiated from the machinery, welcome at first, then overbearing. The CineticS Tausug he'd used back in the day self-cooled, automatically reloaded, and utilized IFF technology to ensure he'd never friendly fire. In comparison, this beast was a dinosaur, all hard edges and utilitarian design.

Cailean had made some modifications here and there, an optical sight and a vertical foregrip chief among them. A faded inscription down the carbon-fiber feed cover read: THIG CRÌoch air an t-saoghal, ach mairidh gaol is ceòl.

"Nice gun." Wil tapped the lettering. "Let me guess: Kilroy was here."

If that was it, Cailean didn't let his astonishment show. "Just finished givin' Neil a lesson, so ye may as well have a turn, too. The way that lad is, he'd miss the floor if he tripped—so show me somethin' better."

The old man yanked his shredded target, replaced it with a fresh sheet, and sent it shimmying on its rail. He offered Wil his ear protection, but he turned him down—with his aural implants, it'd be overkill. The old timer produced his cigarette pack covered in Merovingian symbols, lit one, and waited.

Wil stocked the Kilgour to his shoulder. Awkward. Not only a vastly different make and model than he was used to, but something else. His wrist twinged, dealing with the weight, trying to find the right way to hold it.

If Cailean was judging him yet, he didn't say so.

The paper target halted about thirty meters out. Stock digging into his shoulder, Wil took the first shot. The kick was incredible, immediate, and he needed to lean into the recoil to have any chance at holding it steady.

The target stayed untouched. He put ten more bullets downrange and ultimately punched a single hole in the paper beside the silhouette's head.

"As expected," Cailean said. "Ye go adrift without yer armor."

Wil grimaced. The recoil had woken up some of the hurt from yesterday that he'd hoped had healed by now. "That obvious, huh?"

"It's yer stance. Narrow. Casual. Not relaxed where ye should be, not tense where ye should be. Yer used tae firin' from the hip, geist linked to yer gun, aye? No need to proper aim when your wetwork does it. And ye remember how tae shoot small caliber from muscle memory, but the big guns? Those, ye only got tae handle in yer suit."

Wil pursed his lips. He tried another shot. It went wide, too. "Maybe."

"That, or blame my Rhiannon," Cailean said. "Pick yer poison."

Considering the results of his twelve shots so far, Wil let the barrel swing toward the floor. "No, you're right, I—wait. You named your gun?"

"Stevie Nicks," Cailean declared, like he was invoking a saint. His face fell. "No?"

"Sorry. She a Recreation?"

He snorted. "If anything was good in this world she would be, but nah. Singer, long afore yer time. Mine, too, if we're bein' honest. But she was good. Maybe even the best."

"Never been one for music," Wil said. "Only so many petabytes on the ol' cyber-brain, and I need space for my targeting computer."

"Funny," Cailean said. "Targeting computers come standard-issue fer all Ariadnan soldiers, too. We call 'em eyes."

One chuckle was all that was worth. "At least tell me I'm better than Neil."

He shrugged his lips. "Not by much."

"Well, not like you were ever gonna give me an HMG anyways," Wil said, and held the machine gun out. "I'll stick to the Strela, and you bring the artillery."

Stubbing his cigarette on the divider, Cailean declined. "Practice. Never ken when ye might wish ye learned yer way around a Kilgour. Besides Alastair, ye're the only one who's qualified fer heavy ordnance. S'arnt Dunne's got her Molotok, aye, but she'd tip over after one pull on Rhiannon. And Neil, he'd have the grit fer it if he'd stop treatin' her like a chain rifle."

"What about Saoirse? She's… sturdy."

"Aye, but she's staying home. Alastair's orders."

Wil examined the feed tray, loading a fresh belt by feel. "Does she know that?"

"Fer a man so insistent he's no spy," Cailean muttered and stored his doused smoke back in its pack. "Listen, lad. I've a hundred rounds spare and an hour till sunset. Put it all downrange—we'll see if we can pluck ye from the ALEPH's teat yet."

"Still just 'ALEPH,' man. No 'the' involved."

"Aye, right. Take the shot. Or shall I send a formal invitation?"

Wil pressed the Kilgour's stock into his shoulder. "Aw. When'd you get so nice?"

"Haw, haw," Cailean deadpanned. "Get tae fuck, ye interstellar reprobate. Nice. *Nice*. What a place tae live yer mind must be. I'd snap ye over my knee if I weren't sure ye'd enjoy that, ye dog-sick cerulean clown. Fer the love of God, who let ye out today?"

"More my comfort zone," Wil admitted and pulled the trigger.

††

It wasn't long before Helios slid behind the mountains, dousing the fire in the clouds. The range lights clicked on, and the last empty casing clinked into the ammunition box. After a brief stop by the garage to lock up Cailean's heavy machine gun—pardon, *Rhiannon*—and leave the brass for the quartermaster, they took a detour around the grounds and up toward the DFAC.

And as for the grazed paper target in his hands, Wil couldn't stand looking at it. Didn't even want to do the math on hits versus misses. Damn thing had been standing still, the hell was he doing?

Cailean caught him glaring. "If ye ask me, ye rely too much on yer eyes. A bit of trainin' and we'll get ye sorted."

"And here I thought eyes were integral to shooting."

"Aye, but not eyes alone. Ye've had ghost in yer head, lad, sayin' shoot here. Aim here. Do this, move there, fall back. No thinkin' necessary—bollocks. Need tae find that front sight 'n' shoot like a boxer throws a punch: whole body, toe tae tip. That, or ye'll end up bleeding out in a puddle of yerself afore long, mark my words."

Wil stowed the folded target in his shirt pocket, along with his sarcasm. The old man was doing him a favor. "Yes, sir."

But Cailean seemed to take the respect personally. He drifted to Wil's side, revving up another lecture, and staggered to a halt.

Saoirse sat at the top of the stairway onto the bailey landing, dragging a whetstone along the length of her Teseum claymore. She'd returned to uniform in her grenadier's vest and combat boots, broad shoulders grazed by the exterior lighting. When she saw them, she stood, a lopsided frown on her face.

A hundred unlucky things raced through Wil's mind at once. "Hey, Sersh. Something happen?"

Saoirse propped her claymore against the railing. "Aye."

Cailean cleared his throat. "Anything to do with me?"

"On yer way," she said. "Need words with the PanO. Alone."

Wil gawked at him. "You're ditching me?"

"Yup," Cailean said and headed up the stairs past her. "Good luck."

Saoirse waited, jaw set until the old man had made his way inside. The instant they were alone, she wheeled on him. "You dingey blueberry idiot."

"Me? What'd I do?"

Her boots clomped on the descent. "I ken yer secret now. How dare you?"

Wil swallowed, hard. She'd learned about Svalarheima. She knew what he was, who he was, what he'd done. The back of his neck pricked, urging escape. "Who told you?"

"Alastair. But not till I'd found the photos myself."

"Listen, whatever you heard, I didn't—"

"Ye made me act the fool," she said. "Having a laugh, aye?"

"I didn't want you to know," Wil said. "I'm sorry, okay?"

"Sorry? Sorry ain't good enough, not this time."

Words galloped out from under him as fast as they formed, and Wil struggled to turn the stampede into speech. "Well, it's not like you haven't kept things from me, either. Nora in the bar? Don't lie and say that was coincidence."

"Incomparable!" she crowed. "That was so ye could set her straight, ken like? But this's a matter of life 'n' death."

"Not your life, or your death."

A wry, lopsided smile creased the corners of her eyes. "Issit always gonna be like this with you? I get a finger under the armor, and then it's, 'I'm fine,' and 'not your life,' and 'nowhere.'"

"When did this become about me?"

"Yer takin' the piss, right? Fer the last week, the whole system's revolved 'round yer silly arse."

He gripped the railing. "The hell do you want, okay?"

"Is honesty so difficult?"

"Like it's ever done me any favors," Wil said. "My deepest apologies for pretending I'm a human being instead of an inimitable screw-up for a few days. You want me to crucify myself while I'm at it, or is self-flagellation enough?"

Her face fell. Genuine confusion. "What?"

Wil stammered. "Didn't you—you just said—"

"I'm talkin' about tomorrow, Wil. The mission. You, and Al, and thirteen others traipsin' off tae the DRC. The bug hunt. Not martyrdom, the hell?"

The chill in the air pierced through to his bones. "Oh."

"So many things didn't make sense: Odune not recognizin' you, the secret meetings I weren't allowed to attend, why ye got shot down in the first place. And now I find out yer plannin' tae leave without even sayin' goodbye? The fuck's that about?"

"I wouldn't do that," he said. "Couldn't, after everything you've done for me. I might've been drugged on the balcony last night, but... Saoirse, I wasn't lying."

Her wide, pale Antipode eyes locked onto his. A single step apart, less than a meter. Wil summoned up his courage and closed the gap, but she caught his chest with her palm and held him back.

Saoirse exhaled, anger deflating into something else, something softer, but not better. "Here I am, spittin' on about liars, and... I'm a hypocrite," she said. "I ken what happened, Wil. About Svalarheima."

He fell a step back. "What?"

She dropped her gaze. "The dead folks. You. Runnin' away. Everything."

"Who," he said, barely capable of speech. "Who else?"

"Alastair," she said. "Gordon, and Cailean. Eideard pulled yer information from Arachne the night Alastair called Odune and shared it 'round like it proved him right. I wanted to say something, but the moment never felt right. But that's all, aye? No one else, promise."

Wil swept his palms over his face. So many ignored coincidences through the last week, building atop each other one after the other until he buckled under its perfectly obvious weight. Twice in the bar, Cailean's surprise in the gun range. Had to be willful ignorance.

"I'd thought suicide watch was a bit much," he said. "Handcuffs, too, but… no, it makes sense now. After one disgrace, another might've done me in."

Saoirse laid a hand on his shoulder. "That was Eideard's suggestion, not mine."

"And what was the first thing I did when I got here? Run. You guys must've been howling about that one, wow. Fuck me sideways, that's funny."

"It's not like that," she said. "Everyone makes mistakes."

"Everyone gets fourteen people killed?"

Her hand dropped to her side. "They said *a lot*, but… bloody hell, Wil. Fourteen?"

There it was. The expression that had dogged him ever since Svalarheima. Unbearable. Horrible. Excoriating. Not rage—no, rage had no hold on him, not anymore. It was pity, damnable pity, once and always pity like he was the one who needed sympathy for killing fourteen better people.

Wil pulled away from her. This wasn't her fault. No need to lose his temper. Wasn't anyone's fault but his own, and he knew exactly why.

Just as she began to speak, her comlog dial flared over her wrist. Incoming call. Momentum stalled, she accepted it with a grimace. "What?"

"Hey," Alastair answered. "Is Gotzinger with you?"

Saoirse shared a worried glance. "Why."

"Check the Kildalton Cluster. Main channel. Thirty minutes ago. I've flagged it for removal, but the auto-moderator's not deleting it and Eideard's not answering my calls. What do you see?"

She scrolled her feed. "A video."

Alastair cursed. "Report it, too? We can't let this get out."

Too late.

Even in low-res, Wil recognized that snowfield. And then it began to play.

Snow blankets the substation courtyard, flecks of white drifting past the camera drone's lens. Fourteen PanOceanian soldiers rush over the terrain, taking up defensive positions. An Aquila Guard leans into frame with an HMG in his arms. It's Wil. There's no sound. He gives commands, and the Fusiliers bristle, so Wil lifts his weapon and steps out of cover first.

The plasma flash goes off silent. It's bright enough to scramble the feed. When it returns, Wil is gone and the Fusiliers are on their own.

Fusilier Whitehead stumbles back, coughing. Combi raised, he directs the others. A retreat. Fusiliers Iadanza, Kinney, Nicholls, and Chokshi cluster along the rimed surface of a barricade around him. Whitehead signals, stands, and inside a second all five soldiers are charcoal beneath their melting clothes.

Montgomery panics. Breaks for it, and it happens again. Sankaran, Schulz, Trauma-Doctor Hoffman, and both unrelated Peterses spark and set fire alongside them. Fusilier McCombs sprints through the frame and dies behind a snowbank, frying Auxilia Llano and her Auxbot. Kovac is last, scrambling on his hands and knees in the snow, but the Q-Drone triangulates his path and his Combi rifle sparks like a fork in a power socket before his arms drop off.

Several seconds pass until Wil returns. He's uninjured and unbothered, having successfully avoided notice out of frame. He disappears around a corner for four-point-four seconds before he comes sprinting back weaponless over the field of dead PanOceanian soldiers.

He doesn't notice Llano holding out her hand. The slow convulsions that bring it back to her side, or the fast-forwarded minute of labored panting before she goes. It cuts off before he hunts the second drone with his pistol only. Before he sits amongst their bodies.

Before he realizes he didn't know their names and commits them all to memory.

The soft plink of a comment broke Wil from the replay's thrall. The words were all Caledonian, save for 'galactic.' And then another followed, and another.

Saoirse looked from her comlog to him. Her eyes had changed.

More of that damnable pity.

19

Wil unfolded the omelet left outside his door. Ashes and cigarette stubs darkened the filling. Unimpressed, he left the dissected breakfast on the doorstep and returned to pacing.

It had to have been Talbot, one last middle finger before he lost his permissions. No other possibility, after his comment at the Croatoan. How he'd got access to drop video links onto their cluster's main sphere, that was the real question. Eideard could've helped him if he'd known. Probably ignored Alastair's calls on purpose. Convenient that he'd run into a criminal Eideard had been searching high and low for months for. There had to be some connection there, too, because Talbot wasn't smart enough.

Brick by brick, it all added up... but did it actually matter? Twelve days and a wake-up was all he'd ever spend in Caledonia. Today, he was going home.

Nine days until the *Sword of St. Catherine* arrived in Dun Scaith.

As the morning light overpowered the cloud cover, the castle came alive. Four AUVs rumbled onto the lawn and parked in a semicircle. Soldiers packed the vehicles. Not long after their arrival, a messenger from Alastair swung by to inform Wil of a delay, and that someone would be up to brief him soon.

Hours passed. Dawn became morning. Gordon and Saoirse never came knocking, and no one stood outside his door. Once the clock struck 0700, Wil decided to go and investigate on his own, find some answers, solve some problems—anything to cut his time here in the miserable north one second shorter.

The mood out in the halls was somehow worse than ever. First it'd been being PanOceanian, but now it was even worse—he was a coward, to boot. Every errant bastard with something to prove glared from beneath their bonnets as if Wil was Achilles himself, come to colonize their ugly, lonely hill with its blown-out Teseum mine and its bitter, backward people.

On the second story landing, Nora fell in beside Wil and matched pace. She was in full uniform again, rifle over one shoulder, the other burdened by a satchel marked with a paramedic's cross. Her golden curls were tied back in a tight swirl, laying bare all the little divots in her ears where her piercings had been before.

"How's the nose," she asked. "Feeling better? Any loose teeth?"

Wil stopped mid-flight and turned on her. Her puzzled expression, entirely devoid of judgment, kicked his indignation out from under him. "It's… good," he said. "Yeah. And no."

"Brilliant," she said and giggled nervously. "Were you gonna yell at me?"

"Sorry," he said. "Rough morning."

"I heard. Wanna talk about it?"

He shrugged her off. "Just wanna get out of here."

A few local militiamen maneuvered around them on the landing, coughing words into their fists. *Clara. Luid. Onsha.* One laughed, and they cast glances back before they went outside.

Wil didn't understand, but Nora definitely did. Her luster dimmed, and her smile seemed forced. "Back to the holos and the flying cars! The glitz and the glamor, aye? Frankly, I'm jealous. Your time with us must've been like a tech detox. World's worst rehab center, but…"

"Nora," he said. "Thank you. Not just for saying something, but for doing what was right. I know that wasn't easy, but it's pretty goddamn brave. Keep your chin up, and you'll make a great 112 one day. You're already a damn good person."

Just like that, her smile reached her eyes again. "Aw. Ta very much."

Wil nodded a curt goodbye and made his way to the broad double-doors at the end of the foyer. The two Volunteers holding it open caught sight of him and let it close in his face. Grumbling, he shoved it open, and Nora flit past him, out toward the cars.

He rushed after. "Where are you going?"

"With you," she said. "Unit needs a paramedic. Cailean asked for me because I play the bagpipes."

"And bagpipes have *what* to do with being a paramedic?"

"What don't they?" Nora said, more than a little teasing. "Haldane Reform of the British Army of 1909, Wil. All paramedics in the Highlander Army are required to be proficient at piping. And here I'd heard you were some kinda military historian."

Wil made several noises until he settled on, "Why?"

"Don't look so worried," Nora said and pouted over her shoulder. "I'm a lass of many talents and limited backpack space. Your fragile PanOceanian ears are safe—for now."

Wil stalled for a response and ran smack dab into Saoirse Clarke.

Back in uniform, all the best parts of her midriff were firmly hidden behind a knit undershirt and her grenadier's vest. No more pleasure. All business. A Mk12 hung by a strap over her shoulder, a sleek and technological PraxiTech from the Nomad Nation. Emerald green swathed its barrel shroud to better blend into the forest.

Wil had only ever seen Mk12s mounted on REMs or as emplacement guns—that Saoirse was strong enough to fire it from the hip put her strength into perspective.

Awkwardly, she glanced from him to Nora. "Sorry," she said, and pushed past.

After the video, things between them would never be the same. The way she turned and walked away without a word. The way he stood there, knowing no explanation was good enough. But he didn't care. Dawn would be behind him soon, just another bad dream.

The striped shemagh bunched around her neck was a nice touch.

Alastair wasn't around, but Cailean was, surrounded by a gaggle of Volunteers including three Wil didn't recognize. The old timer was back in full uniform, plaid flung across his chest, FREE CALEDONIA! stenciled on his breastplate in fresh white paint. A cluster of smoke grenades hung along his hip, and Rhiannon laid in the grass at his feet beside a long claymore in a cowskin sheath.

Nora joined the Volunteer circle, singing her good mornings. Neil greeted her with a groan and a "Can ye not?", and spotted Wil over his sister's shoulder. One nigh-imperceptible nod later, he turned his back again. A plastic bag of produce hung from a carabiner on his assault pack, stuffed with a carton of eggs and a plethora of native produce.

Gordon's voice rumbled up from behind Wil, belly-deep. "Neil's shakshouka is heavy brilliant. Delectable, even. Too bad you don't eat black pudding."

Wil gawked. Instead of the big, hairy bastard he'd expected, Gordon had transmuted into his Dog-Warrior self—bigger, hairier, more bastardy. He wore an armored breastplate sized for his tree-trunk body, an enormous length of plaid hung around his waist and pinned at his shoulder with a Teseum-alloy brooch of the MacArthur clan crest. Both biceps were ringed by steel torcs thicker than industrial chain. Strapped to his sides, his twin Yungang Xíng Type 9.0s clinked against a bevy of frag grenades, and a battle-axe sized for his transmuted state hung horizontally across his lower back—the weapon from his saddle, back when they'd first met.

He pried his eyes away. "Didn't know we were on speaking terms," Wil said. "Sure you don't want to ignore me, like everybody else?"

Gordon cocked a canine brow over his primeval eyes. "Sound like my ex."

Wil sighed. "Go fuck yourself, Gordon."

"Still sound like my ex."

Wil regretted the laugh that kicked free from his chest, but it was better than being alone.

Gordon picked at his teeth, pointing out the Volunteers. "On Nora's left is Kelsie, Shaw's sister. On the right is Vern. RTO. Nice guy, even if he is from away. Middle one's Llowry. He's an idiot. Think they gave him a grenade launcher just to see if he'd blow himself up."

Vern. The guy who tattled to Talbot when Nora fetched Saoirse. Stocky, glasses, face like a marmot. He'd have to keep an eye on him.

Wil started to ask about their combat experience when a joyful Highlander in a kilt bolted toward them across the yard. Steel-ringed braids jingled in his mane of wild, dark hair, and he wore an echo of Saoirse's uniform—a tall-collared vest, standard-issue gauntlets, and a claymore. Smoke grenade canisters clustered along his belt beside a boarding shotgun, its barrel sawed brutally short.

Without warning, the Highlander yanked Wil into his massive embrace. "Halò, a charaid! Madainn mhath! Dè do chor? Cha dèan mi steam' dhìot!"

"Whoa," Wil said, and let the guy hug away. "Hey. Hi there. Howdy."

Short as he was, the wild man was almost as strong as Saoirse. Against all expectation, he smelled amazing—like a bottle of aftershave pitched into a gingerbread sawmill. The Highlander beamed and held Wil by the face like one might a brother. His response was in full Caledonian, impenetrable, lyrical. Unrelenting.

Gordon waited patiently for the briefest gap in the one-sided conversation to butt in. "Fionnlagh O'Casidei," he introduced. "45th Highlander Rifleman. He's from Pointed Hill, even norther than our lot. Only speaks Caledonian, like the rest of his clan."

45th Rifle meant Fionnlagh was one of the famous Galwegians—the kind of Highlander that his briefing had warned him about just about a lifetime ago that didn't die when they were killed. "Let's hope the language barrier doesn't—"

"His geist translates the basics," Gordon said and offered Fionn a greeting with his fist. "And he's right here, mate. Talk to him."

Fionn laughed and bounced his knuckles off Gordon's twice more. Sure enough, the comlog on his wrist was higher spec than the one Wil had in his visor. "A Cù-sìth! Goddag! Ciamar a tha thu?"

"Tha gu math, mostly," Gordon replied. "Dè tha dol?"

The Galwegian traded a quick shrug. "Chan eil càil fhathast."

They kept talking, faster and more animated. Gordon laughed—more than once. At least three times. A world record.

"Damn," Wil said. "Y'all are best friends, huh?"

Gordon grunted. "He's saved my life twice, the dumb bastard."

Fionn laughed, amicably disagreeing. He clapped Wil on the shoulder, called him something strange, and disengaged back toward the castle into another excited embrace with another victim of his unstoppable mirth.

"Called me Clara," Wil said. "Second time I've heard that today."

"Cladhaire," Gordon corrected. "Fionn said he's glad someone's coming he can count on to keep camp while we fight."

At least he was nice about it.

Across the crowded green, a woman approached Cailean—the Scots Guard from way back in the library. Sergeant Muriel Dunne. It was impossible to gage her shape through the cloak, but she moved with purposeful grace, cloudy hair braided now and tucked beneath a red-and-black-checkered bandanna. Her patchwork custom Molotok hung on her back, visible over the poncho she wore. With every step, her clothing changed color, soaking in the local area. Photoreactive tech. Primitive, compared to thermo-optical camouflage, but damn if it didn't look pretty.

A tall, scrawny man ambled beside her. Neat-kept brown hair crowned his square head, and a rugged spate of brown stubble raced across his milky white jaw.

He wore a black wool turtleneck under his uniform vest—one shoulder marked with an Ariadnan cross and the other bare. A cornucopia of weaponry hung from his back, his hips, in sheaths and holsters up and down the straps over his shoulders: a flash pulse; a chain rifle; a light shotgun; an assault pistol; a handaxe; two knives; a trio of demolition charges; grenades, grenades, grenades.

Wil nudged Gordon. "Who's the ammo caddy?"

"Robert Hodges. Special Ariadnan Service—SAS. Who Dares Wins; best of the best. Well, ex-SAS, anyways."

"Doesn't look so tough."

Gordon snorted. "Wouldn't be surprised if the men Hodges killed didn't realize they were in Hell till the devil said hello."

"Always the ones you underestimate, huh?"

"'Cept you," Gordon said.

"Exception proves the rule."

"Aye," he said. "Right."

"Alastair said there were five in Dunne's crew," Wil said. "I count three."

"Pyotr MacReady turned the job down," Gordon said. "Heard some bad things out of Odhran's Ford. Got spooked. So he's absent, and Pellehan stays outwith the town limits save for disarmament holidays."

So Alastair's photo had disseminated more widely than Wil had realized. Recent events spurred wild theories, but he knew better than to waste time trying to unravel another pointless mystery. "This Pellehan—claustrophobic, or hates people?"

"Neither. Done things for the clan, years back. Bad things. Honor would dictate his surrender if he'd cross the threshold, so he don't. Odd fellow. You two would get along."

Wil gawked. "Wait—is he a Cateran?"

Gordon rolled his eyes. "Yup."

"Whoa, for real? They're supposed to be—"

"Legendary, yeah, sure," Gordon said. "You going out in a sweater and trainers, buddy?"

"Hope not. How long you think we'll be delayed for?"

Gordon licked the tip of his snout. "Hm?"

"Alastair said we'd be a while. How long, you think? I still need to swing by the garage, see if I can beg Sharlene for a rucksack and a second pair of socks."

"Alastair said, huh," Gordon said and gave him a sidelong glance. "Mate, we're pullin' chocks in fifteen."

Frustration balled his heart to his lungs, forcing a grimace. Should've known—should've confirmed. Some asshole was having a laugh at his expense right now, standing out on the lawn in his civvies. "Right, of course. Fucking fantastic."

Gordon cracked his neck. "I'll buy some time. Start some shit."

Wil paused. "You sure?"

"Not everything can be your fault," Gordon said and pushed him toward the castle. "Go."

With Gordon's size, the spur felt more like a throw, and Wil harnessed the momentum into an unsubtle rush. He ducked a pair of Volunteers team-lifting a sandbag, weaved around the line of approaching soldiers. Aimed for the path to the garage entrance. A near-collision. Another miss.

Bell skittered out of his path, carrying an ammunition box. "Bloody hell," he blurted. "Blueberry's doin' a runner already!"

He was lucky Wil didn't have time to turn around.

⸸

Sharlene was glad to see Wil, though no one else in the garage was. She invited him back to her desk and handed over the Strela, the Detour, and an assault pack she'd prepped. And she'd scrounged up a uniform to boot: standard-issue knee-pads, gauntlets, pants, and flak jacket, all in a muddy Ariadnan green. She shared a few tips on surviving the cold, wet climate: how to treat trench foot, what kinds of ivy to avoid, when to ventilate and when to insulate.

Nothing he didn't already know. But she reminded him of his mom, so he didn't mind letting her lecture.

"There's gel-paks in the pocket for your face," she said. "Doc Crawford said twice a day, so I put two. And some antiseptic cream. Paracetamol will spread the bruise, don't ya know?"

Wil wasn't sure if that was true or not, or what paracetamol was, but he'd take her advice going forward. The pocket had a few other staples: gauze, bandage strips, moleskin pads. "Thanks. Appreciate it, really."

Sharlene leaned onto the armory countertop. "And maybe it's not my place to offer advice, but… The MacArthur are prickly on the outside but twice as sentimental. Either you win 'em over, or give up on caring. Both are fine. Either will make them respect you. Hell, I already do."

"I'll remember that when I open this bag tonight and the mine inside goes off."

She laughed. "How 'bout you open it now?"

He made sure she didn't take cover and unzipped it. Wil's multispectral visor stared up at him from the interior; oculi, radial sensors, and all. Ropes of welding knit new steel to the old, though the paint had changed considerably: A diagonal cross had been airbrushed in white across the visor's cerulean face. With the red of his oculi, it evoked a close approximation of the Caledonian flag.

"So nobody in the bush sees you creeping behind the line and gets jumpy," Sharlene explained. "Lord knows I'd have questions, seeing a galactic sporting the cross of St. Andrew."

He thumbed the extra padding. Soft. "No more AUV battery?"

"Didn't ya hear? Somebody smashed our extra."

"… Sorry."

Sharlene laughed, proud and a little villainous. "Rigged an emergency power cell from a bum Mul. Worked great. Holds enough charge for twelve hours, or so it goes. Still couldn't get the biometrics to start, or diagnostics. If your armor's aux supply weren't shot, different story. But it's better than nothing."

"And the infrared?"

"Like a charm. Should interlink with the comlog in your bag just fine."

Wil dug through the rest: A camouflage-pattern poncho and a matching waterproof woobie; a handful of energy bars, and five plastic-wrapped MREs with flameless ration heaters that must've been sourced from a time capsule; a change of clothes, two suits of long jehans, and four pairs of socks; a flashlight, hand mirror, and a compass; a wet-weather bag; an aluminum space blanket; a combat knife; spare 5.56x45mm for the Strela and .45 for the Detour; an obsolete wrist-mounted comlog with a paired earpiece; a simple medical kit, no frills; and his Aquila Guard duster.

Wil unfolded the duster from the bag and held it to the light with no small amount of reverence. She'd stitched up the rip that Pale Shadow had put across his chest and sewn in the missing parts with cow leather so he could don it without his armor. "Wow. Damn."

Sharlene broke out in a big, pretty smile. "Good?"

"Great," he said, comparing the old familiar fabric to the new. The shoulders were still decorated with all his favorite patches: an oil lamp crested with flames; a numeral '1' flanked by eagle wings; the Capitaline Cross; and the peach fuzz where the rest had been torn off after the tribunal. Along the breast, a newer patch had snuck in among the old: Three crowns atop a blue shield. The symbol of Clan MacArthur.

"To remember us by," she said. "At least, the good parts."

He didn't know what to say.

↑↑

One hurried redress in an unoccupied corner later, Wil made a wrong turn and stood staring down a stairwell into the belly of the castle.

Down would lead to Rajan. A quick explanation, if Alastair hadn't given it already. An assurance. An apology—groveling, more like. And if he was lucky, he'd be allowed to keep hanging on to his demoted rank by his fingernails until he aged out, retired, and died in the same place he'd been born.

Something was wrong with him. He should've been planning how he'd throw the bastard under the bus, not whining about his own bad decisions.

Searching for the exit, Wil wound through the guts of Castle MacArthur. An intense bout of déjà vu struck as he strode into a dead end followed by a dusty Roman bath, and increasingly desperate to not be the one to dumpster their schedule, picked up his pace. Doubled back, and then again.

Up ahead, voices. Wil slowed, unwilling to endure another jab about retreating from another clueless moron. Around the corner, Saoirse stood beside

Alastair. The young chieftain was strapped in heavy armor. Gauntlets, greaves, kneepads, all Teseum-alloy. Azure pauldrons bearing St. Andrew's Cross perched above a dark breastplate, every plane notched and pitted with the evidence of a hundred different battles. The famous heirloom armor of the Caledonian Mormaers. Some parts of that suit were maybe only a few years younger than the castle they stood in.

A length of green and gold tartan hung over his hip, and he had his helmet under one arm, rebreather swinging against the Americolt chain-colt in its holster. His comlog was anchored to his belt over his decorated sporran, to keep it free from Teseum interference.

"Bell?" Saoirse spat. "Fucking *Bell*, but not me?"

Ah, shit. This was personal.

"Sersh, please," Alastair said. "I wanted to hire a Wardriver, but the funds…"

She perched a fist on her hip. "This isn't an Arachne relay check-up, or a 'Pode pack needing scarin' off, Al. It's serious. Bell sucks. Bring me instead."

"I'll be alright, Saoirse. I'm in more danger at home in my civvies than under artillery fire in this getup, trust me. And all Bell needs to do is be competent enough to press a gas pedal."

"Stop actin' older than I am," Saoirse snarled. "All it took was a few people for Rian—or the time before, or when our da——"

Alastair placed a hand on her shoulder. "It's not like that."

"What's wrong, then? I do something wrong?"

Crestfallen, Alastair receded a step. "No, Sersh. Not at all. But someone has to stay with Eideard and protect Kildalton while I'm gone. Gotzinger means well, but I can't trust him."

"Setting aside Eideard's dislike of me, how not? Wil's an arrogant, gloomy wanker, but he's a good man, Al. People change."

"And your evidence for that is?"

"He went tae blows for Nora, and he came back fer me—both times when he didn't need to, both times when he shouldn't. That's proof enough."

"Martial prowess does not an angel make," he said and ran a gloved hand across his face. "You're lucky Gordon got into it with Bell just now, or we wouldn't even be having this discussion."

She crossed her arms. "Don't sidetrack me."

"I don't want to give you a direct order," Alastair said. "Please."

Abruptly, Saoirse turned away. "Aye right, nae bother! Forgot my place. All's well. But, do me a favor though and lead with fuck off next time? Save us both a minute."

Thunderous footsteps echoed along the hallway, drawing closer. Wil hugged the cold concrete as Saoirse stomped by, fists curled like she was searching for something to put a hole in. Alastair clanked after, trying his best hand at a running apology, but the metric ton of Teseum on his shoulders didn't do him any favors.

At least now Wil knew which way was out.

A click from behind jolted Wil around. The flicker of a pocket lighter. Sparse flames illuminated a man's face—the ex-SAS, Hodges. How long he'd been there, Wil had no idea. No clue why this guy was smoking in a basement of all places, but Wil didn't want to ask.

Hodges puffed on his cigarette, encouraging the flame to take. "Bloody hell. Got to work on your nerves there, mate. Almost hit low orbit."

"Nerves? Naw, man, I'm great. How're you, how's eavesdropping? Good times?"

"Only following your lead," he said, exhaling smoke from his nose. "Lot of drama for a simple escort."

"Yeah, well, talk to Alastair about that."

"More curious about you," Hodges said. "Celebrity galactic. Used to be an Aquila Guard, yeah? Heard you're good at sprinting."

More of this. Great. He sifted a sigh through his teeth. "First in all things."

"How you got here. Why your people won't come get you. Why no one's asked around. I knew PanO didn't like you, mate, but this is on another level."

Wil squared with him. "I'm not your fuckin' mate."

Hodges clicked his lighter shut. "Yeah. You're not."

Stance shifted, hand hidden. The oncoming sucker punch was painfully obvious. Wil curled a fist. Grit his teeth. But nothing came. Instead of a swing, Hodges took a long, long drag and dropped the half-dead cigarette.

"Sorry, chief," he said, grinding the stub into the hallway concrete. "Fist fight means the missus starts askin' questions I won't want to answer. Scrap's one thing, but smoking's another. Fight later, aye? Promise."

A strange disappointment coursed up Wil's arms, out of his hands. Whatever frustrations he had, a fist fight wasn't the answer.

But it would've felt good.

20

Fourteen strong, they left Kildalton and Saoirse Clarke behind.

The drive to Odhran's Ford was short and pleasant. Well-kept highways and boreal forest roads sped by until the convoy came to a stop not far from a long stone bridge over a canyon river. Twenty meters across at least, and another twenty down. A starkly out-of-place Nomad comms array tinseled with dead ivy jut up from the green, encircled by an electrified fence and guarded by twin F-13 defensive turrets.

Llowry gestured past the windshield, out toward an empty field. "Welcome to Odhran's Ford."

Wil squinted past the trees and just found more. "Thought this was a town?"

Nora perked up, but Neil spoke first. "Better tae let him see. Easier than explainin'."

The convoy drew up beside a trio of concrete hatches in a grassy clearing, and Cailean disembarked. He ambled over, gave the biggest hatch a few amused stomps. A moment later, the door groaned open and a tide of Caledonian villagers clambered out to meet them. Five, ten, fifteen—and Wil lost count.

He boggled at the growing crowd. "You're telling me the whole place is...."

"Underground," Nora beamed. "Safer than our walls, to be honest. Antipodes don't dig. But I couldn't ever give up the night sky in winter."

"Vulnerable to siege, asphyxiation, disease. I'd prefer walls, too."

Neil shrugged. "Disease en't a problem, so much. Not since Eideard started trading fer medicine. Turrets were his idea, too. Yer lucky Al gave Kildalton's to the homesteaders, or yer palisade jump woulda ended in ribbons."

Nora caught sight of a woman her age waving hello and disembarked into the crowd. Halfway there, she picked up a little girl and carried her into the bustle.

Wil recalled Saoirse's endorsement of the 'offworld-make' drugs from Haqqislam. How a town out in the sticks like Kildalton afforded imports like that, he had no idea. And F-13 defensive turrets—expensive. They needed support tech far beyond any capability he'd seen planetside so far. Couldn't have been legal, or first-party.

Kelsie Shaw lingered in the passenger seat until they were alone. Her brown eyes regarded Wil in the rear-view mirror, laden with suspicion. "My brother. He deserve it?"

"Less than the others," he said. "But yeah."

"Good," she said, and went after Nora.

† †

An hour later, Wil couldn't shake the feeling that another shoe was due to drop.

Ever since Wil was a kid, his mother had said bad things happened in threes. She'd harped on it after they'd run late to the dole and had to pick their dinners from the dumpster behind the strip club. On the third day, the glitter-crusted leftovers had been bleached. His mom had laid up for hours puking her guts out, too worried about the next misfortune to take him to a doctor.

He'd told himself he wouldn't be like that, but he'd told himself a lot of things: that he'd never sell out and leave King's Den; that he'd never join the Fusiliers, like his mother did; that he'd make something of himself.

Still time for that last one. But not much.

In time, the villagers' interest waned, and the vast majority meandered back below ground. The members of the task force mingled about, finishing last-minute checks and preparations. Dunne, Cailean, and Alastair gathered out by the clearing's edge, deep in the midst of private conversation.

A chain-link fencepost caught his eye. Familiar.

Dried blood still lingered in the tension bands.

An elderly man in a ratty poncho emerged from the forest, doddering along the weeds before approaching. His bushy gray goatee bristled wildly, and his leathery, liver-spotted face was wizened with deep, uncompromising wrinkles. A sniper rifle, an AKNovy Zyefir, underslung beneath his assault pack. As he strolled beside the tall grass, his threadbare cloak stained wildflower yellow. Photoreactive.

Wil sized him up and stood in his way. "Can I help you?"

The old man walked around him, then paused and turned back. "When you die," he said. "Your multispectral visor. Can I have it?"

Wil's hand drifted to his pistol. "Hey, uh, guys? Somebody?"

"A simple 'no' would've sufficed," the old man huffed.

Neil sauntered around the lead AUV, weapon in hand, and the moment he saw the septuagenarian, he broke into a grin. He gave him a handshake, a quick greeting in Caledonian, and pointed him on his way. The old man wobbled through their defensive circle, trading hellos with just about everyone before he caught Alastair in a hug.

"No cause fer alarm," Neil explained. "It's only Pell. Might be the only time ye see him."

Wil had to look again and still didn't believe it. "The Cateran? Wait, he's our sniper? Are you sure? Isn't he a bit…"

"Old?" Neil said, and cocked a brow.

"I wasn't gonna say that. But, yeah. He come over on the *Ariadna*, or what? Who's guiding him back to camp when he sundowns?"

Arms stiff, lips pinched, Neil regarded Wil with uncharacteristic severity. "Listen here, mate. That man hung that MO flag in the DFAC, alongside the sword o' the monster that carried it. He stood against the Antipodes at Skara Brae without relief fer sixty days. Folk called him the Dullahan then, for if he saw yer head, he'd claim it. I'll brook no disrespect, aye? Man's a legend—or, at least, he used to be."

In the right light, if he tilted his head, maybe. "Yeah," Wil said. "The Dullahan."

Before Neil could push his point further, Cailean whistled, spun his hand in the air, and the task force collapsed around the hood of the lead AUV. Atop it, Dunne weighed the corners of a topographical map with small stones.

More paper. Did they not know what their comlogs were for, or what?

"Afternoon, everyone," Alastair said, motioning for everyone to fall in closer. "I know this brief isn't as comfortable or traditional as we normally hold, so I'll keep remarks to a minimum."

"Smaller words," Cailean cautioned from beside him. "Ye've already lost Fionnlagh."

Laughter wandered amidst the group. The 45th Highlander froze, caught sneaking a sprig of orange wallflowers over Nora's ear. Sheepishly, he discarded the wildflowers and leaned on his claymore. "Gabh mo leisgeul."

"I'd rather not," Cailean replied. "No tellin' where it's been."

More laughter. Easier going than most of his briefs in the field, but not in a good way. It put a worry into him about their professionalism, whether they'd keep on or bail if things got difficult. He'd trade a hundred Bells for one Saoirse Clarke in a heartbeat, but what about the rest? Vern was a tattletale; Nora was naïve; Neil, a hothead. He scanned their faces, trying to judge which were the dead weight and which were the ones he could rely on.

Something repeatedly clicked, nigh inaudible. The bolt of Bell's rifle. He was bobbing his knee rapid fire, knocking the butt with his thigh, nose the same jaundiced shade bridge to tip.

Gordon tapped Wil on the shoulder. "Oi."

And when he turned back, the entire task force was staring at him, each face somewhere on a sliding scale between pissed off and amused. "Pardon, sorry," he said. "What?"

Cailean barked a laugh. "Bloody hell. Now there's two of 'em."

Another laugh rippled through the group, Fionn's louder than the rest.

Wil felt about as tall as a CrazyKoala.

"Big-shot Lieutenant Wilhelm Gotzinger III, everyone," Cailean said. "Used tae be an Aquila Guard. Now, not so much. Please, be patient wae the lad. As you can see, he's a mite touched, but he's very, very good at shooting."

Wil resisted the urge to shrink farther and gave a half-hearted wave to little fanfare and a lot of judgment. Fionn spat a quick quip in Caledonian and gripped Wil by the shoulders. Another giggle ran through the group, no doubt all at his expense.

"Quiet up now," Dunne said. "It's the MacArthur's turn to talk."

The chuckles died away as Alastair strode forward to address them, hands behind his back.

"Officially, we are patrolling the interior of the AEZ to check for signs of Submondo activity. But by now, you are well aware of the true purpose of our expedition. We have reason to believe that the Shasvastii Expeditionary Army has set roots in the Dawn Research Commission outpost Dun Scaith on the western border of the MacArthur clan lands. Our mission is to confirm the enemy presence, ward away an oncoming delegation of galactic benefactors, and return home armed with proof of alien occupancy."

Wil scanned the assembled faces, expecting worry or confusion. Aside from Gordon, who cast a concerned glance at the back of his girlfriend's head, the task force was level. Prepared. Wil wondered how many of them had been told before yesterday morning, and if any of them held the secret against him like Saoirse did.

Over the AUV hood, Hodges met Wil's eyes with a restrained smirk. He whispered to Dunne beside him, and she hissed for him to drop it.

Llowry stepped forward. He was skinnier than the other Volunteers, cheeks so clean-shaven they shined. "We sure it's aliens? Think I'd prefer Submondo."

"Should be jumpin' fer joy, lad," Cailean said, picking at his armguards. "Shas won't dose ye with Baba/Yaga and make ye *like* getting yer face minced off."

Pellehan combed his beard with his fingers. "Submondo? Meh. Druze, I'd do for free."

Cailean smiled darkly. "Wouldn't we all."

"Pardon, sir, apologies," Hodges said and rapped on the AUV hood, drawing all eyes. "Am I to understand the only proof we have of this 'presence' is the photograph you shared on the private cluster last night?"

Alastair's calm facade slipped, and his tone became curt. "Cailean and I agree it's rather clear. Lieutenant Gotzinger killed a scout of theirs in close combat."

A few impressed glances mingled among the doubtful. Wil didn't like either.

"With all due respect," Hodges said, "I fear next you'll tell me the Shasvastii are stealing the township's chickens."

"Stealing people, more like," Cailean interjected. "Can't all be runaways or traffickers."

"Right. Little green men. Well, gray, in this case."

"Ye've never seen a battlefield after their win. Found corpses chewed on, hollowed out, sucked dry. Human body has everythin' a growin' spawn embryo needs to cook a new bug, ken? Locally sourcin' their own compost would keep things subtle, keep us in the dark."

Noses wrinkled. Flashes of disgust traded among the task force's faces. Hodges put up an unperturbed front, but a momentary grimace gave him away.

Wil thought of the print-out in the fence, the one of the grandmother in the horn-rimmed glasses beaming with pride over her cookies. He thought of her face-down in the muck, pulsating eggs stuffed up inside her withered carcass.

It took a moment to relax his jaw, for his fist to uncurl.

"So, assuming these 'Shasvastii' have invaded the DRC," Hodges persist-ed, "they're stuck in alongside the PanOs, the mercenary galactics, and O-12 staff. Correct?"

"That's what we suspect, yes," Alastair said.

Hodges scanned the crowd, searching for support. "So how's that our bloody problem? Seems to me the bugs are doing us a favor. Enemy of our enemy. And no offense, Gotzinger, but I don't give a damn about some rich galactics' lives. Hell, do you, the way they treat you? Get your bloody Joan of Arc to go save them or something."

Wil wasn't sure how to answer that. Lives were lives. And judging by Dunne's weapons-grade glare, this was what she'd been asking Hodges not to bring up.

Cailean crossed his arms. "Besides the obvious detriments tae havin' an enemy installation within' stone's throw, y'mean?"

"DRC's been there two years," Hodges said.

"And what'll happen if the Shas run tell that *we* shot down the galac-tics? And after, what'll Rodina and the Federation do if they catch wind that Clan MacArthur are risking war with PanOceania? Think, Robert. Ask Fionnlagh for his other brain cell if yer three's nae enough. And if ye still have words, I'll take yer pay back right now if ye like."

In the pregnant moment that followed, Hodges' dumb smirk faltered. Sud-denly aware of Dunne's steady, murderous glare, he shrank like a kicked dog. "Christ, mate. Point made. No need for insult."

"Real or not, it's a perceived threat, and one that must be considered care-fully," Alastair said. "Any other questions?"

Kelsie Shaw perked, and her hand shot up. Like her brother, she was short and stocky, her skin only a shade lighter than his. But unlike Shaw, she carried an ambitious gleam in her eye. "These Shas, they're the ones Cailean fought on Novyy Cimmeria, yeah? Should I be worried?"

Alastair weighed his response. "I would be."

"Sounds like my ticket to the Scots Guards, then," Kelsie said. "Line up the Tohaa, the Yujingyu, the CA. I'll fight anything gets me out of Kildalton."

Dunne nodded, amused. "You and me both, Private Shaw."

"Any other questions?" Alastair asked, and scanned the assembled sol-diers. His patience had thinned since the meeting's beginning, and his normally steady voice tinged with a combative tilt.

Gordon hoisted his massive, clawed mitt and asked, "When we eating?"

††

When the route had been decided and the logistics determined, Dunne folded up her map and the group broke into smaller cliques and shards. Belonging to none of them, Wil skirted the edges, trying to place his finger on the group's pulse and power dynamics.

Alastair knelt in the grass by his open pack, staring into the eyes of his Mormaer helmet like Hamlet with Yorick's skull. Out by the foot of the bridge, Nora engaged in terse conversation with her brother. He gave both a wide berth.

Pellehan had already disappeared. Where the old man had gone, or how he would follow them remained an utter mystery, but Wil had dealt with Hexas and Locusts before in his prime. Best to leave the ghosting to the ghosts.

On the roadside, Fionn and Cailean were deep in discussion, speaking Caledonian. Then Fionn said, "Rhiannon," and Wil realized they were jawing about his Kilgour. Cailean grew somber, somewhat proud, and presented the engraving on his machine gun's stock.

Shouldn't interrupt that, either.

Dunne and Hodges crowded along the trunk of an AUV, eyes glowing with quantronic light. Actual link bracelets circled their wrists—surprising, considering the clunkers everyone else in the task force was wearing. Without his own lens, their halos were invisible, though it sounded like Hodges was trying to catch a private connection to pull up schematics on Combined Army ordnance—grenades, mines, etcetera—and failing.

"Sod it," he said. "It'll be bloody Christmas by the time the request times out."

Dunne drew a gesture on the empty air. "For the record, I appreciate you speaking up, though your methods were decidedly lacking. Rian or Cameron would've never brought us along on a snipe hunt."

Hodges put an arm over her shoulders. "I knew about halfway through that the reason we're here instead of an army is because the other clans said the same things I did."

"Even still," she said, and bumped him with her hip.

"Give the word, darling. I hear Varuna's wonderful this time of year."

"If only," Dunne said. "We need the money."

"To get to Varuna?"

She smiled at him and gingerly touched his arm. "To eat."

Time to move on.

Gordon sat apart from everyone else on a crumbling stone fence, shining the bladed edge of his battle-axe with a rag. Finally—no flirting, no frustration, no drama, just Gordon and his laconic grunting.

He spotted Wil in the axe blade's fresh-shined surface and grinned. "That went well. I expected an argument, but Al handled it good. Should put more faith in him. God knows he puts his in me."

"Same," Wil said. "Dunne's mercs. What's their deal?"

Gordon worked his axe back into its leather sheath. "They expect more. Used to Kosmoflot and StarCo and such. Ran with William Wallace once or twice. They'll straighten out."

The Detour's weight on his hip sparked some of the old Aquila Guard bravado. "And while we're at it, what's yours?"

The big lug's expression darkened, as usual. "My family's always guarded the MacArthurs, chieftain or not. Debt of honor. Goes way back. Besides that, I'm just some asshole following orders and waiting for my turn."

No wonder Gordon was frustrated being Wil's jailer when he had his own asset to protect. Wil considered how things would've been different if he and Rajan had grown up together, and decided he probably would've still hated the bastard anyways.

It wasn't as if Alastair was helpless, though. The kid was Mormaer; unlike Rajan, he could fight. But something Saoirse had said during her argument with Alastair came to mind: *All it took was a few people for Rian—or the time before, or when our da....*

"Your turn for what?" Wil asked.

Gordon didn't answer.

No one wanted to take the risk, he'd said. Alastair's two brothers, gone. Gordon's two brothers, gone. Neil and Nora McDermott, who considered Alastair their cousin—their father, Lloyd McDermott, had died on the same Christmas as Alastair and Saoirse's dad.

The history of Clan MacArthur, written in blood.

Back at Nora's mom's apartment, when he'd asked if Gordon fought in the arena because he liked the pain, she'd said: *That'd make him a bigger idiot than you.* And now he saw the fear in those words for what it was—not for him, but for her boyfriend.

Gordon brushed off his kilt and stood. "This is nice. You finally shut up."

Wil didn't answer, too distracted by the familiar shade in Gordon's inhuman eyes. The same shade that kept Wil from ever looking into a mirror, or thinking too long before sleep. Self-loathing, survivor's guilt, and something else—the need to touch the void.

Six seconds later, the call went out, and they piled back into the AUVs dead set for the DRC-9 Dun Scaith.

21

Across the hundred-year-old stone bridge, past the bunker doors of Odhran's Ford, the convoy descended into the boreal valleys and temperate rainforests of the Caledonian highlands.

Wil rode with the Volunteers, passenger-side front. Neil drove. The descent was uneventful and quiet, save for Kelsie dictating her planned career path to an uninterested Llowry and Vern.

"Beef suet and onions," Neil said, licking his lips. "Stirred intae blood, milk, and oatmeal, stuffed intae intestine. Delicious. Black pudding's pure barry, can't believe ye never had it."

Wil shrugged. "You ever tried choripán, or feijoada?"

"Don't eat fruit," Neil said. "Gives me a headache."

Rolling, empty hills stretched to the horizon, everything stained a listless gray. It rained, and the convoy slowed. A fog condensed after. Enormous trees faded in and out of the murk until one much larger than the others loomed ahead, stretched steel branches dotted with little crimson lights. A radio tower, foundation drenched in mold, wrapped in demolished chain link and rusted beyond repair. How it hadn't tipped over yet, he had no idea.

The going was slow. Some roads had washed clean from the mountainside, others buried under it. Judging by the smooth mud, no one had been this way in a long time, and the convoy doubled back to hunt steadier ground more than once. Twice, a switchback necessitated fording water to open the way.

Soon, Helios fell, staining the temperate Caledonian rainforest in pink and purple hues. The road descended into a broad, forested grotto, somewhere Nora called 'the Brume,' where they stopped. The Volunteers and Wil stacked sandbags from AUV floors to keep cover from the less-protected south while Dunne spaced the AUVs fifty meters apart, and they all clambered onto the high ground overlooking the bend in the road to make camp.

Wil expected portable heaters or something more subdued, but actual campfires brought back memories of training exercises deep in the Aquilan outback. The task force crowded in to warm their hands until Fionn tossed a thick bundle of thin yellow flowers from his pack onto the flames, and the acidic, lemony fumes drove Gordon from the light.

"Dawnwort," Cailean explained. "For safety."

Wil recognized the flowering weeds from the bothy planter he'd nosedived into. "Let me guess—Antipode repellent."

Cailean clicked his tongue. "Aye. Here, the local tribe will keep their distance long as we keep ours, but no sense in being reckless. Not as aggressive as Pale Shadow's ilk, ken, but nevertheless don't wander far for a Jimmy."

"Noted," Wil said. "What's our ETA on arrival at the DRC tomorrow?"

"Tomorrow? Unlikely. Day after next at best, lad, and in the evenin'. We've no less than two ruins, a mountain, and a river tae cross. And *someone* ensured we left near-on an hour after schedule."

Gordon chuckled. "Not my fault Bell needed cutting down to size."

"Only glad ye didnae use yer claws," Cailean said.

Gordon grinned from just beyond the firelight. "If only."

By dark, sleeping spots were claimed and lines were drawn. Everyone slept in shifts: Gordon took first, along with Nora and Hodges; Dunne, Kelsie, Neil, and Wil took second; Bell, Alastair, Cailean, and Fionn, third. Llowry posted up by the road to keep an eye on the AUVs, and Vern pretended he was minding the radio instead of dozing off.

The night filtered on, and Tanit emerged to hide behind the clouds. Soon, the area proved its name as a fog descended from the surrounding mountains and collected in the canyon like smoke in a fireplace, turning the air damp and soaking his hair.

Bell kept looking at him during shift change. Small glances, paired with frustrated grunts. When he'd gone, Wil made sure to double check his pack and his canteen. Nothing strange, but he picked up and moved his sleep area anyways. After picking at the cold remnants of Neil's abhorrent 'shakshouka,' he took off his visor and lay near the fire.

⇡⇡

He woke to a pain in his arm.

Llowry knelt over him, combat knife in hand. "Don't move."

Wil startled. A loop of paracord lassoed his body, pinning his arms to his sides. His right sleeve had been rolled to the elbow, and blood beaded on his forearm. "Hijo de pu—!"

A gloved hand muffled him from behind. Llowry pressed the flat of his blade to Wil's skin. Nerves like overtuned guitar strings, Wil struggled. No use. The hand clamped tighter until he settled enough for Llowry to swipe the blade with blood.

It was nearly dawn. Fog slithered through the boughs above, and the sky burned violet out in the east. The fire clawed at the last dry branches fed into the dirt pit. In its shadows, Fionn stood ready, claymore in both hands. Vern and Kelsie lingered beside him, pistols raised. No smiles, just fear and resignation. Everyone's arms were looped with white bandage in the same place Wil had just been nicked.

Nora slinked into the firelight, her paramedic bag held high like a shield. "Is it safe?"

"We'll find out," Llowry said and plunged the bloody blade into the camp-fire.

Nothing happened.

Everyone released a collectively held breath. Nora drew a cross on her shirt and muttered a thank-you toward the mountaintops and the morning's first light.

The hand muffling Wil's mouth fell away. With a curse, Neil stood up from behind him, unfolded two paper bills, and traded them to Fionn. "So much fer gut feelings."

"Tapadh leat," Fionn said and stuffed them in his shirt.

Wil glared from face to face, confusion exploding into indignation. "Can someone *please* tell me what's going on?"

"Calm down, we had to check," Llowry said. He held up the knife, blood burnt on the steel. "Proof you're not a Shasvastii. Figured if anyone was, it'd be you."

"Wait, what?" he blurted. "How's the—how's burning a knife prove—?"

Nora hunkered beside Wil with her kit and got to work patching the hole in his arm. "Cailean told us how the Shasvastii replace you. How their assassins go so deep, even they don't ken they're the copy. Speculo Killers, he called 'em? And then Llowry—"

"You burn the blood, to see if it screams," Llowry said. "That's how you can tell. My da saw it in a movie, once."

"So everyone's been doing it," Nora said and picked at her bandage. "To make sure."

Their method was bullshit. The only way to unmask a Speculo for certain was to either inspect their blood under a quantronic microscope or cut off a digit and watch to see if the dismembered bit festered back to slug-skin gray.

He stammered. Opened his mouth. Shut it.

It wasn't that Wil didn't know what to say. He just didn't know if he wanted to tell them the truth before they untied him.

†††

Alastair eyed the bandage on Wil's arm. "Strange. I swear Vern had an injury there too."

He tugged his sleeve down over it. "Huh. Weird."

The camp was broken down before sunrise, sandbags stacked back inside the AUVs along with their gear. With how efficiently Hodges and Dunne hid their trail, the fire may as well have evaporated with the fog. Besides the necessary waste buried out in the woods, no trace of their presence remained.

"You're with the Volunteers again," Alastair said, inventorying the day's assignments on his link bracelet's projected holoscreen. "Any complaints?"

"None," he said. "We're getting along great, sir. Trading career advice, sharing recipes."

Alastair pursed his lips. "That bad, huh?"

Neil jogged up, pack over his shoulder. He clapped Wil on the back and carried on without breaking pace. "I see you, PanO, askin' after the management. One day outside the wire and yer already actin' up?"

Wil slipped off his visor to glare at Neil face-to-face. "And then there's this motherfucker."

"On your trolley, tin can," Neil said. "I'm countin' the minutes."

Wil thumped his chest. "Métetelo en el culo, pajero. Feeling's mutual."

Neil sneered, walking backward, and threw a V-sign at him knuckle-first. Wil fired back with his right middle finger and let the Strela swing to his hip to draw the left, too.

Killing a cigarette, Cailean caught the exchange. "Oi, PanO. Don't forget I still got a cartridge with yer name on it."

Wil considered turning the birds on the old man, but holstered them instead. "Acknowledged."

Alastair glanced from Neil to Wil and back, unamused. "Let's keep the hostility at a minimum, please. And try not to use hand signs in camp? Someone, or some*thing*, might confuse it for a salute."

"Apologies, sir." Wil nodded toward the brush. "I got time to piss?"

"Two minutes," Alastair warned. "Stay close."

A few meters out from camp, everything was white-barked trees, dead grass and dirt. Maze-like, almost. He stopped at a fat boulder swamped in moss and almost unzipped until he heard Nora and Kelsie passing by, jawing about Candy Double and her 'candied doubles.' Farther, then, past a copse of vine-choked stumps and into the multiplying trees. Ahead, the ground curved, declining into an overgrown grotto below.

Far enough. Easy to imagine an Antipode scrabbling up the rocky hillside. Didn't want to chance it. Wil undid his belt—and a shift in the air urged him to check his six.

Bell clambered over the boulder, Glengarry in hand. The edges of the purple splotch across his face had begun to line with yellow, and though his shoulders were slack and head lowered in shame, Wil immediately clocked the pistol on his hip and the chain rifle hanging from his shoulder. He didn't slow until they were about four meters apart.

"I need tae talk to you. About what Nora said to Alastair."

Wil wanted to zip up but didn't have the luxury of distraction. His ear itched, but he held his hand near his holster. "No. You don't."

Bell took a step closer. "You gotta tell her, take it back."

He didn't chance looking away. Edged until his footing was almost diagonal. "Fuck off, man."

"Mate, please," he begged. "I'm sorry about the 'runner' thing, alright? Have mercy! I cannae go to space, I amn't a Nomad, mate, I don't belong up there. I belong on solid ground with my family, not in low orbit with a Bearpode up my arse."

"Sorry you got caught," Wil offered.

His beady eyes narrowed. "It's your fault, ken. You coulda explained things better. We woulda listened. But you had to spill that tea."

Wil kept in side profile, forcing relaxation. Subtly, slowly, he shifted his coat to undo the clasp over the Detour. "The guys y'all sent at the Croatoan were gonna kill me."

"I'm sorry," he griped and surged forward. "Please, mate, I'm heavy fu-!"

Behind Bell, something cracked into the dirt.

He crumpled to the grass.

Dead.

22

Wil hurled himself onto his belly beside Bell's still body before he could think. Two thumps soaked into Bell's ribs and a third sheared his tweaked nose, coating Wil's sleeve in a splash of discolored cartilage.

No reports, no muzzle flares. Just the rip of air, heralding the impacts. High-tech suppressors.

Shasvastii.

He crawled into a run and beelined for the boulders. Puffs of turf on the forest floor corralled him, forced him behind a tree. His shoulders coated in bark chips. Needed harder cover.

Rifle off his shoulder. Safety off. Loaded. He tied his belt in a knot and reclipped his holster. Wil spun up his comlog, and static roared back. Had he left Vern's repeater range, or was this a hacker running Oblivion on him? No way to tell.

Wil checked around cover. Couldn't establish a visual.

No time to hesitate. Seconds to act, and he needed help. A shout would draw attention but wasn't urgent enough. Didn't want to chance luring someone into the crossfire. Had to make his situation crystal clear.

Wil leaned out and drilled three shots into a tree.

An instant later, the trunk beside his neck exploded. He skittered back, impact throbbing past the layers of his armor. Bad guess, but the report would bring the MacArthurs running, and he'd learned something besides: By the angle of the shot, the shooter was shifting position, using the hill as natural cover. Forcing him to turn. Opening his flank. All signs pointed to a partner, waiting in the wings for an opportunity to present itself. If Wil didn't want to find out what happened at the end of the rodeo, he'd need to risk his neck and buck the lasso.

First, distance and cover. He launched to his feet and bolted, aiming for the buried boulder he'd climbed on his approach. Silent puffs of moss and dust trailed him but didn't strike home, and he scrabbled into better cover. Knelt behind the granite with safety on one side, he could respond, turn the fight—

A shockwave from behind sent the leaves crazy-dancing. An explosion at camp. The morning silence shattered as shouts became screams, drowned out by concentrated gunfire.

They'd been caught in an ambush.

No help was on the way. No plan from here. No use saving battery on his MSV. Wil spun up his dial, confirmed settings, and the world smeared into infra-red, shapeless save for a single bluegreen silhouette crouched atop the bough of an Ariadnan fir a hundred meters out.

He knew that grim reaper getup anywhere—Noctifer. Shit. Spitfire. *Shit.*

But that wasn't where the shots had been coming from.

A humanoid shape ascended the hillside, barely visible in its purple hue compared to the surrounding technicolor wilderness. TO Camo—thermo-optical, heat-shedding, designed to render multispectral technology useless. By the bucket shape of the helm, a Malignos. Legendarily undetectable. Nightmarishly untouch-able. Its long coat fluttered, rifle primed, and it opened fire.

Wil ducked back. Muted gunfire drilled the stone. Suppressing fire from the Spitfire above swept centimeters above his scalp, keeping him pinned. Their footsteps made no sound, but Wil knew the Malignos was growing closer, closer—

A red-white shape hurdled the bushes into the clearing. Neil, with his chain rifle in both hands. He staggered to a stop, transfixed by the blur that stood over his dead friend's body.

An impact caught the kid center mass. With a flash and a spark, Neil top-pled face-first into the dirt.

Wil dropped the Strela. Lunged out. Gloved fingers found Neil's backpack strap, and he dragged him two-handed into cover.

But before they were totally clear, Neil sucked in a ragged breath and belted a litany of vulgarities so thick, so impossible to understand, it must've been what made him bulletproof. He lurched to a stand, leveraged his chain rifle over the edge of cover, and screamed, "Gie off my friend, ye bloody knock-kneed *in-vertebrate cunt!*"

The Malignos jolted back, chittering, and the crack-flash of the chain rifle swallowed it whole. Sizzling white-hot shrapnel embedded in the dirt, the trees, the hundred pureed chunks of flickering thermo-optical camouflage that'd just been a Shasvastii.

Flank clear, Wil vaulted the boulder and zeroed in on the infrared blob of the Noctifer. Deep breath. Slow and steady. Aim over speed. A Spitfire tracer sliced the fantail of his duster, scant centimeters from his thigh, and only then did he pull the trigger.

Two rounds hit the tree; one disappeared. Gore drained onto the bough below. The Noctifer wobbled, but it refused to die.

Instead, Wil's visor did.

The heavy crack of a large-caliber weapon sent Wil to his knees behind the stone. He wrenched the visor from his face, squinting for the telltale signs of camouflage—pressure, motion, distortion. But the Noctifer was gone. The tree branch was empty.

He scanned the tree, the woods, pulse hammering into overdrive. "Neil! Where'd it go, did it jump?"

Neil panted, keeled against the boulder, and pointed. Blurry air heaped at the foot of the tree, purple blood pooling atop an invisible mound.

"Who—"

Boots crashed through the underbrush, chasing a whirl of sunfire hair. Saoirse sprinted out from the thicket, Mk12 in hand, backpack jumping on her shoulders.

Whatever feelings Wil might've had about her appearance were erased under a second percussive boom from the direction of camp. He vaulted from the boulder and helped Neil into a lean.

Saoirse shoved past without recognition, and her pat-down grew more and more frantic. "Were ye hit, Neilan? What happened, why'd ye fall? Answer me, right now!"

Neil ground his fist against his chest, and only now seemed to realize who was in front of him. "What're you doin' here, are you mad?"

"Savin' you," she spat and located the hole in the center of his flak. She traced it, brow furrowed, until she fished up his jingling dog tags.

Teseum, same as hers and Alastair's. The twin tags had been dented into an interlocked dome, and on Neil's sternum, his full name and DOB laid stamped into his skin. Blood dotted in the base of each bruised letter and number.

The Noctifer's bullet had hit his dog tags and ricocheted.

"Pit air iteag," Neil rasped and glanced skyward. "Thanks, da."

Saoirse thumped him in the arm. "Idiot."

Neil gawked. "The hell's—"

Another boom. More gunfire.

Saoirse turned toward camp and picked up speed. "Go," she shouted. "Now!"

Wil propped Neil on his shoulder, but the kid pushed away and staggered on without help. Mid-rise, Neil fixated on Bell. Grimaced. Cursed again, and charged after her.

Together, the three of them sprinted back to camp, vaulting stones and crashing through the underbrush. Smoke slithered among the trees in tight, circular clouds, cutting visibility almost to nil. Where the MacArthur task force had been finishing final prep for the drive to the DRC was now honeycombed with smoking craters.

A shadow burst from the haze ahead, at a dead sprint aimed for the nearest AUV. Llowry. Right as he tumbled into cover behind a wheel well, a small, black streak arced between his feet with an uneventful whump.

Flash. Crack. Llowry disappeared in a column of dirt. Against all reason, Wil slowed to stare, hoping to see the Volunteer lope from the cloud with a flesh wound.

When the smoke cleared, what he saw was much worse.

A near-miss put a buzz in Wil's teeth. He startled after Neil and fell into cover behind a fallen log. Cailean crouched there with Rhiannon in his lap, craggy face flecked with dirt. Behind him, Kelsie covered Vern with her body, shattered comms tech pooled around his feet. Nora balled up around her rifle at their feet, small and pale and terrified.

A hundred meters out, a smattering of violet lights radiated malice from the high ground of last night's campsite. Judging by the glow, alien MSV. A sniper's nest. The bugs had stolen their defensive position and turned it back on them.

"Haiduks," Cailean advised. "Keep yer heads down."

Wil turned over, shoulders against the log. "Guess who I found."

Saoirse crawled into cover behind a granite slab a meter from their log. "Hiya, Cailean. So this's gone tits up."

Cailean frowned and stretched a fresh belt of H-12 from his ammo pack into Rhiannon's feed tray. "Saoirse Clarke, provin' again yer ears are decoration. Alastair will not be pleased."

Just seeing Saoirse put a dose of bravery in Nora. She crawled up onto her elbows and watched the brush, expectant, but when no one else joined them, her face fell again. "Where's Bell?"

Wil wrenched his visor free and mashed the manual reset once, twice. The blue oculars sputtered back to light. "Someone hack comms? No one's answering."

"No hack," Kelsie said. "Vern got shot. He's uninjured, but our repeater's KIA. So's comms."

He growled, frustrated. "Where's—"

"Bell," Nora blurted. "Bell was right behind you, where'd he—"

"Bell's dead," Neil told her, and she went shock-white and still.

The crags of Cailean's face deepened. "Al and Dunne pressed up. Gordon and Hodges hooked north. Saoirse, Wil—secure the roadway and our exit. We'll join ye, push up outta this tae better ground. Wait fer my signal, and I'll cover you. Copy?"

Visor, on. The infrared was still running—good—but now the display was flashing Low Power again. He'd risk it. Going back to analog wasn't an option, not with this much hostile TO Camo. "Understood."

"Heard," Saoirse barked, and blind fired toward the ridge.

Kelsie flashed hand signals to the other Volunteers, ones Wil recognized. Two fingers and thumb held out, a point toward the smoke clouds. She waved her hand in front of her eyes. *Three. Cover. MSV.*

"Two, now that Alastair's killed one," Cailean replied. "Spot for me."

She blinked. "When did he—"

Cailean yanked the pins on two smoke grenades and planted them at his feet, dousing their feeble cover in a heavy cloud of acrid campfire. Hefting Rhiannon, he stood into oncoming fire.

Two reports. The log splintered. Sawdust flaked into Wil's hair.

Kelsie shouted, "Ridge, left side!" and Neil followed up with, "Two meters above!"

Cailean traced the rounds through the undulation of gray, triangulating his shots, each bullet pounding out the steady bassline of Rhiannon's song. When his heavy machine gun went silent, something trilled over the ridge—deeply alien, and undeniably wounded. "That one's for our lads, ye bug-eyed wank—!"

Two double-action rounds thumped into his breastplate.

The old man spun, off balance, but didn't fall. Didn't go for cover like a sane man would. Instead, Cailean howled like a demon and repaid the quadruple-tap tenfold, burning H-12 into the zero-vis. Up on the ridge, both MSV glows thrashed and fell out of sight.

A shadow materialized inches from their flank. It closed on their position, but before Wil could raise his Strela, it'd already met the end of Cailean's claymore. He drove it to the earth, sweeping Rhiannon across the battlefield.

"Now!" he barked. "Goan, ye weapons, now!"

Saoirse crested her cover and charged. Wil trailed behind, covering her advance. They dashed into the clearing, past the burning AUV, out into the road where smoke grenades twirled on the damp black earth. Vision cut to null. Wil swiped on the comlog screen, activating infrared. In a flash, the world painted over the billow in polychromatic swirls.

One by one, three Shasvastii shapes leaned out to stall them. Saoirse dropped the first with one burst, and Wil nailed the second with a lucky headshot. The third survived to duck back behind a boulder, stalling their rush.

Before they could muster a pincer, a terrible screaming closed on them. Wil braced for impact, but it was Fionnlagh, weapon high, locked in a downhill charge toward the third shadow. His silhouette splashed into the surviving Shas, split apart, intermingled again, and then only Fionnlagh remained. Belting a battle cry—"Buaidh no bàs!"—the Highlander hefted his claymore and streaked back into the brush.

"Ta, Fionnlagh!" Saoirse called. "'Mon, Wil! Keep up!"

Ahead, fire bled white through the infrared, eating up what remained of the second AUV. If he read the signs right, the cause of death was D-charges in the undercarriage—localized demolition charges used by saboteurs and guerilla soldiers across the Human Sphere, designed specifically to obliterate what they were attached to without collateral damage.

"Imagine if ye'd left camp early," Saoirse said, exposed skin practically glowing under his infrared filter. "Tick, tick, boom, and none would be the wiser."

Wil picked around the conflagration, watching for hostiles. "Still trying to figure out how you got here."

"Eideard needed someone tae run the horses back to Odhran's Ford," she said. "Locals said I missed ye by a few hours. Strange smell on the air. Didnae sit right, so I kept on. Kent ye'd camp here—only place safe enough."

The unique chatter of a Molotok at full-auto rattled in the din. The wreckage of an M-Drone lay askew on the roadside, its alien chassis spattered with baseball-sized bullet holes.

"And the horse?" Wil asked.

"Told the mare tae git, but—"

A shrill, strange cry. High-pitched, but from something massive. Labored, heavy breaths drew closer until an enormous, infrared shape lumbered into view, swaying on six legs.

Wil yanked his visor up to get an ID. Not a monster or an alien, but one of the horses from Odhran's Ford, sable fur ran wild with blood.

A humanoid shape braced against its flank. Digitigrade. Alien. Blade-lined hooks dashed along its back, jaw lined with an armored bevor. A Shasvastii Caliban. Its arm was plugged up to the elbow beneath the mare's ribs, bulging the flesh from within. Its mandibles clenched tight against a gurgling slice in its throat.

It gulped.

The horse lowed pitifully, skin crinkling like paper as its ribs surfaced across the svelte expanse of its belly. Its eyes shriveled and its legs buckled as it fell. The Caliban let gravity rip its clawed fist from the horse's side, gauntlet roped with viscera. Its armor creaked, and its body swelled until its gangly physique had thickened to that of a Morat. Blood smeared its chest from the gaps in its iron jaw, and a short blade filled its hand.

Protheion. A bio-genetic enhancement designed to siphon organic matter and repurpose it into physical enhancement: strength, speed, regeneration. Wil had seen it on Paradiso—not in person, but on the security footage left behind after an Umbra Samaritan's death waltz through an entire platoon of heavy infantry.

He discarded his fear and opened fire. Swollen as it was, the Caliban moved hummingbird fast. Nothing hit, and then it was on him. Its blade streaked toward his face.

Saoirse intercepted the Caliban's swing, driving her claymore up over her head. Both weapons screamed in the clash. Steel flashed, weapons blurred. Driven back, it chirped in frustration. Saoirse refused to grant even the slightest escape hatch. Every parry she forced left a trench in her opponent's blade; every dodge sapped its momentum. Despite its bulk, the Caliban lost ground.

Wil aimed, but shooting into CQC without a geist and a Spotlight was too risky. He'd only be a liability in close combat. And one Shasvastii vampire wouldn't stand a chance against Saoirse without reinforcements. So he planted himself beside the last surviving AUV and covered her. He'd be ready when they arrived.

When the next parry landed, the Caliban went to wrench the blade from her grip with its own notched weapon. She kicked it back, changed grip to preempt a second disarm, and lunged in for a stab. It shadowed her motion, faster than her. Ballistic fabric frayed in a line along Saoirse's armored midriff, slash fast enough to be invisible. Her strike whiffed, but the Caliban lagged, showing his blind spot, openly baiting—

Saoirse ducked the feint and anticipated the true counter with a hard right cross. The Caliban staggered, and she snatched its mandible and yanked. Gore spewed from the gaps in its jawplate as she wrangled it by the face and lashed its back with her blade.

Metallic spines clattered to the road below. Thick, meaty slices in its armor welled with violet. It groped for her chest to steady itself, and Saoirse jolted off her feet to avoid its empty hand.

Not empty. A D-charge blinked in its grip.

Using explosives in CQC wasn't novel, but it betrayed the Caliban's desperation. For a TAG, D-charges meant a crippled limb, shredding the toughest armor without difficulty. Versus flesh? If it'd anchored on Saoirse, she'd have been reduced to a flower-petal scatter of blood and bone after three sharp beeps.

Two red shapes lunged over the wrecked AUV, digitigrade and loping. Ikadron Batdroids—techno-organic drone soldiers, each of their arms tipped with an underslung flamethrower. Wil traced their trajectory, rushing to reinforce their master, and emptied his magazine to ensure they didn't.

Saoirse rolled to her feet. Her grin was thanks enough.

In a frenzy, the Caliban ripped its own dangling mandible free. It hunkered low and speared toward her, faster than before. Desperate. She poked, feinted, led its wounded side, retreated from its barrage until she saw her moment and bunted its lead-in with the quillon of her claymore.

The Caliban's forearm snapped. Pain stalled it just long enough for Saoirse to stomp onto its two-toed foot and put her weight into her swing. Its hips hit the asphalt before its torso sailed into the brush. Electronic chirps muffled in the dirt until the D-charge detonated, launching a column of gravel and a reverberation through Wil's chest.

Wiping purple specks from her face, Saoirse rushed to her horse's side. Its chest had stopped rising; blood no longer pumped from its wounds. She reached out to touch but stopped short, curling her caress into a furious clench.

Wil laid her discarded Mk12 beside her. "I'm so sorry."

"These fuckers," she whispered. "Do they regenerate?"

"Don't know," he said, eying the Caliban's two distinct halves. "Unlikely."

She inhaled sharply. "Hope it does. I'd like tae kill 'em again."

Just as he touched her shoulder, Fionnlagh crashed from the brush into the road. Claymore high, uniform soaked in violet blood, he pitched a smoke grenade, screamed "*Air adhart!*" and sprinted into the plume.

Wil left Saoirse behind and dashed after him.

Beyond the haze, a wide boreal field stretched before him, littered with old stone and carpeted in moss. Clouds hung impaled upon the faraway mountaintops. Wil slid into cover behind the nearest boulder and took stock of the vacant roadway.

Fionnlagh came to a stop. He planted his claymore into the dirt and screamed until his echo joined him. When it faded, there was no sound on the highlands save for the far-away burning of the AUVs and the wind across the stones.

Wil donned his visor again just in time for it to sputter an illegible warning and die. He hung it on his belt by the frame, sweat icing his armpits and back without motion. Reloaded—no, he'd already reloaded. When had he reloaded? Dull pressure pulsed inside his shoulder, and he probed it with his fingers.

They came up damp.

He yanked open his uniform, terrified his adrenaline had hidden a gunshot wound in the chaos. But there was no more blood. No hurt, other than the throb that waxed as his fear waned. A tear in the collar of his flak jacket led to an alien bullet rolling around inside the fabric.

Mierda. The blood was Bell's.

Hodges stepped into sight through the fading smoke, shotgun slung over both shoulders. "Oi! PanO! What're you doing?"

Wil paused. Glanced around.

He wasn't sure.

23

Bell laid out in the middle of things, draped in a wet-weather bag.

Neil sat beside him, chain rifle laid over his lap. When the wind blew, it lifted the corner of Bell's shroud, revealing a pale ear. So the kid held it down with the tip of his boot.

Nora sped by with hyposprays and autoinjectors in her little hands and gasped at the red streaks painting Wil's flak, but when he told her it was Bell's blood, he hated the way her eyes lost their light. Cailean stalked the battlefield, listing the dead Shasvastii's ISC—Nox, Haiduk, Noctifer, Caliban—somehow disappointed none were Jayth, or missing limbs, all while Hodges chopped their heads off with his handaxe and stuck his knife up inside their guts to spike their spawn embryos or whatever counted for a gut on a Shasvastii and their entrails were the same color as the dead fish that washed up on the lagoon shore after the artillery barrage back on Paradiso, white and caked with slime. And despite feeling like he'd been cracked in the neck by a baseball bat, pain wasn't pain, and Wil took a long deep breath and unclenched his fists and tried to hear the million different things that everyone kept saying over each other like the radio towers that dotted the Caledonian Highlands all singing in frequencies no one would ever listen to again.

Fionn sat beside him and held out a thermos lid filled with whisky. Wil drank, and the burn helped him turn back into a person.

Vern sifted through his backpack, removing hunks of broken plastic and circuit board. With consternation, he located the hole punched into the side of his repeater node. He tried the switch—no dice—and retrieved the old-world dual-channel comms box from below it. One side sported a spate of blunted ballistic particulate. When the switch flipped, the box hummed, and all the air in Vern came out of him in one depressing wave.

"Wonderful," he said. "Welcome to the 21st century, lads."

Wil didn't need him to explain. Without the specialized repeater node to manage long-distance connections, comms were limited to local devices only. No Arachne meant no calling home, meant no calling for support, meant the mission was well and truly over.

Kelsie paused on her way by and pointed at Vern's arm. "Got some red there, Vernard."

He touched his upper arm above the elbow. The fabric had torn, and a shallow wound lingered underneath. Vern whistled. "Think I got grazed?"

Cailean strode by and paused for a moment to consider Bell's still shape beneath the makeshift shroud. Shoulders slack, he drew a cross over his chest. Said something soft about a stone and a cairn, something in Caledonia that seemed like an apology. And when he turned away, the reverence washed from his face, replaced by stiff professionalism.

He passed Wil and thumped his shoulder. "Good work, lad. Gettin' used tae it without the ALEPH?"

Wil managed a thumbs-up, or something close enough. He still didn't feel like he was piloting his own body yet. "Yeah."

"If ye need my knife fer tallies," Cailean offered and carried on toward Dunne and Alastair. Their conversation was reaching a pitch, so Wil got up and followed after. Might as well learn how screwed they were now.

Dunne paced in frustrated circles, shoulders hunched. She had a few bullet holes in her poncho and a scrape up her arm but was otherwise unharmed. "They knew where we were," she said. "They planted charges. Laid mines. Waited. How'd they know where we were?"

Alastair sat on the burned-out hood of the lead AUV. His armor had been scored with shallow dents, and a purple-gold burn had climbed up the muzzle of his chain-colt. "Unsure," he said.

"We'll be ready next time," Saoirse said and stood beside her brother.

Alastair gave her a long, hard look, blue eyes colder than the mountaintops. Disapproval melted into frustration, into begrudging acknowledgment. "I clearly requested you stay home."

She smirked. "Bet yer glad I didn't."

"That's how!" Dunne said. "They must've followed her."

Saoirse's nose wrinkled. "Hate tae break yer bubble, hen, but I got here after the shooting started."

"So they spaed your route, or hacked your comlog, or—"

"It could be navbots," Wil said. "Dun Scaith sends out automated reconnaissance on the daily to run the AEZ border for orographic data. They're plated with thermo-optical camouflage, silencers, radar shielding. They could've been watching Kildalton—doesn't necessarily mean what you're implying."

"Muriel knows what a navbot is," Hodges said, coming up from behind. He stowed his handaxe on his hip and stuffed a purple-smeared handkerchief into his bag. "She's Atek, not An-idiot, like you."

Dunne scowled. "Robert. Now's *not* the time."

Hodges shrugged, drew his pistol, and counted the rounds in his mag. Gordon approached too, then Neil, and everyone else magnetized over little by little until the entire group crowded in a circle around Alastair.

The Volunteers' faces were awash with concern. Fionn ambled through the group, offering his thermos and words of encouragement to each in turn. When he stopped at Nora's side for longer than the others, it didn't mean good things.

"We're not compromised," Alastair said firmly, and stood. "Only Eideard, Cailean, and I were aware of our route before we left Kildalton. If they had intel we were coming here ahead of time, they would've ambushed us in our sleep. They had the MSV for it."

"You think they're playing catch-up," Wil said.

"Precisely. They arrived as we were leaving, saw an opportunity, and rushed into position." Alastair dropped his hand. "Seems you were right after all, Lieutenant. I'm sorry for not taking you seriously."

He shrugged. "Didn't want to be."

Gordon lumbered up, shirtless, enormous frame riddled with defensive wounds from the aliens he'd shredded. Patches of oily purple shimmered atop his coat. "They were all over, trying to do everything at once. Ended up doing fuck all. Didn't exactly live up to the stories."

"Glad I amn't alone in noticing," Saoirse said. "Only ten, and nothin' flashy? Wil's story had me fearing a missile, or a TAG—if the Shas got TAGs, knock on wood."

Cailean exhaled a single, bitter laugh. He held his pauldron atop one knee, scratching a trio of crosses into the azure paint with the tip of his combat knife. "Oh, they do. Sphinx is a helluva thing. Let's no speak it intae existence."

"Sure." Saoirse rapped her knuckles thrice against the scorched AUV hood. "But they felt rusty, aye?"

He paused. Chewed on his lip. "Aye."

"Two casualties in one ambush," Hodges said. "Direct contact with alien resistance. Fine end to a fine operation, if you ask me. Which way's home?"

"We're not done," Alastair said. "They won't give up while we have what they want."

Everyone turned to regard Wil for a few ugly seconds. Some gazes lingered less affably than others.

Dunne crossed her arms. "Sure they're not in it for you, sir? You're clan chieftain."

"Those D-charges weren't stuck on at random," Alastair said. "Look at the interiors and how little we've lost from our supplies despite the fires. I trained in demolitions in Scone—I know precision when I see it. Those explosives were meant first and foremost to scuttle our engines."

"Idiots," Neil said. "Coulda blown us sky high instead if they'd had some patience."

Kelsie elbowed him. "That's what he's saying. Why didn't they?"

Neil grimaced. "The hell should I know?"

"Why didn't they shoot Vern, instead of putting one through his backpack?" Alastair asked, carrying Kelsie's implication forward. "Why focus on removing our transportation over massacring us? Because they wanted to kill

Gotzinger, and *just* Gotzinger. When that failed, their primary objective became preventing our mission from continuing, and only then did they go weapons hot."

"Well they bloody succeeded," Hodges sighed. "Can't do much now—"

"We're continuing on," Alastair said.

Hodges plodded back a step, dumbfounded. "Sir, wait. You can't seriously be considering Charlie Miking this. No transportation, no comms, no food—no back up. Couldn't we mail a bloody picture to the PanOs and be done with it?"

"Good luck uploading that without a stable connection," Vern said. "If we wanted to attempt a reconnect, we'd need to hike back to Kildalton, and even then, there's no guarantee our relays are up. And assuming it was, the chance we'd catch the attention of PanOceania in an official capacity using a network they're explicitly not allowed to connect to...."

Hodges stabbed his finger at Wil. "Then plug in the galactic's Cube and have him do it."

Vern's eyebrows bobbed up behind his brown bangs. "Cubes don't have quantronic connections by design, sir. Do you mean I should give him a new com-log, like the ones I just said can't connect long-distance?"

"Yes, exactly that, you *glorified deployable repeater—*"

"Stop it," Nora cried, rifle cradled in her arms. "Stop! Stop arguing! I don't want to hear it anymore. Bell died, and—and Llowry is—"

Llowry's grenade launcher sat alone where he'd forgotten it by the fire. He'd thought it was in the AUV and hadn't lived long enough to realize his mistake. There hadn't been enough pieces left to put under a sheet, much less into a bucket.

A chill wind swept through the clearing, rustling the dead foliage and tugging at the corners of the wet-weather bag across Bell's lifeless body. This time, Fionnlagh kept it down.

Gordon broke the quiet with a judgmental grunt. "Funny. Didn't see you durin' the fight, Hodges. And now you're ready to cut and run."

Hodges glowered up at Gordon, scrappy as a rat against a reptilo drake. "Are you wanting me to fetch the Seed-Soldier that tried to check my prostate with a Panzerfaust? At least I'm not Wilhelm-fucking-Wallace over there."

"Enough," Alastair said.

Confusion overrode any offense Wil might've taken. "Wilhelm *what?* Fionn was right beside me, where's his pithy nickname?"

"My battle-brother's none of your concern, galactic," Hodges said. "I've seen your video, watched you run off to hide when you thought no one was looking. You belong on a firing line, mate, not on the frontline, and definitely not beside us."

"Oh, don't start," Neil growled. "He zeroed five of the bastards. What'd you do?"

Hodges spat into the grass. "Piss off, ned."

"I said, *enough*," Alastair said, louder.

Saoirse held Neil back by the shoulder. "Jesus Christ, Robert, stop. Neil's not yer punchin' bag, and Wil's not tae blame here."

Hodges crossed his arms. "Maybe you are, killing that goddamn horse."

Kelsie gasped. Saoirse recoiled like she'd been slapped. When she surged forward, fists balled, Gordon roped her back. Fionn slipped between them, holding them both at bay with practiced disinterest. Everyone started shouting at once, except for Nora, who slid to her knees and clung to her rifle.

Cailean unlimbered his pistol and fired twice into a tree.

The fight died as quick as it started. Silence reigned. Saoirse shrugged off Gordon, though Fionn stayed planted, appreciating the echo that traveled up the mountains.

"Yer chieftain's tryna talk," Cailean said. "So, whisht. Next person tae speak outta turn kisses the Teseum."

Alastair stepped forward, jaw set. "Listen, please. I understand that emotions are high right now. Swallow them. We're continuing to Dun Scaith."

Hodges sheathed his handaxe, lips pursed in silent fury. Neil didn't seem so keen on it, either. Dunne's disapproval was silent, severe, and after a fleeting moment, disappeared from her face.

Gordon straightened out, haunted eyes glowing in the daylight. He stepped forward, silent, challenging. After a few seconds, Cailean begrudgingly ceded him the floor.

"I want to hear your reason," Gordon said. "I deserve that much."

The wind picked up again, providing a momentary respite from the acrid stench of melted rubber and scorched steel. The shroud over Bell's still form wafted, but Kelsie kept it in place with her foot.

"Alright," Alastair said, and his armor clunked together at the joints when he paced. "They want Gotzinger. Sure, we could give him to them. But that won't take them off the planet. It doesn't take their spies out of Achadh nan Darach, or make the Shasvastii our allies. We could run and hide in Kildalton, valor be damned, but we've seen them, killed them, and they won't let us survive that insult.

"And the truth is, this isn't our fight. But it *is* our planet—our Dawn—and our dead friends, our family. And I won't sit idly by and watch yet another army from yet another distant solar system make a beachhead in my father's highlands, the one our ancestors bled for all the way back to Ceilidh MacArthur, to Róisín Kicklighter, the same one Sebastian Bell and Domhnall Llowry died for. Our choice is not *if* we answer, but *how*."

Alastair leveled his arm toward the east. "As it stands, we're going to face these trespassers someday. The conflict is inevitable. We can do it now when they're playing catch-up, like Gotzinger said, or when they're good and ready for us. Between the hunter and the hunted, I know what I choose."

Hodges glanced at Saoirse. He held out his fist, and she knocked her gauntlet against it—an apology. By Hodges' wince, she'd sprained a knuckle, but he checked any complaints and finally mustered the temerity to shut the fuck up.

Jaw set, Neil picked up Llowry's grenade launcher. A third dog tag hung around his neck now, its sheen duller than the others. Bell's. Cailean gripped him by the shoulder with a reassuring shake.

"Dawn is Ours," Gordon said, tail swishing his kilt.

Alastair raised his fist. "Let's show them why."

When he was done, the group had changed. Reticence wiped away, replaced with resilience; frustration and fear exchanged for determination. One by one, chain rifles and shotguns and claymores uplifted until even Nora had joined in, and when Cailean cried, "All or Nothing! Alba gu bràth!", eleven voices shouted back—out of unison, but louder than hell.

Kelsie nudged Wil with her elbow. "God's Perfect Idiot."

He blinked. "Me?"

"Fionn's nickname," she said and weighed the corner of Bell's shroud with a stone.

⚔⚔

Everyone bustled, gathering what they could from the ashes. Alastair stood amidst the chaos, raised voice clear above the commotion. "If we're up against thermo-optic drones, we'll need to be mindful of movement without cloud cover, and it goes without saying we'll be going by foot."

Wil considered correcting him—navbots weren't quite drones, weren't quite TO—but there'd be no point in it. If the rain kept up, infrared scanners would be scattered by the droplets and the fog would be even worse, rendering them invisible even out in the open.

Hodges politely lifted a finger. "I'm raising the possibility of returning to Kildalton to rearm, recruit, and set out again."

"Farther back than it is forward," Cailean said. "We arrive a day late, and the bugs'll have every gun and soldier on that ship ready for us."

Alastair searched the crowd. "Vern! What's the status on comms?"

"Outlook's not good," Vern said, emerging from the back of a burned-out AUV with an armful of toasted components. "With the long-distance repeater in bits, we're on our own. With what's left over, I can jury rig us a local cluster. But it'll be short range—a hundred-twenty meters, tops."

"Great," Hodges muttered.

Alastair ignored him. "Let's talk topography and route next. Dunne?"

"If'n ye don't mind, Muriel," Saoirse said, "I ken a route."

Dunne pursed her lips and unfolded her map. "Alright, Princess. Show me what you got."

Saoirse laid it out atop a boulder and traced a line with her claw, careful to not tear the paper. "When I run patrol, we take this route down the highway at Old Outpost 4, 'round the springs near the Hargreaves, and then tae Loch Eil via the M-828. Normally, we come back west up the ridge, but if we head east, it's a straight shot up the shore to the DRC."

"Shore's a bit open," Dunne said. "Got a detour in mind?"

"If we snake along the lowlands," Saoirse said, and mouthed out silent numbers as she did the math. "That's a hundred sixty-six kilometers. Detour enough?"

Dunne turned to Fionn, and asked, "Dè do bheachd?"

Fionnlagh considered it for a moment. "Sìmplidh agus sàbhailte. Is toil leam seo, a Mhuireall."

"If he likes it, I like it," Dunne said with a shrug.

"Nine whole days o' rough, huh." Neil whistled, soft and low. "Brings me back tae basic."

The pit in Wil's stomach yawned. "Nine? You sure?"

"Round abouts," Saoirse said. "Problem?"

"We don't have that long," Alastair said. "Any shortcuts?"

Cailean tapped on the map with his thumb. "Could skip the 828 and save a day climbing the fells near Fort Resolute. Ford the Burn of Amherst on foot. Thoughts?"

"Might see resistance," Saoirse said. "No tellin' what's there."

Gordon scraped flakes of dried gore from his axe. "Dead motherfuckers, still walking around."

Memories of the red-lit comms array tower at DRC-9 came back strong. "Our objective's on the north side," Wil said. "All we have to do is get close enough to piggyback their signal and broadcast an SOS. PanOceania will handle the rest."

"Won't be undefended," Dunne said. "Might need several attempts before we can connect without being spotlighted and done in by guided fire."

Kelsie crossed her arms. "Bottom of that hill's prob'ly mined so bad, dirt's like kitchen tile."

"Mines? Of course they got mines," Neil scoffed. "What's more galactic than killin' someone without lookin' at 'em?"

Wil wanted to disagree, but honestly—the kid had a point.

"Going through Fort Resolute could be advantageous, then," Hodges said. "The ruins would provide cover, set up a trajectory to scout the DRC, and open a route to the north without needing to skirt the loch. And there should be a supply cache nearby, maintained for situations exactly such as this."

Alastair scanned the group. "Any objections?"

"I don't mind climbing," Kelsie said. "I was born on a mountainside."

Vern smiled. "Same here."

"Two mountains in eight days," Neil said. "I can swing that."

Hodges glanced back to Wil. "Can he?"

"Tha e marbh, Rabbie." Fionn clapped Wil's shoulder and smiled sadly. "Marbh."

Wil blinked. "What's that mean?"

"You'll be fine," Saoirse said, and when she thought he wasn't looking, pulled a face.

The task force spent the next thirty minutes salvaging what they could from the AUVs and camp remains, and took stock of their bearings. Saoirse needed a place to write on the map, and Wil's back seemed like the easiest solution, given the bullet-struck nature of the sole surviving AUV.

Halfway through her sketch, Pellehan descended from the hillside, T2 Zyefir leaned against his shoulder. His trousers were slick with mud, and a ratty red beret rested challengingly atop his bald head.

When he saw Wil, his mood noticeably darkened. "God help me, I'll never get my hands on a multispectral visor."

"Sorry," Wil said. "Still mine."

"For now."

Saoirse glared. "Pell! The hell were ye, playin' bingo? Woulda loved a sniper in the thick of things."

"I was here," he said. "Zeroed the Nox fireteam leader twice, and their paramedic inbetween. What'd you do other than get surrounded and have the galactic save you?"

Her nose wrinkled. "Suck my dick."

As he passed, he swept his poncho back and dipped into a bow. "Thou art wise as thou art beautiful, Lady Clarke."

"Pound-shop Knauf on a good day, and you know it," she chirped back. "Keep walking, *Dullahan*."

He grinned. "Glad to have you with us, *Princess*."

The complex series of gestures she threw at him had him coughing on his cigarette all the way to Alastair. They met and stepped aside, speaking briskly in Caledonian.

Wil zoned it out until Saoirse's scribbles slowed to a scrawl, then stopped. He checked her over his shoulder. Saoirse's pointed ears had perked quite vertical, and her face was set in a toothy scowl.

"Honestly," she muttered. "Utter nark, he is."

Wil dropped his voice to match her whisper. "What'd he do?"

"Pell gave the all-clear… fer *you*. Seems his job was tae monitor our irregularity in the night. All combat, he kept his sights on *us*."

"To make sure we're not—"

"Shasvastii," she said and strummed the cowl of his ear. "Very clever."

Wil flustered. By the time he had words again, Saoirse had long finished her route and traipsed back to Alastair to present it.

He figured they were done, after the video. Apparently, she'd been biding her time. What he'd done to earn back her affection, he had no idea, but he was glad to have it.

And despite Saoirse's frustration, Alastair's plan wasn't a bad one—who watches the watchmen, and all that. But if Pell had been more concerned watching their flanks instead of their friendlies, then maybe Llowry and Bell…

No. Best to not tread that path. And even if he was, it'd been Alastair's orders, not Pell's decision. If he had a complaint, it needed to be with their CO.

Compared to the other officers he'd served under, Alastair was already exemplary for his age. Fusiliers always hesitated; Auxilia never led from the front; riding with the Neoterran Bolts was like playing pledge for a frat house; not to mention the Deva Functionaries, ALEPH liaisons from the Special Situations Section who only communicated in terse, nigh-cryptic decrees as if they were secretly elves or something.

Collectively, they were the reason he'd accepted the commission to The Aquila Officers' Academy in the first place: to be the CO that he'd wished he'd had on Paradiso, tossed into the grinder day-in, day-out while every civilian and official looked down on the Fusiliers like trash—as if they weren't dying every day to hold the line between civilization and total annihilation.

Plumbers of the Human Sphere, his mom had called them. Because if the Fusilier Corps all quit at once, the whole Human Sphere would've gone to shit.

Wil watched Alastair ask Nora what the minimum viable amount of Serum was in case of battlefield injury and asked how best he could enable her responsibilities; stay in constant communication with Cailean and Dunne to keep an angel and a devil on his shoulder; stop to share a drink with Fionn and get a mountaineer's perspective on their situation; and organize their scouts by mediating a sit-down between Saoirse and Hodges. He didn't rest, didn't hesitate, always knew exactly who needed him and where.

The kid really had a knack for it.

In the end, they left Bell and Llowry behind under a cascade of stones and set out across the Caledonian Highlands on foot.

24

If sprinting through Achadh nan Darach at midnight had been tough, the Highlands beyond were worse. The morning rain transmogrified into a slushy particulate, invisible as it froze together on the rocks. The wind picked up and refused to show mercy. Within a day, every single face in the task force had gone windburned and chapped, and with the frequent downpours, wet-weather bags were the sole reason their assault packs didn't soak and rot off their backs.

Before, Wil figured he missed his geist the most. No. What he missed the most was his ORC Combat Armor, and all the little ribbons that entailed: Magnetic clamps locked his guns and gear to his chassis; personal heating kept him from shivering so hard his teeth chipped; artificial muscle bore the brunt of long marches, leaving him pristine in the aftermath instead of gelatinized and crawling.

After the first rain, Nora discovered her poncho and woobie had been shot through during the firefight without her ever noticing. Gordon gave her his, and his kindness inspired Neil to needle his sister about her 'intentions wae the poor, young lad' all through their next rest.

Gordon grunted. "Just a cover, Neil. Come off it."

Neil squared with him. "If yer gonna be family, Gordo, ye'll need mind I tease my sister as I please."

"Whingey, bleach-blond bawbag."

"Furry-arsed lunatic."

They grinned and traded shoves until Cailean forced them apart. In the midst of the brief chaos, Wil caught Neil glancing for Bell between chirps. When the kid realized he wouldn't find him, all the youth sucked out of him and he didn't speak until the next morning.

One thing Wil hadn't expected was arguments over the weather. Kelsie called the drizzle *plowetery*, and Dunne corrected with a *dreich*, and now it was more tense than when Gordon had asked Hodges where he'd been. Someone said *pure Tartary*, and Vern burst out in condescending laughter.

Wil watched, bewildered. If he hadn't just seen these people slaughter an entire strike force of Shasvastii while suffering minimal casualties, he would've already written them off. They were career soldiers, sure, but no one important, no one special. Bumpkins with guns and gumption.

"Watergaw," Nora said, and pointed into the mist. A broken rainbow arched up from the valley, lost in the ocean of Caledonian gray.

The MacArthurs staggered their column five meters apart so that one errant blast or bullet wouldn't fell more than one of them. When it fogged, that five meters felt like five hundred. For hours, Wil followed Neil's solitary shadow through the wilderness, only vaguely aware of the rest of the line. On occasion, unholy lowing would erupt from outside vision—a feidh, Saoirse said. Ariadnan deer.

"Big ones grow to two meters, and we call 'em macrofeidh. Heavy fuck-off stags that would fight Satan himself if he stepped too close. If ye see one, pray tae that Joan of Arc of yours, aye? Then again, if she came tae save ye, it'd prob'ly kill her, too."

Saoirse, Hodges, Dunne, and Gordon scouted the fringes, about twenty meters out and returned to the column frequently to give Cailean updates. To his credit, the old Grey seemed at home leading a regiment in rough terrain, and though his hand signals didn't quite match the ones Wil had learned so long ago on the Neoterran outback, he grokked the essentials quick enough.

Then they descended the first mountain, taking a footpath roughly the width of a pencil. If horizontal had been rough, vertical was hell. Clinging to the smooth escarpments. Balancing on granite scree, toes hanging out over oblivion. He slipped—once—and Fionnlagh had nearly gone over dragging him back. But when he tried to recall the moments between disasters up on the ridge, the entire world wreathed in billowing white nothingness, his heart shivered in his chest until he shoved the memories aside.

How Alastair did it all wearing a half-ton of Teseum, Wil had no earthly idea.

They made camp the first night on a ridge above Old Outpost 4. The settlement itself was invisible until Alastair pointed out the light pole footprints, the water tower struts caging a gnarl of trees, the toppled church belfry. Everything had been reclaimed by Dawn, coated in green and scattered with flowering weeds.

"When the Commercial Conflicts started," Alastair said, "mercenary soldiers paid by MagnaObra arrived, intent on driving us off the land. The mercs would bait the warriors away, then swoop in to set fire to the buildings and shoot anyone who escaped."

Wil crossed his arms. By the number of remaining buildings, the population back then was at least a couple hundred, if not a thousand. "Evacuating this many civilians when already stretched thin by the war had to be a nightmare."

Alastair gave him a soft, sad smile. "When the Druze were done, Wil, there was no one left to evacuate."

Camp was simple: they parted into two shifts, half waking the other at second watch to steal the last few remaining hours of sleep. Only Gordon and Saoirse were allowed to rest all night. Something about their physiology meant they needed double the intake of a regular soldier, and with their dwindling amount of rations, sleeping was the easiest way to control their hunger.

Gordon shifted down at sundown, and very rarely beside. Whenever he returned to his human shape, steam and sweat clouded around him for hours, and once he sat, he'd not be able to stand again till morning. Then he'd tear into Neil's scant breakfast offerings before hauling himself away from camp to transform. Far enough to stay sight unseen, but not far enough that his crunching bones weren't audible.

According to Dunne, Dog-Warriors always succumbed to the blood fury when they shifted. It was why Rodina sent them in as men to soak the first salvo and transmute—the pain maximized their rage and their killing potential. But Dog-face members of the 2nd Irregular Cameronians Regiment transmuted long before the horns sounded and only frenzied in battle. The key was that Cameronians spent years in both forms, honing their minds and their mettle until they harnessed their rage, directed it, controlled it—became it.

"Helps that the CHA is regimented by family," Dunne said. "Harder to eat people you've known since childhood and all. But emergency rations have their use."

He chuckled dryly. "I'll take being called 'Emergency Rations' over Wilhelm Wallace any day."

As the march stretched on, a rotating door of task force members tried their damnedest to keep him going without breaking pace. Every rest stop, someone would swing back to check how he was holding up, share water, to ask to carry his pack or his rifle. Never condescension, but concern. Desperate to avoid the ultimate shame of being carried without sporting a lethal injury, Wil refused to flag, even when it started costing him toenails.

On the second night, Dunne showed Wil how to dig a Dakota hole—an underground fire pit meant to keep the glow low-key beyond a few meters—with an E-Tool, and how to fix a plastic bag into a bellows to feed it. Neil demonstrated how to turn a single MRE into the bare minimum for thirteen people with nothing more than a pot, some water, and determination. Pell explained how to read Ogham hunter's script, tallies left in the trees and stone by two-hundred years of Caledonian frontiersman. The sign for Antipode. The sign for water. The sign for poison.

When they made camp, Nora balanced a stick across the firepit to dry their rain-drenched clothing and collected socks, inspecting feet and microdosing Serum for bad blisters. Soon, the bruise on Wil's neck where his flak had blunted the Shasvastii bullet faded away, and he felt whole for the first time in weeks.

Then they got back up and kept marching.

With Saoirse scouting ahead and Wil near the end of the column, they barely got to speak save for a few brief moments in camp when she tended to a raincatcher made from Bell's wet-weather bag. It chafed him, somehow. In a PanOceanian regiment, the kind of feelings Wil held for Saoirse Clarke would be enough for an immediate change in assignment. Here, Hodges would rub Dunne's shoulders at mealtime and no one said a thing.

Wil hunkered beside Neil and whispered, "Are they married?"

"Keep tae yerself, Wallace," Neil said. "Their business is their own."

Reasonable, but he still couldn't stymie the dissonance. Siblings, uncles, lovers, all beneath the umbrella of one regiment—it felt wrong. A security risk. But then Fionnlagh started humming a tune, and Cailean filled in with the lyrics in Caledonian Gaelic. By the second verse, he wasn't singing alone, and it was hard to remember why those risks actually mattered.

"*The Ballad of Three and Fifty*," Saoirse whispered. "Need a translation?"

"Nah," Wil said. "It's good enough without one."

Past midnight, a high-pitched whistle woke Wil for his shift on perimeter duty. It lasted only a second and repeated in intervals about a minute apart throughout the pitch-black night.

"Ariadnan raptors," Kelsie mumbled past the toothbrush in her mouth. "Birds. Mating call."

Tonight, he had shift with Nora and looked forward to a bit of her wanton cheerfulness. There was none; she was absent. On his fiftieth lap of their campsite, he found her sat atop a great gnarled tree root, muffling tears with her sleeve.

Wil crouched beside her. "Hey. What's wrong?"

Nora squeezed her eyes shut, wiping snot onto her leggings. She breathed, shaky, until she managed, "Nothing. I'm sorry. It's fine."

"Hey, it's okay. If you want to talk, I'll listen. Or if it's blisters, I got more moleskin in my pack. Either's fine."

"No, it's stupid," she said. "You'll laugh."

"Should I get someone else? Saoirse? Neil? I can wake Gordon. He'd be glad I did."

She balled her knees against her chest. "No," she said. "God. I shouldn't be like this. What the hell is wrong with me?"

Wil risked confirming his suspicion. "It's Bell, isn't it?"

Nora met his gaze for just a moment, eyes glistening all over again. "He was terrible," she whispered. "I hated him so much. Should be crying over Llowry instead."

He nodded. Tried to lack judgment. Tried not to show that he agreed.

"Called me a bitch," she said. "Painter's radio. Barracks bunny. And... worse, when no one was around. Always said I joined the Volunteers just to mock him, that it was unladylike. But it isn't like I had anywhere else to go, ken? I amn't smart, and...."

Wil nudged her with his knee. "Hey, hey. You're gonna be a 112, remember?"

Nora shot him a look, its meaning clear as day: *Don't patronize me*. And he hadn't been, but respected the sentiment all the same.

"Neil always told Bell to quit when he got mean," she said. "But they'd known each other so long, and his mum took care of us when our da passed. He'd sit up with Neil till dawn, back when he had night terrors. He was nice."

"Until he wasn't."

"Until he wasn't," she whispered. "It's stupid, right?"

"No, I get it," Wil said. "Now that he's dead, you'll never get to tell him to screw himself proper. And he was a twat, but he was your twat. He deserved comeuppance, not death."

Nora gawked at him with her wide, wet eyes. "If Saoirse heard you whispering about *my twat*, she'd slit your throat, Wil."

"Or rip my dick right off, right?"

"That was *one time*," she sputtered. "And it was an accident!"

She fought back a smile too quick to sell the joke, but Wil laughed anyway. And when Vern patrolled by, he gave them a wide berth with a strange look on his face, and it only made them laugh harder.

⇅

On the third day, Saoirse returned to the column in a hustle, dirt-streaked face split with an eager grin. Whispered rumors became constrained celebration: Gordon had caught a feidh.

1/13th of an MRE and a protein bar a day might've been enough if they'd been driving for twelve hours, but not while at full march in rough terrain. To say they were hungry was an understatement: Hodges had offered Wil a stick of nicotine gum yesterday that he'd considered swallowing since, just to know what it felt like to have something in his stomach. Cailean spoke highly of the emergency cache waiting in Fort Resolute, but that felt like a lifetime away, and Neil refused to adjust the rations in case the whole thing was a wash.

So when the whisper raced down the line, the dream of venison gave them wings. The pace quickened. Faster. Cailean gave the signal for full ahead, and the task force broke into a frantic run. Vern slipped on a root, and not even Alastair went back for him.

Up ahead, in a narrow clearing, Gordon pinned a furry quadruped to the grass. He had his whole face stuffed into the antlered creature's steaming gut, snout stained a vicious red. Down on all fours, sucking up its intestines, Wil hardly saw the human in him.

Then Gordon looked up. His hackles shivered, and he lumbered to his knuckles like an ape, back bent so his withers lifted above his ears. No wasted motion. His tail raised and went very, very still.

"Gordon," Alastair called, fingers brushing his Americolt. "Everything well, brother?"

No. It was not. The salivating black of Gordon's lips thinned against the bloodstained yellows of his teeth. Twitching. Warning.

Fionn strode past Alastair toward Gordon, arms outstretched to them both. Dunne leapt to keep him back, but he wormed free with a nervous smile. "A Chùsìth," Fionn said. "Cuimhnich cò thusa!"

Gordon growled. The reverberation rattled their equipment in their holsters at ten meters.

Fionn didn't flinch. "Tha eagal air Eileanor," he said, and gestured to Nora. "Dè tha ceàrr ort?"

Blank eyes sharpening, Gordon scanned the group till they fell on his girlfriend—small, wide-eyed, hiding behind her weapon.

All at once, whatever instinct that'd had him growling receded, and he rose to his hind legs with a much more human grimace. "Duilich," he rumbled, clawed palm smearing the blood from his lips. "Sorry. I'm sorry."

Alastair exhaled, hand leaving his chain-colt's grip. "Can we come closer?"

"No. Not yet," Gordon said. "I'll leave."

"Gordon," Nora called. "Thank you."

"Always," he said, and stalked into the woods.

Cailean checked the dead feidh for illness, sniffed at its half-munched entrails, and declared it edible enough. In a half hour, with Neil and Fionn's help, he butchered it. He bemoaned that he'd have to leave the hide and rack here—Gordon's messy takedown had ruined most of the kill—but there was still enough to feed the group for more than a day. Cailean washed his hands with some of Fionn's whisky, said it'd be good enough till they hit water, and Neil sat to math out how many meals one feidh would make for thirteen people.

Saoirse crouched on a fallen log, transfixed on the still carcass, dueling bracers jingling as she bobbed her knee in distress. Alastair sat beside her, patient, plying, until her sympathy waned and she allowed herself the concession of eating what organs the others couldn't.

Hodges sauntered over, playing with the strap of his chain rifle. "Pardon, sir, but by my calculation, if we keep up the distractions, we'll have to walk at night."

"When Gordon comes back, we'll go," Alastair said. "Don't worry."

He grimaced. "Wish we still had his brothers around."

By Alastair's solemn silence, he agreed.

Vern took a kneel, tending to his backpack. Not maintenance. Frustrated. He banged his fist on the radio box's metal paneling, slapped the side like a drum. "Bloody hell, come on! Work, you primitive piece of—shite!"

Dunne jogged over, Molotok in her hands. "What's the problem?"

"It's Gordon, I guess," Vern said, flicking switches and dials fruitlessly. "He's transmitting, but this nonsense box isn't—"

Saoirse burst from her spot on the rock into a dead sprint. Unfettered by Alastair's shouts, she crashed through the rough, following the bloody trail Gordon had left.

Wil pursued her without hesitation. Tangled in the first briar. Slipped on a wobbly stone. Lost his wind, clotheslined by a low bough. Others caught up to him with ease, forged ahead while he struggled over the uneven terrain.

Up ahead, another clearing. A few uprooted trees draped precariously over a narrow stream and a long, square pond. Greenery pressed to either side, tilted as if shoved, and in the crater the bony, leaf-strewn carcass of a PanOceanian luxury air vehicle planted nose-down in the earth.

A second Balena.

25

The wreck here was unlike the last one. It hadn't burned; no scavengers had taken it apart. It'd landed somewhere soft so it was mostly intact, and Wil easily placed where the missile had collided dead-on with the cabin. Exposure had cracked the upholstery, and thick tufts of weeds bloomed in the gaps in the nacelles. A narrow creek snaked around the wreckage, runoff forming a pond in the trench dug by the crash.

Wil wasn't a forensic technician, but he was certain he knew the identities of the withered corpses left strapped inside: the missing attaché, Yearwood, and his security detail. Shot down, like he had been, but not lucky enough to survive.

Rajan had been right all along.

Neil swept his Glengarry off his head and let out a low, long whistle. "Bloody hell."

Gordon stood atop the wreck, arms spread proudly. He was wet from head to claw, bloody fur washed clean in the stream. In three bounding leaps, he descended to the forest floor. "Shit parking job, en't it?"

Saoirse stamped to the water's edge. "Gordon, you absolute rocket! We thought ye were in danger!"

His furry brows drew together. "Signal not work?"

"No, I came runnin' fer the aerobics. Love me some fuckin' cardio."

Gordon's ears drooped. "It's my comlog—it—and when I transform," he said, and to illustrate, he drew his massive, clawed mitts together and rotated his thumbs. "Sausage fingers."

"Och, aye," she sneered and hurled a backward peace sign up at him.

Nora struggled over the brush, MediKit in one hand, her pistol in the other. "Everyone alright? No one's hurt?"

"False alarm," Saoirse said. "Big ugly here cannae work a comlog."

"He's not ugly," Nora chided, and her next footstep clunked into a click.

Wil's heart speared up into his throat. Without hesitation, he hauled Nora off her feet and went for distance, two steps, four before he hit the dirt and shielded her with his back.

Silence. No detonation. Not a mine.

Cerulean steel-alloyed plate. PanOceanian. The four-eyed helmet of an Orc Trooper stared up at them.

Kelsie knelt and tugged on the radial sensor. "Friend of yours?"

† †

A meaty hock of feidh thigh, diced into chunks and sautéed. Water from the stream, boiled and filtered. A few spices from baggies in Neil's assault pack, and half a packet of onion soup that Vern's aunt had made him bring along 'for some reason.' Some alien nightshades that Kelsie had tripped over two days ago, purple and bruised. Crushed wildflower petals, thrown in by Fionn against everyone's wishes, and a handful of salt besides.

Best goddamn thing he'd ever eaten. Neil gave him seconds for shielding Nora, and he passed them on to Fionn as a thank-you for not letting him drop.

Afterward, Wil patrolled the clearing's western edge, the crash site on his mind. So it wasn't something Rajan had done, per se, but some transgression the two attachés shared. Had they asked too many questions, or the wrong ones? These dead men had taken five scuffed negotiations over a full year to earn their concrete shoes—had Rajan just been that annoying, or was there another reason?

The four corpses' necks had all been detonated from within. Voodoo-Tech—Combined Army technology, so advanced it may well have been magic. Their Cubes were unsalvageable. That meant true death—permanent death—and an explanation for why the attaché's implants hadn't called out a Cube Jäger by now.

After an hour, Dunne came to get him. Together, they walked back through camp to the wreck. Vern sat alone, glaring at his old-world radio like an anti-theist would the Nativity. Across the clearing, Nora tended to the salvage with her knife. Winter's freeze and the spring thaw had ruined the emergency kits and their contents, but a single waterproof suitcase had survived. Inside, a veritable fortune of silken Merovingian menswear, ripe for processing into fresh bandages.

"They were on the way back from Mariannebourg by the heading," Dunne said. "Missile must've hit them about ten klicks south, but the pilot stayed conscious. Engines dead, he tried to glide, but there's no safe place to land in the valley. So he gambled on finding an updraft near the ridge, and caught a downflow instead. Game over."

Nora jogged over, picking pine needles from her pant legs. "Alastair says they might've been from way back, tricked to land in Antipode country. My gran used to do that—rig Yujingyu SOS beacons and ditch 'em where the 'Podes were meanest."

"No way," Wil said. "That Orc's armor is two years old, tops."

"The divot on the helmet's shallower, right?" Nora said. "Cailean said the same thing."

Out by the crashed Balena, Alastair and the Volunteers were washing their hands in the stream, mouths covered with scarves and shemaghs. Gordon lounged on a large stone with the air of a scolded child, and Cailean sat on the dirt beside him, taking advantage of the rainless afternoon to do maintenance on Rhiannon.

Three piles of river stones lay stacked atop three squares of fresh-churned earth. Cairns. Saoirse and Dunne ambled over from the creekside, lugging the beginnings of a fourth toward a shallow grave beside the Orc Trooper's corpse.

Fionn climbed from inside, folding shovel in hand. He caught sight of Wil and bowed his head briefly. "Mo cho-fhaireachdainn riut, Uill."

Wil slowed to a stop. "You buried them."

"Left the Orc for last," Alastair said. "I wasn't sure if you could utilize the salvage for your MSV."

"Yeah, but... why'd you bury them?"

"Took us five minutes," he said and tossed Wil his shemagh. "Why not?"

No. It'd been more like an hour. "Should've left them."

Pellehan perched atop the Balena nacelle high above them, cigar in one hand, his rifle on his lap. "Then the mountain would ken our disrespect and begin to resent us. Deadly for mortal beings such as we. There are things out here older than the universe, young man. Older than time."

"Cho sean ri ceò nam beann," Fionn said, washing his hands in the stream.

"Best not to challenge it," Saoirse said, unloading her stones and helping Dunne in kind. "The mountain always wins, Wil. It's how it's still here after a hundred-million years."

Pell exhaled out a ring and pierced it with a second breath. "Precisely."

Their weird mythology dragged the Díreach out of his memory, the thing Eideard and Cailean had argued about over the round table. A phantom, or a monster maybe, but he didn't want to risk asking when everyone was so goddamn serious. "Yeah, okay. Older than time. Like what?"

Gordon picked a wad of gristle from his maw. "Dragons."

Wil laughed. "Sure."

"Oh, oh!" Nora perked up with a big, bright smile. "My mum saw a dragon flyin' in a rainbow the day before she had us."

"Right above the Lochnagar, aye," Neil said. "It's how come Nora's bonnie."

"I'll say," Saoirse snickered, and sent her a wink.

Cailean touched the side of Rhiannon and grimaced. Something had gone missing in the reassemble, and he searched as he spoke. "My da had one's footprint mounted in the den. After he passed, my butter-fingered brother dropped it while we cleaned house upstairs. One big piece o' history, smashed intae a million. Went tae bed scared he'd go my dream tae throttle me."

"I'll do you better than a footprint," Gordon said. "My uncle shot one."

"Aye, really? Where?"

"Loch Kirkshaig, up near the white stone."

"Good on him, then." Relieved, Cailean located the wandering bolt tucked beneath the rear sight and went to screw it on. "He strike a telling blow, or a wee graze?"

"Neither. Missed. Bottle of cherry moonshine ain't so good for aim."

"A' marbhadh nathair-nimhe," Fionn said. "Nì mi seo latha brèagha air chor-eigin."

"And when it flies away?" Kelsie asked. "What then?"

Fionn grinned, slowly extending his arms for a practice flap. "Nì mise itealaich cuideachd!"

Wow. They were trying so hard to sell this joke, it hurt. Literally—the hole Llowry had dug in his forearm throbbed. "Very funny, guys. You got me."

"With what?" Neil asked, brow furrowed.

"Dragons are real? Get outta here."

Kelsie's smile died. "We're being serious."

He scanned the group for Nora, expecting to find her brittle deadpan in the midst of breaking. Instead, the same disapproving lip twist as in the Croatoan waited right on her face.

"There aren't dragons on your planet," Wil said. "Or any planet."

Saoirse strolled over, hands on her hips. "Issat so?"

"Someone would've catalogued one by now. The DRC, or O-12, or—"

"Prove it don't exist," she challenged.

"I can't prove a negative, Saoirse."

She snorted, smug. "Our win, then."

"I mean… they're a mythological creature," he said. "Doesn't that imply something? *Mythological*?"

Cailean cocked his brow. "So're Wulvers, lad, but yer standin' right afront of one."

Saoirse curled an arm and flexed her bicep, gleefully taking any excuse to peacock. Nora struck a half-turn pose, told Saoirse to copy her. On Nora's skinny frame, supermodel. On Saoirse's tall physique, Greek goddess.

Wil realized he was gawking too late to hide it and verbally flailed into, "I mean, okay, yeah, okay, you're wrong, but you might not be *that* wrong. Not a dragon, but close enough? An offshoot of some species affected by the cuckoo virus. Or a Steindrage."

"We ken Steindrages," Neil said.

"Completely different," Nora added, in the midst of demonstrating a runway lean. Gordon matched the tilt of her torso with that of his head, appreciating until she caught him looking too—and then, all her poses aimed his way instead.

"I mean," Wil said, "where I'm from on Neoterra, we've got reptilo. That's close enough. They're like a common dinosaur, fairly endemic, if you—"

"Wait," Hodges said and sat bolt upright. "A common bloody dinosaur? Tell me I misheard you."

"No, it's true," Wil said. "They're everywhere, like pests almost. They climb gutters, hang out on rooftops. We used to keep a bat by the door for burglars, y'know, but we mostly used it on reptilo. Some had a bite could dent polysteel."

Dunne's lips twitched into a grin. "The gutters?"

"Wil," Saoirse said humorlessly. "Now yer bein' mean."

"No, seriously."

"Best advice on a lie," Hodges said. "More details makes it less believable. You need to trickle, not spout. Unless you're talking politics, then the opposite applies."

"I'm not lying. Look, if we had Maya out here, I'd show you. There's photos. Mascots. Hell, people farm these big longnecked ones on the Aquila outback, at ranches—"

Pell crooked a thinning brow. "Methinks the lady doth protest too much."

"No, this isn't—I'm not—they're—"

Alastair had his back turned, but the crick in his stance and his hand over his mouth gave him away. "Lieutenant, I'd take the loss on this one. No offense."

Cailean replaced Rhiannon's double-handed backplate with practiced expertise. "First, the lad havers on about planets, and now this? A troublin' pattern of behavior."

Gordon shook, deep baritone gone breathy and chopped. He pawed at his muzzle, turned away. "Hey. Wil. At the ranches. The dinosaur ranches, the great big ones. Do they… do they got cowboys, Wil? Dinosaur cowboys, with lassos and boot spurs and PanO-shaped belt buckles?"

Wil refused to answer.

Filtering out the laughter was more work than disconnecting the Orc Trooper's backpack. The powered armor's artificial muscle was swamped with so much dried mud, it may well have been a fossil. Leveraging a trench shovel, Wil decoupled the protective plate from the backpack and pried open the release. Inside, the primary power supply's battery had ballooned obscenely, bent and puffed like a pillowcase. Lime-green corrosion caked every connector.

But inside the secondary compartment, the auxiliary battery shined. Disconnected. Pristine. Wil picked it from the coupling with the edge of his knife and held it up to the light to check for faults. None.

Alastair hunched over his shoulder. "Seems valuable."

"It'll keep my visor going for more than three minutes," Wil said. "Can't ask for more."

Hodges hovered over the body as well. "We noticed no one's wearing dog tags. What's the usual procedure? Is there someone we should be notifying?"

Wil almost told him to cut the act until in a startled flash he understood that it wasn't, and he knew then what they were doing. Patrol. Stories. Jokes, food, hazing, anything and everything, all meant to keep his mind off the corpses of his countrymen—off the fact that if the cards had shuffled another way, some other Orc might've been looting his battery instead.

He hoped his silent appreciation was enough. Knew it never would be.

Nora wrote 'A PanOceanian Soldier is Buried Near Here' on a river rock with her waterproof marker, and left it atop a cairn when they went.

11

Walking past sunset drove everyone to their limit. Blistered, bleeding, drunk with fatigue, metatarsals threatening to punch through the wet paper of their feet. Even full on feidh stew, the flesh could only take so much. By the time they made camp, the horizon already glowed blue.

Wil woke to Alastair tending the fire in the Dakota hole. Fresh, dry kindling crackled under the earthen shelf, waves of welcome heat dispelling the morning chill. Shirtless and unarmored for the first time since Kildalton, Alastair's flank rippled with lean, visible muscle. Not as skinny as he looked. A thin burl of pink flesh knotted below his left shoulder blade. Not a gunshot scar, but something else.

As Wil sat up, the hurt from the day's march melted into his gut, stirring into a nauseatic soup that warmed every dull joint in his body. "You sleep yet?"

"No," Alastair said. "Still need to scout our bearing."

"But that's Saoirse's job."

He shrugged. "Sharing her burden for one day won't kill me."

"You're gonna blink, and it'll be time to march."

The growing firelight danced over the solid planes of Alastair's face. "My da once said that if you like being CO, it means you're a shitty one."

"Smart guy," Wil said and started coffee.

The sun rose, and so did they. More march. More pain. The steep cliffs and dicey switchbacks softened into hills of rolling greenery, fresh-bloomed after the Caledonian winter. The unsteady footing didn't abate—only worsened. Vern almost ate shit climbing an incline, and Pellehan lectured him about spatial awareness all the way down the second mountainside. Mealtime came and went. Sleep. Then, back to walking. Moments began to pop and bleed into each other until it all became a blur of footsteps, misery, and fog.

The afternoon sun slipped behind the mountains above, ushering in an early twilight. The humid air grew disconcertingly muggy, and traces of something rotten carried on the wind. Along the rocks, an Ogham scratch—*water*—followed by a second.

Antipodes.

A pass less than a meter wide led up the ridge and over the treetops. Ahead, an overhang tucked deep beneath the rock face. More than enough space to stand. A few wiry shrubs tangled together near the edge, and the remnants of several campfires scattered at their feet.

All the energy Kelsie had spent since yesterday morning returned to her at once. She spun endlessly, lips parted in a speculative O. "Cor! Sersh, don't tell me this's the hot springs?"

So that's what the sulfuric tang in the air was.

Ten dirt-streaked, mud-soaked, bone-tired Highlander warriors who'd only washed their hands and faces in muddy creek water in the last five days all shivered at once.

"AEZ patrolman's secret," Saoirse snickered, a clawed finger over her lips. "Hot springs're a boilin' forty degrees, year-round. An' up here, behind the trees, under the overhang? Good as invisible. Stone above keeps the rain out, brush kills the wind, and the 'Podes only come this way in summer tae give birth."

Everyone began to drop gear. Wil got his arm tangled in his assault pack straps, and with a "Fuck it," sat. Didn't even have enough in the tank left to be frustrated.

Dunne threw off her pack and gently set her Molotok beside it. "Who's first?"

"You, the McDermotts, and Shaw, if ye please," Cailean answered, cords in his neck taut as the spring in a bear trap. His silver hair shined with grease, beard blackened by the week's accumulated filth. "Keep a tight perimeter. We'll change at twenty-hundred hours."

Her eyes darkened. "I meant for the springs."

"Then no one," Cailean said. "We'll not drop our guard to pretend this is a university road trip, S'arnt. Clothes on, eyes forward. A little dirt's nae danger."

Nora stomped her feet. "But I smell like the wrong end of an Antipode."

"Which end's that?" Neil asked, and she punched him in the arm.

Hodges threw his pack atop Dunne's and began to strip uniform right there in front of the group. His belt buckle clinked against the grenades on his vest as they dropped to the stone.

Cailean watched him coldly. "Robert. Dinnit ye got ears."

"Oh, I do," Hodges chirped, straining to remove his undershirt. "I'm going to scout up that path—naked. I'm in training to be a Cameronian, you see. About thirty meters, right Saoirse?"

"Once spent twenty weeks outside the wire wi'out nary a wet wipe," Cailean said, voice sharpening like each new word was a whetstone. "You can go twenty days."

"Good on you," Hodges said and ambled away in just his skivvies. "Cheers."

Cailean caught his shoulder. Hodges knocked his grip askew, glare burning with the same flame as the Wulvers from the bar brawl. The old man croaked an arrogant snicker and sized him up, gauntleted hands curled into fists, and Hodges' did the same.

But before the show started in earnest, Alastair and Dunne rushed to mediate. They separated the two. Whispers tensed and then became louder. Wil couldn't imagine a world in which military professionals threw a wobble over getting to wander off to a hot spring mid-operation, but here they were.

And then, he realized, he could—but the wobblers were always officers and intel, never the diggers and grunts who got ground up the worst and needed it the most. On Svalarheima, his Hexa liaison had practically shit himself over a chess game when Wil refused an offer to draw. Of course Wil still lost, but it was the principle of the thing. Playing it out was a sign of respect to your opponent, even if you knew the outcome from the word 'go.'

This was something like that, but there was more than pride on the line.

Alastair worked his way back to the middle, speaking loud enough to make it a group discussion. "Hodges has a point, Uncle. A moment's rest will prepare us mentally and physically for the final push."

"Old man's not wrong either," Dunne interjected. "If we want this, we need to be smart. No lagging. In, out. Half the group on shift, quarter bathing, quarter redressing. Then we rotate. Equal split, co-ed. No complaints."

Gordon glanced at Nora, and then away. "I'll take all four shifts. Nora can have mine. Creek was good enough."

"Not how this works," Dunne said, voice firm. "You need to shift down, Kicklighter. Rest. Burning your candle at both ends is gonna mess you up for permanent, ken?"

Chastised, Gordon grumbled. He chanced another look at Nora and startled when he saw her peeling her shirt open at him with a wink. "I'll wash your back," she said. "It'll be fun!"

Neil perked. "So the backside, that's the right side?"

Nora punched him in the arm two more times.

Cailean raked his beard, studying the task force's hopeful faces, and exhaled out all his bluster. "Alright. Fine. Let's be about it."

"It's just a bath," Alastair said.

"Aye, right. Not the point. It's the vulnerability, and time lost. And if we've a Speculo among us, it's the perfect time tae make their move."

"In all honesty, Uncle, I don't believe we do."

"Neither does the Speculo," Cailean said. "Remember that."

Saoirse sauntered up, thumbs hooked in the armpits of her flak. "If time's the hangup, then I'll scout the next leg now, aye? Should get us movin' long before dawn. Half my fault yer arguin' anyways—if I'd kent the springs would be controversial, we woulda gone southerly."

"Nah." Gordon lumbered to his feet. "You're not goin' alone."

Dunne slapped her palm against her forehead. "Goddammit, Gordon. Vern and Pell, you're with Gordon up to the springs. If he comes back dry, I'm shooting you both in the foot."

Pell laughed, but Vern visibly deflated. Ears flattened on his head, Gordon sighed. "Alright, already. Fine."

Dunne's withering gaze leveled on Hodges next. By his flinch, her disapproval must've stung worse than a T2 bullet. He stammered, searching the group for someone to blame, and settled on the usual target.

"Why not make him do it," Hodges said, and pointed at Wil. "It's his fault we lost two hours yesterday, digging up his bloody battery. He's scarcely pulling his weight as-is, and you deserve a rest."

"He's pullin' his weight," Neil called. The begrudging respect in his glare died an instant later, but Wil knew a thank-you when he saw it.

Truth be told, he'd gone longer than Cailean without bathing when he was on Paradiso, so filthy he yellowed fresh laundry on contact. Even so, giving up a dip in a hot spring—no matter how brief—chafed him. But what Alastair had said that morning rang true.

In Omnibus Princeps. First in all things.

Not just a motto, but a promise.

Tight-lipped, Wil forced himself upright. "I'll go, Dunne. You stay."

Alastair stripped off his helmet, and his greasy auburn hair stuck up at a hundred odd angles. "Are you sure? We can't have any soldiers off on their own later. You understand what you're giving up?"

Dead on his feet. Hollowed out by hunger.

Hazy, and bruised.

Aching. Itching.

But something in Saoirse's admiring smile overruled his better demons.

26

By the time evening hit, Wil would've killed fifty men for a three-legged lawn chair and a shred of wheat bread.

Their tiptoe through the swiftly darkening wild stayed silent—part exhaustion, part his own awkward momentum. He didn't know what he wanted from her, didn't know what to say to get it, and before he knew it, Helios had doused in the west and twilight came to an abrupt end.

Saoirse appraised what little light remained. "Head back, Wil. I've got this."

He paused, halfway through grinding his knuckles up the length of his thigh—anything to get the blood flowing. "Alone? In the dark?"

"Ye got yer visor, I got a nose," she said. "State yer in, ye'll die the moment movement's necessary. Tell Al and Cailean all's well, take a nap, and I'll see ye in the morn'. Alright?"

He didn't like it but didn't have the strength to protest.

Back at camp, the fires had already died. Everyone ready to go on watch was bright-eyed, clean-faced, refreshed; and everyone who wasn't was peacefully asleep. Nora was the exception. Bright and bushy-tailed as the day they'd met, she stole Wil's socks to add them to a bevy of clothes hanging on a paracord rig and brought him a mug of watery soup. While he sat, she took Saoirse's message and ferried it out to Cailean in the brush.

"You're the best," he whispered.

"Aren't I?" she said, and twirled a little on the way out.

Wil curled beneath his aluminum blanket, duster bunched beneath his head. For the first time in years, sleep didn't come. He twisted. Tossed. Waited, impatiently, to fade away. Didn't. Each bone in his knee pried apart in the swell, radiating hurt down his shins, and his back ached miserably no matter which way he laid. One week and a vial of Serum after the bar fight, and his nose still subtly whistled when he breathed.

The sulfur on the wind kept wafting over to taunt him.

At first, he denied it. Warmth was for weaklings. Pain wasn't pain. But the more he lay awake, the more he ached for the dark solitude and the distance he could get from Gordon's unbelievable snoring. When Neil and Fionn started playing cards, it only took three laughs to convince him.

To hell with this.

When no one was looking, he went for it. Half-dressed, Detour clipped to his waistband, Wil navigated the trail up from their campsite. Each ascending step up the narrow pass threatened the loss of another toenail; each loose stone, a long drop with a short stop. The smelled of rotten eggs thickened up his nostrils, and strands of heat mixed among the night breeze wisped over his face.

Ahead, the rock shelf split. Water drained from a winding, moss-damp crack in the stone, filling a series of stepped pools awash with gravelly particulate and dammed by stray branches. Each eroded bowl fed into the next larger, the next, until the overflow dashed over the crags into the dark treetops below. Tanit above had swollen, full now, and its reflected pallor danced atop the flow of the natural spring, cloaking the steam clouds in white.

Quickly, Wil undressed. He folded his clothes atop a flat, damp rock and gingerly took a seat inside the deepest bowl. The water came up to his ribs at first, sweltering yet soothing. When he'd acclimated enough, he sank to his neck and very nearly cried.

While the hurt didn't entirely vanish, the knot in his shoulder where he'd been grazed by the Malignos finally untied itself, and his back loosened enough to crack. Soon, the slow boil became bearable, and he wished he'd brought his razor—getting rid of the week-old stubble might make him start to feel like himself again. He scooped up some of the spring water and poured it over his head.

The instant he was blind, something sloshed in the spring below.

He cleared his eyes. Groped for his pistol. Froze.

Saoirse stood half-submerged below. The moonlight draped across the curves of her wide shoulders, swept down the ripple of her ribs, and puddled along a deep, gnarled scar dashed atop her inner thigh. Her hair had been untied from its greasy bun and clung to her neck in dark, wet ropes. Freckles splashed along her collar and between her breasts, across her hips, under the butterfly tattoos. Everywhere.

On Neoterra, nudity wasn't taboo, but for an Ariadnan—he didn't want or need to piss her off. He shielded his gaze. "Sorry. Sorry!"

A long pause. "Silicone," Saoirse called.

Breath tight, he managed a, "What?"

"Fer my wedding ring," she said. "Please 'n' thank you."

Wil moved to stand. He stalled short of flashing her. Sunk back. "Sorry, sorry. Should I, um…"

"Sit still," she said, and two quick splashes preceded wet footsteps on the rocks and rapid dripping. It grew louder, closer until it disappeared inside a splash. Her shadow darkened the water's surface. A callused hand seized his wrist and pulled him into the pool where she sat down back-to-back against him.

"Work for you?" she asked.

He could feel her heartbeat. "Works."

The frigid mountain air intermingled within the steam above the waterline, encouraging him to stay seated. Wil didn't move. Flirting was one thing, but this felt like the something different he'd hoped for back in the rough.

"What happened to scouting?" he asked.

"Lied," she said. "You?"

"Snuck off."

"S'pose we had the same idea."

"Guess so."

"On the bright side, yer nicks are lookin' better. Seen way worse Teseum scars in my time. Almost handsome, ken like. Assuming ye don't bodysculpt 'em right off when ye get home."

He thumbed the persistent line across his chest. "Uh, thanks."

"Ye wanna go somewhere?"

"I mean, I could get dressed," he said, "but—"

Something unscrewed. Metal. Fionn's thermos of whisky. "I meant drinking. Yer words, not mine, remember?"

"… Where'd you get that?"

"Fionn gave it to me fer pullin' Hodges outta the doghouse. Said I could have the rest, ta muchly, have fun. But drinkin' alone's always baws." Saoirse dangled the thermos over her shoulder. "Unless?"

Wil took the thermos. Weighed it. Threw caution to the wind, and tipped it into his mouth. He hadn't noticed the last time he'd drank Fionn's whisky after their skirmish in the Brume, but comparing it to the swill at the Croatoan was night and day—pleasantly warm instead of bitter as acid, totally absent of the aftertaste of old rubber bands. The first sip spilled into the cracks in his chest, ran across his weary heart, and clouded back up to nuzzle his brain.

"Good?" she asked.

Wil coughed.

"I'll say," she snickered and stole the thermos back.

Their fingers brushed in the passing, touch lingering slightly too long. He urged himself to turn and take her, but every time he gathered the courage, he imagined what'd be waiting for him if he'd misread her intentions—shock, confusion, rejection. A fist.

Hell. With how he was acting, he really should've joined the Military Orders.

Saoirse drank and exhaled an appreciative breath. Within seconds, the thermos dangled over his shoulder again. "So, Wil," she said. "Almost there."

A knot tied in his gut. "Yeah."

"First thing ye'll do when ye get back?"

Nothing came to mind. He swirled the whisky in the container, watching the moonlight catch in the amber. "Sleep, I guess. Shower."

"Boring," she teased, "but understandable. Dawn's filthy."

"It's not so bad."

She nudged him with her elbow. "Don't have second thoughts now, Wilhelm Wallace."

He didn't respond.

"Wil," she said. "Ye still there?"

"No, it's," he started, and sighed. "Just wish you wouldn't start too. Really don't like that nickname."

"How no? It's clever. Wallace crash landed same as you. Won us over. I think it's almost sweet. And no one likes their nicknames, that's almost the point."

He shrugged, awkward and clammy with their shoulders touching. "He meant it like I charge into battle without thinking. Like I'm some kind of frothing berserker."

Saoirse laid her head across his shoulder. The damp mat of her hair iced his skin, and breath clouded his earlobe. "That a bad thing?"

"Good or bad, it's true," Wil said and dangled the thermos over his shoulder. "When I'm in the thick of it, I get this feeling in my fingers. A quickening. A frenzy. And when I start, I can't stop, or I go too far, like with what happened with Stuart Walker, or Talbot, or on the road. I'm not in control of myself."

She touched his hand and spoke softly. "Do ye need to be?"

He didn't have an answer.

The thermos slipped from one finger to the other and splashed into the water. Wil turned to grab it at the same time Saoirse did.

Glittering droplets raced along her freckled skin, across many old scars, down the underside of her breasts. And there it was again—AIRAGHARDT, peeking out from over her shoulder. Not all the lines were straight.

Saoirse watched him. Unnatural hunger glinted in her pale eyes, challenging. Her gaze carried up his arm, to his neck, his face, and Wil turned away, unsure of what the right answer to what just happened was.

A heavy, critical silence fell over the springs. Awkward. Smothering. More liquor might grant him the clarity to redirect the awkward moment into—no, bad choice. He'd have to come up with something on his own.

"So, Airaghardt," Wil croaked. "What's that mean?"

"Oh, aye," Saoirse muttered. "Exactly."

He'd pissed her off, taking his time to turn around. That had to be it. "Did I say it wrong?"

"Dinnae ken," she said and groped for the thermos. "Go ask the ALEPH about it."

"Point me to the nearest Maya relay and I will," he said, but she didn't laugh. "I heard Fionnlagh shout something like it once: *air-arst*. So, it's got to be Caledonian Gaelic—was that right?"

"It's *gah-lik*, not *gay-lik*," she said. "Thalla's taigh na galla leat, twpsyn."

"… What's that mean?"

"It's a boring story, ken like."

"Can't wait to hear it," he said, and bumped her with his back.

Saoirse paused for a long time. Wil wasn't sure if she'd started giving him the silent treatment or if she was thinking things over until she plunked the significantly lightened thermos into his lap.

"*Air-a-ghardt*," she said, mimicking his pronunciation. "The motto of the Calgary Highlanders of Earth, established more than two-hundred years ago. They pronounce it '*airg-hoot*' and say it means *onward*, same motto as the city they hail from. But it's wrong. In Scottish Gaelic, it's *air adhart*, like Fionn said, meanin'· *forward*. Airaghardt don't mean nothin' at all. Not a word in any language, least of all mine.

"What I'm guessin' happened is the guy they got the motto from must've spoke it in a dead dialect, and whoever was in charge wrote it down as phonetic as they could. Worse still, apparently how to say it was one of those things everyone just knew, so as the old guard died out, the new recruits had to make their best guess, and then again, and again....

"Long story short, two centuries and a wormhole later, the Caledonian Highlander Army creates a regiment tae accommodate the first Wulver soldiers two generations after the First Antipode Offensive: the 9th Wulver Grenadiers. They needed a motto, and there it was. Airaghardt. Absolutely perfect, 'cause it's the only motto just as mutt as we are."

"And you liked it so much you inked it on your back?"

"I like what it means," she said. "As much as we pretend, Caledonia isn't Scotland, Wil. Not really. We're two-hundred years too removed tae claim similarity, cultures permanently diverged on the day the *Ariadna* set out. But if Caledonia's not the real thing, it's a damn good echo of it. We pride ourselves on it. It matters. We live and die for that echo, from here until eternity."

He turned the thermos in his hands. "Truth sans authenticity. What it stands for matters more than what it means."

"Yeah," she said. "Airaghardt."

He took a sip. "And on your shoulder, the skull with the roses?"

"It looks cool," she explained, and stole the thermos back.

⇡⇡

After the whisky ran dry, Saoirse told him to go dress and disappeared down the ridge. They met up on the escarpment near the pools, sitting in the loose gravel and soaking in the steam. He lent her his duster, and she lounged across it like a towel, barefoot in her bandeau and pants.

He couldn't help but admire her. The curve of her ribs and how it stretched as she breathed; the feminine line down the center of her abdomen, jagged between her muscle; how she soaked in the cold, toes clawed and callused as her hands.

Saoirse hung a little survivalist's torch on her finger from its carabiner, illuminating the ridge just enough to see by. The shadows on the rock face curved as it swayed.

"I've a personal question," she said.

Wil shrugged. "How personal?"

"Very."

"Alright. Go for it."

She tapped her neck below her ear. "Is it true, what they say? About yer Cube."

Cold weight. Warm whisky. Bad mix. "Yeah."

"You were an Atek."

"A long, long time ago."

Saoirse went up on her elbows, pale eyes eager. "What's it like?"

"I mean, you should know."

"No, not that. To go from being Atek to… having it. The Cube. The implanted comlog. A geist, the sensori-thingie, a soundtrack."

"Disorienting. Like I'd rented a one-bedroom brain for my entire childhood, and then I got a roommate. A lot of noise at first, overwhelming. But you get used to it."

"I heard it's rare tae get one when you're grown."

"Extremely."

"'Mon then," she said and swatted his knee. "Out with it."

"Well, there's not much there, honestly," Wil said. "I got mine from the Neoterran Integration Fund. Not, like, from it, but the alley doc running the Cube drive was a friend of my mom's. I guess he owed her a favor, penciled me in for a couple hundred Oceanas. But it turned out real shit in the end."

"Aye, right." Saoirse set aside the torch and took his hand, inspecting it with her fingertips. Her claws skimmed down the lines in his palm. "Not much there."

"I mean, okay… You ever heard of Ateks Out?"

Her nose wrinkled. "Bio-purists?"

"More like the opposite—they say Ateks deserve being second-class, that they chose that life. That they're all criminals, or lazy, and they were really against giving kids in the techno-favela Cubes. Like, *bombing* against, y'know?"

"Worse than bio-purists," she said. "Morons."

"When we showed up, turns out these assholes had been harassing the clinic all morning. DDoSing their servers, hacking the domotics, recording people. They'd buzz the cops to report fake IDs, loaded weapons, nitrocaine—anything to trigger a mandatory response from the block force. We waited for four hours in this cramped waiting room, emptying and filling our pockets for automated law enforcement drones with the protestors chanting right outside the door. And then, the power went out."

Her face fell. "Christ. What then?"

"Well, the anesthesiologist is like, nah. He deltas. Gone. Private security, too—they don't want to be around when the shooting starts. The doc's ready to cut and run until my mom starts begging, literally on her knees. She knows I won't get another chance for this, not without winning a lottery. So, he says, fine. But with no anesthesiologist, I have to be awake for the procedure."

Wil remembered the halogen emergency lights flickering above the gurney. His blood, pattering along the cardboard below his face. Black plastic, crinkling under his clammy skin as he squirmed in and out of consciousness, forceps nestled in the meat of his neck. And a pain so total that nothing would ever compare.

"Fuckin' hell," Saoirse whispered.

"Loaded me up on little white pills and let 'er rip," he said. "Bit right through the straps of my mom's purse. I was twelve years old."

"That must've been—I can't imagine it."

He shrugged. "Hardly remember a thing."

Judging by the suspicion in her big, blank eyes, Saoirse knew he was lying. "Wilhelm."

"Actually, between you and me? That's not my real name."

Saoirse cocked her head. "What?"

"Yeah. Secondhand Cube didn't get fully formatted thanks to the outage, so I ended up with the wrong name, wrong DOB, and a geist that insisted I was allergic to bananas. Worked out for me, though. Willem Arturo Díaz Ortega would've never made Fusilier—but Wilhelm Gotzinger III didn't flag any medical exemptions."

She gave him a lopsided squint. "… Yer name's not Wilhelm?"

"God, no. Me?"

"And nobody ever figured it out?"

"You didn't give it a second thought until literally right now."

Her brows creased. "S'pose not. How not the ALEPH, then?"

"Well, Paradiso meant they needed enlistment, enlistment meant they were scouting NCOs, and active conflict meant field promotions. I was shipped back to Aquila for Officer's Academy three years to the day after I enlisted. Graduated with honors, top of my class. And it's not like anyone ever called me by my full name, just nicknames until—"

"Willem."

He perked. "What?"

A wry smirk crept onto Saoirse's face. "*Willem.*"

"Yeah, I know. Like you can say anything, Sah-oy-er-see."

"Fuck off." She yanked her hand from his and gave his arm a slap. Her crooked smile did more for his exhaustion than the hot springs.

Wil exhaled a laugh. Whether it was the whisky or the mountain air, he didn't know, but it felt good. He'd never told anyone that story before.

Saoirse squeezed his wrist, then his forearm. "Got a bump here."

"Implanted comlog," he said and jingled the Teseum shackle. "Bracelet here keeps it bottlenecked with a cyclical data dump so its synchronization requests time out. Since the Shas have the DRC-9's datasphere locked down, they could wreak all kinds of potential bullshit via halo if they connected to me."

"Those are words," she said, and ran her hand up his arm.

The dim light cast a shadow down the line in her face. He hadn't thought about it lately, content to see Saoirse Clarke and not 'the scar-faced woman' from when they'd first met, but he still had questions and was finally brave enough to ask them.

Saoirse's smile cooled. "Yer starin' again, Wil. Gotta work on that."

"Your scar," he started.

She held up a claw. "Careful, now."

He hesitated—and committed. "I showed you mine, now show me yours."

"I showed ye mine up at the springs, I think."

"I'm being serious."

She chewed on her lip. "Most folks hate Christmas stories."

"You kidding? I love Christmas."

Saoirse snorted. "Yer so PanO, it hurts. Second favorite's Easter, aye?"

"You're just jealous you don't have Recreations of Santa Claus delivering presents via rocket-propelled reindeer."

Her jaw dropped. "That's…"

"A lie, but I appreciate that you tried to believe me."

Incredulity became exasperation. "Double fuck off."

He liked this. Liked her. The little glares, the joking. It was comfortable. Something kept bringing them together—loneliness, or a kinship of sorts. Both outsiders, both desperate to feel something. It wasn't healthy, but good things seldom were.

Saoirse picked at the stubborn mountain grass along the path until a single blade came loose, and she twisted it around her fingers.

"Christmas Eve at Castle MacArthur, nine years ago," she said. "Tree's up, lights're hung, presents wrapped. Everyone's in attendance. Happy. Rian is makin' the rounds, only twenty but playin' at bein' elected clan chieftain already. Cameron's come back from Scone after his second year away, braggin' about all the pretty Nomad boys he'd rattled on leave. And Alastair is glued to my side, babblin' on about mandatory-service this, AKNovy that, did I see the ruins of the *Ariadna* in Матр?"

"Didn't know the old ship was still around."

Saoirse paused. "And of course, my da was there."

"Awkward?"

"Always," she said. "Who I was wasn't secret, much, and Alastair would scrap with whoever made it an insult. Called me his sister, especially when Rian would insist 'half.' Christ, that boy. Could never leave well enough alone. I don't deserve a brother like him."

Wil recalled a time when he'd mistaken Saoirse for Alastair's girlfriend and decided to never tell her for as long as he lived. "He's a good kid."

"Aye," she said and fell into a restless quiet.

He touched her hand. "You don't have to keep—"

"So, it's half twelve," she blurted, "and Malcolm says Gordon's gone missing. Alastair won't have it, says we got to look. Even back then, the two were inseparable, 'specially with how thick Elijah and Rian were."

With the sympathetic approach dead-on-arrival, Wil chose active listening instead. "Elijah, as in Gordon's brother. Were all his brothers Dogfaces?"

"Only Gordon," she said. "Elijah was a Scots Guard. Worked with Dunne, way back—it's how she kens us, aye? Another few years, and Malcolm and Cameron would've joined the Grey Rifles. They were competing to see who'd make the cut first."

"And this bodyguard practice his family does, is it normal? You said he was sept, but when I asked Gordon about it, he said something about a 'debt of honor,' or…."

"Ol' Ceilidh sheltered the Kicklighters from a mob when their three daughters all birthed Dogfaces one after the other. Kept the crowd from puttin' 'em to torch, kiboshed talk that they'd been consorting with dark spirits." She paused. "Can I tell my story, now?"

Wil relented, palms up. "Sorry, sorry. Please."

Her little smile gave away her false outrage, but it faded fast. The grass in her hands strained, soft fibers tearing. "So, Gordon's gone missing, and Alastair grabs me. Together, we go searchin'. Not fer long, mind. We find Gordon upstairs, crouched in a closet and hidin' from the crowd."

It was hard to picture Gordon as a child, but impossible to imagine him afraid. "Then what?"

"Then, there's a man in the bedroom who weren't there before," she said. "A shinobi. And he's draped in thermo-optical camouflage, carrying a samurai sword, and we're just kids."

Saoirse tore the blade of grass in two.

"Everything went off," she said. "Blood fury took Gordon, and before I knew it, we were draggin' his furry hide down the stairs, tryna keep his insides from spooling out the slice. Shinobi catches up on the landing. Puts an arrow in Al's back. Comes in close fer the coup de grâce, so I snap up a lamp, take a swing, and…."

Saoirse drew a finger down her face, tracing the scar with her claw.

The clean cut, the narrow width. Obvious, now: monofilament. "Hot damn. And you survived?"

"So far," she chirped, but her snicker didn't last long. "Ducked back on reflex, so the blow went shallow. Took years fer the teeth on that side to sit natural. Eye socket healed right, thank God, but even now there's no feelin' in my cheek, like here, or here…"

He'd touched her before he realized, fingers placed alongside hers on her scar. This time, no disapproving look. No recoil. Wil drew a line down the mark with his thumb, and she only noticed when he'd stopped.

She licked her lips, so close he could smell the sulfur in her hair. "Totally numb."

"And the ninja," he asked, careful to back away with all his extremities intact. "What happened?"

Saoirse's brow pinched, tipsy color blooming under her freckles. "Well, I, uh… I thought we were dead. Then, Neil's da, Lloyd, burst in wae his claymore, and scared the piss outta the ninja. Started shoutin', help, help. Didn't last long—died a second later, cut straight in half. And just as the ninja'd done him in, my father charged in, picked up Lloyd's weapon, and…"

She went quiet, picking at her claws. Wil knew what happened next. He'd seen it. The katana, seized into the core of the claymore. Two names, written on the hallway monument. Neil's words to Saoirse long ago in the cell made sense now; she'd inherited Alexander MacArthur's intact weapon, while his inheritance had been relegated to the memorial hall.

They'd both bet their lives on a deathblow.

"Nine months later," Saoirse said, "Rian passed in an ambush alongside Elijah. Cameron and Malcolm followed the summer after. Poison. Alastair's mum that winter, from cancer. And if Kurage hadn't kicked off when it did, I'm sure Alastair and Gordon would've been next."

The history of Clan MacArthur, written in blood.

Wil blew out a sympathetic breath. No wonder no one else ran for chieftain with the katana of Damocles hanging over their head. Words didn't seem enough.

"Funny," she said, drawing lines in the dirt with her claw. "Alastair's older now than Rian was when he went. Never thought of that till now."

"Are they still a threat?" he asked. "The ninja."

"Not after the Uprising. Eideard says their clan got wiped out. Figured the Teseum were the reason for the contract, ken? Lotta folks said it must've been PanOceania. MagnaObra had hooks in our mine, lost it, wanted it back. No way to be sure. But, funny enough, the moment the DRC broke ground on that mountain, the very first call we got… I bet ye ken what it was for."

He chuckled nervously. "No wonder no one liked me."

"I liked you," she said, flattening his guard. "But then ye kept secrets, and you lost yer mind when Talbot leaked what ye'd done. Ye fancied me, then hated me. And now, I cannae tell at all."

"I don't hate you," he said. "Never have."

Saoirse wrestled with herself for a moment, but her conviction flared. "They say yer a coward, Wil. They say yer the worst there's ever been. But ye stormed the Shas with me at the Brume, killed five, and were the only one beside Fionn itchin' fer a hundred more. Ye coulda ditched Nora in the garage, and no one would've seen. Could've run at the Croatoan. I caught the moment you thought it, too, gawking at the stairs, but then ye came back."

"C'mon, Saoirse. Not this."

She placed a hand on his chest. "Wil, please. Talk to me."

Pinned against the mountainside, there was only surrender.

27

Wil took a deep breath.

"So, three days after I make captain, we're outside Ulveslør. The location's secret, but the mission is routine: reinforcing ALEPH's Special Situations Section as they closed in on a suspected Shasvastii cell. T-minus five, the SSS were en route to engage, we're bunkered at an adjacent block to provide fire support, and then the Shas make first contact. With us."

Saoirse settled back, her knee touching his. Listened.

"At first, it was comlogs disconnecting. Bad signal. We chocked it up to the blizzard. Then the Dazers kicked in—alien tech deployables. They broadcast this frequency that fucks with your inner ear, kills your balance, and these nanobots that make the air, like—thicker. Harder to move.

"So we collapse in. Trade some fire, fall back. No visual. We're prepping to receive their spearhead when I get a call. It's the Hexa, this inimitable asshole named Gavon Fhorst, and he tells me ALEPH is ordering our retreat.

"I don't get it. In my opinion, we're stable. Backup is on the way. We can hold out versus some terror tactics, buy time for the main force. But Fhorst says, listen, you might not know it, but you're overrun. Totally surrounded. Fall back, and let the Proxies handle this. So I order our withdrawal, and the moment my guys are about to break cover, a Q-Drone stands up from behind a snowbank."

Saoirse narrowed her eyes. "Q-Drone?"

"They're like the Shasvastii version of a Katyusha Mul, or a Sierra Dronbot—unloads on anything that moves. But instead of a rocket, or 5.56 rounds, a Q-Drone's rocking ionized gas cartridges loaded with actual, literal plasma. Cartridge hits, E/M field breaks, plasma expands. Boom, zap."

"Jesus," she breathed.

"I take a hit. My armor suffers the brunt of it, but I'm separated. I shout for the Fusiliers to scatter, and neutralize the threat to cover their escape. What I don't do is anticipate the second Q-Drone. Twelve plasma rounds later, and that was fucking *that*."

"Then, the video…"

"A WarCor was on scene. We were recorded, the footage was edited, and it got leaked."

"So, out of frame," Saoirse said. "Yer not hiding?"

"Fighting for my life, actually. The moment that plasma shocked me, I lost it. Charged. All I could think about was neutralizing the Q-Drone, safeguarding my men. But by the time the quickening was gone, everyone was already dead— everyone but Llano. I went to carve a path for MedEvac, but it didn't get there in time."

Saoirse touched his arm. "How long till they come back?"

"Never," he said. "Plasma fried their Cubes, and it'll be a cold day in hell when rank-and-file can afford a back-up like that."

He could tell by her expression she'd never once considered that resurrection in PanOceania was unavailable to the lower class. She wet her lips and leaned closer, insistent. "Alright, but new comlogs have all kindsa tech, right? Satellite feed, battlefield visualization, AR—so, how they dinnae ken ye were surrounded? Where was your support?"

He saw what she was doing. "That's the thing, Saoirse. In debriefing, Fhorst explained that ALEPH considered the loss of our small support force as acceptable to draw out the hidden elements of the Shasvastii assault team, that it worked to the main force's advantage. 'Sometimes, you have to sacrifice the rook.'"

Saoirse's scarred face stayed frozen in crooked shock. "What?"

"Fhorst's words, not mine."

"So where's that fucker now, then?"

"Six feet under. Some schmuck on Paradiso saluted him near a deployable repeater, and his Tubarão ate a direct strike from a guided missile."

Her glare deepened. "When's *he* come back?"

"I get what you're saying," Wil said, "but it's not his fault. ALEPH made a mistake. Publicly, on-camera, resulting in loss of human life. That couldn't get out. Someone had to take the fall."

"And so you played the rook."

He nodded. "The Human Sphere needs ALEPH, Saoirse. Some cowardly Aquila Guard? Not so much. So they cited conduct unbecoming, stripped me of honors, and stuck me in solitary until the public forgot and the evidence got scrubbed from Maya. That took six months. After, I was demoted, but not discharged, and for two years I played sentry to an unused garden elevator at the Hexahedron in San Pietro until they sent me to Dawn with Rajan."

"Six months solitary? Christ, Wil, I'm so sorry."

"I deserved it," he said.

She recoiled. "Fuck's sake, what?"

"I could've refused ALEPH's orders. Could've been smarter. Could've disagreed, or improvised, but I did what I was told. If we'd bunkered in, if we'd ignored the command, my soldiers would've lived. Going out into the open was suicide. Two years of tactical training, an 'acceptable' in battlefield acumen, and I didn't ever stop to think for myself."

Saoirse gripped his wrist. "Wil, no. I felt the same way about my da—if I'd only done this, or that. But the truth is, I hadn't any power, I only—"

Wil tugged free. "ALEPH advised. I complied. End of story."

"Tell someone," she pleaded.

"Never."

"*Wil.*"

"Ten years," he said. "I've been in the PanOceanian military for ten years. More than a third of my life. So they blackballed me, so what? Outside of boosting lockers, it's the only stable income I've ever had. It's my entire life, and if I cross that line, there's no coming back. But once we save this delegation and stomp out these Shasvastii, things'll change."

Saoirse's brows pinched together. "Change, how?"

"I'll get my life back, for starters. Prove I'm not the coward everyone thinks I am. Get my old commission back, my old apartment. Be the hero for once in my goddamn life, and after all that, maybe I'll be able to look at myself in the mirror again. Someone recommended me for this, Saoirse. Someone's got faith in me—at least, besides you."

She stilled. "Thought this was about helping people."

"It is," he said. "But this might finally get me back to where I'm supposed to be."

"Where yer supposed to be," she repeated, and drifted from the torchlight.

The hole inside him widened, draining away his borrowed courage. No. This was good. He'd suck it up, be the villain, end this. She deserved better. Someone stronger. Someone who would give up the stars to stay in the mud with her—someone who could.

He needed to keep looking up, not looking back.

Saoirse lunged. Fast. Her fingers knotted the collar of his shirt. He shielded his face with his arms, but she shoved past to press her lips against his. The shock jolted his push into a grip. Recoil became reciprocation.

There was vanilla in the whisky on her breath.

Caramel on her lips.

And when Saoirse pulled away, the creases beneath her eyes doubled. Pain. It reminded him why he'd tried so hard to avoid this, how pathetic he was for giving in. He should've gotten up and gone back to camp the moment he saw her in the hot spring.

He opened his mouth, and Saoirse muffled him with her fingers. "Don't," she whispered. "More for me than you. I don't do regrets, Wil, not any more. Call me selfish, sure, but yer priorities are as fucked as mine."

Her hand relaxed and fell away, calluses brushing his cheek. "I think ye should take a long, hard look at who yer burnin' away the total of your life for. Those fuckers used ye, ruined ye, abandoned ye, and yer dream is to beg to be their hound? Wilhelm Gotzinger, sure, but I ken Willem Ortega's better than that. An outcast, like us. Like me. And if ye don't fancy any particular Nomad Nation, I'm certain our Clan MacArthur would be glad tae have ye."

His first instinct was indignation. Then, rebuttal, but he didn't know what to say. There was no convenient joke, no easy out—because she was right.

Saoirse released him and stood. Tanit's light caught in her hair, illuminating red and redder strands. If she'd reached out for him now, he would've taken her hand and followed her anywhere in the goddamn universe.

"Give it a think," Saoirse said, and went back up the ridge.

ᛏᛏ

The way down was much harder than up. Despite a hundred new worries, Wil barreled on with overt confidence. Treetops swayed without wind. Rocks shimmered and wobbled underfoot. More and more, the descent shifted until it coursed out from under him, and he sprawled on his ass in the middle of the path.

His head spun. His heart kicked. Thin, red scratches glistened on his palms. A meter to his left, the rocky cliffside threatened a long drop into absolute nothingness.

Shit, had that really just happened? He'd choked. She'd kissed him, and he'd choked. He needed to apologize. Had they been trauma bonding?—ugh, that wasn't good—he'd been such an asshole—damn good kisser though, fangs hardly in the way—and why was his face so hot?

Ah, balls. He was drunk.

Guiding himself along the ridge with his hand, Wil plodded on. Each wobbly step threatened a deadly fall, each loose stone a broken leg, and he only remembered he'd left his Detour behind when he was way too far to possibly go back.

Ahead, a shadow lingered below a crop of dewy nettles. Hodges. He sat on a stone with his balaclava removed, and the cherry of his cigarette glowed in his eyes when he dragged on it.

Mierda. The one guy who had it out for him, the one guy who—

Hodges perked. Stared directly at Wil through the dark.

Gave him a thumbs up.

Rocks shifted down the path. Footsteps, announcing another person's arrival. Hodges swiftly ground the nub under his heel and wafted the smoke—but when Dunne rounded the corner, by her crossed-arms demeanor, Wil knew the poor bastard was busted.

With a beleaguered sigh and a, "Yes, dear," the deflated ex-SAS escorted his Scots Guard back to camp.

Their footsteps faded. Wil shivered and clambered down the path to sit on Hodges' newly vacant ridgeside seat. It wasn't warm or comfortable, but stasis stopped the ground from rolling. He'd sober up here before heading back, rest a moment, wait for the mountain to settle down. The air tasted bitter, tinged with menthol and ash—no wonder Dunne despised it on her partner's breath. Why they were still legal on Dawn, Wil had no idea.

And the hell was that thumbs-up about?

His duster pocket emitted a muffled crackle. His comlog. Wil extracted it with great effort and laid it on his lap. The screen flickered, the dial projected, and the words CALL WAITING impatiently hung in mid-air. No callsign. No image.

Had to be Saoirse.

Earpiece in hand, Wil answered. "Hey, listen. Can we pretend that didn't happen? I should've stopped talking, and, uh—"

"Lieutenant Gotzinger." A small voice. Feminine. Not Saoirse. "We don't have much time."

The night's persistent chill penetrated him and constricted around his heart. His temples throbbed. Mouth, dried. There was protocol for this, priorities, but they faded before he spoke. "Who is this? How'd you connect to this network?"

"Nomad satellite uplink. We're speaking via free-space optical communication."

"Tell me who you are, or I drop the link."

"A friend," the woman answered. "You don't seem to have many of those lately, do you? Friends. I want to help you. I know about what's going on in Dun Scaith. The Shasvastii. The delegation."

His fingers hung over the touchscreen, ready to cut the call. "Name."

"Scáthach," she answered. "While you're no Cú Chulainn, you'll do."

Wil blurted the first thing on his mind. "He's one of them, isn't he? Odune."

Scáthach paused. "The Counselor has grown unstable."

"Called it," he said. "Bet you're one of them, too. Power struggles getting that desperate, huh? Hoping I'll vacate the position so you can snag a promotion?"

"A small PanOceanian contingent arrived in the DRC recently, looking for you. Your absence has alarmed some very powerful people."

Couldn't imagine who. Couldn't even speculate.

"Things are spiraling out of hand, and the scope of our purpose has been lost," Scáthach said. "Reinforcements have been called in from cells all across the continent. They're preparing for something massive."

"*Purpose*. Great euphemism for speciocide."

"Humans are locked into an endless cycle of misery and death. Interesting that you insist being freed from it by the firm hand of true civilization is wholly impermissible."

"No more war when there's no one left to fight. I get it."

The channel popped with the uneven timing of her breaths. "The Counselor—Odune—should have never shot you down. Not only did it violate his directives, but it's endangered our purpose. A certain level of controlled rebellion is necessary, but this has gone too far."

The idea that the EI allowed its soldiers to step out of line only to prop up an illusion of freedom struck him as both funny and sad. "I'm not your fucking hitman."

"The uncertainty. The conflict. The *violence*. You can lie and say you haven't missed it, but I've read your file. You're truly skilled at hurting people."

"Yeah well, y'all are aces at dying."

"My kind, on the other hand, are more subtle. Intelligent. We would do well together. Complement our strengths. Both gain. You'd like your reputation restored, no? Your position reclaimed, your power returned?"

"You can say you want peace and ascension and all that other shit, but I don't believe you. I've seen what your Combined Army does to civilians, to prisoners of war, to medics on the frontline."

"And I've seen your kind do the same to mine on Paradiso." Scáthach paused. "What do you hope to gain by resisting an alliance?"

"Ain't about gain. You're about to kill a lot of people who don't deserve it."

"I want the same thing. To save innocent lives, placed into jeopardy by the unconscionable actions of my superiors. We're both fighting for the greater good, for the survival of our species, for—"

Wil breathed out a little laugh. "You practice this sales pitch in the mirror this morning? You're kicking ass. Keep going."

A pause, then the connection severed, leaving him alone with the cold.

Wil spun the dial. Shook it. Held the comlog up to the stars, if only so that it might reconnect and he could give this 'Ska-hawh' woman a reason to really hang up on him—

"Who was that?"

If Wil hadn't been drunk, he would've jolted off the ridge. Instead, he swiveled toward the voice, brain spinning like a pinwheel—all torque and flash without purpose.

Alastair stepped out from the dark, thinner without his armor but not by much. The dip in the hot springs had brought a semblance of dignity back to his boyish good looks, and he seemed half as ground down as when he'd tended the Dakota hole that morning. His Teseum dog tags jingled together when he sat down, a deeper and heavier sound than Wil would've expected.

"Lieutenant?"

"Shasvastii," Wil blurted and presented his comlog. "Check the transcript if you want."

"Unnecessary," Alastair said but paged open its history, regardless. Network connection data and incoming/outgoing addresses blurred by under his careful ministration. "Seems she wasn't lying about the satellite uplink. Our location is still secret—wide-net method is surprisingly unreliable at geolocating, considering her Nomad network and this comlog were fabricated about two decades apart. Though, how she got this device's address to seek it out specifically, I'm unsure."

The kid's aptitude boggled him. It was easy to forget that his Mormaer training had included closer contact with the wider Human Sphere than most of his peers. Wil admired his penchant for playing dumb to set his opponents at ease and wondered how often he'd taken that bait before Alastair had stopped setting it.

If he'd stopped.

"Might've grazed a hacking area or something back at the Brume without realizing it," Wil said. "Or one of the ghosts that jumped me might've been a hacker, or deployed a repeater we didn't catch."

"If they sent a hacker to kill you, that's just more proof to my theories about their sloppy incaution."

Whatever response Wil had cooking to that ten-dollar word disappeared along with the drunken lean of the mountainside beneath him. A prickly burn trailed up his throat from his gut, and he swallowed it back down. "Sure."

Alastair returned the comlog. The screen blinked and displayed the manufacturer's boot logo, a telltale sign of a successful reset. "Keep this handy. The next time they call, let me know."

"You're not angry?"

"The enemy of our enemy might prove useful, and all that. I'll inform Cailean and Dunne, but try to keep things hush around the others."

Wil bowed his head. "Yes, sir."

"What I *am* angry about is you sneaking off to get drunk. While on mission. With my sister."

"Yeah, I," he said, and his brain caught up to his mouth.

Alastair set his jaw, eyes the same as in the library the night after his escape. Like he was willing to use words but wouldn't mind it if he had a reason to draw his Americolt and settle things the old-fashioned way.

The brief expectation that Alastair was about to break his deadpan with a grin knocked a laugh out of Wil that he instantly regretted.

"Is there something funny about this?" Alastair asked.

"We were just talking," he hurried. "Swear."

"For two hours?"

Wil rotated the comlog in his hands, trying to summon up the right words from the inebriated pinball machine of his brain. He mashed the paddles until a bumper set off a chain reaction that lit the backboard with digital fireworks.

"Saoirse's, like—I've never met someone like her before, man. Someone who's not afraid of anything, who wears her heart on her sleeve all devil-may-care. I wish I was like that. And what she's done, and gone through? I mean, Al, your sister, she's kind of amazing. Even smiles when she sees me, man. Makes me feel like I'm... seen, I guess. Listens to me. And I listen to her."

Alastair's glare melted into confusion, then awkward concern. "You really were just talking."

Wil slumped against the rock. "Have you seen her calves?"

"A bit too much, there."

He shrugged. "Then don't ask."

"Just... whatever happens, Wil, be kind," Alastair said, and stood. "You're not going to be here for much longer."

"I know," he said and wished he was wrong. Together, they headed back to the campfire.

Saoirse didn't come back until well after sunrise, Detour and empty thermos akimbo. Despite her sparkling skin and voluminous curls, she stunk of sulfur so badly they shifted her scouting position based on the direction the wind turned for the whole next day.

28

On the sixth day, the rocky ground curved into grassy flatland. The fog came in worse than ever before. Freezing rain haunted them from morning to night, flooding their Dakota hole and leaving them shivering. Wil slept, but many others didn't. And then they were walking again by the time Helios crested the horizon, uniforms caked in mud.

Three days until the *Sword of St. Catherine* reached the DRC Dun Scaith.

No further contact, via text or call. As ordered, he hadn't told anyone about Scáthach. Of those told, Cailean seemed ambivalent, almost approving of Wil's rejection. However, from that morning on, Dunne kept Wil firmly planted in her line of sight.

The day wore on, and the remnants of a broken roadway coalesced underfoot. Hundred-year-old surface markings mottled the asphalt path, alongside stretches of rusted signage, tilted light posts, and corrugated guardrails. A wide sign streaked with old growth above the abandoned highway, arrows declaring destinations on a roundabout long since swept from the road: KILDALTON. OUTPOST 16. SCONE. FORT RESOLUTE. OUTPOST 4. DAL RIADA.

An unfamiliar warmth bled into the wind, and the fog died away fast. The overcast broke, and through the cracks in the sluggish clouds above—blue. An actual spring day, for the first time since he'd arrived on Dawn. The evergreen branches danced in the breeze.

The group slowed to a stop beside an upended lorry. Only two klicks to Fort Resolute. After a quick conversation, the forward scouts set off eastward with Alastair, leaving Wil behind with the fireteam.

"Hodges said he spotted trace of a landing craft," Cailean said, Rhiannon loaded and ready across his lap. "Stay ready."

Nora perked up. "Isn't that a good thing? Means Wil's people came to find him, yeah?"

Cailean picked his last cigarette from the pack. "Here's hoping."

Further evidence that Scáthach hadn't been lying, but it didn't bring him relief. No matter what might happen next, Wil didn't want to chance losing his

MSV again. He pried open the visor's compartment, discarded the dead Mul battery, and mashed in the ORC auxiliary unit. It took some negotiating—he wasn't a Machinist, after all—but it fit. The HUD railroaded him through new user setup for the fourth time since the crash, but the diagnostics said FULL POWER, and infrared was one gesture away.

A quick crackle over comms silenced the Volunteers. Hodges. "Victor 6, this is Foxhound. Check, over."

Vern held his comlog to his face, choking the hologram with his other hand. "Foxhound, this is Victor 6. Loud and clear. Over."

"Victor, be advised, Papa Oscar is confirmed on-site. Rally to Sunray. Over."

Papa Oscar—PanOceania. Relief and impatience swirled together in Wil's chest. This long, horrible chapter of his life was about to come to a close.

Or the Shas had sent a kill team wearing blue berets.

The group jogged over the rough. More mud. More roots. A derelict bus tilted half-sunk into the mud, and ten meters away, a jungle gym lay sheeted with vines. Mud hardened into pavement, and yesterday's rain collected in missile craters in the road. Unlike Outpost 4, fire hadn't flattened Fort Resolute. The clustered, multi-story buildings still stood, though many hadn't survived their abandonment unscathed. Balconies sagged, signs eroded, and great splotches of moss and mold intermingled up the facades. Trees punched through rooftop tile all along the thoroughfare, roadways lined with the rusted chassis of centuries-obsolete gasoline automobiles.

On the horizon, what remained of the Fort's docks tilted below the waterline into Loch Eil, rusted struts and slabs marking the shallows like a graveyard. A concrete drum of a building squatted beside the eastern wall, the same make as the Croatoan in Kildalton. Another bunker, though judging by its access to the highway, this one must've been a fuel depot.

Alastair crouched behind an overgrown bus stop, scanning the clearing with a pair of black binoculars. Wil hunkered beside him, and Alastair offered them over. "Middle clearing," he said. "Past the collapsed wall."

The clearing was, in actuality, a parking lot—or what was left of it. The blackened husks of more modern prefabs lay on the other side surrounded by Zion-style palisades. He could easily imagine the barracks, the admin facility, the DFAC beside them both. Atop a leaning, moss-soaked watchtower, a sun-bleached Ariadnan flag hung dead at the top of its pole.

A Tubarão hunkered amidst the tangle of cars ahead, turbines still and silent. Two Fugazi Dronbots perched atop its winglets, red oculi dim. In standby. A small accompaniment of PanOceanian soldiers milled through the grass, their smart-fabric uniforms blending in to the natural greens.

Saoirse's voice crackled over comms. "Sunray, this is Princess. Looks like a search party. Over."

Alastair muted his comlog and glanced at Wil. "Seems your friend was telling the truth."

"She's not my friend," he said and dialed up his visor's magnification. Within seconds, the four-hundred meter distance zoomed into a manageable fifteen. He clocked the scattered forces' loadout: An Orc Trooper HMG, two Fusiliers, a Pathfinder Dronbot, and a Bulleteer Spitfire with its Optical Disruption Device deactivated—for now. Plus the two Fugazi, that made seven.

If Rajan had to bribe the officials a hundred Oceanas for Wil's MULTI Marksman to clear customs, this must've cost a fortune. "If they're a search party, they're loaded for Bearpode."

"I'm only counting seven," Dunne said. "TO or TAG, place your bets now."

"Neither," Saoirse answered. "Comlog's pinging at least three more Fusi near the ruins. Gonna take a closer look."

"Acknowledged, Princess," Cailean said. "Though, tread lightly. I wouldnae trust these degens tae ken a Wulver from a Tartary brown bear."

Gordon huffed a laugh. "Don't mind if I stick prone, then."

Alastair drummed his fingers on his ballistic shield, deliberating over a holographic representation of the battlefield. The positions of each forward scout bounced around the map, lagging harder the farther they strayed. "Victor 6, is there a chance we could connect to their repeater network, open a channel?"

"If we piggyback their net, they'll no doubt think we're attempting a hack. Assuming they're friendly to begin with." Vern rapped his knuckles on the clunky box inside his backpack. "Assuming this baby doesn't shit out again."

Wil considered the options and sighed. "Only one way to find out."

It only took a moment to shake out the battle plan. Alastair marked the map of Fort Resolute on his comlog with Markers Alpha through Juliett, as well as where and how to approach each site to regroup with the others when this inevitably went sideways.

Wil slipped his Strela across his back and stepped out from cover, approaching the Tubarão and the PanOceanian fireteam with a wasp hive buzzing in his guts. Felt wrong. Couldn't be this easy. Too much cover in every direction, too many places to watch all at once.

Vern dictated a quick broadcast from Alastair: "All units, be advised. Errant is making contact with Papa Oscar. Stand by, over."

Hodges chuckled in Wil's ear. "Wish you all the Caledonian luck, mate."

Wil drew his Detour and removed the magazine. "Jokes on you, Foxhound. If I didn't have bad luck, I wouldn't have any at all."

Alastair requested radio silence, so Wil muted his comlog. If one of the Fusiliers heard chattering in his earpiece and got jumpy, this wouldn't go good for the boys in blue.

A tall, bone-white billboard teetered precariously over the overgrown crawl between the PanOceanian transport and their location. For an instant, Wil's visor flagged motion atop its corner, and then the outline vanished. "Watcher in position," Pell transmitted. "Errant, I'm counting two more in their ship. CSU. You're safe for another fifteen meters."

As if cued, two men jogged out of the open Tubarão cabin. Wil recognized them—Fontaine and Ghent, the two security officers from Odune's office who shared a crew cut and mirrored shades. They were already whipped into a frenzy, unlimbering weapons and shouting in garbled unison: "Contact, contact, contact!"

Wil stretched his arms up, dangling the unloaded Detour from his fingertips. "Lieutenant Wilhelm Gotzinger, 3508-9469. DOB, 16/6/41 NC. It's empty."

"Gun, gun, gun!" Fontaine barked, shotgun wobbling as he ran.

Ghent groped the air until the manual safety on his Combi Rifle switched off, and the Breaker ammunition in the magazine flared the color of the Concilium Prima sky. "On the ground! Face down! Hands in the air!"

The Orc Trooper disengaged from the bewildered Fusiliers across the yard and rushed over with his MULTI Rifle magnetized to his back, forest-green fist raised. "Stand down! I repeat, stand down!"

The two idiots hesitated, confused. They let the barrels of their weapons fall, oblivious of how their lines of fire intersected each other. "Sir?"

Relief cut through Wil, though he didn't lower his hands. "Appreciate it, fellas."

The Orc Trooper closed in on Wil, four red eyes taking in Wil's slapdash visor, painted with the Caledonian flag; the Ariadnan-issue AKNovy Strela dangling on his back; his boots, kneepads, and standard Ariadnan flak. He cleared his throat. "There's been a murder."

A challenge-and-pass. It was near-ancient now, used last during the Commercial Conflicts, but it'd been in the intel Wil had received before landing. So much had happened since then it took him a full six seconds to recall. "Check the purple burglar alarm."

"Which foot fits which foot," the Orc replied, passing Wil's own challenge, and lowered his weapon. "With all due respect, Lieutenant, what the hell are you wearing?"

Wil lowered his arms. "It's a long story."

"Command would love to hear it," the Orc said, waving Fontaine and Ghent off. "We'd retraced your flight plan on the ground for the last two days. Nothing. No charred fuselage, no sign of conflict. The Fusiliers were taking bets on whether you deserted, got black-bagged, or the Antipodes found you."

"Not bad," he said, and went for a handshake. "Two out of three."

The Orc double-tapped his proffered forearm, but Wil didn't have the patience to explain why the permission exchange wouldn't work. "Are you alone?"

"Escort's in the trees. They're friendlies. Promise."

The Orc's four red oculi scrutinized the outskirts, searching. Judging by his subtle backstep, Wil was sure he'd put eyes on more than a few. "Mother of God. Alright, 'friendlies.' Is Brizuela with you?"

"Not currently," Wil said. "We're headed east to the DRC."

The Orc's gauntlet tightened on the grip of his MULTI Rifle. "Odune said you'd turned traitor."

He suppressed a bitter laugh. "No, I haven't. Listen—Shasvastii have in-filtrated the DRC-9 Dun Scaith. Odune's one of them. They're planning to hijack the *Sword of St. Catherine* when it sets down in three days. You need to relay that message, right here, right now."

The Orc tilted his head. "What? Wait."

"They hit our transport with a missile, openly attacked us on the highway, and—"

"Wait, wait, you cut out," the Orc said, voice muffled—his vox had gone. "Apologies, soldier, my geist's going hay—"

The Orc clapped a hand to his radial sensor and froze. The glow in his oculi darkened, and his armor cycled from camouflage green to PanOceanian blue. The servos in his joints all hissed at once when they released pressure, but none of them unlocked.

Wil's visor pinged an unknown target within a tangle of brush atop a rusted watch tower, twenty meters out.

From beneath the notification, a spark. A plume of light speared into the Tubarão. A cloud of fire engulfed the clearing, the Fusiliers, the Dronbots. The explosion shoved Wil off his feet, but the Orc remained planted, artificial muscle bulging as he raged against his armored coffin. Shrapnel decorated his armor all along the side where he'd shielded Wil from the worst of it. His eyes reignited, free of the Carbonite, and as he dropped his hand, a hole cracked dead-center through his Adam's apple.

Warm mist spattered Wil's face. The tang of iron jabbing up his nose was enough to shock him into motion, and he was on his feet. Old automobiles laid abandoned in the adjacent parking lot. Steel chassis. Engine blocks. Cover that'd do more than obscure his silhouette. At full tilt, Wil sprinted from the overgrown parade ground and slid behind a wheel well.

No missile impact. No sniper shot. He sat there, panting, for longer than he should've before returning the mag to his Detour. Comms spun up easy and played back static. Hand to his earpiece, he spoke into the white noise. "Victor 6, this is Errant. Where are you? Copy, over."

Nothing but static. Again. Had to be a hack, but the only repeater near the Orc was his own deactivated Fugazi.

Uneven footsteps approached his position. Limping. Fontaine and Ghent. The two CSUs struggled into cover a car-length away, faces coated in sweat and smoke residue. Blood drooled through the gaps in Fontaine's fingers, hand clutched over his stomach—bad, but not immediately lethal. At least Ghent seemed strong enough to carry him.

The cynic in him faltered, replaced by cold relief. Not everyone had died in the missile strike. Not who he might've chosen, but better than no one at all. "Hey. Hey, guys!"

Ghent didn't hear him. He breathed hard, readied his Combi rifle, and prepared to stand.

"Don't!" Wil shouted. "Stay low, dammit. There's a Noctifer out there, and a sniper—probably a Haiduk—best to keep—"

Fontaine sputtered. He jabbed his boarding shotgun down the row like a saber. "Hey, it's him! Ghent, it's Gotzinger!"

Ghent jolted, Combi instantly at his shoulder. "Hands up! Face down, now!"

Wil narrowly contained the impulse that shocked along his arm, magnetizing his fingertip to the trigger of the Detour. He pried it back, and kept his weapon lowered. "Don't."

"You led us into this," Ghent shouted. "You're with the Highlanders!"

"Should've known," Fontaine said, and his red stain slicked deeper, dripped darker. "Traitor! Knew it all along!"

The pavement unsettled beneath Wil. A crack popped and formed, and then another. Dust puffed from the gaps in the asphalt, carrying the heavy, bitter stench of expired gunpowder. Something was burrowing under them. Something big.

Wil held his breath and propped his weight onto the open car window beside him until his feet floated. "Shut up," he hissed. "There's—"

"I said hands up, now!" Fontaine shouted, and tried to rack his shotgun. The forestock didn't budge without the release depressed, and he banged it on the rear-view mirror above him. "You don't—"

Something growled beneath the asphalt.

The broken ground beneath Fontaine ripped open, and a rocky, squat creature the size of a German Shepherd lunged out, scrabbling on two enormous, fin-like forearms. Its mouth gaped in a sawtooth grin, eyes masked with metal laced in strobing diodes. A massive steel collar burdened its neck, notched with a single rifled pit.

Wordlessly, Ghent turned and sprinted away.

"Ghent!" Fontaine bellowed. "Ghent, wait—"

The creature shot forward and axed a jagged fin through his face. Mirrored shades and fragments of shattered mandible scattered together on the asphalt.

Ten meters away, Ghent sucked below the earth. His scream halted abruptly, replaced by guttural barking and a loud, wet rip.

Taigha. Asteroid-dwelling monstrosities from beyond the Human Edge that hunted by vibration, affixed with a sensory-overload-inducing faceplate to better drive them into a berserk rage. The Shasvastii were said to use them like the ancient Romans did attack dogs—cannon fodder to soften the enemy for the more sapient troops that followed.

They were supposed to be cryptids. Not real. But there one was, unsticking its claw from Fontaine's face and licking the gaps in the keratin. Its glistening, purple tongue lapped up the pinkish grain dripping from the crack, and when he twitched—it bit down.

An errant thought, amongst the quickening: Fontaine's comlog might still be intact, and with it, a chance to send that distress call via direct line.

Wil shifted from his anchor on the window. Heart hammering against every breath, he stood. Silent and slow, he leveled the Detour on the creature's unsuspecting back. Fontaine's linklet jingled on his wrist as the creature sucked out his eye.

He pulled the trigger; the Taigha jerked left. Fontaine's corpse danced, skull popped by a narrow miss. Whirling, the creature steadied itself. One foot planted on Fontaine's wrist, snapping his linklet in half, and the pit in its collar sparked.

Wil ducked. A plume of shrapnel cut above his head.

Nope.

He bolted away, slamming from one derelict to the other in his rush. His gear scraped and clanged on rearview mirrors and door handles. Braying followed him through the lot. First one voice, then a cacophony. A second Taigha swiped at his shins from the undercarriage of a van, and he vaulted the hood to keep from its reach. Ahead, a third blocked his path, arms cocked high like a praying mantis. He ducked left, and it launched toward his face.

Thump. A small dark dot knifed through the center of its chest. The impact torqued it in midair. Entrails streaked from its back like ribbons as it flopped dead to the asphalt.

From the corner of the billboard, far, far away—the report of a rifle.

Behind him, the monstrosity that'd killed Fontaine hollowed out in a splatter. Out from beneath the van, another, and in the span of one distant pop it went limp and fell. Its metal facemask curled open, steel bent like flower petals. Smoke hissed from the damp cavity beyond.

Not normal bullets. T2.

Wil pitched atop the nearest vehicle, kneepads scuffing the rust. Back flat, still as he could get, he listened for more. The barking in the lot grew louder, then faded. They'd lost him—at least, for now.

Comms crackled in his ear, revitalized. "Errant, copy," Pell said. "Hey, Errant, you die? Say something soon, or I'm coming for my visor."

"Copy, Watcher," Wil said. "This is Errant. Nice shooting. Where'd you all go?"

Pell grumbled, inaudible, for a good four seconds. "Errant, main force is en route toward the city center chasing three PanO survivors. Sunray wants their comlogs, says it'll bypass the Arachne problem. Any down there salvageable? Over."

He scanned the wreckage of the Tubarao. No bodies, at least none that had all the parts of a comlog intact enough to swipe. The two Fugazi Dronbots stood vigil beside the smoldering wreckage, riddled with shrapnel and deactivated. In the cargo hold, a single Mulebot idled, red optics blinking. Fire curdled the paint on its chassis but it made no move to save itself.

A distance away, the Bulleteer laid half dismembered but unmoving. Farther, where the Orc had once lain, a reddish scrape dragged its way into a fresh-churned hole in the earth.

"Negative," Wil answered. "You sure it's three?"

"Sure as the sun's up," Pell said.

He'd clocked nine. Three made twelve. Plus the Mulebot, thirteen. Strange number for an op, and he didn't like it. "Watcher, this doesn't feel right. I think we're getting baited."

"Tell Bleeding-Heart MacArthur that," Pell chortled. "One idiot making a bad move is a mistake, lad—thirteen is a plan of action in itself."

He had a point. "Alright. Got a bearing for me?"

"You're safe to cover due east, fifty meters—but mind we still don't have eyes on what took out their air transport. Watcher, out."

As Pell cut out, another voice spoke in his ear. "Errant, this is Victor 6."

His anger flared too quickly. "Comms goes out on me one more time, motherfucker, and I'll—"

Vern spoke over him with enunciated calm. "Do not answer. Rally immediately to Marker Echo. I repeat, Errant, this is Victor 6, do not answer..."

A recording. Wil choked on his frustration, breathed it out. This wasn't the time for anger. On his comlog's holomap, the pin of Marker Echo hugged the edge of Fort Resolute where the quay fell into the loch. He'd give Vern a piece of his mind there when he wasn't walking in a minefield of monsters.

The percussive echo of gunfire bloomed up from the ruins—more resistance. More Shasvastii. The beginning of a firefight. He stood, traded his Detour for the Strela, and sped down the row of derelict cars, hopping from hood to trunk to hood as light-footed as his skinny six-foot-four ass could manage.

He'd made it twenty meters when a scream cut up from the lot.

A human one.

His rush slowed. Stopped. It could be a trick. A distraction. The gunfire harmonized, joined in by more weapons, louder ones. Grenades detonating hundreds of meters away rattled the few surviving windshields in the lot. He'd gotten the MacArthurs into this, and he needed to be there five minutes ago.

But despite the heat in his blood and curdling shame in his gut, Wil turned back. Even if it were a trick, the chance that it might not be was worth the risk. If he were alone on this godforsaken planet, surrounded by monsters, he'd sure as hell want someone to come save him.

Hell, they already had.

Ten meters out, a Fusilier stumbled around the corner of a ruined box truck. He'd lost his Combi, and his pistol, and a finger-sized strip from his thigh. Panicked face mantled in blood and ashen residue, he shouted, "Help! God, please, help!"

Two Taigha trotted after him. They nipped at his knees and feet, clubbed him in the buttocks and hips with their fins. The Fusilier stumbled, and they grunted deep and nasal before clubbing him again.

Playing with their food.

The next club put the Fusilier on his back. He wailed and curled into a ball. When their toothy motivation didn't spur the right entertainment, the Taigha grew impatient. Jaws clacking, they huddled close and tongued his leg wound—like Fontaine's killer, testing the taste before committing to a bite.

Wil braced himself on the hood of the next truck. Took aim. Exhaled, anticipating their supernatural reflexes. Three shots, two hits, and down went both Taigha, corpses draping the Fusilier's shaking form. Both corpses were frighteningly heavy despite their small size, but he dragged them away enough to free the man beneath.

"On your feet," Wil said, and held out his hand.

It took a moment for the gesture to register. "You," the Fusilier stammered, and nothing else. Blood oozed from the new bite marks along his forearms and his leg. Shallow breaths along with Palbot-sized pupils in the Fusilier's eyes spelled shock. He took Wil's hand. On his wrist—a PanOceanian military comlog.

The relief nearly put Wil on his ass. This was enough, just this. One comms broadcast, and everything would be over. The Shasvastii had tried so damn hard to keep them at bay, and in the end, it was a trembling Fusilier who'd make the call and put an end to all their alien bullshit.

An echoing machine-gun burst brought him back to reality. Even if they had won the war, the battle was still being fought about three-hundred meters away. He needed to get there five minutes ago. No time for a victory lap.

Wil hauled the Fusilier to his feet, snapped off their beret, and compressed it to his dripping thigh. "Focus, man, focus. You're gonna live. It's just blood. Where's your Combi?"

The Fusilier made a distressed sound, leg shaking. "Dropped it."

"Pistol?"

He pawed at his empty holster before finally taking the beret. "I dunno."

"Okay, that's alright. Here." Wil unlimbered his Detour and slipped it into the Fusilier's free hand. "Good pistol. Very reliable. You got a name?"

With trembling fingers, he pointed out his name badge on his vest. Without a lens, the surface of it was blank. "Glasscock," he said. "Daniel."

Wil swallowed his sympathy. "Hey, man. Your comlog still work?"

"It should be," Glasscock said, "but the DRC cut the channel. Did—did I get hacked?"

Wil swallowed his frustration. Of course they'd have safeguarded themselves already, cut Glasscock off from the network. "No. Disconnect yourself from your datasphere, right now. Everything. Don't turn it back on, no matter how much your geist cries. Can you fight?"

He shook his head, quaking through a few comlog gestures. While he worked, Wil scanned the horizon. A tall sign for a gas station stuck up from the brush a quarter mile away, not far from a leaning water tower.

Wil pointed it out. "Now, I want you to hide. The top of that tower's good, or the gas station roof if the ladder's padlocked. Stay there. Hide. We'll meet their force head-on and draw them away, but they're gonna be looking for you."

"Me?" Glasscock said. "Why?"

"Because you've got this," Wil said, and gripped Glasscock's comlog. "If I don't come back for you by sunrise, turn that comlog on and send an SOS on every channel in its registry. Tell them that the Shasvastii have infiltrated the DRC Dun Scaith on Dawn. Tell them to delay the *Sword of St. Catherine*. Tell them to send everybody, okay? Can you do that?"

Not as easy as he'd hoped, but this would work too. All it required was a distraction, and time. And for Glasscock to show about a hundred percent more competence than at current.

Worst case, it made a good back-up plan.

Glasscock's expression steeled. "Alright. Can do."

"You got something to fix up that bite?"

"My kit was in the Tubarão," he said and inspected the Detour in his hand like it'd teleported there. "Isn't Shock ammo against the Concilium Convention?"

Wil pressed his assault pack into Glasscock's chest until he took it. "Congratulations, you're a war criminal. First-aid pack, side pocket. Got it?"

Glasscock touched the wrong side. "Got it."

"Now, on the count of three, I'm gonna go, and you're gonna hide. Got it?"

"Got it."

"And stay disconnected, or they're gonna drop a Cadmus on your head."

"Okay," Glasscock said. "Okay, I can do that. Hell yeah."

"You're gonna be alright. Ready?"

"Wait-like, a *Shasvastii* Cadmus?" he called, but Wil was already moving.

29

A century of freeze and thaw had ground the asphalt roads of Fort Resolute to gravel. Vines draped along the power lines, anchored in the gutters. Businesses and apartments loomed, brick facades smeared with grunge. Wil charged past it all, Strela in hand, chasing the fresh plumes of smoke.

He crashed into cover below a rust-clad rooftop access ladder. Shapes darted through the street ahead, low to the ground—Taigha. Down the sidewalk, past a bevy of ancient, hollow vending machines, Cailean crouched within an empty doorframe. The Volunteers spread out behind him, chain rifles and shotguns locked and loaded. He saw Wil and flashed a hand-sign before prepping two smoke grenades.

Hold position.

Heavy footsteps and the rattle of gear announced Dunne's semi-invisible arrival. Her poncho shimmered as its photoreactive surface shifted rapidly to match the ruin, its nimbus of blurry color extending to her boots, her mask, her weapon.

She hit the wall beside him breathing hard. "Didn't think you made it."

"Almost didn't," Wil replied.

Dunne cast him a withering look and turned her attention to the road. "Pity. Least then we'd know if you were a Speculo or not."

He opened his mouth, seconds from blurting out Glasscock's existence and their mission's incidental success, and closed it. Something about her suspicion felt correct, almost like advice. He didn't know her. What proof did he have she wasn't a Speculo, either?

It felt shitty, but smart things often did. The information he had now was for Alastair only, and in confidence. Everyone else could wait.

He cleared his throat. "Status report?"

"Shas have Sersh pinned," Dunne said. "A whole fireteam, and there's a big fucker. Bug wings."

Wil's heart sank. He had faith in the MacArthur's Teseum chutzpah, but that wouldn't counter Tactical Armored Gear. Among the TAGs of the Combined Army, the Sphinx was legendary, both in its ambush capabilities and its vicious persistence. "Tell me you're joking."

Dunne replaced the magazine in her Molotok in three seconds flat, tucking the fresh empty into her vest pocket. She squared her Molotok's sight and slid her goggles over her eyes. "Cailean called it a Gwailo. That better?"

No. Not at all.

Gwailos were a first-class combat troop, heavily armed and armored. On Paradiso, old soldiers who'd survived the Second Offensive whispered of the time a battalion of Shasvastii armored infantry single-handedly conquered Xiongxiang City, brushing off the StateEmpire forces that outnumbered them ten to one. A total slaughter. It'd earned them the ISC 'Gwailo,' Cantonese for 'foreign demon.'

While their armor wasn't as tough as an Orc's, their bio-technical shielding was second to none, nigh impenetrable thanks to the nanoscreen that swarmed around them like a sentient sandstorm. Gwailo didn't need cover: their nanobots were the cover. The VoodooTech substrate caught bullets, dissolved rockets without detonation, diffused Viral rounds mid-flight.

He had one question. "Do we know where it is?"

"We will soon," she said and took off at a hard run, each step muffled by her active camouflage. Wil stayed on overwatch down the lane until long after she'd gone, drinking in the quiet before the inevitable chaos.

Alastair barreled from a side street along with Fionn. The belt of H-12 hanging from his Drozhat AP HMG clinked like crystal against his armored thigh. "Sunray and Forty-Fiver, in position."

"Foxhound, in position," Hodges transmitted.

Dunne panted. "Orwell, almost there."

"Princess, stuck out like a knob," Saoirse said. "Clocked some TO, out by Marker Echo. Location uploaded. Smells godawful like Taigha in here. Over."

"Victor 1 here, Princess," Cailean said. "We're workin' on it. Keep prone, over."

Vern cut in. "Sunray, this is Victor 6. Supply cache is guarded, please advise, over."

"Copy. Hold position. Watcher, report?"

"In position," Pellehan said. "Eyes on a Nox fireteam. Sending details. Out."

Wil's comlog lit. Piece by piece, visual by visual, the battlefield scribbled across their shared canvas. Geometric overlays established known firelines. Cailean marked a Taigha warren. Nora called out towers. The enemy troops assembled, their locations guesswork, their armaments unknown. Over the next four minutes, the Caledonians cobbled together a facsimile of the battlefield that would've taken a well-supported PanOceanian contingency six seconds to request from an eye in the sky.

By the time the lengthy procedure finished, Wil had no doubt the Shasvastii not only knew their precise positions and specific loadouts, but their blood types and zodiac signs.

"This is Errant," Wil transmitted. "Glad to see the network's back online, Victor 6. You figure out how turn it off and back on again? Over."

"Apologies, Errant," Vern responded. "With the distance, and the Combined repeater network, there's nothing I can do about frequency interference. Over."

Wil grimaced. Another misfortune to add to the pile.

"Wagtail, at the ready," Gordon transmitted. "Hey, Errant. Are Nox good in CQC? Carry Viral? Any shotguns, chain rifles?"

"Negative," Wil answered. "Poor meleeists. Some carry Zappers—pocket-sized E/M pulse emitters—but all that'll do is turn off your comms."

Gordon chuckled darkly. "Shame."

Pertinent details and enemy positions flicked by on his comlog screen. So many Shasvastii, all deployed along enclosed spaces and balconies. HMGs, MULTI Snipers, light grenade launchers—this wasn't like them to take a fair fight. They were survivalists and terrorists, not shock troopers.

Still, his heart beat with white-hot fire, fingers quickening alongside his—his...Saoirse's position noosed by enemy markers kept breaking his concentration. He tightened his grip on the Strela. Focus. Focus, goddammit, focus.

"Engage on Watcher's signal," Alastair said. "One. Two."

Pellehan's sniper rifle erupted, its report shattering the silence over Fort Resolute. Gordon charged, grenade in one hand, battle-axe in the other. Fionn split from cover. A quartet of smoke grenades rattled out, choking the street in Caledonian fog. The report of Shasvastii Combi fire whistled like birdsong in tight, semiautomatic chirps. Bullets pierced the haze in blind and ineffectual clusters. No visors.

Alastair buzzed through a mixture of hand signals and comlog broadcasts—move up, take space, covering fire. His ballistic shield clattered, drilled by a pair of high-caliber impacts, and he answered with four shots from his Drozhat HMG that left Wil's ears ringing.

"We need to defang that sniper!" Alastair shouted, leaving out the comlog middleman. "Errant, take point above and cover our advance!"

Boots against rung, Wil scrambled up the ladder and onto the roof with a splash. Icy cold sucked inside of his boots, up the legs of his pants. From parapet to parapet, a hundred years of rainwater flooded the roof up past his knees. He pushed past the initial startle and made for the east side. Smoke blanketed the building's edge, obfuscating a nest of Nox on the other side. Shoes squishing, Wil sloshed into his best range without the slightest resistance.

He could get used to this.

A swift gesture activated his MSV. Beyond the smoke, a cluster of Shasvastii shapes bearing heavy arms crouched along the shattered face of an office building. A skywalk connected it to the taller building on Wil's right. That nothing controlled the walkway's dominating sightlines terrified him. Visions of TO camo missile launchers twisted his gut and left him scanning windows.

In the street below, Gordon stalled at the edge of the smoke cover, still himself enough to not rush headlong into certain death. By his frenzied pacing, not for long.

Dunne materialized from behind a tilted light pole. The Nox reacted fast, but not fast enough. Glass rained down onto the fireteam support hiding below, preceding their sniper and machine gunner all riddled with holes from her beloved Molotok. Wil took a potshot at their helpless flank through the smoke, but his intended victim skittered back behind cover unharmed.

Patience snapped, path opened, Gordon bellowed and bolted across the clearing toward their defenseless remainder.

A rush of air. A thunderclap. Flame and smoke. Gordon was gone. Debris rained over the rooftop, rippling the water. No point of origin—nothing to confirm a visual—just a strange cluster of shifting distortion—

Albedo. White noise, intended to jam multispectral vision.

Wil yanked up his visor. Where nothing had stood just a second before now stalked a black-carapaced monstrosity of steel and alien tech. A long-barreled rocket launcher balanced across its pauldron, smoke licking from the barrel. Between two enormous spikes that flanged up from its back like a dragonfly's wings, an enormous, angry cloud of dark substrate whorled.

The Gwailo.

Dunne chanced a shot. Her bullet sparked into the cloud and disappeared.

The Gwailo braced itself against the skywalk railing. Its rockets hissed and took flight at nigh-supersonic speeds. She barely outraced the impact, the pyroclastic flash. Dead vines ignited in the aftermath, lacing the ruins with veins of fire.

They'd been had. The Shas had anticipated their arrival and placed their best roadblock front and goddamn center. They weren't fighting from the back foot at all—that position had calculated sight lines on Alastair, on Cailean, on Wil, on Gordon. And judging by the violet glow radiating from its faceplate, it wore a multispectral visor, too.

The smoke thinned as the first grenades died, revealing Gordon sprawled behind the rust-struck carcass of a burned-out Traktor Mul. Still moving. Still alive. Where his gear had set fire, his flesh held fast—something in his Antipode physiology rejected the flames, healing too swiftly to burn.

But he was hurt. Badly. Blood glistened on his hide.

The Gwailo leaned left and right, searching for an angle. Couldn't let it get one. Strela stocked, Wil lit the Gwailo's position in suppression fire, begging for the ounce of distraction Gordon needed. The ashen cloud of nanobots swarmed to intercept. Bullets blunted across its undulating patterns, swept out of existence. Nothing so much as touched the armor underneath.

Slowly, almost indignantly, the Gwailo turned to face him.

Wil dove on instinct, breaking the rooftop pond with his face. His aural filters maxed out. Deafening. An incredible heat seared through his clothing from behind, duster hissing as it caught fire and doused in the same split second.

The world groaned. Tilted. The water surged away from his face, his hands. The roof was collapsing.

He stuck out a leg to brace himself. Slapped the solar tiles. Palmfuls of sediment slicked up from their surface, and he fell. An aluminum bar speared toward his face. He took the hit across the gauntlet, spun. Daylight grazed every jutting pipe and duct edge just before he struck them. Pain. Forearms, then his knee. His hip. His back. More pain. He spun and twisted and knocked about until he impacted a firm rectangular platform that put the break in breaking his fall.

Wil coughed. "Fuck."

His legs tangled atop an ancient cash register, duster tented on a wire display stand. Empty shelves surrounded him in every direction. Water drained from above in rivers past a network of struts and ducts. A mass of dried, dead flowers swamped the cooler interiors, and murky water churned restlessly on the tile.

He'd fallen into a corner store, or what was left of one, and landed square on the countertop.

A bullet punched through the boarded windows and into the register at his feet. Another. More. Wil rolled from the counter with a splash and bunkered behind the rust-cloaked time-lock safe, weathering the momentary follow-up. A yellowing pinup of a Caledonian lass in a sheer top and tartan miniskirt still stuck to its side.

His earpiece crackled. Alastair. "Errant, copy. Copy! Wil!"

"I'm good," he managed, all pretense of comms etiquette abandoned. "Gordon—is Gordon—"

"Clear," Gordon said. "For now. Gwailo saw Pell and noped back up the road. Mad amount of Taigha en route. Gonna bait 'em up a wall. Going silent. Out."

Saoirse cut in. "Gordon, I'm clear! Comin' to get you. Hold fast!"

"Break, break!" Hodges barked. "We need to stop screwing around and fall back, before—"

Cailean shouted over him. "Incoming!"

Another wave of gunfire swelled within Fort Resolute.

No time to lick his wounds. No time to hesitate. Wil stood, eyes affixed on his comlog—watching the markers rearrange, listening to the chorus of battle grow closer. Pellehan's sniper rifle rippled the air, then again.

The closest source of Shasvastii gunfire went silent.

Now.

Wil sprinted through the shop, out the glassless sliding doors and back onto the street. To his left, Dunne and Alastair choked the side street with suppressing fire. A crowd of Taigha swam along the river of bullets until their skittering luck ran dry. One fell, then another, and then a third was scrabbling at Alastair's ballistic shield, lower half ravaged by Molotok fire. Alastair went one-handed on his Drozhat HMG, drew his Americolt, and finished the job with a flash and a crack.

To his right, Fionn bellowed, mid-vault over a concrete barricade. He buried his claymore into the first incoming monstrosity and carried on toward the second, disappearing into a smoke cloud.

Behind him, the Gwailo loped into the street, footsteps unnaturally silent. It raised its rocket launcher. Aimed toward Dunne.

Wil snapped his rifle to his shoulder lanced it over with bullets. Nothing penetrated, but the distraction was enough, and it turned on him instead.

He bolted. Ten meters away, the street engulfed in flame. Chunks of asphalt scattered against his boots, under his feet. The force buffeted him back. Slip-sliding, arms wheeling, he swerved left and threw himself prone.

Rust, moss, and fresh blood loomed over him. The dilapidated Traktor Mul. Gordon's axe lay buried in its ruined chassis, steel scorched black. Thinning spatter trailed north, source lost in the fog.

Pain. Heat. His sleeve flickered and he—he was on fire. A nearby pothole brimmed with murky water. Wil doused his forearm in it, clenching his jaw through the sizzle. Better sick later than charcoal now.

Cailean barked in his earpiece, "There's too many of them!"

"Not leavin' him behind," Saoirse said. "Almost there!"

"Princess, you're clear for fifty," Pell said. "Good luck."

Hodges chimed in. "Princess, three en route to intercept. Can't identify—targets are under ODD. Caution."

"Got it," she replied. "Princess, out!"

ODD. Optical Disruption Devices. Working under the same principles as thermo-optical camouflage, ODD bent light around the wearer, distorting their outline and obfuscating their true position. Where TO Camo was passive, ODD was active—the photon-bending field spun their position like a prism but didn't hide their presence.

Shasvastii with that kind of tech only meant one thing: Jayth Cutthroats, guerilla soldiers from a vicious high-gravity system. Instead of chitin and slug skin, they were wreathed in thick, almost prehistoric hide. Where Shasvastii were spindly and lithe, Jayth were swollen and thick. Where Shasvastii were predictably cruel, the Jayth were somehow worse.

"Cannae support shite wi' this racket," Cailean growled, brogue thickened by fury. "Either we zero the Gwailo, lad, or Saoirse 'n' Gordon are dead when it pincers us."

Across the intersection, a rocket punched into the rotted interior of a shop. Fire belched onto the street. Gentle, mechanical footfalls betrayed the Gwailo's position as it walked one way, then the other. Pacing. Searching. Click, click, click.

Wil appreciated the candor. Their armor was famously soundless—the footsteps were purely to intimidate. Arrogant, but they'd definitely earned it.

The vox of its helmet cracked, and the Gwailo spoke, voice more feminine than he expected. "Lieutenant," it beckoned. "Oh, Lieutenant? I'm glad I've found you, Lieutenant. You have the power to end this. Please surrender."

Wil unseated the mag from his Strela and paused. He'd prepared himself for a lot of things from the Shas, but politeness wasn't on the list.

"I would have very much liked to have never worn this armor again," the Gwailo said. "If you could reconsider your course of action, I and many others would be most appreciative."

Across the street, motion. Dunne and Alastair, crouching low and zig-zagging cover to cover. He met Wil's eyes as he came to a stop behind a concrete bollard. No way they were reconsidering jack all, not with Gordon and Saoirse alone in the thick of it. If they wanted to give chase, the Gwailo would have to go.

"Victor 1, rally at Marker Hotel," Alastair broadcast. "We'll cover. Sunray, out."

"Ack-fuckin'-knowledged," Cailean answered, and the telltale song of Rhiannon echoed over the Fort, mixed with the plunk-whump of Llowry's leftover grenade launcher.

Alastair pointed up the street with four fingers, then chopped vertical downward from the top of his head. *Coordinated attack. Spread out. We'll go together. On three.* Dunne tugged her poncho's hood up. With silent acknowledgement, she disappeared into the closest building through a broken window.

Alright. So they were doing this. The entire Yujingyu army at Xiongxiang hadn't put a dent in a single battalion, but the hell did they know? They didn't have Teseum-coated ammo, or gumption. Just artillery support, TAGs, and cutting-edge powered armor. Maybe they'd had more than three exhausted soldiers, maybe that was why they'd lost. Too many cooks in the kitchen.

A knot tied in his chest.

One.

The Gwailo sighed. "Or I can kill every single one of you. The easier option, but diplomacy was worth the attempt."

Two.

Steady breathing kept Wil's resolve steeled, his hands from shaking. This wasn't a good time to remember he should be afraid of dying.

Three.

Alastair roared "Eisd, o Eisd!" and hurtled out of cover.

A streak impacted his ballistic shield and rebounded from its surface into the open window of a pizzeria. An explosion within shattered every window, washing a decade of rotten leaves back onto the street. Brickwork debris rained after, rattling Alastair's pauldrons.

The Gwailo lowered its rocket launcher and laughed. "Good reflexes!"

Wil vaulted his cover. His Strela kicked into his shoulder. One shot. Two. Both hit, both erased by the whirling black cloud. Alastair leveled his Drozhat and set their pace with a machine gun metronome.

The nanoscreen danced like a sheet in the wind, scarves of dark substrate soaking in every projectile without the faintest ablation. The Gwailo's feet puddled with pearls of snubbed lead. Nothing pierced.

But killing it didn't matter. What mattered was forcing it into a losing decision—into zugzwang. It might've been invincible, but it was alone. It couldn't see everywhere at once. No matter how tough its armor, how endless its ammunition, its attention was finite and perhaps its most valuable resource. Once Dunne got behind it, they'd see how thin that nanoscreen stretched.

Alastair winded and slowed. Wil had to pause to reload. Their offense disorganized, and the covering fire thinned. Without the benefit of a rush, the Gwailo saw their plan and jolted back, narrowing her actionable angles. The substrate solidified like an eggshell, protecting it from all sides.

"*This* was your plan?" the Gwailo clucked. "Suicide?"

A heavy metal rattle echoed from above, joining their barrage. Dunne, feet planted on a third-story fire escape. She'd not been going around, but above. A river of brass scattered across the steps, playing them like a pachinko machine. Impact points dashed the Gwailo's helmet, drawing a constellation down its armored torso. Periphery sparking, it dropped low.

Two rockets speared toward Dunne.

The first detonated halfway through, struck by an errant bullet. The second veered off course to burst along the facade of the building above her, showering the street with flame and debris. The fire escape pried free from the wall and fell. The flash enveloped Dunne, and then she was gone.

The Gwailo wheeled on them. Its nanoscreen parted like the loophole in a rampart wall, and the barrel of the rocket launcher slotted perfectly into the gap. "One down, two to—!"

The egg cracked. Substrate scattered as its helmet rocked sideways. The faraway report of a sniper rifle snapped over their position.

The hand signs. They'd not only been intended for them, but for the man watching through his scope a hundred meters away—for Pell. And now the substrate piled together where his bullet had pierced, threat assessment automating its response. For a split second, the Gwailo's anterior was open and its chassis, unguarded.

Dunne burst from the smoke cloud and rolled onto an adjacent roof. Her poncho had tinged an ugly green, photoreactive cells melted by contact with the flame. Semi-automatic fire abandoned for a mag dump, her voice rose along with her Molotok's rattle until the two were screaming as one.

The violet oculi in the Gwailo's helmet flashed and sparked. Its nanoscreen surged back to safeguard it a second too late as its tendrils thinned: bulged: punctured. The salvo of armor-piercing high-yield ammunition lanced into its carapace, bolting cracks through its breastplate and thighs. Desperate to escape the crossfire, it dashed headlong into the face of an adjacent shop foyer. Glass smashed in its armored wake as it scraped through the window, but its wing-like flanges hooked in the frame. Unbalanced, it stumbled and went to one knee.

Alastair closed in fast. His Americolt filled his hand. Scrabbling to stand, unable to maneuver, the Gwailo unlimbered a snubbed ring-grip alien pistol. Visceral licks of crimson arced from its periphery, trailing up its armor in the draw.

Breaker. A nanophage, contained in a brittle E/M field. No matter how heavy Alastair's Teseum armor, if the bio-technical round touched his organic matter, its self-propagating payload would eat him from the inside out.

Wil's Strela had a chance of neutralizing the Gwailo. A small chance. One solid burst, point-blank, to put it down before it recovered, to capitalize on Alastair's distraction. He needed to pull the trigger. This was the only opportunity they would get. It wouldn't underestimate them a second time.

But he was already shoving Alastair out of the way.

Three gunshots. Wil hit the asphalt, scouring his duster for an entry wound he knew would spell his long and painful death.

None. It'd missed.

Electricity crackled from the middle of Alastair's ballistic shield. The Breaker bullet hung there in its impact crater, wide as a fingertip and glowing like the sun. It sizzled along the Teseum, melted a path through the unicorn heraldry, and rolled from the shield's edge to pit into the damp concrete underfoot. With a gasp of steaming ozone, it gnawed into the earth, boring a cylindrical hole, and disappeared.

Alastair watched the Breaker round go, eyes wide past his goggles.

Inside the shop, the alien juggernaut laid among the racks, eviscerated as the feidh back on the mountain. Inert substrate littered the violet-soaked floor, intermingled with a thousand silvery specks of Teseum chain ammunition.

"Well struck," the Gwailo gurgled, and died.

30

Dunne descended the facade to rejoin them, coughing a lungful into her bicep. Every fiber of her photoreactive poncho had scorched the same useless color. "Motherfucker burned my camo. She dead?"

Alastair stared into the deepening dime-sized hole embedded in the street, and then at the Gwailo and its growing bloodstain. "I thought I missed."

"Apologies, sir," Wil said. "Didn't think. Just moved."

"Wil," Alastair said. "Thank you. Sometimes, I trust this Teseum more than I should."

"Had the same problem in my ORC. And don't touch the impact trail for 72 hours. The nanophage will stick to your skin like grease on parade blues, and it'll hurt the whole time that you're dying."

Alastair cracked open his chain-colt, emptied the cylinder, and filled it with a fresh clip. "Acknowledged. Dunne, you alright?"

"Takes more than one rocket to kill a Dunne," she grumbled, engrossed in a quantronic distraction. "Comlog says the Victors are pushing up from Marker Bravo toward Hotel. Fionn cut a path through six or seven Taigha, an M-Drone and a Dazer, and set off two mines on the way."

"Shit," Wil said. "I'm so sorry."

Dunne cocked a brow. "Why? He's fine. Sizzled a bit by the M-Drone's electric pulse, I suppose, but chipper as he always is."

Wil raised a finger. Thought better, and lowered it.

Alastair holstered his Americolt and stretched a second belt of H-12 ammo from his pack into his HMG's feed tray. He clicked it shut. "On me."

"Sir," Wil said, "there's something I need to tell you. In private. It's important, about the mission."

Alastair shook his head. "Not now. No time. After."

He briefly considered sending the good news via comlog message, but the unsteady nature of his own comms kept his hand from the touchscreen. "Understood."

The urban center of Fort Resolute deteriorated into ruined brickwork, swathed in a hundred springtime colors of green. Streetlights stuck out at peculiar angles, foundations tipped by surfacing roots. They cut north, following the path of destruction—a dying Nox gurgling by the roadside, a dismembered Taigha in the gutter. The bulky shadow of the Croatoan-like fuel depot loomed two streets away, casting a shadow across the ruins.

The ground broke and tilted. On their next left, the quay stretched out before them, partially submerged in the still shallows of Loch Eil. Warehouses caked with rust and slime bent like the bodies of fat worms along the collapsed boardwalk into the lake, crowded with flowering water lilies.

In his time under Gavon Fhorst, Wil had been inundated with chess terminology and metaphors to the point that they'd stopped being words and started being dog whistles. One specific phrase that'd stuck with him was *zugzwang*, a German word his geist had failed to translate. It meant, 'the obligation to make a move causing a serious and decisive disadvantage.' Fhorst shortened it to, 'no matter what you choose, you lose.' That seemed closer to how he meant it: 'go fuck yourself.'

Unlike most things he learned from Fhorst, zugzwang wasn't just applicable to chess. Zugzwang was your girlfriend asking if her dress made her look fat. Zugzwang was every day in the barracks with a CQ with a mean streak. The Gwailo had been under zugzwang, facing their unrelenting advance. And right now, committing to a battle in Fort Resolute felt like zugzwang, too.

Just before Wil was about to ask if either of his accompaniment had ever put eyes on these missing Fusiliers, Alastair raised his fist. They stopped. Forty meters away, the water rippled high along a building corner. Something was approaching, splashing through the shallows.

Saoirse rounded the corner, kicking a wave with every step. Her uniform was drenched with oily Taigha blood, and her Mk12 was brutalized, steel layered in gouges and bite marks. Gordon limped after. Whatever state he was in after the Gwailo's rocket, now he was worse. The ragged scraps of his armor barely held together above his shredded kilt, an enormous combat knife occupying his clawed hand. With a point and a grunt, Gordon clocked their approach.

The wall beside them exploded. Two shapes burst into the street. Motion. Sparks. The scream of steel. Blurred silhouettes warped drunken among an invisible field of mirrors. Tall, gray-green humanoids with digitigrade legs solidified in the fractal. A weight class above their compatriots, but unmistakably Shasvastii.

Smoke wafted from a massive impact point along Saoirse's claymore's fuller, dulled Teseum scored a brighter silver. Her Mk12 bobbed atop the frothing water, sheared completely in two. It wasn't a sword that she'd deflected.

"Jayth!" Dunne shouted and dove for cover.

The taller, more disfigured of the two wore a massive false right arm wreathed in fiberweave cables and punctuated with incandescent couplings. Its hand was substituted by a formidable flat-tipped spike—a pneumatic hammer— and its left leg ended abruptly below the knee, fashioned with a simple crow-bar-shaped runner's prosthetic.

Thick keloids melted together across its exposed flesh. Burn scars.

With a hydraulic hiss, the spike sucked up into its owner's fist. "Pitiful creatures," he said, voice harsh and throaty. "You've strayed too far inside my abattoir. Time to die."

"How abattoir ye fuck off," Saoirse growled, and kept her stance wide.

Alastair lifted his Drozhat to cut the hammer-handed Jayth down. A hail of bullets sliced the water at his feet. Not the two in the road—a third, suppressing from the rooftop above. Wil ducked behind Alastair, joining Dunne behind a reedy dumpster piled with cinderblocks.

Three shots blunted against Alastair's Teseum armor as he fell into cover beside them. "Red Fury! Care!"

For a brief, critical instant, Saoirse had the chance to disengage. A tight retreat paired with one of Gordon's smoke grenades would've left the Jayth easy pickings in the street. Wil hoped—prayed—begged that she would make the right decision.

But she saw Alastair stumble, and blade met spike. The opportunity passed. Fangs bared, Saoirse surged into motion, forethought crushed by the grip of her blood fury.

The hammer-handed Jayth commander weaved through his nimbus of afterimages, each strike improvised, lethal, without hesitation. Her barrage sliced air; so did his. She jockeyed for footing, denying his offense; he did the same. Wil had never seen anything like it, two brawlers anticipating each other's lethal improvisations at such a speed it was almost a dance.

If so, Saoirse wasn't leading.

Alastair didn't stay down. He propped his HMG over the corner, searching the rooftops for their attacker. Dunne tried to spot for him. The moment she called out, a bullet streaked from the opposite building and cracked into the center of Alastair's goggles. His shots went wide, and he fell back into cover.

Alastair hooked the now-opaque bulletproof goggles away from his eyes, brushing glass dust from his rebreather. Bruises already decorated the tops of his cheeks. "Victor 6, ETA. Saoirse needs back-up, and—"

"Break, break!" Hodges shouted over comms. "Six Taigha, en route Marker Hotel. Thirty seconds, over!"

Vern's voice followed after, chopped with heavy machine gun fire. "Sun—tor 6 is en rou—der enem—ETA two minutes—"

"Hostile's on the move," Dunne said, scanning the vacant rooftops. "Victor 6, street is not clear. I repeat, not clear! Red Fury is active and in suppression, please copy!"

Alastair's blue eyes were haggard above his rebreather. "We don't have two minutes," he said, but when he went to stand his balance got the better of him.

Wil braced him. "Shake it off. We'll triple-team it, like the Gwailo."

"Can't." Alastair coughed. "No time."

Wil stocked his Strela to his shoulder. "Then I'll make some."

Pressed to the dumpster, Wil crawled to its edge. Lake water sucked up his duster, soaking his sleeve to the elbow. Strela cocked, he chanced a look. Nothing on the rooftops. The Jayth Red Fury had moved, fighting like how a real guerrilla should.

Five meters away, Saoirse parried a strike aimed to open her throat, and Wil crushed down the instinct to hit the infrared and mag dump. Didn't trust himself to not clip Saoirse with a burst at this range. Had to trust her, same as with the Caliban, had to take his time or the Red Fury above would keep them pinned until the duo closed in and decapitated them. Every second counted.

Past the melee, Gordon struggled to his feet. He'd been upended by the initial strike and only now the wound had healed enough to stand. With a feral snarl, he barreled toward the fray—only to stumble and fall. A tide of golden chyme surged from his throat, clouding the water's surface. In an instant, he was human again. The steel torcs fell from his arms like anchors.

Saoirse was on her own.

The second Jayth drew his machete and rushed in, and with it, the tipping scales painfully unbalanced. Saoirse fell back, parrying blows in a mad flurry, unable to attack for defending. Their combined efforts left her nowhere to reposition, no space to breathe. The tempo of their melee peaked, and Saoirse's breath steamed from her mouth like smoke from a furnace.

She tried for a low blow; the hammer-handed bastard jerked into a headbutt. When she went to swap grips, he caught a handful of her scalp. She lurched back. Her hairband snapped, giving enough leeway to catch the Jayth's machete across her dueling bracer instead of her neck.

The near-miss almost distracted Wil from the shimmer of light that craned over the warehouse roof above. With a gesture, the ODD melted away, replaced by an infrared blob. The Strela punched into his shoulder before he knew he'd squeezed the trigger, and the Red Fury startled back behind the lip of the roof.

Alive.

Hammerhand caught sight of Gordon slumped onto his elbows. Pivoting, he raised his weapon. Saoirse intercepted the rush, stalled his advance. Her defense unraveled. The top of her thigh bloomed a fiery red, and then her cheek, and when her focus broke, he grabbed her by the collar and slammed her into the shin-high water. His spike jumped, and she barely deflected it in time to spring from the water to her feet.

Cracking his neck, Hammerhand regarded both of the Dogfaces with a leathery sneer. "The Counselor guaranteed me and my Taigha a challenge! Instead, I find disappointment."

Saoirse stepped in. Her claymore flashed, spun, changed palms. Hammerhand planted his prosthetic like a pole-vaulter and speared both feet into her ribs. The pneumatic spike retracted, and he atop her before she could react.

The prosthetic thumped against her collar. Discharged. A last-second flinch turned a mortal wound into a vicious one. Her shoulder flooded over, skin tented grotesquely until Hammerhand hoisted her off the ground, meat hand caging the guard of her claymore.

"Embarrassing," Hammerhand said. "The last Wulver I killed cost me my arm, my leg. You haven't laid a scratch, nothing more than a feeble—"

Her forehead cracked against his. And then again. "Stop," she roared, "talking!"

With a visceral rip of fabric and flesh, Saoirse kicked free, sailing from Hammerhand's hold into a belly flop. Howling in pain, she rose, fell, rose again. Her claymore's warding swings went lackluster and frantic.

Hammerhand smeared the blood from his forehead. Mandibles bruxing, he clipped his taunts short and maneuvered in for the kill.

The Red Fury sprayed Wil's position, bullets striking the water like raindrops, drumming the dumpster. Stepping out now would be suicide. He had to force himself not to.

The comms barked. Hodges. "Taigha! Hotel! Any bloody second!"

"Almost there," Cailean said, "almost—"

Hammerhand dodged under Saoirse's arm and pressed his spike to her throat.

Alastair leapt up. His Drozhat roared. Hammerhand's arm sparked, and his strike went off-kilter. A trench ripped across the second Jayth's face, temple to temple, dislodging its eye guard. Before his dead partner fell, Hammerhand had its corpse hefted like an improvised shield. Flesh and armor stood no chance against the concentrated burst of Teseum 7.62mm. In seconds, the corpse was limbless, then bones, then a loose fistful of viscera.

Sparks dashed from Hammerhand's arm again. Cleaner. The force of the impact bent him onto one knee, and the second bowled him into the water.

Belt spent, Alastair shouted, "Saoirse!"

Two impacts against Alastair's armor. One went higher pitched than the other. Alastair's eyes blanked. Pink mist puffed from his collar, speckling the exterior of his rebreather's mask. Listed to one side, arm raised skyward, the MacArthur dropped his weapon and collapsed. Water splashed heavy and high around his armored bulk.

Blood spotted across the gold and green above his belt. Pooled along the neckline of his armor. A thin hole threaded the Breaker round's pit in his shield, skimmed the leather of the inseam of his gauntlet, and disappeared into his gut.

Red clouded the shallows all around him.

Guttural chirps echoed up the street. Splashing. Closer. Taigha rounded the corner of the farthest warehouse, slowed by the water, but not enough. Dunne sprayed a feeble burst into their approaching mass, but nothing struck home. Resistance only encouraged their rush.

Shadows filled the alley opposite: Cailean, and the four Volunteers.

The shooter above flickered wildly below his ODD. It craned over the building's edge, preparing a spray into the approaching Volunteers. Cailean saw. Barked a warning. His fist shot to his smoke grenades. Too slow. Nora jolted, scrabbling to find safety where there was none. Neil shielded the two women with his back.

The Strela in Wil's hands came alive for a brief, perfect moment. Fury extended from its barrel, rage focused into force. Four bullets pierced the mirage. Four bullets struck true. An arterial squirt strained to touch the sky, and the dead Jayth pitched from the rooftop and crashed head first into the alley below.

Gordon heaved a final rope of vomit into the water and lurched onto his knees. His glazed eyes took in Saoirse's wound, Wil's struggle to stand, and the toe of Alastair's boot, stuck up from the water where he fell.

He howled. Loud enough to startle the Taigha. Loud enough to flinch Hammerhand. Transmutation wracked him, anatomy bulging grotesquely. Black fur raged over the whole of his body. Blood cascaded through his fangs, out his nose, and the lattice of old scars up his trunk stretched and melted open like a plastic in a fire.

Gordon lunged, closing in—on Saoirse. He snatched her by her belt and whipped her down the street, ten meters, fifteen after she skipped on the water's surface.

"Yes!" Hammerhand bellowed. "A feast, after such famine!"

Gordon answered him with a point-blank, blood-soaked roar.

Hammerhand pounced. His pneumatic fist shot forward, and Gordon caught it with both hands. The spike fired, impaling his enormous black paws. Stalled. Tangled in Gordon's ligaments, the pistons slipped in their housing and the spike lost pressure.

Gordon took grip. His teeth flashed and buried in Hammerhand's neck. Leathery flesh split. Scales cracked. Fangs gouged lines in his meat. Worried by the throat, the mouthy Shasvastii abandoned language for shrieking.

Saoirse staggered to her feet, disarmed yet still claimed by the blood fury. Against all reason, she turned and charged back with both claws raised.

Cailean bolted from the alley and caught her around the waist. But when the 3rd Grey saw Hammerhand and Gordon locked together, he froze as if he'd laid eyes on the devil himself.

"Díreach," he whispered, and went for his pistol.

Saoirse's headbutt snapped the old man back to reality. Dazed, nostrils dripping red, he shouted for help. Wil held himself together long enough to sweep her legs, and Neil tangled up her arms. Together, they towed her kicking and screaming from the street, demolishing the water lilies as they passed.

Vern needed both hands to carry her claymore.

The last thing Wil saw before they lost visual was Gordon, teeth caught up in the meat of Hammerhand's neck, swarmed by six Taigha—and laughing.

31

Cailean breached the stairwell door back-first. Wil skimmed the perimeter, clearing empty offices and side rooms. Sunlight trickled through spidering vines that'd grown over the shattered windows and their security grating, illuminating the walls of a hundred empty cubicles.

"Clear!" Cailean shouted and made way.

The rest of the MacArthurs piled after. Neil hefted Alastair by the arms, and Fionn carried his legs. Blood spattered across the carpeted floor, soaking into the faded pattern. Nora screamed orders. "There! Stop! Get his breastplate open, and—he's aspirating blood into his rebreather, someone—"

Alastair's helmet sucked from his head. Beneath, he was sweat-soaked and pale, eyes pinched shut. Crimson foam bubbled along his lips, smeared his stubble orange.

With great haste, Neil undid the buckles of his chieftain's breastplate. The uniform underneath was more blood than cloth, dusted with silvery fragments of Teseum armor. Fionn cut his ballistic shield's straps and hurled it into the corner, keeping what might've remained of the Gwailo's nanophage far from Nora's workspace.

"Watcher," Cailean spoke into his wristlet. "Tell me we're clear."

"M-Drone sniffed by, didn't stop," Pell answered. "Third floor?"

Cailean peered through a slat in the security grate. "Fourth."

"Then you're out of sensor range. You're clear."

His eyes glowed with vehemence. "That Jayth."

"The Díreach," Pell said. "So he survived."

While Cailean quickly gave Pell his orders—watch their ass, keep hidden—Dunne guided Saoirse to the corner. The blood rage had faded once she'd laid eyes on her brother, though its last whispers still kept hold.

She struggled against Dunne's push. "Alastair," she said. "He needs—"

"You'd get in the way," Dunne said, firm. "Let Nora work."

Saoirse's face fell, and she backed away into a pillar. Trembling, she slid to the floor against it, smaller than Wil ever thought she could be.

With incredible care, Nora slit open Alastair's uniform with her knife. Two holes bubbled beneath: one inside his clavicle, and the other above his hip, diagonal to the navel. With every ragged gasp, the gunshot wounds bled darker.

"One shot," Wil called. "Ricocheted off the shield, into the hip, out his collar."

Nora sent him a bare nod and tossed her Glengarry aside. Two fingers probed the entry wound, inking her cuticles red. "Shock round."

Shock meant anti-coagulants. Shock meant bioengineered anaphylactic shock. Shock meant skipping triage straight to Cube retrieval procedures. Wil swallowed hard and tried not to betray any of that with his eyes.

"How?" Vern asked. "Then why isn't he dead?"

"Teseum soaked the hydrostatic force," Nora explained, dismissive. "Fionn! Keep pressure here—Neil, here—now, *now*, right now—"

The bore in Saoirse's shoulder oozed into her grenadier's vest. "Please, God," she whispered. "Please, don't, not both. I'm beggin' you, please, no more. *Please.*"

Cailean whistled at Wil. "Lad! Help her."

Wil left his Strela propped against the wall and hurried to Saoirse's side, inspecting the hole punched in her shoulder. Not cleanly lethal as Hammerhand intended. No broken bones. What wound remained had already begun to knit together.

When he took her hand to check the gash there, she yanked it away. "Don't touch me."

"Let me look."

Her lips curled, crooked and shaking. "I don't—*don't.*"

Red blotted the synthetic leather of her gauntlet. Gingerly, he peeled it back, revealing the deflected chop. Bone-deep, but non-lethal. Nora's second or third priority, depending on if she realized she'd just watched her boyfriend die or not.

The way Saoirse begged him with her eyes was so unlike her. "Wil."

"I know," he said and took her hand in his.

Alastair groaned, and her grip tightened. Then more, and worse, until it threatened to rearrange his knuckles. But pain wasn't pain. He considered it sharing. Didn't mind lightening the burden she carried, watching her little brother bleed out in a cubicle farm.

Nora unfolded her paramedic kit with a swiftness. She drew two autoinjectors from its straps, stripped their release tabs, and hammered them one after the other into the fabric of Alastair's thigh. Painkiller cocktails disappeared into his meat with a hiss and a puff.

"But it hit a lung," Vern muttered, transfixed. "That trajectory, it had to—"

"Vernard, dear," Kelsie said gently. "Shut the fuck up?"

Nora retrieved a silver cylinder from her kit, similar to a pen light—a low-tech telescoping bioscanner. With a twist, its end flared, and she peered into a lens on the other side. She traced a methodical trail up Alastair's abdomen, to his chest, to the pumping wound below his neck, turning the cap to change the depth in which she inspected his innards.

His gasps hastened, growing heavier and more agonal by the minute.

"Is it bad?" Neil asked. "Say it's not bad."

Nora collapsed her bioscanner. "Bullet didn't fragment. Deflected off the hipbone, nicked the liver and lung, missed the heart—but cavitation strained an artery."

A cold inevitability settled in Wil's chest. They'd already spent minutes retreating to safety thanks to Gordon's distraction. How much longer did they have until Alastair went into hemorrhagic shock? Until he died?

"Say that's not bad," Neil insisted.

"Coin flip if he dies now, or tomorrow," Nora said. "Serum overdose is our only answer—but outwith active fire, I need familial permission."

Versus mortal wounds, even nanobot-laden Serum like the vials in Nora's MediKit would be utterly useless unless an overdose was purposefully induced. Three to five rapid-fire injections would either snap the dying soldier back to fighting condition, flooding their body with a tidal wave of synthetic hormones and reconstructive nanobots, or collapse their system beneath the hemodynamic shock, instantly snuffing their life.

"We don't got another choice," Cailean answered. "Quick, now, lass. Go on."

Nora ignored him and locked eyes with Saoirse. "Love, it's your call."

"Don't let him die, Nora," Saoirse said. "Please."

"Not without a fight," she swore and drew her archaic MediKit gun from her pack. One vial of Serum locked into the chamber. Another two set aside, pull-tabs yanked and ready for injection. More than half of her remaining supply. "Neil, Fionn—hold him."

Neil braced his arms. Fionn braced his shoulders. Vern did as he was told. Kelsie slipped her glove between Alastair's teeth like a bit and cradled his head in her lap, swiping the bangs from his face.

Nora discharged the MediKit gun against his neck, leaving behind a bright red semicircle. Reloaded, and fired again, this time into his breastbone. Again, over the hip.

His wounds sizzled and bled clear.

Alastair's glazed eyes short open, and he screamed through clenched teeth. Convulsed. Fought to escape, lips foaming as his eyes rolled, head tossed, fingers curled wildly to claw at the carpeting, fighting to kick, to roll, to escape the chemical cocktail turning his blood to acid in his veins—

Saoirse hid her face in Wil's chest, but he refused to look away.

The shaking died. Nora brushed the froth from Alastair's mouth with her sleeve and laid her ear onto his chest. A deadly calm washed her expression away, and in three swift, mechanical motions, she retrieved another vial, stripped its tab, and zeroed it into Alastair's chest.

He tremored.

Exhaled.

And jerked upright, bowling Vern off his feet with a shrill, desperate breath, pupils so dilated they left no room for color. Coughing, Alastair pawed the floor for his weapon. Paused—and licked his purple lips. Sweat beaded on his forehead. He groped at his neck wound.

Nora slapped his hand.

Alastair sucked a breath through his teeth. "Ow."

She shrank back. "Sorry."

All at once, the MacArthurs burst into motion and noise. Fionn punched the air, braided beard dancing. Neil and Vern fell back, shoulder-to-shoulder, queasy from relief. Dunne chortled a posh impression of Alastair's 'ow,' and Kelsie echoed 'sorry' back to her until both of them were breathlessly laughing, laid together on the floor.

Saoirse rocketed to her brother's side, whimpering a litany of curses and struggling to find a place to hold him without stubbing his wounds. "How dare ye scare me like that, what's the matter with—"

"Hey," Alastair said, too weak to raise his arms. "Hey."

Cailean's eyes creased, hand clasped over his beard. By Wil's guess, he'd gone somewhere else for a moment—to other places on Dawn, other battlefields with other soldiers who hadn't survived what Alastair just had. "Eleanor McDermott," he said. "Thank you. Truly."

"I just—with the vials, it's not much," she protested. "Anyone could've…"

"Volunteer, lifesaver, future 112," Neil said and looped his arm over her shoulders. "My sister's one-in-a-goddamn-million, aye?"

In eight words, Nora's perfect, professional calm shattered. Nervous giggles, at first, and then tears. Her lips screwed up, and she hid her face in the clean crook of her elbow. Neil mussed her hair and hugged her to his chest as her shoulders jumped.

Blood-strewn. Dirty. Exhausted. Low on ammunition, surrounded on all sides, outnumbered and outgunned. Three casualties deep, Gordon was missing, and they had fifty-four hours to reach the DRC-9 before a lot of innocent people died.

Wil shouldn't have been smiling.

† †

Ten minutes later, Hodges clambered through the stairwell door and paused, somehow surprised to find so many guns pointed in his direction. A cluster of shallow stripes dashed across his flank, balaclava and grenade belt both absent. Dunne swept to his side, embracing him before even considering his wounds.

Alastair struggled to his feet and limped over. The two men took in the state of the other, trading the usual remarks with casual confidence. All posturing—the strain in their smiles gave it away.

"Glad you made it," Alastair said. "Your side—"

Hodges shrugged. "Scratches, sir. No bother. Like you should talk."

Dunne squeezed his arm. "Next time you don't answer your comlog, I'm feeding it to you."

Hodges held up his link bracelet. The light didn't blink. "Couldn't, dear. Caught an E/M grenade leaving Charlie Foxtrot."

"Better than a frag," Dunne muttered and slipped the linklet off his wrist. "I'll reset this for you. Rest."

"Thank you," he said, and when she turned her back, gave in to a tight-lipped grimace.

Alastair gave him an empathetic nod. "Status report?"

"Frankly, sir, we're outnumbered. Camouflaged scouts. More Jayth, more Taigha. Drones. More guns than we've got, more guns than should've been here." Hodges teetered for a moment, as if he didn't want to continue. "And Gordon is alive."

Nora shocked into stillness over her paramedic bag, frozen mid-motion.

Saoirse shot to her feet. "Then let's go get 'em!"

"Not possible," Hodges said.

Wil's legs screamed when he stood. "Where is he?"

Hodges paced to the eastern windows and pointed past the vines and dislocated security shutters, far out into the ruins. A small, silver building glinted in the fading sunlight along the shoreside road near the quay—a diner, not yet sunk into the encroaching lake. Tall, yellowing roadside signage teetered above the adjacent parking lot, its sole surviving fixture a grimy OPEN 25/7.

"Saw him limp inside," Hodges said. "Kitchen freezer's my guess. Armored as a vault, surrounded by a pack of Taigha. Worse, I saw some trees wriggle out near Marker Juliett—reinforcements from a ghost ship. And if you see one, there's another three you didn't."

Ghost ships. Shasvastii craft layered in camouflage systems until they were nigh invisible to all but the most advanced sensors. But they were corsairs, meant to harry targets in deep space skirmishes, not to reinforce battlefields. That they were engaging in an open battle like this must have meant things were particularly desperate for them, too.

"Explains what they've been doing while we were marching," Kelsie said. "Entrenching here, readying their intercept. Think these reinforcements are from near the M-828?"

"Possibly," Vern said, turning dials on his box.

Cailean finally escaped the long silence he'd fallen into after Alastair's revival. "Never did find those Fusiliers on the comlog."

"Seems like they knew just the right rabbit to get us to chase," Dunne said.

Saoirse grimaced silently, eyes downcast.

Try as he might, Wil couldn't bring himself to blame her. She'd been doing a good thing, going after the fleeing marks, and he'd rather know this version of her than the one that'd let three grunts go to their death without a second thought.

Alastair locked eyes with Wil over a cubicle wall. "I've been mulling on this for a while, Wil, but... the more the Shasvastii insist on stopping us, the more I'm certain they weren't trying to kill Rajan."

Wil's blood went as cold as the lake water still dripping from his duster. He tried to shake it off, but a moment's consideration only made it cling tighter. "His file was full of redactions, and his father's an influential man. There's another layer to this, I promise."

"Don't matter," Saoirse said. "Gordon needs help, so I'm going."

Hodges swiped his palm over his face, muffling a rueful laugh. "Don't know why I talk, sometimes."

"The Jayth and Taigha? Easy slip, far as I'm concerned. Gimme yer shotgun and I'll manage."

"Saoirse, please," Nora whispered. "He didn't do what he did because he wants someone to save him."

Expression falling, Saoirse turned to face her. "The hell's that mean?"

"He's not been in good sorts for a while, love," Nora said, tone same as the widows Wil had met after Svalarheima, tight and controlled. "He's wanted this for a long time. Let it be. It's okay, yeah?"

Saoirse scanned the MacArthurs, confusion whiplashed into fear. "Wanted what," she said. "Wanted *what?*"

Wil's stomach turned. He'd thought he'd find Saoirse's outrage mirrored on Alastair's face, on Cailean's, but they didn't seem surprised. Gordon's self-destruction, his bitterness, the secret pain—Wil hadn't been the only one who'd noticed. How could he, when they'd all known him so much longer?

Neil tugged his Glengarry from his head in a daze. "I thought... I thought he was joking."

"Well, he wasn't," Nora snapped and curled inward. "He wasn't."

Saoirse spun to face her brother. "Hey, no, we can't—"

"He gave us an escape hatch," Alastair said. "We need to take it."

She braced back a step, mouth agape. "But it's Gordon."

"I ken that," he said and shot Wil a glance. He'd privately shared Glasscock's existence with Alastair not long after the celebration faded. It'd only taken a moment for their mission parameters to go from 'forward' to 'fighting retreat.'

"He'd go back for you," Saoirse said.

Alastair clenched his fists in his lap, unable to look her in the eye. "The lives of the many outweigh the few, no matter whose they are. If we stay here, we'll die."

"But it's Gordon," she insisted. "Right?"

Cailean retrieved his empty Merovingian cigarette pack and glared into its hollow. "It's a good death," he said. "His da would be proud."

Saoirse's lips twisted. She snatched up her claymore from the wall, and for an instant, Wil was certain she would charge the door. But she turned in a tight, disoriented circle instead, hurled her sword aside, and stormed away from the group.

Nora unstuck herself and hurtled after her.

Hodges waited a beat, and then asked, "So, we're leaving?"

"Those are the orders," Dunne said. Her suspicious gaze stuck to Wil for as long as Hodges' comlog took to reboot.

"Excellent," Hodges said, and tapped on Kelsie's comlog. "Pellehan is securing an extraction lane as we speak. Here, and here. If Marker Echo is clear, we can make for—"

"Robert James Hodges," Cailean said, soft, and crumpled the empty pack in his hand. "Yer not wrong, lad. But perhaps gie it a moment."

Kelsie had daggers in her glare. "Nicer than what I was gonna say."

Fionn stepped away from the group and drew a cross over his chest. "Cuiridh mi clach air do chàrn," he whispered, and kissed the knuckles on his left hand.

Outside, an Ariadnan raptor whistled a mating call as it drifted from the dying light into the shadow of the fat drum of the fuel depot spreading over the ruins. Soon, night would fall, and Saoirse needed to be ready to fight. Wil meandered her and Nora's way. No matter how he felt, Alastair was right, and saving Gordon meant throwing themselves back onto the pyre. This was the reasonable, pragmatic course of action. Didn't mean he had to like it, but reasonable was what kept people alive.

Saoirse and Nora sat on a threadbare couch tucked into a corner office. They were holding hands, whispering. Comforting each other. He lingered close enough to see, but not to hear, and after a moment, even that felt too much. Wil turned away and stared through the gaps in the rusted security screen out across Fort Resolute.

His comlog, losing connection when the Orc got sniped. Dropping out during the initial ambush back at the Brume. Ghost markers baiting them into armed resistance. The Gwailo, its quantronic presence loud as a klaxon yet suspiciously unmarked on their map. How long would it take an EI hacker to spoof coordinates? Ten seconds? Five? Scáthach had pinpointed him on the mountainside—had she taken aim for Saoirse as retribution for his abrupt dismissal? She'd not mentioned the opposition assembled in the Fort. Was it actually bait, like Wil's gut feeling, or were her intentions pure and her security clearance minimal?

Wil's earpiece crackled. An incoming comlog call. He accepted without hesitation. It was thick with distortion—suppressed, but audible, intelligible. "Hey. Wil. You there?"

Gordon. His words had lost their Dog-Warrior edge, and he seemed very tired.

"Hey, buddy," he said. "You alright? You're not broadcasting to the group."

"No," Gordon said. "Hurt. Hurt bad."

"Listen, everybody wants—"

"Don't want everybody. Just you. Because you get it. Because you can help."

Wil began to pace. "Doesn't sound like you're about to ask for a rescue."

"Nah," Gordon said. "Chain rifles, gone. Axe, gone. Don't even got my knife. Can't stand. Just dead weight, now. Would only slow you down."

"Not true."

"Should've died," he said. "Almost did. Then instinct kicked in and I ended up here. Big bloody sacrifice that was. Didn't even die proper."

"Glad you didn't."

Gordon clicked his tongue. "I'm not. Was looking forward to Valhalla."

"Hey buddy, listen, Nora is right here, and—"

"You've got friends on Neoterra, Wil? Mom and dad?"

His heart sank. Gordon wasn't listening. "No, buddy. I got nobody."

"Me, too. Rian and Cameron. Elijah. Malcolm. My da and mum. Alastair's da, and Alastair. Seen so many people die who should be alive instead of me. And I'm too much of a coward to follow."

"You are *not* a coward."

"So I need your help. Because I see it in your eyes, Wil. You're like me. Empty inside. Cold. I know you've been on this ledge before. Talk me through what helped you step back, so I can step off."

A breathy sob broke Wil's concentration. In the office, Saoirse held Nora close. Gentle strokes along her back coaxed the silent tears that followed.

Wil shook his head. "You're wrong. I'm not empty, and Alastair's alive. Nora saved him. She saved him, and she's here crying over you."

A long, grateful pause. A heavy sigh of relief. "Good. That's good."

"She wants you to come back. Saoirse, too. And me."

"You all deserve someone better."

"Yeah, well," Wil said, "nobody gets what they deserve."

Gordon grunted. "You're supposed to make this easy."

"Motherfucker, when have I ever made *anything* easy?"

His snicker was short, forced, and his uneasy breaths choked away like water down a drainpipe. "Still sound like my goddamn ex."

"I'm being serious."

"So am I," Gordon said. "I thought when I died, it'd be a relief. Peace, finally. No more guilt. No more what-if, no more fear. That it'd make a good story, and that's how I'd stay alive forever. A legend, like all the dead heroes in that upstairs hallway. Instead, I'm just another one of Saoirse's boring stories, eh?"

A shadow blotted out the light through the security screen. Helios had finally sank behind the bulky fuel depot bunker, and its corona—

Wil's mouth went dry. "Gordon. We're gonna come get you."

"Don't, pal," he said. "They got me surrounded."

Wil cast a long look over the assembled MacArthurs. Downtrodden. Beaten. But he knew without a doubt that they would march into the fires of Hell to pull their brother from it. All they needed was a plan—one glimmer of hope to take grip and hold on to, white-knuckle, until the bitter end.

"Tell me you want to see Nora again, and I'll make it happen," he said. "All you gotta do is ask."

A long pause.

A shuddering breath.

"Wil," Gordon grunted. "Don't make me beg."

32

Helios set behind the western mountaintops and set fire to their peaks. As the cold, purple shadow of twilight reclaimed Fort Resolute, one building held back the dark, ancient chrome-plated surface shining like a beacon: the diner along the quay, not yet sunk into the loch. From their vantage point in the ruins of a burned-out motel room, it didn't seem so far. Only a flooded roadway and a parking lot between them and Gordon.

The antiseptic soaking the bandage on his forearm itched. Or maybe it was the burn. Nerves. Or yet another infection setting in.

Saoirse descended from her perch on the second story above, clawed hands caked in chalk. She'd abandoned her blood-soaked long-sleeve shirt long ago, preferring only the bandeau beneath the flak. Arms bare, tattoos and old scars visible, same as the day of the crash. Her wounds had all closed, though the flesh of her shoulder still blemished a furious red.

"Lot's still hoachin' with Taigha," she said. "Outwith the diner, mostly. More n' what Hodges said, ken, but fuck-all for Jayth."

"Our Hodges, round down?" Neil said. "Don't sound like him. We sure he's not a Speculo?"

"Let's not start that again," Wil said, feigning a massage over his bandages. "My arm hurts enough already."

Saoirse didn't laugh, even though she laughed at everything. Focused on a loose scrap of leather come undone from her claymore's handle, she asked, "Is this gonna work?"

His brain ran the numbers. His heart said, "Yeah."

"Has to," Neil said. "After what you promised my sister."

"I said, it will."

"Y'think what Dunne said was true," Saoirse asked, "about the rabbit?"

"Nothing we can do now," Wil said. "It's my fault you're out here, so if you gotta blame someone for this shitshow, blame me."

"Fuck off," she said and flashed an unconvincing grin. "Your fault, aye, but don't mean it can't be *our* fault, Willem Wallace."

Neil slapped his thighs and stood. "Been too long. Hodges should be here by now. Gonna go make sure he's still inbound."

"Keep your head down," Saoirse said. "You see movement, you run."

"Copy that," Neil said and picked through the rubble back out into the yard.

Alone with her again, Wil saw his opportunity. "Personal question?"

"Not in the mood," she said. "But sure. What?"

"Back at the shallows. Cailean. When he saw that Jayth with the prosthetic, I got the feeling they'd met. He said a name."

Saoirse opened her mouth, and faltered, shock shifting into disdain. "I didn't... but no, has to be the same one. How many Shas lose an arm and leg, and don't regrow 'em? Shoulda kent. Shoulda never picked that fight."

He pinched his brows. "Did him wrong?"

"Was a Jayth done him wrong, back on Novyy Cimmeria," she said, and thumbed the nine of diamonds tattooed on her forearm. "His wife. But it's not my story to tell."

The idea of gruff, irascible Cailean married to anyone gave Wil pause. But if it was like that, then the only answer was that she'd been killed during Kurage. No wonder he didn't get along with anyone without his better half.

Saoirse nudged him, and her blank eyes trailed out the window. An impenetrable knot of smoke cover had begun to wind down the streets of Fort Resolute, one six-meter billow at a time. Along the north side, to the south, the west. While they watched, a fresh pair of columns snaked skyward.

Rhiannon's song echoed from the ruins, percussive and steady like a double-time march. The rip of chain rifles and shotgun claps filled in the metronome. Saoirse hovered at the corner, close to going after Neil when Hodges scuttled into the room with his finger over his mouth.

A chirp. A bark. Louder, closer. The three of them packed shoulder-to-shoulder below the window and held their breath. Heavy, keratin clacks echoed over the rubble, moving fast. Taigha, herded toward the sound of combat by the fire in their blood.

Exactly as he'd thought. There was no way that the Taigha's handlers had enough wherewithal to micromanage every target, every movement, every moment. Chaos complimented a shock force like the Taigha, and the Shas had leveraged that in their favor during the skirmish. Now, they were tasting the backbite of relying on expendables as their advance guard.

The herd passed, and its din faded. Seconds went by without the clunk of claws or shrill gibbers until finally Hodges exhaled and said, "Almost caught out. Told Neil to go back."

Saoirse glanced at Wil, her jaw tense. "Alone?"

"Better that than Taigha chow," he said, swiftly taking stock of the weapons hung on his shoulders and from his bandoliers. Without hesitation, he drew his shotgun and spun it to Saoirse stock-first. "You can't go unarmed. Here. Time to go."

Her fingers lingered around the trigger guard. But she shook her head, accepted it, and vaulted through the window.

Out in the alley, over the chain link, down into the flooded roadway beyond. Tall grass ran the length of it, greenish water floating with tiny aquatic clovers. Wil boosted Hodges and went after, ascending and descending with nary a sound.

Across the flooded road, the diner glinted in the center of the abandoned lot, surrounded with the scattered, ruined chassis of vehicles both military and civilian. Teseum-coated shells lingered in the pavement cracks alongside decades-old stains from stray Viral rounds. Weeds flowered up through the wheel wells, flourishing in each automobile's shadow.

Saoirse took a deep sniff of the air. "Care. Some Taigha stayed behind."

They kept low, kept quiet, kept moving. Saoirse took point into the maze of cars; Hodges went last, chain rifle cocked to cover their six. Row by row, the diner grew closer. With great care, they passed through the cargo bed of a tattered Tartary troop transport, tarpaulin wagon cover swaying in the chill highland breeze. Decades-old Combi rifles stained the asphalt in rust-red blooms.

Under the shadow of the yellowing roadside signage lay a century-old museum. Bar stools, booth seating. Vinyl records, framed above a jukebox. An antique soda fountain perched atop a bed of moss the size of Wil's leg. Daily specials still survived, scribbled on a tall board propped in the glass double doors: Tattie scones with egg, fried chicken with rashers and American dressing, iced drinks.

Bloody streaks marred the time capsule inside and out. Red pawprints smeared along the foyer, over the countertop, and into the kitchen.

Hodges nudged him. Pointed. Two Taigha crouched beside the curb, claws tucked under their leathery haunches. Another scrabbled at the pull doors listlessly, jingling its bell. Motion and diode flashes from the darkened kitchen interior suggested these three were on the low end of what was left behind.

Wil tried a hand signal. *Good range. All three of us. At once. On my mark.*

Hodges cocked his head, surprised, and reciprocated. *On you.*

Wil counted it down on his hand—three, two one.

Mark. They shot to their feet, and the Taigha speared toward their cover in the same motion. Their collars plumed and spared. Saoirse yanked Wil down as shrapnel scoured the surface of the trunk top.

A second rise, a second chance. Hodges' chain rifle sent white-hot chain cords pummeling into the crowd, pitting the asphalt and shattering diner windows. Rifle bullets bit into their hides, slowing them enough for shotgun slugs to finish the job. And when one closed the gap, Hodges had his handaxe in hand before his chain rifle hit the floor, and the Taigha stumbled dead behind their line. Two chops to its jugular, faster than sight.

Saoirse huffed three swift breaths and vaulted the hood as the front door smashed open. Strobing diodes and bladed fins struggled to press through all at once, bottlenecking each other. She plucked a grenade from her belt, yanked the pin with her fang, and lobbed it underhand into their midst.

The diner doorway exploded. Concrete dust launched up and slowed to a crawl in mid-air. By the time the cloud faded, the Taigha had all gone still in their perfect little pile.

A pinprick in Wil's scalp drew his attention. The sting intensified. Probing through his hair, he brushed a sizzling steel ember from it. Blood smeared his fingertips.

That close.

"Robert," Saoirse barked, "watch the door! Wil, with me!"

Saoirse bypassed the corpse pile through the obliterated front window and jumped the counter into the kitchen. Wil followed close behind. The blood trail ended in the kitchen proper at the foot of the walk-in freezer door. A network of deep scratches tore into the steel panel along its lower half.

Wil turned the handle. Locked. No hinges to shoot out on this side, no power to the keypad. He knocked it with his shoulder. No dice. Sturdy as a Jotum's shield.

"Move," Saoirse said and unsheathed her Teseum claymore.

The blade slipped into the steel like fingers through water. Once, twice. Scattering ribbons of titanium at her feet, Saoirse julienned the door until her claymore caught the bolt, and the whole thing tilted. She checked it with her shoulder, and the steel door toppled inward with a massive, hollow thud.

The stench hit them first. Sweat, sick, and blood. A very human Gordon curled against the far wall of the empty walk-in freezer, head slumped against his shoulder. The tatters of his Dog-Warrior sized armor was wholly gone, and only his plaid remained, stretched over his crumpled form like a blanket. Blood from a thousand fresh wounds slathered what unmarred flesh remained.

Saoirse dropped her sword and slid on her knees to his side. Ear over his nose, she jumped. "He's breathin', Wil. He's still alive."

"Then let's get him to Nora," Wil said and called out for Hodges.

Thirty seconds later, they emerged from the diner with Gordon balanced on Saoirse's back as if weighed nothing at all. Wil bore Hodges' shotgun now, his Strela hanging limp along his back, and Hodges took point with his chain rifle.

Gunshots echoed in the west. Shasvastii weaponry mixed among the cacophony.

"Jig's up," Hodges said. "What now?"

Wil took point, speeding into a jog. "First, distance!"

Under a chain link, over a low wall. Asphalt gave way to grass, and grass to pavement. The shoulder of the fuel depot blotted out Helios, growing closer by the minute.

To the west, a pair of streaks fell from the clouds and spiked down into the ruins. A fireball blossomed there. Then a second, followed by pieces of the Tubarão whipping listlessly a hundred meters in the air. Glass shards rattled in their panes. A trio of Ariadnan raptors squawked and flapped away from the rooftop gardens above.

Wil knew it. No way they'd waste their chance if they pinged their target standing stationary within repeater range. All it'd taken was a knife, some persistence, and Fionnlagh to run the pearl of Wil's amputated internal comlog back to the Bulleteer left in standby at the burning Tubarão.

"Bloody hell," Hodges muttered. "The plan's actually working."

"Don't sound so surprised," Wil said. "Hit the button."

Almost begrudgingly, Hodges pulled the detonator from his bandolier and thumbed the little red button. A hundred meters of dilapidated parking lot behind them, the foundation of the tall, yellowing roadside signage exploded.

Bright smoke enveloped it. The individual numbers of the 25/7 swung free and fell. The sign swayed, steel moaning louder and louder before it finally axed down into the diner's face.

The ground shook. Glass shards glinted in midair around the impact like a snow globe of the NeoVatican before the dust cloud swallowed it whole. Out in the surrounding ruins, a handful of car alarms blared.

They'd pushed the Taigha away from the diner with the distraction. Now, it was time to pull them back, to see how they reacted when things got louder and if competing prey split their attention the way he hoped.

While the Taigha yo-yoed, a concentrated force of Shasvastii would press back to confirm the kill. Attention split, they'd inadvertently open a path toward the fuel depot and its bunkered interior—somewhere safe in plain sight where nothing short of a nuclear option could reach them.

And while copying the Croatoan maneuver just to batten down and hide might not solve the problem of the delegation, it's what would keep everyone alive. For now. And, hell, maybe Glasscock would come through. They hadn't lost, not yet. Not as long as they were still breathing.

They snaked down an alley, past the rubble and debris and thickets of weeds. It exited into a long street run with old rail, same as the one beside the palisade at Kildalton. At the end, the fuel depot's hydraulic blast door yawned, wide-open and inviting.

He stopped Saoirse before she crested the corner. "Not yet. Wait. Need to make sure it's clear first."

"Clear enough," she huffed, Gordon hanging over her back. "Go."

"TO Camo might be hiding on any of those rooftops, in any of the windows," he said. "Wait. Be patient. We need to wait for the signal."

Her lips pulled back, baring fangs. "Forget the signal, Wil, he's dying. *Go.*"

"Saoirse, no. Please trust me. All I'm asking is one minute."

Fire lit inside her pale eyes, and for an instant, Wil thought he should raise his guard. But she exhaled and stepped back, vein prominent in her brow from exertion. "Fine. One minute, nothing more."

Silence fell among them. The distant cracks and pops thinned. Staggered chain-rifle bursts echoed off the surrounding brickwork labyrinth. A shotgun report sounded. Far. The whump of a grenade launcher, twice.

An enemy location pinged fresh on his comlog. Out in the ruins, the tell-tale sound of a 9mm pistol, and the marker vanished.

Silence again. Saoirse rocked on her heels.

Inside the bunker, a torch blinked: Short. Long. Long.

"Alright," Wil said. "Depot's clear. On me. Three, two—"

Wil crested the corner, Hodges' shotgun braced against his shoulder. The others followed after. He paced himself to within a few meters of Saoirse so that if she fell, he could go back for her, for Gordon. Ruined buildings crowded the lane, empty windows glaring. Motion within. Maybe. No time for a second look.

Two canisters clattered into the street in front of the bunker door. Smoke grenades. Shop fronts and second-story windows faded away under the undulating gray. Beyond the whorl, two shapes—Cailean and Neil, beating a swift retreat from raising hell in the west.

The brittle, crumbled asphalt crushed beneath their feet. The safety of the wide-open blast doors closed in fast, and the cover of smoke along with it. Safety. Close. Only a few seconds more. Fionn dashed from the door, arm raised, but not in celebration—in warning. He shouted, arm pulled back for a pitch when his grip sparked and a smoke grenade slapped from his hand. It burned brightly, once, and died smokeless, its label soaked in red.

A single severed finger lay beside it on the street.

"Pit air iteig!" Fionn yelped and bolted back into the bunker. Violet lights ignited in the empty windows. Five, ten—more than Wil could count.

The world slowed. Terror swelled, strangled by training. The Shasvastii had caught on. Come in force. Laid a trap. Mired in the smoke, they were targets in a shooting gallery. Unarmed and encumbered, Saoirse would be dead in seconds, and Hodges not long after.

Someone needed to slow them down.

Wil spun up his MSV, painting the world in stark infrared colors. Their smoke cover turned transparent. Behind them, a Shasvastii-colored blob, pitched at a full run. Above them, two more.

The color inverted. Glitched. Not like before. Fractured. Broken. Stuck between modes. Static ripped across his vision in waves of distortion, and every errant rock and blade of grass highlighted with a full read-out.

A piece of shrapnel pierced his visor lens, centimeters from his eye. A glancing hit from the Taigha when Saoirse had shoved him behind cover. His MSV had finally been done in.

But the Shas didn't know that, and neither did his allies. Their shapes faded beneath the white noise, seconds from the door. Impacts rattled the road around him and him only.

Good.

In one eye, the smoke glowed red from his periphery. In the other, unfiltered data arranged into humanoid shapes. His pant leg blustered. His duster whipped. A near-miss. Wil rationed shells into the occupied positions, scraping a windowsill with one slug, bulls-eyeing a shop window with the other. No dice—no blood, no scream, no kill. Shells rattled hollow to the pavement, one after the other.

Useless. Toothless. He brought up his dial and spun to comms, searching for back up or explanation or a single iota of reassurance—

Nothing. Dead again.

Enormous weight speared him in the center chest. Wil went down gasping. Another bullet. No penetration. A lucky blunt. The stitch in his ribs overstretched, and when he stood, it tore loose.

In the distance, Nora screamed. Happy. Frightened. A mix.

They'd made it. They were safe.

His shoulder seized, locked his hand. Pain wasn't pain. His lungs knotted as he gulped down mouthfuls of bitter gray air. Two slugs, reload, two slugs, keep limping, moving toward the bunker door. His chest seized, and he coughed, and the pain was enough to force him to stop for a single—

The ground pitched. Wil's left leg kicked from under him. The road rushed toward his face. Impacting face-first, he flailed onto his back. Agony and nausea struck without delay. Adrenaline kept him conscious. Too hurt to be afraid. The leg of his muddy fatigues raged with a torrent of fresh red blood, fabric frayed at the bend. Inside, his kneecap jut off to one side, upending the topography of his leg.

A Taigha's claw jut from the road where he'd stood. Ground bulging, the rest of the creature punched free, leathery body swathed in dark earth. Wil turned his shotgun on it, caught it just before it reached him. Two slugs hollowed its face into a wet cavern. The next Taigha out of the burrow shoved it aside, died the same, and was vaulted by a third.

It barked. Rabid. Closed fast. Wil squeezed the trigger. Nothing. Out of ammo. He fumbled for his pocket, for the shells. One left. His grip quaked, the shell dropped from his hand, and the charging Taigha was atop him.

Greedy chirping. Tearing. Pain. Clawed fins like axe blades cracked against his armor. The shotgun splintered. Bent in two. No air left to shout. Too heavy to flip. Too strong to hold back. The Taigha pinned him down and lunged for his face.

A gunshot.

The Taigha juddered back, facemask dented. Its diodes flared and popped. Black blood foamed past its broken teeth, and then it danced back, jaw split, face carved, anvil-shaped skull degloved until the point-blank fire from the approaching machine gun shredded it wholesale off of Wil's chest.

Alastair stood behind him, sweat-soaked and unarmored. All that was left in his Drozhat HMG was tangled belt casing, its barrel white hot and glowing from the sustained pull. He reached out, but when Wil tried to take his hand, it seemed so far away.

Slimy mucus wet his Adam's apple. Warm.

Red. Not mucus.

Blood.

A lot of blood.

The empty Drozhat bounced off the broken asphalt. Alastair hauled Wil over his shoulders.

And then they were running.

33

An ancient, yellowing light glared from the water-stained ceiling. Dust motes floated heavy in the glow. Vents hummed. A hinge creaked, so gentle it scarcely registered, and footsteps receded from the room.

Breathing hurt. Seeing hurt. Thinking hurt. Every part of his body burned when he moved, like his skin had torn away from the skeleton underneath. He swallowed, and it felt tight. Swollen. Silk strips tightly wound his neck from jaw to collar. His left pant leg had been slit open up to his thigh, and his knee was hot and thick with malaise.

He'd lost his duster. Again. And his visor. *Again*. Reduced to his shirt and pants, shoeless and cold. He ran his hands against his face, and Taigha skittered in the red-black nothing behind his eyelids along with Indigo River's jaws and Keyes' near-miss.

His voice came out in an unfamiliar, gravelly crackle. "Fuck."

Snippets of memory remained. The crunch. His wheeze. So much blood, and Nora's total calm. The last vial of Serum, split two ways and chased with morphine—lots of morphine. No wonder he barely remembered.

He'd gone from the smoke cloud to a small, antiquated office, a time capsule to the earliest days of Ariadna. Ancient, pre-quantronic tech littered the desks, stacked dot-matrix paper beside long-obsolete fusebox towers and keyboards caked with decades of dust. Barren cupboards lined the walls, cream finish rotted jaundice-yellow under the bunker's decayed emergency lighting.

The bunker. Saoirse and Gordon. Mierda. He needed to find them. Needed to get up. When he sat upright, someone grunted beside him.

Saoirse. She sat beside the table, face buried in her folded arms. Her grenadier's vest was folded into the pillow he'd rolled off of, wrinkled and beaten and bloody. She stirred, eyes half-lidded, and saw him. "Wil, wait. Don't. Calm down."

"What," he started, and failed to swallow the lump in his throat.

"Taigha dislocated yer knee, gashed your windpipe," she said, and stood to check his bandage. A few thumps on the back loosened the web in his lungs for him. "Nora says yer lucky. Says its only fractures in the—not bones. Cartilage.

Says the Serum should knit ye well enough, if ye rest."

"No. With the Shas. How long have I been out?"

Saoirse found his hand and squeezed it. "Hours. Past midnight now. Dinnae ken how you slept through the D-charges, or the missiles. Nothing worked. They're locked out, Wil. We're safe."

Two days until the *Sword of St. Catherine* arrived.

Dread clawed at his innards, tying his entrails into pretty ribbons. They still had time. Barely any, but time. The only question was if they could utilize it, or if the mission was unsalvageable.

A cough punched out of Wil. He muffled the next in his palms, webs of mucus thick as plastic wrap dislodging from his gullet. Antibacterial film. Residue from the Serum, chock with inert nanobots encased in protein slurry. Saoirse wrapped his hands around her canteen, and he finished the contents in three hard gulps. He wasn't hungry until she put half an energy bar in his hand, and he demolished it in seconds.

"The smuggler's run," he said, breathless at first but gaining momentum. "That's the only way Stuart Walker could've got into the Croatoan without someone clocking him on the street. And Eideard's too paranoid to agree to have the whole town bunker in one place if there weren't a secret way out—because of the Druze—"

Saoirse steadied him against her. Her lips grazed his forehead. "Shh. It's okay. Pell saw the door, all hid under a mountain of barrels. They're diggin' it out as we speak. You were right, Wil. You were right."

The tension across his body slacked all at once. His head swam, and Saoirse nestled him in the crook of her neck. Warm, and soft. Her heartbeat drummed through her ragged undershirt. Sweat and smoke mingled with the tang of sulfur in her hair. Not the best, but... her.

"So glad yer okay," she whispered. "Everyone keeps scarin' me lately. And those regrets keep comin' tae mind, and..."

Her primeval eyes drank him in, and then they were kissing.

It only lasted a moment. But it was good. For a few seconds, he wasn't aching, wasn't hurt, wasn't scared or wracking over his dwindling ammunition supply, wasn't terrified of PanOceania or Dawn or the Shasvastii or Antipodes. The only thing on his mind was her.

Saoirse pulled away, red curls curtaining her eyes. "Sorry."

"Don't be," Wil said and drew her back in.

She resisted. "No, your breath. It's rank."

He wiped his teeth with his glove but knew that wouldn't change anything. "Right. My bad."

"I'll manage," she said, and came in for seconds.

Now, the kiss was more of a need than a want. Primal. Not like he minded. He'd known necking with her would always be a contact sport ever since she'd put him on his ass in the infirmary, but he didn't care—about bite-marks, about consequences, about being kind. Dawn would be behind him soon, but there was no reason she couldn't come with. Problem solved. That's how he would do this. That's how he would keep her.

No. The idea of a woman like her 'kept' defied logic. Trapping her in sterile, soulless Neoterra was the worst thing he could do. San Pietro was no place for her, away from her family, away from her highlands, in a place where she could never be more than an Atek, an outsider, a pariah. Hell, it wasn't a place for him either.

So why then, exactly, couldn't *he* stay instead?

The office door clattered open. Saoirse shoved away from him, but not fast enough. Neil stood frozen in the doorway.

His jaw dropped, and then he grinned. "I've won ten pound."

"Damnit, Neil," Saoirse growled. Her cheeks flushed bright beneath her freckles. "We were havin' a *moment*."

"No worries, already could tell," Neil said. "Figured he'd rattled you off on patrol when ye came back steamin'. Laid money on it with Fionn. Ta much, Princess."

Wil flashed a thumbs-up. "Doing great. Thanks for asking."

"Bet ye are," Neil said. "Listen. Vern and Kelsie found something. A panel."

Saoirse slid to the table's edge. "Tell 'em hit 'open,' then. How you askin' me?"

"Not you," Neil said. "Him. It's quantronic."

Wil blinked. "In the hundred-year-old building?"

"Aye, now yer catchin' up."

He ignored the hurt and swung his legs off the table. "Show me."

†††

The fuel depot's interior was a mirror-version of the donut-shaped Croatoan layout: sans bar, sans caged arena, sans cloud of smoke and spilled beer and neon-soaked walls plastered with decades of bloodstains, signed photographs, and trash-metal band posters. A network of rusted pipes traced overhead, like roots in a wine cellar, and stacked steel drums ran the perimeter of every floor.

Wherever Glasscock was, Wil hoped it was better than this.

Battered knee numb enough for an assisted walk, Wil followed Neil over a cross-shaped catwalk suspended through the center of the structure's ground floor. On the way, they passed Pell and Dunne, resting near the blast doors with their firearms in hand.

When Pellehan saw him, he produced Wil's dented multispectral visor from his assault pack with a cheeky grin and offered up a cigar as a peace offering. "Long live the Aquila Guard," he said, and fished an old matchbook from his poncho.

Dunne snatched it up with silent, precise fury, and thumped a steel drum with the butt of her Molotok. "Whole depot's packed with expired gasoline, Pell.

One spark," and she gestured out an explosion. "One!"

Pell croaked a solitary laugh. "You're being paranoid, my dear."

"Light up then, see what happens."

The geriatric sniper considered it, but bowed instead, and stowed the cigar in his coat pocket. "After then, Wilhelm. After. When all this smoke clears, we'll make some of our own."

Fionn sat at the top of the stairs, vest removed, shirt soaked with sweat. Gauze packed tight to the wrecked stub of his left index knuckle, and he was finishing off his canteen when they approached.

"Shit, man," Wil said. "You alright?"

Fionn wiped his lips and grinned. He said something in Caledonian that must've meant *It's bad, but I've had worse*.

"Yeah, same. Hurts?"

What do you think? or something like it, and the two of them had a laugh.

More of the MacArthurs gathered on the second floor. Hodges sat beside a steel drum, lining varying sizes and calibers of ammunition atop its lid. Cailean hunched over his pauldron in the corner, knife in hand, decorating the last stretch of unbroken blue with a fresh line of tallies. There was only enough room for four or five more.

Gordon occupied the farthest corner, giant frame swathed in his bloody tartan and what had to be all the remaining bandages. Nora curled in his lap, jacket folded for a pillow. Her eyes were red and swollen, and she smiled in her sleep.

As for Alastair, some of the color had come back to his face. He'd sourced a fresh shirt, chest plastered with Wild Bill's crossed-revolver logo, and only a few scant pieces of his Mormaer armor remained buckled to his frame. Wil counted the missing pieces on the others: Hodges wore a pauldron; Neil, the shin-guards; Cailean, his gauntlets. On the table, Alastair's Teseum helmet sat upside-down, filled with blinking comlogs and lidded by his scorched ballistic shield.

That was one way to keep their quantronic presence hidden.

As they approached, Alastair limped to Gordon's side and placed a hand on his friend's shoulder. Paused a beat, held the gesture. Before he continued on, Gordon took him by the forearm and looked into his eyes.

Tacit acceptance. Brotherhood. Solidarity. Everything Wil had never had, and for a moment, a pang of bitter envy lanced through him.

All that mattered was that Gordon was alive. He'd finally dug his fingers into that void he sought so desperately to grasp, scraped along its rim, and pulled himself back out. He might keep climbing. He might not. But for now, he was surrounded by family, and if they won free of this place, he had a chance.

Gordon's eyes leveled on Wil. Without disdain reflecting back, they almost seemed a different color. He nodded, once, and looked away.

When Wil checked his six, the others were staring. He braced himself for Hodges' smart comment, for Cailean's grumble, and limped across the room with as much dignity as he could muster.

"Lieutenant," Hodges said, tone sharp. "Glad to see you up and about."

No edge; no double-meaning; no hidden dig. The shock of it had him wrestling with the sudden notion he should cut off Hodges' finger to make sure he wasn't a Speculo.

Cailean jumped up and slapped his knife flat on the table. "Throat ripped out, and already standin'! That's our PanO for ye, *our* goddamn—"

"Oi," Saoirse hissed and gestured madly toward Nora. "Wake her, old man, and so help me."

"Galactic," Cailean finished, voice cut to a whisper. "Pardon, but—didnae guess ye'd walk that off, lad. Thought ye'd go, but here ye are. Only glad is all."

"Same," Wil said. "Nicest old timer in Kildalton, everybody."

Cailean grimaced. "Sick cerulean bastard."

Alastair approached, gait hastened from a limp to a stride. Wil extended his hand, but the young chieftain wrapped him in a hug, instead. "I owe you a debt, Wil, one I can scarcely repay. Thank you."

"Something cart, something horse," Wil said and made space. "We're not out of it yet."

The brief exertion had already tapped Alastair's strength, and he needed to lean on the wall for support. "True. But because of you, we're halfway there, even if our injured are starting to outnumber our able. And Gordon's alive."

"I just gave you a plan," he said. "You guys did the work."

Alastair simply smiled. "Of course."

Cailean sidled closer, concern writ large on his silver-bearded face. "Breathing's easy? Serum do its job? And the knee, it can bend?"

"Seems healthy enough," Neil said and wriggled his eyebrows. The glare Saoirse gave him could've stripped the SymbioMate off a Sukeul.

"I'm good," Wil said, and hated that he had to clear his throat and repeat himself. "I'm fine. Really. Pain isn't pain. Nothing I can't handle."

"Well, if you need something, ask," Hodges said. "I've not much left, but there's rations, water—or antiseptic cream? Mayhaps a pistol? My Groza's got eleven rounds, and I've the flash pulse in a pinch. I'd offer Llowry's grenade launcher, but all we've left is improvised smoke."

Wil sighed. "Don't tell me: there was only 9mm FMJ in the supply cache."

"Actually," Alastair said, "it was destroyed."

His surprise muted under the obvious signs: energy bars, empty canteens, rationed ammunition. A hundred possibilities came to mind: Antipodes, inclement weather, mold, hit by a lucky lightning bolt. Judging by Alastair's demeanor, his guess was Shasvastii, which meant it was either comlog eavesdropping, a lucky discovery, or Scáthach.

As long as they didn't lose anyone else, Wil was okay with that. Their trek back to Kildalton would start on a low note, sure, but as long as Glasscock was still alive with that comlog on his wrist, they'd won. It was over.

From Alastair's expression, Wil knew he felt the same.

One quick conversation about ammunition rationing later, and Neil led the way to the final subbasement. They hadn't made it halfway when Cailean called out down the stairwell after them.

"Hold, hold," he said. "I need tae speak to our PanO, alone."

Neil acquiesced and descended to the next flight without slowing. Concerned, but trusting, Saoirse followed. "Don't push him, please. I fancy this one."

"Would never," Cailean said and waited until they were alone.

Wil kept balance on the railing. "What's up?"

Stone-faced, Cailean dug in his pocket and pressed something familiar into Wil's hand: A Holland-12 cartridge, brass casing engraved with the name WILHELM.

He stared at it for what felt like a long, long time. Searched Cailean's expression for an explanation, and didn't understand why the old man was smiling.

"For if you ever return here," Cailean said. "When you do, my home is yours. Dear old da might spin out his grave, me breakin' bread with a galactic, but far as I'm concerned, yer already sept."

"Alastair told you," Wil said. "About my Fusilier."

Cailean nodded. "And Saoirse, and Dunne. Seems we've succeeded. Less dead Shas than I'd hoped for, but ye have to ken when tae call it."

"You sure you wanna give this up? Might be your last shot."

"Still got Alastair's spare belt, and Neil's extra besides," Cailean said and turned away. "Turns out Volunteers are good fer more than cheerin' me on, aye? They also carry things, sometimes."

Wil caught hold of his plaid. "Wait up."

Cailean turned back. "Dinnae make this weird, lad."

"No, it's just—back in Kildalton," he said. "Eideard said you were hunting ghosts. Named one. Jeerack, or something, and when you saw that Jayth you said the same thing. Saoirse told me who he was."

His mirth and gratitude faded behind a haze of solemn anger. "Aye. The Díreach. My old friend from Novyy Cimmeria."

"She said it was personal."

He nodded. "Back then, he was some bastard Shas thought he was a Morat. Tussled more 'n a few times, at Johnny-5, Duban, the Aplekton. Hated the bug. Last time I saw 'em was back at Lafayette, caught up in the flames of his own side's firebomb. But when I went back, he was gone, and so was Rhiannon's claymore."

It was an instant before Wil realized Cailean wasn't talking about his gun.

"No one believed me. Said I was mad fer revenge. Haunted. But there were whispers, ken. A ghost, huntin' homesteaders on the fringes. Not an Antipode, but somethin' else. Locals called it the Díreach, after the one-armed, one-legged giant of legend. Five years of dry leads, and now… well, to put it lightly, I've a chance tae finish what she started. Or would, if this wasn't all but over."

"Rhiannon was your wife," Wil said. "She's the Wulver who took his arm and leg."

Cailean shared a rare, non-sardonic smirk. "Aye."

"What happened to Stevie Nicks?"

He laughed. "Same thing she was named for, and a canny excuse besides. The Kilgour could never match her volume, or her warmth, but it helps me feel like she's still beside me in the thick of it. Might sound sad to a man from where folk come back tae life."

"Not in the least," Wil said. "Bet she would've broken my nose by now, the amount of fuck-ups I've pulled?"

"Her fury was bar-none, aye, though she woulda kent yer worth when I was still spittin' on about Tech Bees and made-up planets. She always had a ken for what I lacked."

Saoirse leaned into the stairwell below, checking in on him. Wil caught her curious glance and held it till she smiled. "She sounds like a badass."

Cailean chuckled. "Now, stop me if ye've noticed…"

"I have," he said. "Saoirse's a badass, too."

"Had me waxin' nostalgic, you two. Saoirse Clarke, in love with a Pan-Oceanian. Never thought I'd see a stranger thing than an Überfallkommando, but here we are, living in the interesting times the Yujingyu go on about."

When Saoirse left his sight, Wil knew then and there that 'love' wasn't far-off after all. What other explanation could there be? "Yeah. Chimeras. Weird."

"My secret: Socks o'er the claws," Cailean said, and started back up the steps. "That, an' only tellin' the truth. Rhiannon and I coulda gone another thirty years with truth and love alone."

Strange terror choked him. "I might stay."

"In the bunker?"

"On Dawn."

Cailean held out a biding hand. "Careful, lad. Expatriation's a dangerous game."

"I don't want to go back."

"S'fine. Ye don't have to."

"But I do," Wil said. "I owe a debt to PanOceania. They fed me. Clothed me. Gave me a Cube, and a purpose. I can't turn my back on my home. And this place doesn't want me."

"After what you've done for us, I can say yer unequivocally wrong," Cailean said. "Squeeze the H-12 in yer palm if ye got any doubt of that."

The primer indented a circle in Wil's thumb, so deep it might've been permanent.

⁜

Vern swabbed the dust from the narrow window embedded in the lower-level's storage room floor and let Wil take a look. "Don't know how it opens. But you were right."

By the concentric rings of rust, the hatch into the smuggler's run had been covered with fuel drums. Now, most of them laid stacked outside beside a trio of tall storage tanks marked in triplicate with faded warnings and smeared with pinkish residue. If there was a competition for Most Flammable Thing in the Human Sphere, they would've taken gold, silver, and bronze, to the chagrin of every Gorgos pilot ever.

Wil cast a long glare in Vern's direction. He hadn't forgotten the cut comms, but their current situation was more pressing. "Neil said something about a panel?"

Kelsie ran her hand in front of a seam in the wall. A dot in the concrete twinkled and cast a steady holopane. Modern, but still rigged with a projector for Atek usage. "Et voilà."

"Thought this place was built a hundred years before the Commercial Conflicts." Wil swiped his fingers through the holo. The implanted haptics in his fingertips buzzed, and the display reconfigured into a six-digit numerical input. "The hell is this doing here?"

"Your guess's good as mine," Vern said. "There was one hidden outside the front door, too—at least, before Dunne smashed it. Didn't want to risk the Shas letting themselves in."

Kelsie shrugged. "I say Yuan-Yuans. Vern says Submondo. What's your take?"

Wil shook his head. "Both stick to outer space. This is something else."

"Lovely, more complications. Whoever had 'it gets worse' on their bingo card, mind you can't mark it off more than once."

Wil shined Vern's flashlight into the window. Past the glass, a narrow staircase led to a length of smooth tunnel wide enough for two men to walk side-by-side. By his amateur judgment, the run bore south—away from Fort Resolute, and the DRC-9.

"Perfect," Wil said. "Absolutely the direction we need."

Kelsie sat cross-legged on a fuel drum. "You're usually not one for sarcasm, PanO. What gives?"

"I'm not," he said, and made the decision to trust them. "Assuming the asset I rescued doesn't bleed out, our job here is done. DRC, warned. Everyone who made it to the Fort is alive. Time to hit the bricks."

Vern furrowed his brow. "Wait, what asset?"

"Aye, turns out not every one of those dummy markers was noise," Saoirse said, and helped Wil back up. "Gave 'em a gun, told 'em to hide, right?"

"Yeah. And if they're doing what I said, every channel's getting flooded with distress calls right about now."

Kelsie's smile spread across her whole face. "Really? Really really?"

"Really," Wil said. "Broadcasts will trigger scrutiny. Scrutiny means satellite footage of the Tubarão detonation. That alone will belay the *Sword of St. Catherine*, trigger an official response, draw attention to the DRC-9—everything we set out to do. Once we rescue the asset, we're home free to tuck tail back to Kildalton."

"Hell," Saoirse snickered. "Ye really are clever."

"We still don't have food, or ammo. We're not out of the woods yet."

"But that's it, it's over?" Vern asked. "We're going home? We won?"

Kelsie tossed the closed canteen back to Saoirse. "Once you get this door open, sounds like. You tried 06126? That was the side door up at the mine when I was a girl. Standard safety protocol, ken?"

Vern went to his feet, dazed with relief, when a metal clangor rang out above them. It was Neil, stretched over the second floor railing and drumming the steel with his rifle. The moment he saw them look, he flashed hand signs. *Danger close—come here—Wil and Saoirse.*

Upstairs, the MacArthurs gathered near Gordon, encircling his makeshift seat. Nora stood beside him, worry writ large in her little blue eyes; Alastair was already reaffixing his armor to his body. A miniscule sound emitted from a pair of small, dark earpieces laid on Gordon's palm.

A voice.

Wil's gut jumped. Of course—his implanted comlog. No way to hide his quantronic presence short of cutting it out. They'd been careless, and Scáthach had found them again.

"I'm so sorry," Gordon whispered. "With everything, I didn't think."

Alastair swiped his comlog from the improvised bowl of his helmet and affixed it to his wrist. "It's alright. It's not like it's a secret we're in here, we'll figure this out."

But when Alastair spun up his comlog and connected to Gordon's, the voice on the other side wasn't female.

"MacArthur regiment," the caller said, voice deep and tinged with self-importance. "This is your final warning. You are surrounded, and I am growing impatient."

Odune.

Something didn't seem right. A familiar itch unsettled in his brain, begging to be scratched: Where had he heard that tone before, cut up by the vox, transmit over a comlog….

"Outside wall's likely flush with repeaters," Hodges said. "If they've accessed Gordon's halo, they know where we're all standing."

Nora's eyes widened. "Are we gonna get all missiled like Wil's comlog?"

"Needs an aperture fer speculative fire," Cailean said. He'd donned his armor again—claymore sheathed on his back, Rhiannon at his side. "There's no path in or out of this crypt, but get geared. We'll move soon."

Alastair buckled his breastplate with a wince and spoke into his comlog. "This is Alastair Lucas MacArthur, chieftain of Clan MacArthur of the Achadh nan Darach. Who is speaking?"

A pause. "It seems that crash wasn't as lethal as you purported."

"And it seems you've killed two Volunteers. Their names are Sebastian Bell and Domhnall Llowry. As a mercy, I'm willing to give you twenty-four hours to remove yourself and your miserable infestation from my planet before I come and do it myself."

"*Your* planet," Odune balked. "Is that a threat?"

"It's an oath," Alastair said, and counted the last four cartridges into his chain-colt.

Odune broke into heavy, dry laughter. "An oath—my god, an oath! Human arrogance never ceases to amaze. If you're baring your fangs, I'm unimpressed. This kind of game doesn't resign on time, little prince, but luckily I'm amicable to a draw."

More chess terminology. More—

Terror jolted him awake. Realization warred with impossibility inside his staggered mind. The vox over the comlog, the incorrect rank, the echoes of memory, chess terms, zugzwang, the itch of déjà vu in his gray matter all tied tight into one horrifying idea.

The Hexa liaison to the OSS on Svalarheima, Gavon Fhorst.

Xandros Odune, Counselor to the Dawn Research Commission.

They were the same person.

34

Wil grabbed for the comlog, heart pumping white-hot fire. "I knew I recognized you, I fucking *knew* it! You're dead, you hear me! Veta al carajo, hija de—!"

Saoirse shoved him away from Alastair, bowling him onto his back. For the first time since they'd met, she was stunned into silence, staring with her jaw agape as if she didn't understand rage.

"The guy from Svalarheima," Wil shouted. "Fhorst! Odune and Fhorst, they're the same guy! Same Shasvastii, two different skins—like a costume change, he's the one who—my soldiers, he said we needed to retreat—"

"Ìosa," Saoirse gasped. "Seriously? Ye sure?"

Alastair muted his comlog. "Enough."

Wil doubled over, fighting down the words. So many things clicked now. Their last-minute reposition. Orders to retreat arriving just after they'd reached position. Fhorst's convenient death by guided fire. And then Odune had slipped back in the lobby, and called him *Captain*....

Deep gulps of air. Counting in reverse. Halogen lights, black plastic, and cardboard. Saoirse braced him until he was in control of himself again.

The MacArthurs gathered, armed. Below, Vern and Kelsie's voices pitched. They were arguing. Now did not seem the time.

With quick gestures, Alastair doled out new orders. "Eleanor, Neilan—head downstairs. Help the others. Pellehan, Fionnlagh—pack what supplies we have left. I intend to evacuate this place posthaste. Saoirse, can you see about the hatch? Use your sword if you must."

Saoirse seemed reticent to leave Wil's side. He waved her off, muttering assurances. Hesitantly, she led the twins downstairs, her Teseum claymore catching the emergency light in its draw.

When Alastair unmuted the channel, Odune was laughing. "Wow. Wow! And here I thought I'd jumped the gun by ordering his vessel scuttled. He's sharp, isn't he?"

Alastair secured his Teseum vambraces over his gauntlets. "You're talking about Lieutenant Gotzinger."

"Captain when I met him, but yes," Odune said. "Too smart for his own good. Hexahedron said the boy had a millstone for minutiae and meaningless things, reciting apocrypha and mission parameters to the letter—more impressive when you know his geist is always on silent. And then, it turned out he had half a brain besides. Turned down our lethal injection, donned his suit to avoid the gas seeping from the vents, clocked our agents on the road. Dangerous instinct, that."

The medtech and his booster shot; the strange smell in his domicile; the repairmen in the road, so surprised to see him. Something had been off that day, something his gut had caught that his mind hadn't. Now it all made sense in the worst possible way.

"So you had him killed?" Alastair asked.

Odune's smile was evident in his voice. "Unsuccessfully, it seems. What terrible luck to meet again here. For both of us. Imagine if he realized who I was when I was still in his reach! Or if he actually told someone who mattered, instead of a cabal of drunken Ateks squatting on a Teseum vein."

Dunne handed over Alastair's helmet—empty, now that she'd doled out the comlogs. He hooked his trenched ballistic shield onto his left and balanced the helmet in his right. "And the other attaché. Did he find you out, too?"

"Almost," Odune said. "I hired Yearwood precisely because I believed he'd relax, guard down, too distracted by his relief at escaping his position on embattled Paradiso. Instead, thirteen months into his long vacation, he came to me with whispers of a wild theory that members of the DRC staff had been replaced by alien infiltrators."

"Rajan Brizuela did the same?"

A laugh. "Oh, no! Did he strike you as intelligent, MacArthur? I toyed with the idea he'd been sent by the Hexahedron, the way he deftly avoided the welcoming party for Gotzinger in Fort Resolute with his little flyover game. But, alas, no."

Another near-miss, without either of them ever knowing. No wonder Keyes had been so concerned, and Odune had jumped straight to the missile—from an outside perspective, their lucky fumbling must've seemed like precognition.

Alastair met Cailean's eyes. "So. What now?"

"What now is, you decide," Odune said. "You control tonight's outcome, MacArthur. Until Captain Gotzinger complicated things, I would've gladly let your people live out their insignificant lives, pointing your guns in vain at the heavens above. But now, you've pointed those guns at me."

Dunne stood beside Hodges. He whispered in her ear, and she took his hand in hers.

"It doesn't have to be that way. I'm willing to let your rag-tag group of insurgents go free, no questions asked. All you have to do is deliver Gotzinger to me, and never speak of what happened here. If you can do that, we will not harm you—this, I swear upon my people, the Continuum, and our Shaviish."

The lines in Cailean's face deepened, fingers tightening around Rhiannon's pistol grip.

"Leave Captain Gotzinger behind, dead or alive. It doesn't matter to me. Do what you want with Rajan Brizuela. His life is of no consequence. If he'd kept his hands to himself, instead of liberally applying them to his superior's wife, he wouldn't have set foot here in the first place."

Gordon bared his teeth, bloodshot eyes burning.

"In three years' time, and with your clan's support, the DRC Dun Scaith will succeed in our petition to expand into the natural marina of Loch Eil with a space port, connecting your lonely holding with the Human Sphere in ways you could never dream of. Technology. Medicine. Jobs. Drill equipment, sold at a reasonable bargain with no expectation of Teseum in return. With that autonomy, you'll no longer need to beg for scraps from Rodina's table."

Wil shoved his broken visor back onto his head. It'd saved his life too many times to be abandoned now.

"But if you don't—if you resist us—then none of this will happen. Terrible gears will turn into motion, ones that *cannot* be stopped. Defiance here will not slow the sunset on Judgment Day, and when it comes, MacArthur, your people will *burn*. Everything you have ever fought for will fade into ash and obscurity. All we ask is symbiosis. All we ask is peace.

"We can share this world, human," Odune said. "What do you say?"

Cloaked in sweat, Alastair dredged his damp hair from his face. His dark eyes blazed with an inner flame, a warrior's pride, a lionheart.

He said, "Dawn is Ours."

Odune transmitted a full six seconds of stunned silence. "I—"

And Alastair closed the call.

"Christ Almighty, lad," Cailean laughed, face beaming with pride. "*Now* yer soundin' like yer da."

A soft whirr. A pop. Dust coughed from a fresh crack in the concrete floor. Blood cascaded from Cailean's collar, into his plaid, across his boots. He touched his throat, gurgled red into his beard, and fell.

Alastair screamed. Dove for him. Gordon caught him halfway. A second bullet flit like a dragonfly through the thin opening in an air vent and grazed the helmet in Alastair's hand. The force sent it whirling over the railing.

Hodges screamed, "Guided fire! Smart ammo!" and covered Dunne with his body. "Stay—!"

A third shot buzzed between Wil's legs and thumped into a gas drum.

The air went bright and then black.

Heat, and force.

Steel grating ran rough against his hands. He had fallen atop the catwalk—when had he fallen?—and the surface of a restless ocean surged above him. Not water. Smoke, black as hell itself and roiling. The yellowing light burned a brighter orange, now. Flames coursed along the ground floor in a widening pool.

The gasoline was on fire.

Wil's eyes watered. Lungs ached. His first desperate gasp seared through to the core of him, and he coughed it back out until he acclimated to the scorch.

Alastair was gone. Gordon, too. No sign of the MacArthurs at all. Only raging black and roaring red remained. Metal creaks and pops preceded splashes, bursts. Ignited portholes atop the drums flared like pilot lights. One by one, they burst, imploded, toppled stacks. The conflagration grew until the pool had become a swell and fire cascaded in sheets into the basements below.

Wil stood and limped for the stairs.

Tinnitus bubbled up inside him. The ground clouded away, and his limbs swung wild on reflex alone, muscle memory all but erased. His vision blurred and threatened to double, and the catwalk floor shot toward his face. Wil staggered to keep balance and nearly tumbled over the railing, clinging to the thin steel bar with every ounce of his focus. Coughs wrung blood from his throat and kept him pinned in the open.

A steel flower unfolded near the cluttered office door, pulsing with wisps of green light. A Dazer. Same model as back on Svalarheima. No clue when it'd gotten there, or how it'd activated.

Hodges voice carried over the chaos. "How! There's no entry for smart ammo, we *checked*!"

"Robert!" Dunne cried. "Not now!"

Her Molotok rattled. Grenades cracked. Their voices faded.

Nora screamed from down below, "Wil! The hatch, below! It's open! Wil, we—"

Her cries were swallowed by the snarling of the flames.

Wil refused to stay down. Had to follow them. Pain wasn't pain. His fingers quickened, along with his pulse, but his hands were naked without a weapon and his ruined knee slowed his run into a drag. Smoke replaced air. Every breath tangled in his lungs. The edges of his vision squeezed.

Wind sucked through the bunker, engulfing him in a freezing whirlwind before the heat redoubled. The blast doors groaned open. Violet lights beyond erased what visibility remained, smoke silhouetted with tall, gangly Shasvastii.

He urged himself on. Used that one cold breath, held it, leveraged it to give him another step. Almost there—almost to the stairs, almost outrunning the fire.

The click of a prosthetic rushed close. Hydraulics sucked in behind him, and then its bearer had him by the shirt. Wil slammed against the railing, air crushed from his lungs under the enormous weight of Hammerhand's bionic arm.

"Lieutenant Gotzinger," Hammerhand growled. His leathery face and neck was sewn with stripes and gouges, each roughly the width of one of Gordon's fangs. "Such a terrible price for such a pitiful creature. Your pound of flesh will be paid in the blood of the innocent."

"Combined Army, my ass," Wil choked. "The fuck combined to make you?"

Its mandibles creased. "Filthy creature. Maggot-thing. *Human*." Hammerhand unhooked a dark discus from his belt—a D-charge—and primed it. Violet light traced across its surface. "Hardly fit to play grenade."

He affixed it to Wil's visor and bent him over the edge.

Beep.

One floor beneath, shapes darted across the open subbasement. The MacArthurs, racing for the smuggler's run. A violet-lit shadow braced to open fire, tracing a shock of red hair.

Beep.

The burning bunker split with the staccato drum of heavy machine gun fire. Shasvastii silhouettes ripped apart beneath its obliterating line. Hammerhand spun wild, meat shoulder shocked with two fresh holes, and Wil summoned up everything in him to wrench free his visor and hurl it away before the detonation seq—

Beep.

⇡⇡

Darkness.

Thrumming.

Heat.

Wil coughed, and his eyelids scraped open like sandpaper on glass.

Above, the catwalk moaned, wedged askew along the concrete pillars meters above his head. Cables swung loose, curtaining the floor.

They'd fallen. The catwalk had broken. Smoke billowed all around him, thick with glottal Shasvastii clicking. Fire washed along the bunker's upper levels on gasoline tides, spilling from floor to floor and growing ever closer.

Wil leveraged one arm forward and dragged himself. Couldn't leave Saoirse. Not now. The thought of her gave him the strength for another pull. To raise onto one knee. A hobble. One clumsy step, and he went down gasping. A blue-and-white shard of scorched steel slipped from an indent in his flak and clinked on the concrete. Everything that remained of his visor and Sharlene's hard work floated in the blood spatter below him.

Shadows gathered on the railing above. Alien firearms primed, leveled down on him. And a new shadow, a taller one, broke the smoke at the edge of his vision, striding along the fire's limit. Their weapon rang out with mechanical precision, scattering the Shasvastii above. Each shot, measured. Each step, calm. Green and gold tartan billowed in the heat haze, heavy footfalls accompanied by a whistling rendition of *The Ballad of Three and Fifty*.

Cailean. He'd survived. Wil crawled toward him, and the old man bent down mid-burst to drag him by the collar. The shot had been a graze. Cailean was alive, somehow he'd managed—

No.

Arterial red sputtered in Cailean's neck, white strips of exposed muscle plucked among blackened threads of flesh. Dark lifeblood caked his breastplate and filled the divots of every cross he'd etched onto his shoulder. Fire climbed his pant leg, but he didn't seem to notice.

He'd heard that if you killed a Highlander, their corpses got back up and kept fighting.

Dunne was at his side. "I've got him, sir," she said, and froze.

Cailean swayed, eyes bloodshot and unfocused. His whistle ended with a labored cough, far too damp to spur hope. "Alright, Rhia, alry," he said, smile feeble and kind. "Straight to the helo, mo chridhe. No dawdling this time."

Hammerhand impacted the concrete fist-first, meters away. The holes in his shoulder dribbled rivers of wine-colored ichor as he stood. Violet connections flared. With a roar, he launched toward them.

Hodges burst from a side chamber, chain rifle braced against his hip. Flash-forged shrapnel exploded from its muzzle, pitting the concrete and the false arm's armored surface. It failed to stop the rush. Hammerhand flickered stop-motion in Dunne's Molotok's flare, and then he was atop her.

His leathery fist cracked her in the jaw. Dunne stumbled. The spike in his fist sucked back and buried in the wall, impaling her through the breast.

Dunne shrieked and hurled herself aside, photoreactive poncho tearing from the pneumatic hammer's spike until it was clear the hit had been offcenter. A graze. Deep and bloody, deadly but not mortal. Hammerhand snatched at the tatters of her poncho, leashing her back and off of her feet.

The spike sucked into his fist as he rose above her. "More meat for the warrens!"

His shout woke Cailean from the waking dream he'd fallen into. The Grey hurtled forward. Shoulder met rib. Stock met jaw. Hammerhand's strike went askew, spike overshooting Dunne to punch a hole in the concrete instead. Unbalanced, the Jayth faltered, and Rhiannon's barrel pitched point-blank into his face.

The first shot scoured his eye guard from his face. The second blunted on his prosthetic as he collapsed behind its bulk. Sparks choked the air. Coated the floor. The relentless hammering of unstoppable force versus immovable object screamed like a chainsaw on glass.

Pink hydraulic fluid splattered them both. Muzzle flare clawed the steel, hungry and alive, until the plating warped, buckled, sawed clean at the elbow, and cartwheeled into the fire. It turned the flames blue as it passed.

Hodges dragged Dunne and made for the open hatch. Faraway voices urged Wil to follow, but he couldn't. With or without a weapon, he needed to be next in line. Someone had to slow him down, and Cailean—Wil couldn't leave him, not now, not like this.

On the rings above, two Nox attempted a desperate ambush. Cailean pivoted, and Rhiannon cut them in half.

Her song stammered to a halt. Out of ammo.

Hammerhand roared and barreled forward, hide shocked with bleeding wounds. An alien D-charge primed for in his remaining hand. A duck, a headbutt, and it knocked askew. So did Rhiannon, rattling along the concrete to stop at Wil's feet.

Both warriors stepped back, sizing the other up. Hammerhand paced, searching for an opening, a way past. Cailean matched him. Left none.

Mid-stride, Hammerhand paused. "I know you," he growled, and his mandibles jerked in an alien grin. "Novyy Cimmeria. Lafayette. The old human, with the old Wulver, the one who took my limbs. The one whose sword I made my arm."

Cailean drew his pistol, though it sagged in his bloody palm. "Aye."

"And you remember me?"

He breathed hard. "*Aye.*"

A burst up above chained into two more, a third. The smoke above pressed lower, black tendrils scraping the tops of the fuel storage tanks. Heat rolled from the floors above, washing the subbasements in waves of mirage.

"You've dreamed of this, haven't you," Hammerhand said. "Honoring your female. Killing me. I can see it in your dying eyes, human. So fortunate that after so much chattel waits a kill worth savoring. Don't you feel the same?"

"Yer just another notch," Cailean said, and went for his claymore.

Hammerhand rushed in before he finished the draw and plowed him into the storage tanks with a heavy, hollow drum. Cailean's pistol barked. Elbow met nose. Blood spattered the floor, both purple and red. They pushed apart, and in the whirl, Hammerhand stole the claymore from its sheath. The blade shrieked across its owner's decorated pauldron and in one smooth motion tunneled up through Cailean's back into his heart.

Hammerhand held him close. "Keep dreaming," he said, and twisted the pierce.

The hatch groaned. Closing. Saoirse screamed their names.

But Cailean didn't fall. He dropped his pistol, braced against the storage tanks, and shivered. Flame climbed his plaid, licking at his cheek. Each breath grew slower, louder, wetter than the last until it became something else entirely.

Laughter.

Grinning with blood-black teeth, Cailean bent down and picked something up. It blinked. A dark discus. The Shasvastii D-charge, lost in the fray.

"All or Nothing," Cailean gurgled, and slapped it to his chest.

Hammerhand's eyes bulged. He dove back, but Cailean had him by the arm. Nothing he did broke the Grey's unshakeable grip. Headbutts washed off his gleeful face like rain on a mountainside. The last-ditch, desperate bite didn't register at all.

Three beeps. The D-charge detonated. Both soldiers erupted. Disappeared. Teseum shrapnel scoured the storage tanks. Vaporized gasoline surged out, touched flame, and ignited.

The explosion transmuted the air into light.

Wil slid for the hatch just ahead of the blast wave, dragging Rhiannon along with him.

35

Despite Neil's fractured ribs, he was the first to notice Rhiannon.

Nora's hand had set fire, and her melted knuckles glistened with human oil while she wrapped them. Gordon shivered like a nitrocaine addict, ruddy skin beading with sweat. Hodges had inhaled too much smoke waiting for Wil, and Dunne pinned what was left of her ruined photoreactive poncho against the growing stain over her ribs.

Saoirse's pale, freckled face was smeared dark from smoke, bright red hair matted with blood. Alastair had reclaimed most of his Teseum armor, save for the pauldron Hodges now wore. The trenched ballistic shield held fast on his arm, ravaged helmet hung from his belt.

Pellehan and Fionnlagh were missing.

Cailean was dead.

It'd only taken a glance at Rhiannon for Alastair to realize what had happened. His usual calm shattered into shock, into fury, into resolve. And while Neil muttered, "No," loud and then quiet, Alastair laid his hand atop his uncle's weapon.

"Soraidh slàn leibh," he said, and went to comfort Neil.

Nora understood, then. So did Dunne, who stripped off her bandanna and left it crumpled on the floor. Hodges stood beside her, forcefully disinterested, and took stock of the remaining links in his chain rifle's mag. Lost count. Keeled against the wall and fell into a litany of curses, mostly directed at himself.

Vern held his distance, but Kelsie kept murmuring, "Right past my face—that last bullet, like a hornet, right past my face..."

Saoirse struck the concrete with her fist and bent against the wall, face contorted in furious agony. Gordon placed a hand on her shoulder. "Flame won't keep them back long," he said. "Might be more guided fire coming. We've got to go, Saoirse."

She nodded, not quite yet able to speak.

Solemn, Wil held out Rhiannon to Neil. "This doesn't belong to me."

"Nor me," Neil whispered. He took up Rhiannon, regarding her with reverence. "But as long as the old man's watchin' over us, this'll do."

The long, wet expanse of concrete seemed to carry on forever. Smoke hazed the tunnel rooftop for a time, until it crawled up a vent and disappeared into cobwebbed darkness. The heat of the bunker died away, replaced by the merciless highland chill, and their breath became visible again. Moisture bled from the walls, feeding broad patches of black and brown mold.

Cailean had relied on him, and Wil had watched him die.

This had been his fault. All this had been his fault, ever since the beginning. If he'd had the courage to swallow a Double-Action round and join the choir invisible back on Neoterra instead of taking his assignment to Dawn with a wish and a grin, so many people's lives wouldn't be ruined.

His surgery, Svalarheima, and now this.

His mom always said bad things happened in threes.

After what felt like an hour, they reached the tunnel's terminus where a second hydraulic hatch barred their exit. To the side lay a small antechamber, lined with crates and occupied by a pair of deactivated, weaponless Traktor Muls. The floor coated with sawdust, and a rack on the wall held several dusty flashlights.

Saoirse gave them a sniff. "These've been used. Recent."

"Weeks?" Alastair asked.

She shook her head. "Days."

Out in the hall, Hodges coughed, doubled over onto his knees. His chain rifle dangled to his shins—the last loaded weapon in his ridiculous arsenal. "Thought joining the army meant I'd avoid the black lung. Right, love?"

Dunne peeled her shirt from her side, torch gripped in her teeth. The patch Nora had fixed over her wound was already sopping, and they didn't have a replacement. If she'd heard Hodges, she didn't show it.

Hodges paled. He scrubbed his palm against his eyes and summoned up a watery smile. "This tunnel, eh?" he said, and his words firmed quickly. "Bloody hell. Brings back memories."

She dropped her shirt and clamped down on her side with her hand. "Would've preferred to forget."

"It's only a few Shaolin Monks," Hodges mocked in a feminine falsetto. "What'll they do, pray at us? Throw beads? Mumble a particularly worrisome koan?"

"I do *not* sound like that," she said.

"Afraid so."

Dunne's grimace cracked into a grin. "Keep at it love, and you're going to Varuna alone."

"Wouldn't dare," he said and took her hand when she offered it.

Nora bounced from person to person, mechanical and swift. But with her medical supplies critically empty, she couldn't do much more than apologize.

Her eyes didn't move from her empty bag. "Wish I could ring my mum."

"Yeah," Wil said. "Same."

It was a few minutes until Saoirse came back from talking to Alastair and Gordon. Nora walked away, but Wil didn't know if he deserved to.

Saoirse took his wrist and pulled. He didn't stand, so she pulled harder. When he still refused, her brows pinched together and she knelt beside him. "Givin' up, are we?"

"Thinking about it," he said.

"Don't make me make you."

"Just go. Please. I'll make do. Slow them down my own way."

Saoirse's eyes blazed the same way they did at the DFAC, same as at the spring, furious and sad and compassionate all at once. "Wil."

"I killed them," he said. "Llowry and Bell. Cailean. I'm killing more of you every minute I stay. Saoirse, Hodges was right. I should've done this a long time ago."

She looked away but didn't let go. "Don't talk like that."

"Give me this. I need it. Please."

"We owe 'em better."

"*Saoirse.*"

She loomed over him with a lopsided snarl. "Bell and Llowry. Rajan's assistant, the girl with no name. Those diplomats, yer pilots, yer fourteen soldiers back on Svalarheima—Cailean—we owe 'em better, aye? To never give up, not now, not ever. We gotta keep going, Wil, 'cause they can't. Precisely 'cause they can't."

"What if my better's not good enough?"

"I'll be the judge of that," she said and pulled at his dead weight.

And just like that, Wil knew Saoirse was right. This wasn't a wash, but a gift in disguise. Not to save people who might need saving, or to fight for some nebulous something worth dying for, but to take revenge. The universe had put Odune in his reach twice already, and he'd let those opportunities slip through his fingers.

He wouldn't waste the third chance that Cailean had died to give him.

Wil stood on his own, and Saoirse kept him from falling.

Kelsie discovered and activated the exit's hidden holopad within a minute flat. She thumbed in a guess, and the mechanisms inside the tunnel door ground to life.

"I told you!" she said. "06126, same as the mine. You always ignore me, Vern. Why?"

"I tried your code," Vern protested. "They must be different on each side."

"Then what opened it? Hm?"

"I don't remember," he said. "Didn't you do it?"

Neil sucked in a breath, eager to scold their argument to its end. But when the others saw him with Rhiannon in his arms, straight-backed and tense, a pained quiet fell among the Volunteers until the run's exit had fully opened.

Outside laid the T-junction of a mud-swept storm drain, cloaked in the stench of old water. Tight-packed boreal wilderness obscured the tunnel's end where the trickle from the drain dripped into a wider, placid reservoir pond choked with reeds and nightsong. Tanit glowed from on high, wreathed in misty fingers of the returning Caledonian overcast. Remnants of a half-collapsed radio tower shadowed their position, and in the distance, the dim corporate signage of a gas station stuck up through the trees.

Wil squinted. In the dim light, he wasn't sure if it was the one he'd spotted from the parade ground or not. If it was, there was no hint of Glasscock's presence from this far away.

Hodges and Neil cleared the landing while Gordon thumbed a smoke grenade from the rear. But no shots rang out, no ambush, and when Neil gave the hand signal, the remainder of the task force followed them out.

Alastair pointed toward the gas station. "Shelter. Dunne, thoughts?"

"Go without me," she panted. "I need to sit down."

Hodges jut his thumb over. "Hey, Gordo. Come watch my back while I meander."

"No way," Gordon said, eyes on Nora and her perpetual daze. "I'm useless now, mate. Burned everything in the tank and then some."

Alastair glanced from face to face, chain-colt in his hand. "We find cover, manage our wounds, scavenge what we can—and start moving. There's a second cache a day's walk south, nearer to the M-828. Once we're out of the hot zone, closer to civilization, we'll ring the 112 and risk evac."

Swinging his backpack from his shoulders, Vern knelt to tend to the old comms box with one ear folded under half of a headset. "What about Wil's Fusilier? We're just gonna leave him behind?"

"Fusi-what," Neil said. "Thought those were fake-outs?"

Kelsie shrugged. "Apparently, one lived."

"Still should be," Wil started, and cold terror washed over him. Instant panic, total fear. Both tempered under the quickening in his fingers. With only an instant of hesitation, Wil stole Nora's pistol off her hip and shoved the barrel up under Vern's ear.

Vern startled to his feet, arms held high. "Wait! Wait, no!"

Everyone froze. Wide, terrified eyes shadowed him on all sides. Nora stammered and fell back, hands tight around her rifle. Neil shielded her with his body. Before Alastair had registered what happened, Gordon lurched between them swaying equal parts wounded and tired.

Saoirse's hand jumped to her claymore grip, and she hesitated. "Wil, what're you doing?"

"Stay back," Wil said. "Keep away from him. Arm's length, everybody."

The barrel of a chain rifle settled point-blank against Wil's temple, brutal and angular. The stench of scorched metal wafted from deep inside the mechanism. "Shoot, and you'll wake up in the NeoVatican," Hodges said. "Drop it."

"He's one of them, Hodges. Vern's a Speculo. Been one since—had to be the second night. Nora and I saw him. He caught us laughing and frowned. You remember how weird that was?"

Pawing at her empty holster, Nora shook her head.

"You're wrong," Hodges said. "Drop it."

A nervous laugh escaped Wil's throat. "Honestly, man? If any of us were a Speculo, I figured it was you. I mean, the way you weaponized being an asshole, always picking fights? But you can't be. No Cube means no brain drain, no personality download—and definitely no in-jokes with Dunne."

"Wil," Alastair said, cold and calm. He let his chain colt hang by the trigger guard and placed it on the floor. "Please. There's no need for violence."

"No, sir, no way. Hanlon's razor saved our boy here till Occam's did him in. Never said the guy I found was a Fusilier, *Vern*. Never said he was a guy at all. So how'd you know?"

Vern hiked his shoulders like a frightened child, raised hands shaking. "I don't—someone said. You said, you called him a guy, I promise, I swear! Please!"

"Like hell I did."

"Or I did, talkin' while you were out cold," Saoirse said. "Does it matter?"

Dunne raised her Molotok one-handed, squinting for an angle. She listed to her left, stance wide to keep balance. "Robert, love. Move?"

"Don't, darling, please," Hodges said, and blocked her shot with his back. "The man's confused, that's all."

Sweat dripped from Wil's brow. "On the outskirts, everyone was chasing ghost markers while I got jumped by Taigha. I thought it was someone in the DRC, fucking with us over the repeater network—or maybe it was the person assembling all our call-outs into one shared holomap."

"Coincidence, er, I don't," Saoirse said. "Wil!"

"Then, the second time was a coincidence, too? Outside the fuel depot, my comms died right as the Shas collapsed on my position."

"Distance, shieldin', fuckin' gamma rays," Saoirse pleaded. "Don't, Wil, yer not right."

"Kelsie! Her code worked. Why didn't he try it?"

Vern's face screwed up like he was holding back tears. "I did, I swear, I did, please!"

"Why wasn't the Gwailo on the comlog map?" Wil said, and ground the barrel into Vern's neck. "Guided fire needs a spotter and a method of entry. He did something. Opened a vent. Let them in."

"Shaw was with him the whole time," Hodges said. "Did he seem strange?"

"No," Kelsie sobbed. "It's Vernard, dammit, he's always strange. Please!"

Gordon plodded forward. One step. Two. He reached for the pistol. "Hey, buddy. That's Nora's. Give it back."

Wil flinched away. "Why isn't he hurt?!"

"He got his elbow grazed in the ambush," Hodges growled, voice deadly and low. "Please, mate, I'd like you to live, but you're making it so very *fucking difficult*—"

Nora perked. "No, he didn't."

"I saw it," Kelsie said. "A graze, on his arm. Left side."

"If Vern got grazed, I would've known," Nora replied and hunted up her rifle from the floor. She propped it over her forearm, unable to grasp the stock with her hand caged in gauze. "Grazes need more than a bandage strip. They're half-burns. He'd need debridement, disinfectant, dressing—medical treatment."

"I didn't want to bother you," Vern stammered.

"Then the wound will have worsened. No way it's healed clean in a week, sweating down two mountains and sleeping in the dirt. He would've complained, gone sick with fever."

Dunne looked at Hodges. Hodges, at Alastair.

Saoirse drew her claymore, right hand over left.

Vern blinked, mouth agape. "I—I mean—Nora, come on, don't—"

Alastair's chain colt snapped back into his grip. "Wil. Check him."

Wil ran his hand down Vern's sleeve until he found a tear. Old bloodstains discolored the rip in his field jacket, but no evidence of injury remained.

Vern blurred, ducked. His elbow spiked Wil in the solar plexus with perfect precision, and he flit forward, flowing through the rip of Hodges' chain rifle, around the rattle of Dunne's Molotok, past Nora's startled shots. Gordon swung wild and collided with Saoirse as he ghosted between them.

Wil impacted the drainage lip, fighting the spasm in his lungs. By the time he recovered, Vern had Alastair's neck sickled by a burning, golden monofilament blade. Alastair's Americolt weighed his other hand, scorched barrel swaying from target to target.

Gordon ripped to his feet. "No!"

Saoirse was right behind him. "Al!"

"Quiet," Vern snapped, eyes flickering with quantronic violet. His field jacket twisted, holomorphing before their eyes into the dark, tall-collared coat of the Combined Army. "We have one minute before my allies arrive. I have one demand. Let's talk."

"Shoot him," Alastair said. "Now!"

Saoirse took a step forward, roaring curses. The Speculo clicked his tongue and skimmed the blade along Alastair's neck. A thin slice of translucent skin peeled from his jawline and fluttered onto the surface of the pond. Alastair grimaced as the red, raw oval beaded with blood.

"Don't do that," Vern said.

Saoirse seethed, claws wracked around her claymore's handle.

Hodges sidled toward Vern's blind spot, handaxe in his grip, when Dunne slumped into the grass panting shallow and fast. Torn between his leader and his lover, Hodges chose Dunne and flew to her side.

"Tell us where the Fusilier's gone, who he is, his identification code," Vern said. "Anything at all, and you can walk away. I'll even pop smoke to give you a head start."

Alastair locked eyes with Wil. "Don't. Not even a word."

"Al," Wil said.

"Not a damn thing!"

Neil crept forward, careful. He dragged back Vern's abandoned RTO backpack, all but forgotten in the chaos of the last few seconds. He exchanged a glance with Wil, with Gordon. Took his sister by the arm, and guided her toward the underbrush.

While aiming felt impossible, providing a distraction wasn't. "Che, puta de madre," Wil shouted. "You killed Cailean. You're dead."

Vern—no, the Speculo—minimized himself behind his human shield. "I didn't kill anyone. The Malignos who arrived before us is the one who Spotlighted the Grey, and the one who hacked open the vent in the tunnel to enable the guided fire. I was insurance."

"That's not your face," Kelsie whispered, breath shrill and shallow. "That's not your face! What'd you do with Vern, what's happened to him?"

Lines dug across the Speculo's nose and face, shallow, and his cheekbones wriggled like a stretch. In a shuddering instant, his eyes clouded over into a putrid cataract as his nose and jaw tore open, revealing the veiny mess of his gumline tented by alien mandibles. "I ate him. This better?"

Kelsie's eyes became more white than iris. Her hand snapped over her mouth, her shoulders jumped, and she doubled over. Vomit filtered through her fingers into the grass.

Neil and Nora were already gone. Leaves danced in their wake.

The Speculo straightened the monofilament's edge parallel to Alastair's collar. "Look at me, dammit. Ten seconds until I turn Prince Charming here into the Venus de Milo. Fusilier. Where. *Talk.*"

Violet optics burned trails through the dark. Shadows surged after. Boughs bent without sound, bioquantronic camouflage displacing through the wilderness. Reinforcements. In seconds, they'd be outnumbered.

"Talk!" the Speculo shouted.

Dust puffed on the edge of the drainage canal, centimeters from the Speculo's foot. A gunshot. Not Wil's pistol—not one of them—and not one of the Shasvastii, either. The Speculo's focus broke for a single, critical instant, and Alastair snapped his head back into its face. He shoved the monofilament aside, shouted "Eisd!" and was silenced by the butt of the chain-colt.

Gordon surged forward. His bones rearranged with a decisive crunch. Paws replaced feet; claws, fingers. Faster than a DA round, he'd hulked above them all, fanged maw slavering. Blood rage. Unstoppable. Howling, he hurtled toward the Speculo, claws firming as his hand outstretched—

A smear of fatal motion. The monofilament blade scorched a neon trail in the night. From full run to stumble, Gordon plunged into the reservoir pond. Entrails clouded the water's surface and stained it a brilliant red.

Alastair hit the concrete, brow gushing. "Gordon!"

There was no answer.

Metal scraped concrete. A smoke grenade spun in their midst, already ignited, belching a roiling gray wave. Gordon's final gift. The Speculo left its flowing stance and moved to kick it aside, but Wil's fingers pulsed and the quickening propelled him into its chest.

Sword arm seized, they tumbled to the concrete. Wil triggered Nora's pistol until the rack punched back. Nothing landed. An elbow struck his nose. A fist, his eye. The chain colt bashed against his ribs, face, throat, but Wil held the Speculo down until Saoirse barged through the smoke and dragged her brother to his feet.

"Go," Wil said. "Go!"

They hung for an instant, looking back, but didn't stay.

Shadows traced the MacArthurs' retreat through the clearing, spraying the foliage with particulate ammo. Wil ripped the chain-colt from the Speculo's skinny hand and fired blind until a metal boot arced across his jaw and sent him rolling. He slipped from the canal's edge, sprawled across the muddy grass, and bled.

Nox surrounded him. Alien Combi barrels ringed his forehead like a halo.

The Speculo limped to its feet, blade humming faintly in its hand. Purple light flickered on the surface of his eyes, and he nudged his allies' weapons aside.

They chittered. Clicked. One Nox clenched its fist and argued, but the Speculo insisted. With a disappointed brux, the fireteam leader swung its barrel aside, and its soldiers followed suit.

"The Counselor's changed his mind," the Speculo said. "We're going back to Dun Scaith."

36

The interior of his prefabricated domicile pod stared back at him from the dark. A dim green bulb deepened the shadows from above the door. From where he was seated, he could see a surgical tray but not what was inside it. Something in the room smelled sour. Old milk, or rotten meat. A mix.

Wil lifted his head. Jerked his arm. His old, familiar Teseum shackle clinked against newer, sturdier restraints. In the low light, he took stock of himself: His wrists and ankles were anchored to limbs of the chair he sat in, and a broad belt secured his waist. He'd been undressed to his skivvies, and his beard had been shaved. Three old puncture-marks lined his bare bicep, and on his right thigh—a tiny, nigh-invisible suture.

He had no memory of what had happened. A gap stretched from the drainage canal to here. When he summoned up the focus to remember, only images, sounds, and the prick of a needle remained.

He'd been drugged.

The bandages atop his left knee had been undone, and the gashes there had turned the color of sour milk. Red trailed from the wounds, tunneling into the healthy mass of his thigh. Pulsing, unwelcome heat radiated from its surface, and a constant itch squirmed inside the joint. An attempted bend was all it took to brace him back into the chair, biting back curses.

The Taigha swipe. The cuts from its keratin fins. They'd gone taut with infection. That was the smell—Wil's own body, rotting out from under him.

He might lose the leg.

Waves of nausea grew inside him, reeling his stomach into his mouth. The Shasvastii had him. He was their prisoner. They'd kept him alive, kept him conscious, and there could be only one reason why.

No—no panicking. Wil controlled his breathing, strangled the caged beast inside that wanted only to smash at the bars. Remembered his training, remembered SERE, steadied himself. Had to keep control—

Two enormous hands gripped him by the shoulders from behind.

"Good morning, Captain Gotzinger."

Odune.

A click. Bright light blinded him, sent him wincing for the dark.

"It's time for us to talk," Odune said. "Over the board. Face to face."

Tall. Pale. Bearded. Odune stuck to the shadows, pacing a circle around him. His eyes were still human, but Wil saw it now—the alien under his skin, in the way he moved, in the way he manually breathed. The deep lines in his cheeks neatly delineated where his mandibles hid, propped in the facsimile of a human face. How Wil had gotten so close without noticing, he didn't understand.

Odune's eyes smoldered with quantronic violet, lit from within by his neural comlog. "Oh, don't look so unsettled. If anything, blame your culture for creating a hunting ground where the digital world is as valid and real as the material. Put it on a feed, paint it on your datasphere, shout it into the net—there, lies solidify into truth. Delusion becomes reality, disbelief is discarded for novelty, and in that liminal space? My people *thrive*."

Wil raged against the manacles, digging lines into his skin. The chair shifted centimeters, at best. He tried again, and the lines deepened and blossomed up crimson.

Odune exhaled patiently, almost parental. "You're going to hurt yourself."

"Shut the fuck up!"

"Please, no screaming. I'm right here."

"I'll kill you," Wil growled. "I'm gonna rip your throat out, you hear me?"

Odune rolled a chair up beside the surgical tray, outside the halo of light from above. "Come, now. Anger doesn't suit you, Captain."

"You did something on Svalarheima, I know it. Sabotaged us. Fourteen people. Whitehead, McCombs, Nicholls, Sankaran, Kovac—"

"That was war," Odune said, and sat. "Don't be such a sore loser."

Blood-red hate ebbed from Wil's vision. "A... what?"

"Where's the animosity toward PanOceania, for knowingly placing you in harm's way? Hm? ALEPH failed to analyze through my obfuscations to the truth and even agreed with my assessment. You're just angry at me because you can see me. Lashing out is the only way you can feel in control."

"Fuck you."

"Is it because of Cailean Rutledge?" Odune said, folding one leg over the other. "Did you forget that you brought him to me? If you had died in my Balena like I'd politely requested, none of the MacArthurs would've ever been hurt. Hell, if you'd stayed put, you'd be sipping a beer with that Wulver girl naked on your lap by now."

Lightheaded exhaustion unbalanced him. Wil sank back into the chair and let the anger throb, stowed tight in his chest. He'd need its strength for later.

"Those poor, poor Ateks, tricked into joining your pathetic crusade. Too frail to cope with your own shattered dreams and delusions of grandeur, you led them to their deaths. Aquila Guard—don't make me laugh. You've never been worthy of a higher honor than digging latrines."

"When the others get here, they'll crucify you."

Odune shifted his legs. "Is it the Dog-Warrior? Gordon shouldn't have tested his leash when death was on the line. But then again, he *wanted* to die fighting. Told them many times. Putting him down didn't bring me any pleasure, but I'm sure he's content with how it ended."

The pit inside his stomach yawned. "You're guessing."

"On the contrary, Captain, I know everything. I'm omniscient. Ever since the moment you slid screaming into this world, I've watched over your shoulder. Judging. Knowing. How else would I know where the tunnels under the fuel depot emerge?"

Forming a coherent theory was like sculpting La Pietá out of fog. "The smugglers who own that run work for you," Wil said. "That's how you had Teseum cufflinks to give to Rajan. You source it from somewhere, and sell it on the side—or—"

"How else did I know you'd go off the flight plan the day after your arrival? Or where to judiciously position the WarCor on that snow-cloaked scaffolding, perfectly angled to capture your failure? His datasphere was easy to siphon. Leaking the footage, child's play. Tricking your ALEPH into sacrificing you was even easier—like Abraham and Isaac, but I sent the angel."

Wil shook his head. "You're not God."

"Am I not? When you received notice of your mother's suicide, I was there watching you weep. Discharged from the Fusilier Corps for sleeping with her superior officer. Undiagnosed schizoaffective disorder. Surgical removal and sale of her own Cube, spurred by hallucinatory paranoia. It took her eleven years to understand that the decision to leave you unupgraded at birth ruined your future. You hated her until she died, so why venerate her now?"

"Stop."

"Cuando me muera, right? Over and over. Very annoying."

"Fucking *stop*."

Odune tilted his head and grinned. "As you wish, mi corazóncito."

Terror. Then, reason. Vern's elbow and Wil's thigh, two small wounds, similar to a graze, small and unobtrusive. That's how the Speculo hid its DNA sample and how Odune knew—a Speculo had already copied him, and his Cube. Become him. No need for interrogation when you could clone your subject into a more cooperative state. Which begged the question of why drug him, why keep him alive, why take the chance.

His neck throbbed.

"Soon, the remaining MacArthur forces will be routed and killed," Odune said. "There's nothing you can do. I already know everything, and your usefulness has come to an end." He paused. "Well, actually—there is one use for you. But, you will not enjoy it."

Wil spat. The spray dotted Odune's knee. The smart fabric of his slacks zeroed out the droplets in seconds, leaving only the flecks across his knuckles. "Go to hell."

With a broad, bright smile, Odune opened Wil's palm and placed something hard into his fist. Roughly cylindrical, like a toy block, and sticky with blood. Four connector points ended in little jagged frays.

His Cube.

"The *Sword of St. Catherine* will be here soon, and this installation's purpose will cease to exist," Odune said. "Then I will leave Dawn, and never return. Until then, you and I are going to get to know one another."

"I'm not telling you shit."

"Didn't I already say I have no use for you? No one is coming to save you, Captain. The ill-named Glasscock is already a bloodstain. Alastair MacArthur will be a corpse by sunrise. And I have your Wulver girl kenneled on the other end of the hall."

Wil clenched his teeth. "Don't touch her."

Odune watched him for a moment. Purple light lit the creases under his eyes. "Do you know why I chose this place, Captain?"

"All-you-can-eat researcher buffet."

"That, and something else," Odune said. "It was to retire."

"Bullshit."

"No, no, I'm being serious. You see, my species is not made for open warfare, Captain. We aren't persistence hunters like humans, no. We're survivors. Your species goes from world to world, building new and better Earths. We adapt. And after our beachhead on Novyy Cimmeria was destroyed, I and the other survivors, we did just that. We adapted. Hid. And when Xandros Odune came to Dawn and landed only miles from our listening post, well, it was an advantage I could not deny."

Wil focused on breathing, trying to dispel the unease. Focused on how he'd keep Odune here, far away from Saoirse Clarke.

"Here, as far from your ALEPH as I could be, Odune's kingdom became my kingdom, became a place of healing. Paradise. My handlers in the Continuum believed my choice tactically motivated. They thought if I held the illusion long enough, eventually, the DRC-9 would attract a high-value target, and we'd return to the front line after securing our kill.

"But I had already decided the moment I set foot here we'd never succeed. That we'd fail. Forever, if need be. To never give up our Eden, to never return to the battlefield. And in lieu of serving the EI, of feeding my people into the grinder of the Human Sphere, we'd begin a new life here. Build something. And we were so, *so* close to realizing that dream until you stole it from us."

"So what," Wil spat. "The *Sword of St. Catherine*—you were gonna let them go? You expect me to believe that?"

Odune hummed, amused. "Yes, actually. We've let several HVTs slip free over the last two years, content to jealously keepsafe our home. But now, after having to tap reserve forces and sleeper cells all across Dawn to slow your advance? My masters expect results. And all the usual excuses—failed construction, inclement weather, Antipode assault—count for nothing."

In Odune's eyes, fear. Fear, and a glimmer of truth.

"You should've died," he said. "Instead, I'm yoked by scrutiny. Do you think I wanted psychopaths like the Khurland Jayth here, breeding their pets and drawing attention? Much less a dead Armed Imposition Detachment trooper. Do you know how many people I'll have to kill to keep it secret Gwailos can die?"

"The surprise guest in the delegation," Wil said. "That's your target for your trap. And now, with all eyes on you, you have to spring it. Or the EI will know you're afraid. You won't have a use. It'll kill you."

Wordlessly, Odune stood and removed his jacket. "Or worse, yes. Very clever."

The echo of Saoirse in his voice sent a fresh shiver of concern up Wil's spine, but he couldn't let the fear distract him. "Who are they? Who's the surprise guest?"

Painstakingly, Odune rolled his sleeves to the elbow and placed his link bracelet beside the surgical tray. "We've thirty-four hours until the delegation arrives. Two days to get to know one another. I'm very excited."

Wil tensed his jaw. "Hope you like disappointment."

Odune tugged a pair of white polymer gloves onto his fingers, making a fist to test the smart fabric. Pressure colored the nanoweave an oily, unnatural black, and release made it white again. "Oh, Captain. I only want to make you pay—to know what it sounds like to have everything taken from you. And then I'll feel better about what you've taken from *me*."

Wil couched into the chair and swallowed the growing fear that flooded the hollow of him. No escape? No problem. This would be nothing. Pain wasn't pain.

Delicately, Odune steadied Wil's jaw with one hand and slapped him across the face with the other. Light. Testing. The second was stiffer. The third, bracing. Wil's teeth grazed the inside of his lips. Iron splashed across his tongue. The fourth snapped askew against his nose, and he bit back a grunt.

"Two years on and still getting used to this body," Odune muttered and hooked a kick into Wil's solar plexus.

His lungs spasmed. A knot tied in his chest. No breath. The chair juddered and tipped. Wil writhed, unable to roll, unable to find the configuration where his throat would stop seizing and let him draw air. The corners of his vision dimmed and his head bobbed and he finally, finally managed a gasp.

Odune shadowed the light above, studying his face. "Seems I'm a quick learner."

Mucus leaked from his wracked lips. Blood spiraled in the bubbles as he fought for every wheeze. His Cube laid scattered along the wall, settled into a groove in the prefab tile.

Odune tipped him upright again. He placed the toe of his ivory shoe atop Wil's swollen knee and pressed.

Wil bit his tongue. Clenched his teeth. The wounds bulged and overflowed. Mostly white with streaks of red. Strawberry cheesecake. For an instant, relief, and then the hurt deepened, carving to the other side of his leg and back again. Pus turned from abundant to scarce, chased by watery blood.

"You're so quiet," Odune cooed, and ground down. "Come on. I want to get to know you. Do you still play chess? Are you still bad at it?"

His voice came out more animal than man. "My name's Wil. I like shooting, and the color blue, and long walks—"

Odune reared back and stomped. The wound exploded. Pain became him. Overflowed. Wil slammed his head back, fingers twisted into claws.

A cold patch spread across his scalp, and he savored every centimeter of distraction the bleed gave him. Then, the adrenaline ebbed, and the pain sharpened until Wil was only his next inhale, exhale, teeth creaking as they viced together.

Odune didn't pull away until the white of his dress shoe had turned pitch black. He receded, paced. Watching, waiting, anticipating as his toes brightened. "Do you know how much time and effort went into securing our home here? How difficult it was to replace Xandros Odune? How much trust I had to engender to ensure the DRC-9's total autonomy from the Expeditionary Army and O-12? My Eden, my Paradise, my *great work*—all erased in one week thanks to the efforts of one imbecile and his gormless Atek warband."

"Don't pretend," Wil panted, "like you didn't start this."

Odune reached into the surgical tray and withdrew a thimble of gauze. He dabbed at Wil's scalp with a patient smile. "True. Perhaps we're both at fault."

Wil nodded to the chair. "Alright, then. Your turn. Let's swap."

"*Boni pastoris est tondere pecus non deglubere*," Odune said, and lifted an alligator clip from the tray. He squeezed the teeth apart, frowned, and discarded it in favor of a thin titanium probe with hooks on both ends. "Unfortunately, I am not a good shepherd."

Wil gathered his strength in fast, wet breaths. The MacArthurs were still out there. They had a chance. He wasn't alone. And if Saoirse was here, the longer Odune spent away from her, the better.

The thin, blunt tip of the sterile probe scraped along Wil's temple, across his face, feathering his eyelashes. Odune wriggled it, forcing the cold hook under the lid, and... pursed his lips.

He drew back without further harm and tossed the probe aside. "So quiet. You're killing this for me, you know. Can you beg, or something? Make even a little noise so that I know I'm on the right track."

Wil said nothing.

"Anything?"

Silence.

"Alright." Odune stood and gathered his coat. "If you're not going to entertain, I'm sure I'll have more fun with your woman next door."

"Pain isn't pain," Wil blurted.

Odune stalled. "Incorrect. Pain is everything."

"No. I control it. It doesn't control me."

"You're wrong," Odune said. "Hunger. Fear. Grief. Everything links back to inefficient neurons present in every sapient species—pain. Pain is the undercurrent that fuses together the infinite civilizations of the universe, living or dead. Pain is, perhaps, the only thing our two peoples have in common."

"Pain isn't pain," he repeated.

"You say that with such familiarity. Ever since the doctor bored into your skull and laid the egg of ALEPH there, you've thought you'd mastered pain, hm? So much suffering to earn something others are gifted by virtue of birth. Did it ever feel worthwhile?"

"You tell me, you omniscient prick."

The spear-hand strike to Wil's throat left his lap soaked in sour vomit. Wil hacked feebly, trying to spit out his Adam's apple until it recentered with an agonizing click.

Odune circled the chair. "I asked if it felt worthwhile."

Bile coated his teeth. Wil gathered and spat it out. "You. Tell. Me."

Fingers tightly grasping his shoulders, Odune spoke against his ear. "I'll make you a deal. If you scream, even once, even for an *instant*, we'll be done and I'll go play with the Wulver instead. But if you remain silent—if you, in all your PanOceanian arrogance, can prove this irrefutable truth of the universe false—I swear I will not harm her."

Wil measured his breaths. Forced the tremble from his fingers by crushing his fists shut. "Zugzwang."

"Oh!" Odune jerked Wil's head back and smiled down at him. "A situation in which the obligation to make a move becomes a decisive disadvantage. Do you feel like that now?"

No. Wil was still holding out hope that Odune would lower his guard, get too close, slip up. But now, he'd need to lose something for that opportunity. His pride, or his body; Saoirse, or himself.

First in All Things.

A brutal grin strained his cheeks. "All or Nothing, motherfucker. You're on."

Odune gently slapped him. Let go. His eyes flickered with quantronic communication, and the prefab door hissed open.

A narrow hallway lay beyond—not his domicile, not a building he'd been in before, but discernibly DRC. A single light hummed along the ceiling, casting a pale, predatory hue.

Out of the darkness, nine reflective orbs. Eyes. A horror slithered after, wreathed in pulsing Combined Army nanoweave tech. Mucus dripped up its length in paradox to gravity, staining the very air—a nanobot swarm. Twin forelegs capped in pincers extended from its armored sheath to steady his knee. Red light bathed his leg, projecting a tangle of veins on the skin.

Odune pointed. Spoke in the chittering Shasvastii language, incomprehensible and strange. "Alright, Captain," he said. "Let's see how long pain isn't pain."

A probe covered in helical grooves needled from the worm's chest. A drill bit. The end lengthened, and sharpened.

And revved.

37

The darkness thrummed. Pain burned through the totality of him, every ragged breath echoing in the hollow of his body. Wil tried to detach himself, pretend this was only a sensaseries, that it was happening to someone else. Sleep, while he could. If he could, with the drip from the holes in his leg keeping time atop his stomped foot.

Two days until the *Sword of St. Catherine* arrived. Or one.

Or had it only been an hour?

Voices muffled out in the hall beyond the closed door, towing Wil from his half-sleep. Odune, and a man with a soft Caledonian accent. They grew closer, and their words clear enough to hear.

"We had a deal, Odune. You said you wouldn't hurt them."

Eideard.

"I'm so, so sorry about the loss of your men," Odune said. "We attempted negotiations, but things became complicated. Bullets were exchanged. We lost some on our side, too—three Fusiliers, two CSUs, and an Orc Trooper."

"Has the galactic's fingerprints all over it," Eideard said. "The moment they got caught up in his insanity, I knew there'd be hell to pay."

Wil sucked in a breath and froze. What would calling out do? Eideard stood no chance against the Shas in close combat, not at his age. Warning him would only ensure his death. And worse, what if Odune considered it a scream, what would happen to Saoirse then?

So he exhaled, low and miserable, and strained to listen instead.

"Peaceful contact proves difficult when you have a man like Wilhelm Gotzinger levying accusations of alien infiltration," Odune said. "His delusions are spurred from the traumatic events in his past. Views everyone as a potential Shasvastii infiltrator. Schizoaffective disorder, inherited from his mother—it's all rather very sad."

"I tried to convince them," Eideard said, raspy voice breaking. "There's no way you could be what they said. I'd ken a Shas if I saw one, aye? But Cailean couldn't let go of what happened to Rhiannon, and now—"

"Mr. Rutledge *was* very obstinate, indeed. He refused to capitulate and absconded with a group of mercenaries after detonating the fuel reserve in Fort Resolute. Hopefully, we can still find a peaceful resolution to this bloodshed."

This motherfucker.

"Let me talk to him," Eideard said, "and I'll straighten things out."

"In due time."

He paused. "And I know you said I couldn't see Alastair, Counselor, but…"

"Time, Mr. Carr. Give it time. The liaison from O-12 will help sort everything out when she arrives from Cailleach tomorrow. You may not be able to see your nephew now, but you're more than welcome to remain in our care."

"And in the meantime, I trust our arrangement will continue? Teseum for medicine? 'Guests' for the mines on Tanit, for a little extra in the monthly?"

"But of course," Odune said, and their voices faded along with their footsteps.

He'd always been curious why Eideard had been so terrified of letting Alastair speak to him, or why the Wulver smugglers had been so brash in the Croatoan, or why Alastair had never met with the DRC despite six attempts over two years. Never would he have thought Eideard would be the one pulling strings for Odune in Kildalton, funneling Teseum and people through Fort Resolute. Wil wanted to hate him, so gullible and so, so stupid. But the tenuous connection of Alastair's mother's cancer and Eideard's noble insistence on medicine almost made him pity him.

Almost.

The door hissed open, spilling sickly white light onto his bloodstained toes. The worm swayed into position in front of his chair, gangly forceps slithering out from its collar.

"Good morning, Captain Gotzinger." Odune was already behind him. "I hope my guest and I didn't wake you. Today's the big day."

The forceps began to sizzle, pulsing a mirage through the teeth of their grip.

"We're having a cookout."

††

Burning bone smelled like corn chips. Burning flesh like searing steak. Each new brand laddered down his left arm like grill marks on a sausage link.

His stomach refused to listen. Growled, long and loud.

Odune dabbed Wil's forehead with his handkerchief. "Oh, I understand. There's something about human flesh that's uniquely palatable, isn't there? I've eaten your dead several times on Paradiso, but never cooked so… well-done. Calories are calories, I suppose—whether they come from an insect, a plant, or a person."

The armrest creaked. Reflex. Wil tried not to tense. It'd only thicken the surface area, give the iron more to bite down on.

"One human carcass can feed twenty Nox for a day," Odune whispered. "That, or gestate a single spawn embryo. In that way, each enemy killed becomes a reinforcement. When I'm done with you, would you rather be fertilizer or food?"

The worm's forearm retracted, sticky with fond.

"Choke on me," Wil said.

† †

Saoirse drew her finger down his chest, breasts warm against his face. Her breath was intoxicating, her heartbeat a north star. "Where does it take you," she whispered, never expecting an answer.

Here, into this. Into night as dark and empty and frail as what lay beyond the Human Edge, fallen into the cracks in the universe. Raw, and unrestrained. A lifetime of biting back and clenching his fists and lying face-first in the dirt led to the prefab and this chair.

Where he found himself.

Where he was truly free.

All this time, Wil had been lying to himself. He didn't belong on Concilium Prima, not anymore. He'd changed from the boy in the strip club dumpster picking glitter-covered leavings to feed his drug-sick mother, from the cynical Fusilier eager to leave his past behind, from the broken man who spun like a cog in the heart of the Beast. He wanted to say he belonged with Saoirse, but another hour here and he'd belong to Odune.

No. Couldn't let that happen. Wil wouldn't leave this place whole, but he wouldn't leave this place changed. Had to hold on to who he was. Had to hold on to the flashes of good.

Saoirse, half-dressed in the torchlight; his mother's joyful tears at Christmas Mass when the pastor gifted her the day's donations; Caledonian rain blanketing the highlands in mist; the hour-long winter sunsets on Paradiso, and how the fading light never struck the clouds the same colors twice.

But the black nothing of the prefab already churned within him. When his rage surged and his blood boiled, it wasn't halogen lights, cardboard, or black plastic that he saw—it was the line of sterile light, burning beneath the door. Muffled footsteps forcing panicked breaths. The slow whirr of the worm's tentacle drill, gaining speed before it pierced.

He refused to let it replace his anger. In here, it was all he had.

A shadow graced the glow beneath the door. Not dreaming. Real. His entire body tensed, exhausted heart gurgling in his chest. But the door didn't open. The worm didn't come.

"Lieutenant Gotzinger," someone whispered. "We have only a moment."

Scáthach.

"Things are spiraling out of control," she whispered. "After the delegation from the ship arrives, there will be no going back. I am powerless to free you. After disagreeing on our course of action, I've been stripped of my security clearance.

Tonight is our last opportunity to save who we can." She paused. "Are you still alive?"

"Yeah," Wil said. His voice no longer sounded like his own.

"I've added you to the private access list for Room 2968. Within are arms and armor. Good luck."

Too many questions. No time for answers. Why had Scáthach called PanOceania? Who were the innocents she was trying to save? Was she Shasvastii, or human? Wil didn't comprehend her motives, her drive. She was playing a game that he'd never seen in a room he wasn't allowed in.

"And you," he said. "What do you get?"

No answer.

Her shadow receded from beneath the door and left him alone in the dark.

↟↟

A flick to the chin woke him. White. A dress suit. Odune. He held something against Wil's face, turgid and sharp. Clawed. Callous as sandpaper on his lips.

Saoirse's finger.

Odune stole Wil's hand. Pried his grip open. "You did this."

The stiff nub lingered on his palm. One end cold, the other damp. Frayed. It slipped through his quaking grasp and pattered to the floor, lost amongst their feet.

"I was bored," Odune said. "You should've let me win."

Wil made several sounds. Crushed his eyes shut. Sputtered things like words, fighting against the manacles until he bled. This wasn't possible. None of this was real. He didn't want it to be.

Odune removed his suit jacket and hurled it over his chair. "Beyond belief, how indestructible Wulvers are for a genetic dead-end. The opposite of my people, really, but I find them endlessly fascinating. Her tolerance for pain is so much *higher* than most females of your species."

Halogen lights.

Each sleeve rolled to his elbow. His comlog linklet and wristwatch laid atop his chair. "That's not to say you yourself aren't an interesting specimen, Captain Gotzinger, but her natural talents outshine yours so brightly. Not uncommon, frankly. As far as extraterrestrials go, humans are somewhat tragic. Take me, for example: I am the product of a thousand years of meticulous, sophisticated progeneration, stretched across many, many instances of parthenogenesis and time. And you're... some guy. That you think me your equal is simply astonishing."

Cardboard.

"A low-born plebeian, rising through the ranks to protect and serve his homeland—a riveting story. Born into another era, your people would've celebrated your tenacity, your bloodlust. Sang songs. Wrote poems. Made of you a hero, worthy of the highest honors, perhaps even Recreated." Odune picked over the dishevel of the surgical tray, casting aside several stained instruments until he lifted a mallet. He turned it, testing the weight. "But in the now, you're no one at all."

Black plastic.

Odune knelt beside his chair, so close Wil could taste his breath. "Unfortunately, our time is at an end. I've come to say farewell. The delegation is due to arrive soon, despite the inclement weather, and I must prepare to receive our—"

Wil lunged.

Bit.

Odune's neck bulged in his mouth. His voice spiked, and the mallet slipped free and clanged on the floor. Hands slapped. Pried. Failed.

Wil chewed. His jaw locked. The belt of the chair cut into his belly, wrists torqued against the cuffs. A foreign moisture ran warm over his tongue, off his chin and down his neck. More iron. Odune howled, and a thumb ground into his eye. Hard. Harder. Purple flashes blinded Wil, droplets raged over his nose, and reflex alone slacked his jaw just enough for Odune to rip free.

Through the blotches, a white shape stumbled, whimpering, clutching his pumping neck wound. Each red spatter that graced his suit jacket vanished into the fabric.

"Told you," Wil said and spat the pink chunk from his mouth.

A fist knocked his jaw from his blind spot. A second hit his good eye. More. Even more. The ceiling tilted one way and then another as Odune shouted, roared, demanded for Wil to scream, to submit, to die.

Fingers wrung his neck. Thumbs atop his windpipe.

Odune put all his weight atop them.

Wil shuddered. His throat folded shut. The lamp above swayed, and its bright corona spread. He gurgled. The pressure in his chest doubled, pulse loud as a waterfall inside his ears. Reflex rattled his manacles, forcing the curl of his toes, and the door sighed open.

Fear and shame sparked in Odune's eyes. He hastened to let go and swept the loose strands of his hair back with bloody fingers before he even thought to clamp at his wound. "Fetch me the Medchanoid!" he shouted. "Now!"

A tall, broad soldier stood in the doorway, dressed in a security officer's uniform. A muttonchop beard frazzled over the collar of his strained dress shirt, and in one hand—the limp torturer-worm, eight-eyed head concave and leaking.

Gordon threw it at his feet. "Done."

Odune brayed. Recoiled.

Too slow. Gordon seized Odune by the wrist and hauled him back, bashed him against the walls, the door frame. Kicks and punches smashed the mirrored shades Gordon wore, buffeting harmlessly from his skin. And then he had Odune by both arms, back to chest, arms outstretched to either side. Dress shoes squeaked on the polymer floor until they left it.

Gordon transmuted. His bones rearranged as his clothing burst. Black fur raged across his expanding form, jaw snapping and extending as his muzzle took shape. And as his size swelled, so did his arm span.

Odune's did, too.

Elbows taut. Back arched. Shoulders stretched, popped, dislocated. Fabric blackened, then tore. Odune's voice raised from human to inhuman, trilling as his arm ripped from his trunk with a loud, damp pop. Blood splattered the floor, and Odune crumpled into the corner opposite his dismembered limb.

Gordon rushed over, searching the seat for a panel. "Hey, pal. Cavalry's here."

Couldn't be real. Had to be another hallucination. Wil took the deepest breath he could and said, "Buddy. You died."

Thumb wormed under the manacle, Gordon pried it from the chair like a nail from a door. Then the next, and the next, until they all broke open, and Wil's disbelief ended as he went up over Gordon's back, but when his knee dangled—

—impossible—like it would fall off—searing, melting—

Wil tried to point, but Odune—

Gone. The splatter snaked toward the wall and disappeared.

—the tile rushed by, he was floating—

"C'mon, Wil," Gordon said. "Stay with us!"

He didn't.

⸸ ⸸

A gasp woke him. His gasp. Wil's chest was filled with broken glass, his veins scored in a tingling frenzy, and every breath was like swallowing razor blades. His fingers pricked. Heart, gurgled. He was on his back, lying on the floor. On the tile. Why was he on the floor? He needed to get up. Run. A heavy column held him prone, and he pried at it, but it didn't release, didn't abate no matter how hard he—

"Chill," Gordon said. His dark, clawed palm blanketed Wil's torso, disconcertingly clammy, utterly immovable. "Let the Serum do its business."

A MediKit gun sucked to his chest. The electric rush of steroid nanobots awoke other, older pains, and washed it all away on an anesthetizing tide. The last drop of blue slurry disappeared with a bubble, and Gordon withdrew the injector.

The puncture barely bled.

Gordon had seen better days. An ugly bald gap in his fur dashed up his torso from sternum to navel, still raw and red and swollen. His CSU uniform had disintegrated when he'd transmuted, but he'd sourced a boarding shotgun somewhere between death and rebirth: A CineticS Barong, far and beyond what Wil thought attainable on backwater Dawn. It looked new. Sawdust clung to the ribs on the forestock.

"Your intestines," Wil said, testing his swollen throat. Four syllables seemed his limit. "They fell out."

Gordon rapped his belly with massive knuckles. "Funny thing about guts is, they know where to go. Stuff 'em them back in and it all works out."

"How."

"I dunno. Biology."

"Did you live."

"Oh," Gordon said. "Morons left me in the puddle. Must've thought the mono killed me. Sharp as, but I'm tougher. Woke up at sunrise. Hocked up a lung of pond water. Took a day to knit up and find Al, the others. Nora says hi. Her MediKit, after all. Figured you might need it."

"Wait," he winced. "Everyone? Where?"

"Raising hell. Slipped clean and hit the cache at the M-828. Still good. Medical hypos and emergency rations kept us going. Extra bullets got us in here."

"Saoirse, she—she wasn't—she didn't—?"

"She's fine," Gordon said and steadied him. "Once Saoirse kent they took you, she about lost her mind. Wanted to come save you herself, but with her 'Pode eyes she wouldn't have made it ten steps. I'm a big, hairy bastard, but at least I can pass. Radio silent, or I'd have you two talking already."

The tension strung through him from toe to scalp faded fast, and he weathered the burn and throb of nervous laughter. Everyone was alive, and Saoirse was safe. She'd never been captured. That wasn't her finger. Of course Odune had been lying. But it'd felt real—how did he fake it? Or had Wil just strayed so far from the path of reality in all the pain and fear that he'd seen something else?

Gordon held up the boarding shotgun, gunmetal bulk dwarfed by long, dark claws. "Richard here's gonna take care of you. Bring you somewhere safe. I'm headed back."

"Richard?" Wil said and glanced up.

Perched across the room with a bottle of Coca-Cola clutched in his filthy fingers sat Glasscock, blue Fusilier's uniform turned brown with bloodstains and mud. "I said my name is *Daniel*."

Behind Glasscock, the walls of the room were lined with packed shelves. Steel glinted; diodes glowed. Straw-packed crates laid lined with TauruSW and CineticS weaponry, fresh from PanOceanian production lines; Teseum jewelry piled high in sorting bins; collapsed F-13 turrets, ready to deploy on any battlefield or perch; a whole pallet of chocolate snack cakes; a hundred glowing Nomad hacking devices arranged in a server tray, identical to the one on Keyes' wrist in the bothy; four refrigerated cabinets filled to the brim with vials marked with Haqqislamite medical logos; and a pallet of Coca-Cola, straight from their packing plant in Springfield, USAriadna.

A suit of ORC Combat Armor laid out atop a table on the far wall. His duster was already anchored to the breastplate, Sharlene's cowhide additions ripped away to fit the armor.

"Caught this bellend crouched atop that petrol station, twenty meters from the drainage canal," Gordon whispered. "Been giving us no end of whinging."

"Listen, Gotzinger, I'm sorry," Glasscock said. "After you left, I couldn't get through. The DRC withdrew my clearance, and I had to slip a hunting party. Twice! And the connection up here's total garbage, I mean, it's nothing but static and Arachne, okay? But I did take a shot at that guy in the coat! When you came out of the sewer, remember? That's something, huh, right? Right?"

Gordon quieted him with a gesture. "Christ on a bike, Richard. Leave some words for the rest of us."

"Time, buddy," Wil rasped. "How much time."

"By my guess, your ship's due any minute. Storm outside might slow them down, but not for long. Alastair's planning a break for the comms array. System lockdown means we need a physical jack, and Hodges' comlog is new enough."

"Glad you're," Wil managed and lost the rest into a painful shiver that started in the core of him and radiated through every spongy fiber and fried nerve ending in his body.

Gordon waited. When Wil couldn't finish, he stood. "Alright, PanO, he's all yours. Wil dies, I skin you for a coat. Got it?"

Glasscock nodded feverishly. "Hell yeah, got it. You can count on me! Uh, do I get a gun?"

Gordon lumbered across the room and paused, attention stolen by something silvery and massive resting atop a shelf: his battle-axe, leather grip scorched, but the alloyed blade pristine. He hefted it and slid the boarding shotgun over. "Sure. Just found better."

Wil could scarcely bend his leg. Almost make a fist. "Hey, wait. Take me—take me with you."

His enormous lupine shape shadowed the door. "Debt repaid, brother. Mòran taing. I'll see you in Valhalla."

The door hissed shut, followed by the crunch of glass from outside. The interior panel died along with it, sealing them inside the room. The instant it closed, Glasscock zipped to his side. "Alright. Next move is—"

Wil pointed at the ORC on the table. "Get me in that armor."

Glasscock's eyebrows touched his beret, and then he was smiling. "Okay. Yeah. Hell yeah!"

"The vials, the MediKit," Wil said. "Load me up. Triple dose me. I have to get out there, and help. Got to—got to back them up. Finish this."

The automatic door rattled. Loud, chittering Shasvastii voices muffled on the other side of the prefab door. The steel squealed but didn't budge. It shuddered, dented twice, and fell silent.

Nothing. No voices.

The emergency lights hummed.

Glasscock stifled a giggle. "Was that their best—"

The polymer prefab wall crunched. Dented. A second time, in the same place.

Boarding shotguns. The Shasvastii outside had decided to forgo the painstaking process of sawing through the armored door in favor of making their own instead. Red light cut through from the outside hall, fluttering with movement. Sharp, ugly chirps bled through the breach. Two minutes tops until the anti-material slugs cut an entry point and the Shas were on top of them.

Wil grabbed a fistful of Glasscock's pant leg. "Armor. Now."

Right leg, left leg. Belt, breastplate, biceps, gauntlets. Pauldrons went on second to last, then the helmet. Cables connected. The ORC Combat Armor's periphery ignited. Servos cleared their mechanisms with a hiss. Artificial muscle sucked to his skin, peeling the scabs from his burns, and the diagnostics blared all-green.

Glasscock returned with the vials from the cooler. "Like, in your ass?"

Wil curled his fist shut. While his meat hand shook wildly, the gauntlet's motion held stable. "Knee. Chest. Neck."

His faceplate shut, and darkness took him, alone with the persistent screech of new tinnitus and the gurgle of his sluggish heart. Sour breath misted back onto his face, and the initial startup of his ORC finished with little fanfare.

Pain. Incredible pain. Sharp, deep, burrowing. A spike, tunneling a hundred meters into the cavern in his ribs. The air froze in his lungs. His throat locked. Static pops turned to lightning in his veins that blew every nerve they passed, cooking him from the inside out so fast there was no time to gasp or grind or fear.

Again, in the shoulder. A third time in his thigh. His bones kindled, and his organs shriveled to feed the surge. The cauterized holes in his kneecap unplugged and his eyes blurred. An intense sensation of impending disaster, chased by motionless falling. Wil slumped into the armor as his legs gelatinized, and the sound in his ears muffled away save for the slosh in his veins as blood puddled and stilled.

The wall burst, leaving a hole large enough for a person. Alien shapes flit along the other side, inhuman eyes burning in a slew of quantronic violets. Gunfire. Glasscock slammed Wil's breastplate shut, shoved the boarding shotgun into his arms, and dropped out of sight.

A bullet blunted on Wil's forehead and staggered him into the wall. His heart jumpstarted with a machine gun beat, first eager breath choked by a bloody deluge. He slid his left foot forward. Minimal pain. The suit bore his weight. Hostiles silhouetted across both lenses.

His boarding shotgun connected to the suit's rudimentary onboard geist, and its safety flicked off on its own.

NEW USER DETECTED. DO YOU REQUIRE CONTROL INSTRUCTIONS?

38

The first Shasvastii to stick its head into Odune's treasury lost it.

The boarding shotgun slug detonated like a firework centimeters from its face, turning its sinus inside-out. Chitin fragments embedded into the polysteel, and the decapitated Nox slid back into the hall.

Lines of stinging pinpricks crossed his body from toes to tip. Autoinjectors, delivering numbing agents. His own silhouette snapped into the corner of his HUD, flashing desperately. An emergency pane warned him of severe lacerations, internal bleeding, contusions, hairline fractures, hypoxic shock—and asked his permission to order an ambulance.

He dismissed the notification and directed his geist into silent.

Wil braced against the hole's edge. Beneath the swiftly collapsing notifications, a half-revealed camouflage shadow gawked at the remains of its friend. One slug, two. Thermo-optical camouflage sparked along the tunnel wall and died. A corpse with its innards splayed across its lap like tarot cards lay there, spawn embryo a wet crystal ball.

He climbed through the gap, one leg at a time. The hall was crowded with Nox. Eight in all. Shotguns and Combi rifles. The crowd of line troopers froze until one chirped in the Shasvastii bug-language, and they all opened fire at once. Everything they put on him bounced off his powered combat armor and caromed away, shredding his duster and leaving him battered.

And angry.

Wil stocked the shotgun to his chest.

The lead faltered. The others followed suit.

The instant their courage failed them, the ORC's rudimentary combat geist snapped the boarding shotgun's loaded shell from spread to slug, and Wil planted two shots into the lead. Its trunk exploded, coating its allies' faces in a deluge of violet slime.

The Nox's punctured spawn-embryo drained a translucent, yolky fluid along its thighs, and Wil stepped over it to get the ones in the back into his shotgun's effective range.

"Next," he called, and racked the weapon for effect.

This time, they made the unilateral decision to fire. Slug to spread, the shotgun barrel automatically choked, and the hallway filled with light. Shrapnel burned the room numbers from the walls and the paint from the ceiling. One Shas split in half with a visceral shriek. Its partner loosed its Combi to clap its groin, stifling but not stopping the unfurling of intestinal ribbons. Another fell rigid as a board, gaped mandibles flooding with lavender soup.

Three more, done and done. None of their low-yield particle ammunition penetrated his armor.

The first brave Nox broke from the pack to sprint into close combat. Wil met them with his shoulder and shoved it aside. The Nox slip-slided in what remained of its friends until two armor-piercing slugs drilled its mandibles out the back of its head.

Wil licked the nosebleed from his lips. "Next!"

One survivor broke formation and fled. The other two lingered, mag-dumping down the hall. Both caught individual slugs, tangling in each other's arms as they died.

Wil gave chase. Rounded the corner. Sighted the last remaining Nox, locked in a dead sprint with its weapon cast aside. His geist triangulated the shots from his hip, but he didn't pull the trigger when it told him to.

Because he was better than them.

A warning blipped into the corner of his HUD. Hostile motion. Hack in progress. Shotgun slung over his shoulder, Wil strummed the trigger with his thumb. Even point-blank, the boom failed to penetrate the polysteel of his helmet.

Down the hall, the dead camouflage shadow from the entryway crumpled, gurgling from the remaining half of its face. A hacking device glitched madly atop its spindly, twitching forearm. It'd regenerated.

"Damn," Wil said. "I forgot you guys did that."

Barrel to its forehead. Trigger.

Done.

Even in emergency lockdown, the DRC's domotic functions were still active. Sonic waves dispersed the blood puddles into tiny, paper-thin gaps in the floor, cleaning his path as he went. Steadying himself on the wall back to the treasury, Wil failed to avoid tracking their mess with his boots. Looked like he'd been stomping grapes in a winery.

As he fumbled back into the treasury, Glasscock leapt up from behind the deactivated F-13 turrets with Wil's Detour in his shaking hands. Fear became glee. "Aw, hell yeah!"

"You hit?" Wil asked, and his voice sounded wrong through the vox.

Glasscock wriggled a shaka at him. "All good, sir. But we gotta go."

"I need a sidearm. Which box?"

When Glasscock indicated a crate, Wil pried it open. Combat knives in foam cutouts—Teseum-laced, but nothing you couldn't find on the street for a reasonable price. He magnetized one to his hip. "Sidearm. As in pistol."

Stammering, Glasscock pointed out another. Already open. In the sawdust, firearms. Nothing caught his eye that was worth the extra weight until he saw a snub-nosed Americolt Bulldog revolver gleaming in the red light, barrel as thick as his leg. When he cracked open the cylinder, the fat .600 cartridges shined the same silver as Alastair's armor-piercing rounds. T2. Five rounds—enough to put a serious dent in a TAG, and a lockpick in a pinch besides. Outside his armor, it'd splinter his arm like a toothpick. In it, the artificial muscle would bear the strain.

He clicked it to his leg and knocked his duster with his hand in the process. His pocket had a weight to it—a single H-12 cartridge, case carved with the name WILHELM. For an instant, he felt the old man behind him, arms crossed. Judging his stance. Saying he needed to aim with his eyes.

"Let's roll," Wil said, and Glasscock led the way.

⇈

Up the steps. Down the halls. His geist drew signage on the walls and arrows on the floor, though none of it led him toward an exit until he nearly tripped over the corpse of a Nox he didn't remember killing, and then another, and the bloodstains became a trail.

Gordon was doing well.

"Door, door, where's the door," Glasscock muttered. Detour in hand, he lingered behind, crowding Wil as much as any one man could.

A broad door marked EXIT stood at the end of the hall. His shoulder opened it, and when the one beyond refused to yield, the Bulldog convinced it with one point-blank round. The instant he wrenched back the stubborn metal, a curtain of mist swept across his oculi. Rain struck his armor like a million particle rounds, swiftly muted by his aural filters. Emergency lights stained the night a deep crimson, every shadow darker than the last.

Glasscock sprinted into the storm, splashing into the trees. "This way!"

Wil gave chase, descending from the path to the grass and down the hill. Faint streaks of faraway lightning lit his path in millisecond bursts. Far away, gunshots popped and grew quieter with distance.

Glasscock exited the thicket onto a wide, muddy incline. A switchback curved toward Loch Eil's shore, and he descended with aplomb. "Home stretch, let's go!"

Wil lagged behind. "Where are we going?"

"Away, mate," Glasscock said, and slicked to a stop. Beret swamped, water trickling from his brows, he had to shout to speak over the gale. "Five minutes, and this boondoggle won't be our problem no more! Move it!"

"You know something," Wil said, and closed on him. "What?"

Glasscock backpedaled, slipped, balanced out. The constant rush of rain turned the slope into a muddy waterslide. Without armor like Wil's, he was at the current's mercy. "What's your problem?"

"Tell me. Now."

"Listen, asshole—"

One shove was all it took to put Glasscock on his ass. He flailed, tumbled, failed to stand and then again until the blue of his uniform sopped brown from muddy water.

Wil dredged him from the muck by the collar. "Talk!"

Glasscock struggled and surrendered in the span of a breath. "Alright, stop! Stop. I got through, okay? No one's coming. No delegation, just like you wanted. Congrats."

The pit in his stomach yawned again. "But the MacArthurs—"

"They said to make our exit subtle. Let the Caledonians draw fire."

Wil let him go. "What?"

"Our extraction's due at the bottom of the hill, any minute now. We gotta go. The DRC isn't gonna be here much longer. The stabilization systems have this failure point designed into them as a last resort, right? One D-charge and the whole bitch goes down the mountain."

"How the hell do you know that?"

He shrugged. "Operator says they don't know what the Shas will do when they learn the party's canceled. The only way we're living is if we go for distance."

In the storm, the incline they'd clambered down would be unassailable. Searching for a shortcut would burn too much time. He'd bite the bullet and go the long way, follow the road. Kick down the front gates if he had to.

"Alright, wait," Glasscock said. "I know what you're thinking, okay? Don't. If this gets out that a PanOceanian outpost was turned by the Combined Army without any higher-ups noticing, do you know how it'll make us look? Make *me* look? I don't want to be the next you, man."

Anger flared in him again. "Excuse me?"

"I know who you are. What you did."

"The MacArthurs are our allies," Wil said. "I won't abandon them."

"Why not? Someone's got to keep the Shas pinned down until the fireworks show. Better some hillbilly Atek inbreds than us, you know?"

A dawning realization. "When Gordon left, you knew."

"So what?" Glasscock said. "That dude isn't even human."

"What about the scientists in the DRC? Security. Non-essential personnel. They deserve to die, too?"

"Yeah, because any could be Shas! Let the NeoVatican sort 'em out, man, I don't get paid enough for this. I signed up to flirt with Tech Bees and now they make them wear pants."

Wil's fury doused beneath a cold, painful truth. "ALEPH advises, you comply."

"Good soldiers follow orders," Glasscock said, pounding his fist into his palm. "What about that is so hard to understand?"

What Saoirse had said on the ridge echoed back to him. She was right. Glasscock wasn't PanOceania's exemplar, but he was its messenger, cut from the same cloth as the man Wil had been before Svalarheima. The MacArthurs had come to fight this battle, to rescue PanOceanians in their time of need, and the one PanOceanian they'd rescued couldn't see past his own self-assured superiority long enough to dare humanize them.

Not worth convincing. No time besides. Wil started back up the mountain alone.

Glasscock's tantrum faded, replaced by growing gunfire.

↑↑

The switchbacks up toward the DRC's gate proved flatter than he remembered, easy to maneuver on foot. As he rounded the bend, the forest parted to reveal the comms array spires glowing an idle red through the network of boughs above. Beyond it, the elevated heliport's darkened surface blushed with pale greens and blues.

The rain stopped. The wind died. Water still fell five, ten meters out, but none hit him, and Wil looked up. Above, the rainfall traced the faint outline of something geometric and large but silent and wholly absent from sight. Its belly distorted like thermo-optical camouflage when the faint DRC light hit it just right.

A Shasvastii ghost ship.

It didn't slow or open fire. It didn't seem to notice him at all. Swiftly, the shape ascended into the storm and vanished behind the clouds. If that was Odune, there was no way Wil could catch him now.

Around the final jackknife in the road, the front gates loomed. Barbed wire jingled and swayed atop the wide-open sally port. Crimson floodlights turned every raindrop into a tracer round. Signage marked with the elephant and lotus of Bureaus Ganesh and Gaea threatened lethal consequences for unauthorized visitors, first in English, then Caledonian.

Two scorched F-13 turrets hung limp on the battlement, riddled with bullet holes and finished off by grenade. Not willing to chance a hidden third, Wil went wide on the approach—and reconsidered. Abandoning caution, he broke for the sally port.

Behind the floodlights, a flash.

Fifteen meters to his flank, the fist of God hit the mud. Fire filled the knuckle print. Sound became force, became motion. Dirt struck him like a hammer, upending him onto his head, his feet, his shoulders, until he crashed into a flooded roadside ditch meters from where he'd started.

Groaning, Wil shook off the stun and dragged himself into the ditch. Water filled the inside of his armor, vaguely cold against the bodysleeve of artificial muscle. Even if he didn't submerge wholly, more cover was better than none.

That'd been a Needle missile. Hit-mode.

Nothing on his HUD indicated internal damage that wasn't already there, nothing superficial, no gelatinized flesh or pulverized bones. He'd expected a jolt like that to jar his knee and leave him gasping, but the Serum and his suit's auto-injected painkillers had him wondering if he'd been hurt at all. His legs moved.

Arms, raised. His combat armor had eaten the brunt of the explosion and didn't even dent.

God, he missed this thing.

Ten meters into the pitch-black forest, a blinking light bounced into view and bounded toward him. Keratin clunked against fallen trees. Gravelly lowing amplified in volume. A craggy, dog-sized Taigha creature burst from the undergrowth and charged.

Wil fumbled for his shotgun. Before he could take aim, impacts spattered up the Taigha's chest, and it toppled face-first into the ditch water. Convulsing fins scraped his armored cuisse as it died, and its blinking mask shorted out as it sank.

"Stay down!" Dunne called. "That was the last of them!"

No visual, only voice. A quick glance confirmed the advice. If he stood, he'd be visible in all directions for a hundred meters. But staying here wasn't an option, either. Someone invisible was out there packing more overkill than a Szalamandra TAG.

A Noctifer.

Like a jump scare in an old film, his HUD blared with images, information, artwork—a social halo permissions share, foreign now after three weeks without. Dunne's fresh-faced academy graduation photos blocked his sight, framing picturesque Varuna beachfronts and Kildalton wreathed in snow.

"Identify yourself," Dunne transmitted via comlog.

Wil coughed. "Reptilo ranches don't have cowboys."

She paused. "Wil?"

"El único e inigualable."

Pellehan's gravelly laughter cut into the conversation. "And here I thought *we'd* come to save *you*. The hell are you wearing, son? Almost clipped you on reflex."

"It's complicated." Wil sunk lower to ensure his radial sensors didn't give up his position. "What's the sitch?"

"You've met our dance partner," Pell said. "Orwell and I can't catch him out, and he's in the same boat with us. We're keeping him occupied until Sunray's done searching for survivors up the hill."

"Probably the same bloody bug who blew up that PanO transport we found," Dunne said. "Maybe yours, too."

She had a point, but it wasn't important now. "Last I saw, you were basically a casualty. Glad you're vertical again, Muriel."

Dunne scoffed. "Only just, but I'm fit for it. You?"

"Seen better," he said. "Where's Princess? Everyone safe?"

"Safe is stretching it," Dunne said. "While Sunray, Victor 2, and Victor 5 clear the dormitories, your jo and mine are out with Victor 4 pulling a reverse Croatoan, if that all makes sense?"

While Al, Neil, and Kelsie swept the area, Saoirse, Hodges, and Nora were utilizing the chaos to take cover deep in enemy territory. "Got it. Patch me to Sunray. I've got intel that changes everything."

A flash. Smoke speared through the storm. The explosion dismantled a copse of trees, coating the outer ward in a million wet splinters. Flame roiled through the splinters and died as the rain overpowered it.

Wil twisted, attempting to establish visual. The rain was too thick. If he stood, the Noctifer would already be gone. "Orwell, Watcher, copy. Copy, goddammit. Hey!"

Coughing, and the crash of brush rattled in his ear. "Bastard's getting brave," Dunne growled. "Problem first, then discussion. No more distractions."

"Understood," he said. "Please advise. Over."

"I'll pincer. Buy time until I find a way around. Five minutes, max."

"Don't have that kind of time. Trust me. Life or death."

"Frontal assault, then. All three of us at once?"

Pell filtered a sigh through his teeth. "At this distance, in this downpour… The night bringer will bide his time, Muriel. Wait us out. That's the game he wants us to play, aye. Played it many times before, myself. Only way we'll see hide or hair is if he wants us to."

"Alright, so let's give him what he wants," Wil said, and magnetized his shotgun to his back. "Odds on a bite if I feed him a hook?"

Dunne's stunned silence melted into an incredulous chuckle. "You can't be serious."

"I'm wearing ORC armor, Dunne. If it's not T2 or monofilament, I'll manage."

"And I'd believe that if I'd not served with Mobile Brigadas. Heavy armor looks braw till you remember there's a human inside no tougher than a plastic bag."

Ditch water drained from his duster. "Well, let's hope Pell's a faster draw. Heard he used to be the Dullahan."

"Used to be," Pell balked. "Used to be?"

"So prove it," Wil said, and clambered into the light.

Knee stinging, chest burning, he broke into an awkward run. In ideal circumstances, the ORC's automated systems would stabilize his movement, propel his steps, optimize his gait. In the slick, with only a rudimentary geist, it didn't fare well. Clumsy as a newborn deer and just as defenseless.

A blur flickered atop the DRC's walls. Not from the sally port or the watch towers, but the limp F-13 turret. A shadow scuttled atop the spindly wreck, enormous launcher balanced on one scrawny, insectoid shoulder. A pinprick of light bolted from its aperture and streaked toward Wil's feet.

He zigged. Zagged. Hurled himself prone.

A second thunderclap kicked him across the yard and into a tree trunk. Fire lit the outer ward in blinding orange and faded.

Head spinning, HUD flashing, Wil failed to stand. Failed to move. He'd lost his bearing. Loose needles washed over his arms. Déjà vu. Not pine, but scattered debris turned shrapnel by the blast. Flame kindled along the hem of his duster and doused under the downpour.

Thought, impossible. No sound but ringing.

The Noctifer hefted its weapon. The barrel yawned down toward him. Within, a spark. A flash. The F-13 perch disintegrated under a crescendo of light and force. The smoke cloud wisped away with the storm winds, dissipating instantly, and only the twisted remains of the DRC's perimeter fence remained.

Its own missile had detonated centimeters from the barrel.

"Pound-shop Knauf," Pell grumbled and racked his Zyefir's bolt. "*Used to be*, eh? Well, where's your patter now?"

Lightning struck the mountainside, thunder bursting concurrent. Out in the flash, a massive, mechanical shape appeared crouched against a tree. Flanges like wings glowed with malevolent light from behind it. An enormous alien Spitfire wreathed in amethyst flame filled its hands, and it opened fire.

Trees splintered. Rain evaporated. A silent spray of high-caliber ordnance sliced through the wilderness, leaving nothing standing in its wake. As the first trees fell, the shape faded like a ghost into a mirror.

That was a Sphinx.

"Watcher!" Dunne cried. "Watcher, copy! Can you copy? Watcher—Pell!"

A crackle. A wheeze. "I'm hit. Watcher, down. Need assistance. Bleeding."

"Fuck," she breathed. "Fuck! I'm en route, hold tight. Wil, I'm patching you in. Can you stand? If you're hit too, I'll bloody kill you both."

He forced his legs beneath him. "Yeah."

New permissions raced across his HUD. Callsigns and sigils populated a list along his left lens; vitals and approximate distances, his right. The cold comfort of modern warfare felt almost nostalgic after so long without it.

SUNRAY lit, and Alastair spoke. "Orwell, copy. Is the Noctifer still active? We've got survivors who need an exit route, over."

"Gate's secure, sir, but Pell's been hit," Dunne transmitted. Far away, a shadow threaded through the undergrowth, headed east. "On my way to CasEvac, over."

"Lot of personnel need a bearing, Orwell. Some, medical. Press down the mountainside to Marker Echo, and send coordinates. We'll have—"

Wil cut in. "Breaker breaker, Sunray, this is Errant. Bad idea."

A pause. Several names lit along the side of his HUD, talking all at once. A shout. Incredulous whispers. Laughter. Alastair silenced them with a curt, "Clear comms. Copy, Errant. Go ahead."

"The DRC is rigged to blow," Wil said, limping across the outer ward. "One point of failure, one linchpin keeps the DRC stabilized. One D-charge, and the whole outpost takes a shortcut into Loch Eil. We've got to pull out right now."

"Not until we warn the delegation away. A direct jack—"

"Glasscock says he got through, that no one's coming. I don't know if I believe him, but he ran off to save himself and left y'all with the bill."

VICTOR 2 lit briefly. "Fuckin' galactic," Neil spat.

"Fuckin' galactic," Wil echoed and grinned despite the needles it pushed through the bruises in his face. "Orders, sir?"

Alastair's name lit up, but he didn't speak for several seconds. "Orwell, send coordinates. I'm pointing survivors your way. Medical personnel, and scientists. Take them as far as you can get. Stay lateral, look for shelter. Once you're on stable ground, retransmit coordinates and go silent."

"Acknowledged, sending now," Dunne said. "Orwell, out."

Wil's heart sank into his legs. "You're staying?"

"I can't abandon these people to their deaths, not in good conscience. Saving lives is the whole reason we came here—that, and ending the threat to Kildalton. I'd like to do both. Errant, rendezvous with Princess and Foxhound at the comms array, bring them up to speed. With PanOceanian comms tech, zeroing in on that linchpin should be nigh effortless."

Ping disconnected devices, paint their physical locations on the digital patina, and then go by process of elimination. Simple. Pressed for time, they might get one good guess before Odune caught on and sent them all to kingdom come.

Aimed for the red lights of the comms array, Wil sprinted through the sally port. "And then?"

"I do something stupid," Alastair said. "Let's make Cailean proud."

39

The rain fell harder, ran colder, rushed from every rooftop and flooded every gutter in the DRC. Fixtures washed away in the deluge, carrying parked AUVs from their spaces and into the night. Guided by the lazy glow from on high and dodging dislodged detritus, Wil sprinted up the communication building steps.

The glass doors wooshed open. Minimalist corporate décor and prefab necessities cast geometric shadows across the wide open space. A front desk stretched out ahead, flanked by a pair of iron staircases to the second floor. Blue light faded through the frosted control room doors above.

Wil took his first step onto the carpet and something clinked against the side of his helmet. He froze. Raised his hands. Slowly, imperceptibly turned until he saw Saoirse glaring down the barrel of Hodges' chain rifle. And though she looked exhausted, bare arms streaked with blood and dark earth, she still had all her fingers.

Her nose twitched. She sniffed, and her expression changed. "Wil?"

It wasn't the joy he expected, or relief. But fear.

A shadow crossed the lobby. Hodges, with his pistol and knife together in a CQC grip. His wrist was naked, comlog removed. "They're almost done upstairs. Who's this?"

Without explanation, Saoirse bolted. Wil followed. Hodges grasped it an instant later, gasped "Bloody hell, no!" and chased after them.

The stairs creaked with the force of their ascent. At the end of the hall, a dim-lit control room spread out in all directions tucked behind a glass partition. Holopanes flit through the air, orbiting in AR above the workstations proper. Nora stood at a console in the center of the room, typing on Hodges' holographic comlog dial with her bandaged hand. A tall, olive-skinned man with short dark hair and a patchwork beard stood behind her, short-handled knife in his grip.

It was Wil.

His mirror-image clocked their approach with stiff-lipped urgency. Quantronic light sparked in its eyes. The security screen over the control room hall deployed and hissed shut like shields closing rank in a phalanx, leaving them only seconds before the room sealed shut.

Nora startled from the console. "No, no way! I must've—"

Saoirse cupped her hand to her mouth. "Nora! That's not Wil! Nora!"

Brief confusion. Then horrified understanding.

Nora dove over the console. Wil's doppelgänger lunged for her, and the knife in its hand shimmered and holomorphed. Golden light ignited from the extending blade, slicing a glowing semicircle through the dark. The end of her field jacket rushed into the air like a streamer, followed by the vomited contents of her paramedic bag. But Nora was unharmed. She burst to her feet, rifle raised, but everything past the trigger guard had been amputated.

By the time Wil's doppelgänger had vaulted the console after her, he'd donned a familiar long, black coat. It was the same Speculo Killer, down to the scuffs on the lapel.

Saoirse picked up speed. The security screen was closing too fast. They weren't going to make it. But Hodges caught a second wind and sped into a slide. Flat atop the tile, he slipped beneath the falling gate with only centimeters to spare.

Wil impacted the screen with his shoulder. Shoved a foot forward. The shield wall knifed into the greave of his armor, crumpling it. A celery-crunch of broken bone preceded the hiss-pinch of painkillers, and a second later, he wasn't certain he had toes at all.

Saoirse slammed beside him and hauled the screen up with both hands. It lifted only barely. Inside the walls, a metallic groaning doubled in volume. "Wil! Motor!"

He'd already drawn the Bulldog, aimed for the sound. Two shots, left and right. The crack-boom of each .600 shot overwhelmed his aural filters and left a ringing in their wake. The groaning stopped, and the screen shifted up a few centimeters. Not enough space for Saoirse to go under, but enough to free his foot. He bent at the hip and added his strength to the pull.

A readout in the corner of his HUD warned his ORC was approaching its lifting limit. More than 250 kg, and that was with Saoirse's help. "On three!"

On one, gunshots. 9mm. Hodges had already engaged the Speculo inside. Trails of golden light painted a whirling fractal through the dim lit comms room. A glimmer, a vibrato, and Hodges' assault pistol launched into the air in two clean halves.

Hodges' handaxe caught the light as he pulled it free. "Hello, Vern. Was hoping I'd see you again."

The Speculo swayed forward, giving its weapon a spin. "Robert Hodges, ex-SAS. Best of the best. Ready for that scrap now, mate?"

"I'm not your fuckin' mate," Hodges said, and charged.

The Speculo kept distance. It probed in small jabs, growing in speed, in intensity and swiftness until Hodges anticipated the rush, moved to intercept and counterstrike, and right at the start of its motion the Speculo halted on the tip of its toe. It pivoted toward Nora, monoblade aimed for her face.

Hodges seized it by the collar and yanked. The monofilament cut short, and her bangs cut shorter.

The Speculo broke free with a backhand. Kaleidoscope nightmares carved in the shadow of its wake. Hodges ducked a swipe level with his eyes. Then, his throat, and the follow-up aimed for his inner thigh. In the flicker of light, only focus in his vision, the perfect clarity of the zone. Another swipe, and he moved with prescient confidence. His off-hand went up. Jerked like a sewing machine needle, and he leapt back.

The Speculo's eyes pried wide and its jaw dropped, staggering a step to grip at the knife embedded in its neck.

The handaxe streaked toward its forehead.

Monowire trilled like violin string.

Hodges' forearm flung from his elbow to the floor, handaxe clanging away. His head followed after. Blood squirted from the clean stump of his neck, painting the tile in arterial stripes as he fell.

The Speculo slowed to a halt, gulping down agonal breaths. Four deep puncture marks from breastbone to jaw pumped a river down its holomorphic trench coat. But the Speculo was standing, and Hodges was not.

"Best of the best," the Speculo sneered. "Maybe in *your* galaxy."

Saoirse gasped. Strained. Her shoulders bulged, veins shivering to the surface of her arms. Lips taut, fangs gleaming, the cords of her neck unearthed like the roots of an ancient tree. Blood vessels burst in her eyes and her temples, and her scream of exertion rivaled a Balena at full burn.

The security screen racked up. Crunched. Folded in on itself.

No more resistance. She catapulted beneath it. Ruptured servos screaming, Wil kicked her claymore after.

The Speculo turned on Nora, and Saoirse hit it like a fucking missile.

They smashed into the far wall and rebounded. Saoirse's offense was immediate and feral. No gaps, no hesitation, no careful probes to press defense. No pause. Only pure, berserk fury guided by a lifetime's worth of killer instinct fueled by limitless rage.

Desks carved aside. The prefab walls laced with crisscross blows. The floor trenched, wires sizzling beneath. The Speculo glided away, graceful, incorporeal through her assault. It cartwheeled into a half-spin, a jeté, twirling in the air as its monofilament sang, and she drove her fist forward through all the flouncy bullshit and left a crater in its face.

Two mandibles, pulverized. Brow, dented. Eye flopping in the wreckage of its cheek, the Speculo stumbled for a second time. Totally defenseless. Saoirse followed through and skimmed its chest with the tip of her Teseum claymore.

Too shallow. Its coat shredded, but the Speculo underneath didn't.

Gold light twisted in a spiral. Saoirse howled. Her claymore dipped. Blood veiled the lower half of her face. A horizontal line across the bridge of her nose from temple to cheekbone bubbled red, tilted against the perfect verticality of her scar.

Somewhere in the motion, lost between seconds, Hodges' knife had left the Speculo's neck to plant in Saoirse's ribs. Her shirt stained dark, and the hilt drooled like a loose tap in a keg.

The Speculo skipped back, spitting blood past an alien grin, and caught Wil aiming the Bulldog beneath the screen. It sidestepped to keep Saoirse in his shot. "Look at you!" it barked. "Pathetic. Can't even control yourself."

Fangs bared, she tore the knife from her side. "No one can!"

The instant she went one-handed, the Speculo speared in for the kill.

Their blades met. Monofilament carved the Teseum, filling the air with the shriek of metal on metal. Sparks showered their boots, the tile. Yellow light bit into the claymore's fuller, straight toward Saoirse's face.

And the carve slowed.

Stopped.

Blood sped down the groove.

The Speculo shuddered. With wide eyes, it considered the notched and ruined weapon buried in its chest, and the coursing torrent racing down the blade. It flailed its weapon's hilt, but the monowire had tangled in the dogtoothed claymore and disintegrated.

Saoirse was unharmed.

"Impossible," it gurgled.

She howled back, "I DON'T CARE!"

Claymore dropped, she hilted Hodges' knife in the Speculo's wrist. With its arm pinned to its chest, she fell upon it unarmed. Claws rent flesh. Broke bone. Joints snapped, bent, dislocated. Fangs met throat, thrashing until its neck snapped in her jaws and the Speculo's lifeless body slopped to the floor where she went on all fours after it.

Wil strained up and struck the interior security panel with his fist. Red turned to blue, and the screen screeched up from his aching shoulders back into the ceiling. Limping into a walk, he crossed the comms room and stalled for a moment beside Hodges' decapitated body. A twinge of grief, a pang of respect.

A bastard, but *their* bastard. He deserved better.

Wil slowed, angling himself between Nora and Saoirse. He held out his hand. "Saoirse. You alright?"

Saoirse twisted over her shoulder and growled. Bubbles foamed across her sliced nose with every sharp exhalation. Hands clenching the blossoming hole in her side, she rose and took a step toward him. Another. Fingers wracked, claws dripping, she paused and swallowed a moan, eyes crushed shut—

And when she opened them, the fury had died and the inner light had returned, along with a shadow of pain and fear. "Someone," she panted, "someone oughta tell Dunne."

"After," Wil said, and braced her before she lost footing. "There's a lot of shit going down right now. Nora, is she gonna be okay?"

Nora unstuck herself from the corner, fear substituted with cold professionalism once again. "If I can slow the bleeding. Saoirse, love, let me see."

Saoirse collapsed into a rolling chair, sucking pained breaths past bloody lips. A wince spurred an inspection of her dominant hand, knuckles bearing the same centimeter-thick stripe as her face. "That close, three times," she whispered. "Christ almighty."

Brow furrowed, Nora peeled back the soaked shirt. "Hypo'll stitch it for now," she said and touched her bisected bag. Cursing, she wheeled around, scanning the floor. "Wil, my things—painkillers, coagulants, styptics—they've gone everywhere!"

A plastic cylinder laid centimeters from his foot. "Got one," Wil called, and bent to pick it up.

When he stood, a shadow cast upon him. His dopplegänger. The Speculo. Standing. Alive. Wet entrails dangled down to its knees, the inmost cords tense within the wet mess of its throat. Hodges' handaxe gleamed at its side, and its sole surviving eye raged with a horrible, alien fire.

Calmer and more casually than the most hardened operators he'd ever served with, Nora McDermott plucked Saoirse's pistol from its holster and put four bullets into the Speculo's back.

It dropped. Convulsed. Went still.

She shot it twice more, and held out her hand.

"Hypo?"

⇈

Over two-hundred connections each maintained a constant network presence throughout the DRC-9. The amount of disconnected devices that'd come through the DRC was in the quadruple-digits, and they lacked the permissions to do more than stare.

Until Nora hefted the Speculo's hand and plopped it beside Hodges' comlog. The loading wheel spun, and the login screen unfolded into a mosaic of security cameras, navbot frequencies, and comlog clusters.

She held a watery smile. "Another thing Llowry's dad said. Speculo's got a whole armful of Cubes, apparently. Download all their identities there for safekeeping. Guess one had security clearance."

Saoirse held Nora's wadded jacket to her side, every breath laborious. "Find it?"

Wil brought up a network map of the DRC across his visor's limited AR. He pinged blocked ports rapid-fire, tracing the connections in real-time until one caught his attention. South. Below ground. Buried beneath the Administration Building, meters beneath Odune's office. Its first connection to the network was less than three days ago.

He spun up his dial. "Sunray, this is Errant. Clocked a suspicious connection, forwarding the details."

A pause. "Copy, Errant. Reviewing now—and aye, suspicious is right. The last of the survivors are en route to Orwell, so Victor 2 and I will rendezvous. ETA, three minutes. Over."

"Copy," Wil said and unholstered his Bulldog. Two shots left. Shouldn't need much more to cross the DRC unless he met that Sphinx on the switchbacks. Or another copy of himself.

When he turned back, Nora was raising from the comlog screen. Eyebrows folded inward, back of her hand against her nose, she breathed in the slow cadence of someone who'd finally seen too much. "Wil. I found something."

A few quick swipes brought the source of her horror into focus on Wil's lens: a map of the shore of Loch Eil, running from the Campbells in the north to the O'Brien in the south. A hundred little dots blinked, nestled within the wilderness, the settlements. Nora tapped one on the comlog, and it widened to a video feed of a Caledonian man's perspective. In first-person, they watched him chop a carrot at a cutting board while two children played at his feet.

None of the words or numerals on the UI were human. Most, he recognized from Paradiso, from a scrawl left behind on an abandoned bunker wall below a gift-wrapped cluster of grenades. Combined Army script. Alien.

Nora flicked through the feeds rapid-fire. Men and women, young and old, then gray-skinned limbs, extended mandibles, then human again, then Shasvastii, then...

Agents. Infiltrators. The motherlode.

Wil loosed an incredulous breath. "Holy shit."

"So much for what the Stavka says about the Combined Army on Dawn," Nora whispered. "What now?"

"You and Saoirse follow Dunne's lead, get clear. We'll deal with this after."

"I'm comin' with," Saoirse huffed. She stood, but halfway up, her freckled face turned a brighter shade of white and she fell back to the chair. The underside of the jacket wadded on her ribs sopped with fresh red, and her grimace stretched open the line across her face.

Nora kept her from trying a second time. "Saoirse, no! Any more fighting, love, and you'll bleed to death."

"Can't stop now," she hissed.

"You have to," Nora said. "I need you here. With me. Someone needs to scrape this data and send it along."

Wil shook his head. "Nora. If we fail—"

"Then don't fail," Nora said, hunched and swiping at the comlog already. "I don't see the issue."

He grimaced. Didn't like it. Didn't have time to argue. "Good luck, Nora," he said, and went for the door.

"Hey, Wil," Saoirse called, gritting through the pain. "Promise me that when it's over, you won't leave without sayin' goodbye. Give me that."

Wil paused at the door. "Never said I'm leaving."

Across her bloodsoaked face—a flicker of joy.

Beautiful.

Outside the comms hub, the storm had run its course. Torrents of rain had diminished to meandering bursts, no longer cutting visibility by half, and the slow migration of so many things not bolted down had come to an end. Smoke clouded the roads, along with dismembered Shasvastii corpses. Fionn's work, judging by the cleaves and sizzling shrapnel.

The Administrative Building stood above the carnage, frosted windows casting red out into the night like the eyes of a demon. The front doors had shattered open, and the lobby was strewn with what remained of eight dead CSUs, Breaker Combis and light shotguns scattered amidst their bodies. Wil paused and turned one over with his foot, discontent at how far the mandibles sagged from its near-human face after death.

Neil jolted out from behind the front desk, Rhiannon stocked to his shoulder. Fine strips of Mariannebourg silk decorated his torso, bracing his broken ribs, and a graze beneath his cheek burned a line through his ear. Not much of it remained.

"Speak o' the ol' tin can," he said, and grinned painfully. "Never been one for PanO blue, but on you, it actually looks good."

Broken glass crunched underfoot. "Damn, man. Your ear."

"Eh, it's alry. Had better days, but not dead yet. Kelsie and Al are over by the lifts if yer lookin' for 'em. I can hold my own out here against these invertebrates all night if need be."

"Copy that," Wil said and nodded at Rhiannon. "How's she handling?"

"Makes noise, and sometimes I get lucky. Why? Tryna Pellehan me for it?"

"I mean," he said, and paused.

Neil laughed. Then braced his ribs and glared.

Deeper within, Alastair and Kelsie stood in the elevator lobby, leveraging a knife between the doors of the lift. Neither seemed at full strength: While Alastair's patchwork armor had returned to him, the pieces worn by Cailean and Hodges were still MIA, as was his helmet and shield. Both bore superficial wounds—bruises and scrapes—though the gash across Alastair's brow from his chain-colt looked deep enough to scar.

"Excuse me, sir," Wil said, and stepped past them. His fingertips wedged into the gap without problem, artificial muscle more than strong enough to pry the doors apart. Above, the elevator hung suspended on the fourth floor. No access. But below, the shaft stretched down at least twelve meters, descending two full stories into the mountainside.

"That's what I thought," Alastair said, sawing at the straps of his breastplate with his combat knife rather than painstakingly removing it plate by plate. "Hidden in plain sight."

Wil reached into the shaft and tugged on the cable. The steel chirped, but held steady. "I'll go first."

Alastair's armor impacted the tile, Teseum denting the prefab floor. "No. I'm going. You two stay here with Neil and cover our exit."

"You sure, sir? I'm the one wearing a tank."

"It's not about can," Alastair said, unstrapping the greaves off his thighs. "It's about should. I'm the MacArthur, Wil. I can't ask you to do something without asking myself first. And besides—I trained in demolitions in Scone, remember?"

Wil noted Alastair's empty holsters. "No gun?"

"Not yet," Kelsie said. She checked the magazine of her Kremen and held it out. "Six rounds, sir. Use 'em or lose 'em."

"Thank you." Pistol in one hand, he regarded the drop. "Wil, give me a hand?"

Carefully, Wil lowered Alastair into the shaft until he'd taken grip on the service ladder tucked into the anterior wall. When the sounds of boots on the rungs faded below, he doubled back to the lobby and caught a bullet against the side of his helmet.

Wil stumbled. Hand on Kelsie's back, he launched her forward and fell against a prefab pillar, cracking the holo-ad screens with his face.

Reeling toward the lobby desk, Kelsie skidded on broken glass. Pistol shots snapped and barked from outside the lobby, followed by the click-pop and flare of a flash pulse. Her bonnet whipped off her head, and she went down hard clear out in the open.

"I can't see," she gasped. "I can't—!"

Neil stood. Rhiannon roared. Her telltale H-12 drumbeat sent the glass across the floor dancing. And while the trigger only lasted a second before his eyes whited out under the flash pulse focus-fire, it gave Kelsie all the bearing she needed to crawl through the glass into cover.

A pop. Splatter. Neil's forearm sliced open from knuckle to elbow. A deep graze, disabling. Kelsie yanked him down before he caught a more lethal second shot. Still alive, but neutralized.

Footsteps clicked on the lobby tile. Closer. Boarding shotgun at the ready, Wil chanced a quick look.

An Ikadron Batroid stood in the lobby, lanky bio-organic frame shivering from the cold. Little puffs of flame from its underslung flamethrowers sent glints of light dancing up its crimson chassis. It crept forward with halting steps, joined by a second, a third—a gaggle of the goddamn things, all flocking like geese toward their position.

If they reached Neil and Kelsie before the flash ammo cleared from their eyes, they wouldn't stand a chance. If he stepped out, he'd catch six flamethrowers at once. No way he'd survive that unscathed. No guarantee he'd survive at all. But there was no way in hell he was letting another goddamn Combined Army drone kill somebody he knew.

A terrible howling erupted from beyond the admin building, primal and animal and deep. Close, and growing closer. The Ikadrons spun, flamethrowers level to cover the single entrance and exit. The screaming grew loud, louder, until it was right atop them, bouncing off the vaulted ceiling, then louder somehow still—

The lobby window erupted. Claymore-first, Fionnlagh barreled through the shatter and hewed the lead Ikadron from forehead to hip. Columns of flame streaked toward him, but only touched air. Mid-roll, his sawed-off swung into his hands. One pump cut their number by half. And when the last few recovered, flamethrowers primed to incinerate, the boarding shotgun in Wil's hands swapped from slug to spread and put another hundred nails in their coffins.

Fionn swaggered to his feet and drew his claymore from the twitching Ikadron where he'd left it. "Uill! Halò!"

"Fionn," Wil said and accepted the fist bump. "Howdy."

Kelsie chanced a glance over the desktop, brown eyes bloodshot and streaked with fresh tears. "Cor, Fionnlagh. All of them, just like that?"

Fionnlagh took it as an invitation to bow.

Neil staggered up with his left arm soaked in red from elbow to fingertip, hissing curses and gripping his wound. Reeling a Merovingian auto-tourniquet from his belt that looked like it belonged best in a museum, Fionn hurried over. Neil's protests were both immediate and futile.

Out beyond the entryway, four blinking blue lights faded through the storm.

A dropship. The delegation.

Something had gone wrong.

One by one, the lights of the DRC switched from furious red back to its original calming yellow. The heliport wreathed in a crown of spectral light, silhouetting cargo containers and a waiting third Balena. A one-armed man in white hurtled up the stairs.

Odune.

Wil's earpiece crackled. Incoming call from an unknown person, though he knew who it was. "Lieutenant Wilhelm Gotzinger, speaking."

"I have to hand it to you," Scáthach said, and by her tone of voice, she was smiling. "You've done such a marvelous job."

Unable to clearly hear over the sound of Neil's groans and the motorized tourniquet of the Merovingian tourniquet, Wil stepped away from the group. "Thanks for dropping off the armor. Al's offer stands: leave and we won't follow."

"I'm afraid that won't be possible."

"Dawn's got a space program now. You'd be surprised."

"I meant, for me."

Wil licked his teeth. "I was afraid you'd say that."

"In the morning, the Human Sphere will learn of a devastating Ariadnan terrorist attack on a remote scientific outpost on Dawn, claiming well over a hundred innocent lives and one very, very important one. The period of mourning will be long, and the resulting Conflict even longer. By the time the dust settles, I will be gone, Odune will be dead, and you will be an unvisited memorial page on MayaNet."

"You were the one Glasscock talked to," Wil said.

Her mandibles bruxed together. "Guilty."

"Listening stations will have already registered the gunshots. Automated warnings are blaring on a hundred different channels. No one in a cocktail dress is setting foot in Dun Scaith, lady. Even if you kill us, that special guest y'all are so focused on? They're never showing up. We don't win, but you still lose."

"On the contrary, Captain," Scáthach said. "I was counting on this."

Between the comms array and the heliport, the engine whine of the approaching landing craft intermingled with the unmistakable roar of a TAG's primary engine.

A colossal camouflage shadow lurched atop one of the prefab buildings. Wings jut up from its back, stabilizing its stance as it leveled its enormous weapon skyward. Burning periphery trailed up the rail of its alien Spitfire.

The Sphinx.

The transport craft listed, curving toward the DRC. Its engines whistled, windows misted from its descent through the straggling rainclouds. Fog billowed from its engines, smeared by mirage waves clouding from the port and starboard thrusters. It crested the heliport but didn't stop, lowering down farther, farther, until the starboard doors racked open.

Within, the transport filled with crimson optics and glowing periphery. Swords and MULTI Rifles caught the barest flash of light from the DRC below.

An armored young woman emerged from the throng of waiting knights with a Spitfire in one hand and a gleaming longsword in the other. Blonde hair whipped against her face. With a point of her blade, two gatlings unfolded from the dropship's starboard side and spun.

Their volley rivaled the thunder for control of the sky.

Caught beneath twin lines of destruction, the Sphinx vaulted off its prefab perch and faded between the trees. Scarves of smoke trailed from its ravaged armor in its flickering, thermo-optical wake.

The ship lowered, and the woman disembarked, dropping ten meters to the waiting mud below. She recovered with perfect grace and launched herself across the promenade, screaming, "Knights of Skovorodino, fear nothing! Trust in God, and follow me! *Follow me!*"

It was Joan of Arc.

40

A lifetime ago in Odune's office hallway, he'd swatted away images of the Maid of Orleans and discounted Rajan's knowing grin when he'd insinuated her attendance at the upcoming award ceremony.

But Rajan wasn't guessing. He knew.

There will be no going back.

Scáthach had known, too. Goading them into battle. Forcing their hand. The game in the room Wil wasn't allowed in had been over since the moment they'd left Kildalton, giving them just enough rope to trigger security protocols and bait the security team onboard the *Sword*.

Wil swallowed the lump in his throat. "Odune doesn't have the detonator, does he?"

"Don't worry, Lieutenant," Scáthach said. "The Counselor will die with you. Our masters have endured his vainglorious delusions long enough, and he, too, has outlived his usefulness."

No wonder the Shasvastii had gone so far to slow them. A small army fed into the meat grinder to buy enough time to kill Joan of Arc was only logical, especially in the wake of her first death at Strelsau. But unlike then, there would be no opportunity for escape—nothing left to chance—no third resurrection. With no warning, even to their own allies, Joan's crushed body would sink forever into the cold dark loch with no hope of recovery or rescue. The surviving Shasvastii in the DRC-9 were already burning on the EI's victory pyres.

The ramifications of this moment shook him to his core. The loss of the Maid of Orleans would be a deathblow to the PanOceanian Military Orders that no amount of damage control would ever remedy, widening the pathway for the Combined Army's total victory in the Human Sphere.

Scáthach sighed. "Goodbye, Lieutenant."

Through the comlog, a metallic click.

White light flashed out in the storm. The soft, hollow pop of an air burst brushed down across the administration building lobby. A thousand meters away, a streak of flame tumbled from the clouds, detonating twice more before it went dark within the wide, black expanse of Loch Eil.

Scáthach transmitted static. Signal lost, the connection closed.

Footsteps echoed from the elevator lobby. Alastair, soaked with sweat, face contorted in alarm. "Wil! Wil, I found the support column, but there were no D-charges, no explosives. Are you sure you heard correctly? Are we in the wrong place?"

"I'm sure," Wil said. "Just give him a second."

Alastair paused, and his comlog lit. He stared at its surface for a long moment, face set in grim determination before he accepted the call and shared it to the cluster.

Xandros Odune.

No video. Only a voice, laced with stifled amusement. "Do you think Melantha truly believed I wouldn't notice eight pounds of explosives left primed directly below my office? Three would've sufficed—look what it did to her vessel. Not like it matters. The day, it seems, is yours. Celebrate while you can."

"It's just war," Wil said. "Don't be such a sore loser."

The smug chuckling halted. "You. How."

"Got bored waiting, thought I'd come settle things. Where you at?"

"Would love to meet offline," Alastair said. "If I recall, you and I have an oath to discuss."

Odune cleared his throat. "MacArthur. Captain Gotzinger. Good day."

"Have it your way," Alastair said, and the connection closed.

As Odune's call ended, a second broadcast to the wider network. "Caledonian regiment, this is the PanOceanian Military Order of the Hospital of Skovorodino. We are here to assist you. Please, do not be alarmed."

The red Balena atop the heliport thrummed. Its engine whined, swirling the mist beneath its turbines. Lights flared on its wingtips. Wouldn't be more than three minutes before it was in the air.

Wil racked the boarding shotgun. His fingers quickened along with his pulse.

He made it one step before he forced himself still. No. As much as Odune needed to die, as much as it would guarantee Kildalton's safety, he couldn't leave the MacArthurs behind. Not now, not after everything, not when they had so many wounded. Back in the tunnel, he'd have given anything for revenge—but this was the better he owed them. That he owed himself. The one Saoirse was talking about. And as much as it pained him, Odune would live, but so would the MacArthurs. Even trade. Even—

Steel scraped along the floor. Something heavy impacted his boot.

It was Rhiannon.

Pale and shaking, tourniquet strangling his bicep, Neil still had it in him to flash a cocksure smile. "Give that space invader our Cailean's warmest regards."

Wil hesitated, looking from the machine gun at his feet to the faces all around. "But—the Sphinx," he said. "Our injured."

"All or Nothing," Neil spat. "That's our way."

The dropship crested the ground, and a fireteam of PanOceanian Knights joined Joan of Arc in her dead-set charge after the retreating Sphinx. Its wings flapped, casting violet light over the prefab rooftop. A cascade of Spitfire bullets burst the windows all along the second story promenade.

Fionn stepped forward, claymore restless in his hands. "Nathair-nimhe!"

Kelsie pulled Neil onto her shoulder. "That is *not* a dragon."

Two gouts of flame surged from its forearm into the street, swallowing an abandoned DRC-make AUV. The LAI-piloted vehicle ignited, steam clouding from its chassis before the fuel reserve burst and the air thickened with cascading debris.

Fionn stared at Kelsie, eyes round and insistent. "Bheil thu cinnteach?"

Alastair lifted Rhiannon with reverence. He ran his hand down the engraving on the cover, and traded it for Wil's shotgun. "Not the best at close range, but the most ammo out of anything we've got."

Not as heavy as she was outside of his suit. Not as heavy as she should've been, after everything that'd happened. He opened up the feed pouch to check the remaining H-12. Just enough left over to make some bad decisions.

His armored finger laid comfortable inside the trigger guard. "Orders?"

"We'll rally with the Hospitallers and handle the Sphinx. You pin down Odune and don't let him leave. I don't want to know what kind of evil he might put into the world if—"

Fionn raised his claymore, screamed "Cha gheill!" and sprinted into the night.

Alastair closed his mouth. Suppressed a laugh. "Eisd, o Eisd," he said, and followed after.

And then they were running, the three of them, side by side. Rockets and frag grenades and Double-Action rounds chased them through the fog rising from the ruin of the DRC, splashing up what remained of the storm in their wake.

Passing ordnance buzzed the polysteel of Wil's armor. His periphery stained the mist a hell-bent crimson. Every step sent blades up Wil's legs. Every heartbeat strained and tore the veins that hadn't burst yet. Every meter he bled more, hurt more, breathed harder than the last.

And it felt right.

Fionn closed on the charging Knights Hospitaller. They bristled at his approach until he waved, greeted them with a "Halò!" and joined their formation, gaining on Joan of Arc.

Alastair fell behind, shotgun barking as he clocked and dropped a pair of approaching camouflage shadows. "Give him hell, Wil!"

An enormous cannonade interrupted his charge, sending columns of mud into the air and cutting his path short. The Sphinx, attempting one final stall. He braced himself and risked the gap—only to find a smoke grenade hissing down the lane, covering his flank.

Gordon perched atop an adjacent prefab, a struggling Noctifer choking in his paw. It went for its pistol, but he juiced it with his grip.

A single, solitary nod.

Wil returned it.

Ten meters farther, the foot of the heliport materialized out of the smoke. The whine of the Balena's aerodyne was palpable in his bones, even from six stories above. One-hundred twenty-six steps, same as when he'd came in.

His comlog pinged. Odune. "Let's not be too hasty."

"Let's," Wil said, and took the first step.

"Think of everything you have to lose. Your victory is already apparent. Take it! Celebrate! No need to risk more, to perish seeking something as petty as vengeance. A wise man once said revenge is like drinking poison and hoping the other party dies."

First flight behind him, Wil picked up speed. "Gonna puke it into your fucking mouth."

Around the bend, the air thickened, and the stairs beneath his feet softened like rubber. The railing pivoted and carouseled toward his head. He caught himself on it, just short of careening off the side. His ears buzzed, and a migraine pushed up like a bubble from the core of his spine.

Dazers. Of course. Tucked behind a pair of intersecting metal struts bracing the heliport's support pillar, a small green flower spun. Four H-12 rounds broke it into a million pieces, scattering the last raindrops clinging to the struts.

"My death won't make the Ariadnans accept you," Odune said. "Surely, on some level, you understand that, right? You're an outsider. A *galactic*. Your ancestors murdered theirs, and that grudge will carry on forever, no matter who you marry, no matter who you save."

"Ain't about acceptance," Wil groaned. He righted himself on the steel rail, fanning dead nanobots from the air around him, and carried on. "This is about Cailean. About Hodges. About Bell, and Llowry, and fourteen other people. About me."

Odune clicked his tongue. "First arrogance, now sanctimony. You really are PanOceanian, aren't you?"

A camouflage shadow lurched out from behind the next corner. A silent shotgun burst caught Wil in the chest and keeled him against the railing. Rhiannon dangled over the side. As he recovered, the shadow rushed in. The blade of a translucent CCW refracted against the scant ingress lighting.

Wil unlimbered the Bulldog and sent a to-whom-it-may-concern round up the steps. The T2 .500 bullet transformed the charging thermo-optical trooper from a living being into the approximate contents of a single heavy-duty garbage bag.

Wil spat a mouthful of blood onto his faceplate. Magnetized Rhiannon to his back. Stepped over the mess, and kept climbing.

"All alone, once again, stalking a battlefield with no greater purpose than bloodlust," Odune said. "Some things never change."

"What you said, back in the room. A place of healing, searching for Eden, Paradise—it's all bullshit. Worse, you know it's bullshit, right? You're not on some grand expedition for the Promised Land, man. You're just scared. Hiding. If you really wanted peace, you'd fight for it."

"Jealous words from an imperfect creature," Odune said. "I have no interest in your feeble projections."

Wil refused the bait. "And the worst part is, you and your people had so much in common with the Caledonians here. If you'd only stopped for one second and thought of them as your equal, maybe your dream would still be alive."

"Humans?" Odune stifled a laugh. "*My* equal?"

"I looked down on them, too. On their eccentricities, their superstition, their insistence in living in some bygone era. Took me this long to realize I was laughing at a mirror. And the more I think about it, the more that describes you, too."

"Next you'll say, 'we're the same, you and I.'"

"Nah," Wil said. "In two minutes, I'll still be alive."

The lip of the heliport glowed far above. Close now. As if afraid, the shrill whine of the Balena intensified into a scream. Only one Bulldog T2 round remained; thirty H-12; and after that, his knife. Couldn't waste anything. Had to listen to Cailean's voice in the back of his head and shoot with his eyes, not his geist.

"So quiet," Odune said. "Are you sure you want to do this?"

Wil rounded the corner on the final flight of stairs, Bulldog steady. "Are you? You were scared back in the chamber, talking circles around what the EI would do if you got caught. How long you think you got when you escape—a day, a week? An hour?"

"Don't concern yourself with my future."

"If you have one."

"So presumptuous," Odune seethed. "Humans, disgusting humans with their simpering little jokes, the only animal that doesn't consider itself an animal. Primitive, ultraviolent, uncivilized. You'd all rather die than give up one iota of your precious individuality, one single square inch of your godforsaken planets!"

Wil laughed, dry and soundlessly. "Please, no screaming. I'm right here."

Odune closed the connection.

Past the anchored containers across the heliport, the Balena's aerodynes had entered final prep, maglevs spinning so fast their rush became a constant hum. Rainwater collected in the dips and bumps underfoot, reflecting up the glow of the Balena's myriad lights.

The reflections wobbled. A splash. Light and fire blinded him. Submachine gun. Twin spreads impacted his pauldron, his chest, and the full weight of an invisible assailant slammed against his chest. He stumbled, lost footing, and fell against the railing.

Steel creaked. Bolts ripped free. Gravity took hold, carrying him toward the ledge. Over it.

Red flicked to green in the corner of his HUD. The soles of his feet buzzed. Magnetic anchors clamped to the edge of the pad, arresting his fall. The Bulldog tipped up. One shot, and the camouflaged Shas erupted into bloody purple fireworks.

His visor darkened. An errant splatter. Only lights and vague shapes penetrated through the patina of gore. Wil wheeled his arms for balance, barely returning to the heliport instead of carrying on off the edge. As his visor swiped itself clean, he realized he'd lost the Bulldog to the darkness below.

Nails pushed through his veins with his pulse. He stumbled, shouldering a cargo crate. Hung off it. Fought for breath. All that movement had torn something inside and the anesthetics from the suit had begun to wear off. Exhaustion and bone-deep hurt noosed every joint and muscle in his body, but there was no stopping now.

Wil hefted Rhiannon and limped to the Balena's open cabin doors, clearing corners along the way. Inside, the polished, faux-leather interior gleamed back at him. Empty.

He circled along the cockpit. It was unmanned.

From behind him, words. "Last chance, Cap—"

Wil turned and opened fire. Odune wriggled back, ribcage bursting, and winked out of existence.

Something struck Wil across the back of the helmet. A sledgehammer, or a lightning bolt, or a single shot from a pistol. He hit the concrete in a pile.

"To come this far, to succumb to your injuries," Odune said, ambling out from behind a cargo crate. "So unluck—"

Four HMG shots drew a line up Odune's body from shin to forehead. Knocked off his feet, he vanished in mid-air.

A holoecho. Of course. Nanodirectional, tridimensional, pseudo-solid. The same tech that made Shasvastii vessels invisible, that hid the Sphinx in plain sight. No wonder Odune sometimes felt like he appeared in the torture chamber without ever entering—it was his nanobots, taking his shape as he ghosted on the datasphere using the same real-time projection as Wil's geist did displaying his Neoterran apartment on the DRC domicile walls.

Saoirse's finger had probably been a carrot. The sheer audacity of it gave Wil enough strength to pull to his feet one last time.

Clicking footfalls announced the presence of an Ikadron. It barreled around the Balena, flamethrowers igniting, and Wil's first instinct was to scramble for cover. It didn't fire, only picked up speed, wobbling strangely until it fell into a sprint and its body washed away in a shimmer of color.

Beneath, Odune. One-armed. Wounded. Fast. His heel snapped up and scythed across Wil's chin. Rhiannon's feed tray yanked open, and the remaining belt of H-12 hurled into the night.

Wil swung. Missed. Rhiannon clattered away, and he groped for his knife. Odune's white-gloved hand caught Wil's maneuver mid-draw and slammed the blade back into his thigh. Heavy armor provided little shielding versus Teseum. Blood welled in his boot. Artificial muscle bulged, but he failed to dislodge the knife.

Eyes glowing with violet light, Odune's face split—first into a wicked smile, and then a mess of sloppy mandibles. "Captain Gotzinger! *My word.*"

The steel plating of Wil's thigh screeched. The puncture deepened, and the blade gouged lengthwise along his cuisse and into his rotten knee.

Odune finally earned his scream.

The knife plucked free. Hilted in his stomach, then again. Wil fell, and Odune stomped the side of his helmet hard enough to crack his faceplate open.

Wil writhed. Bled. A thousand competing synapses all screamed to get up, that pain wasn't pain, but his body wouldn't listen, wouldn't move. His vision dimmed, but the quickening in his fingers kept him white-knuckle hanging on to consciousness.

Breath ragged, Odune stared down without expression. Strands of his dark hair splayed over his face. "I warned you," he said. "I tried so hard to keep you away. But you didn't listen. All we ever wanted was to be left alone, Captain, and you refused. Why? Tell me."

Clumsy and shaking, Wil steadied the knife in his stomach. Removing it would only worsen the bleed. Red rushed down the inseam of his duster, clouding the shallow surface of the puddle below, and something small clinked after.

The engraved H-12 bullet.

Rhiannon was not far away.

A flash of white. Of pain. His lips tore against his teeth. The toe of Odune's dress shoe retracted, mottled red and black. "No witty repartee, no *first in all things*? Where's your bravado, your certainty? Or did you really think I wouldn't put up a fight?"

He kicked him again. Wil groaned.

The lights of Dun Scaith below them flickered. The red swapped back to bright, sterile whites, casting a sorrowful glow over the sum total of the night. Shattered windows gaped over broken doors, over the mandibled bodies of Shasvastii pretenders, over piles and piles of H-12 brass.

Odune's mandibles sagged, eyes creased strangely below his ripped-wide mouth. Clumsy, trembling, he raised a hand and drew lines over the landscape.

"The pavilion would've been completed by summer," he said, and the severity and rage in his voice died away. "Live music. Games. Better food than commissary slop, imported fresh from Xanadu, prepared by our people to mimic cuisine from as far as Djassah. Luxury prefabs, there and there, all along the ridge. Our own Shaviish, and with it, actual children. Another year, and there would've been no remaining humans among the personnel. Just my people. And it would've been the closest thing to home in so, so long."

Deep breaths. Slow. Muscles coiled, Wil waited for his moment.

"I can only remember a few things," Odune whispered. "The color of the sky. City lights, receding as the morning arrived. Music—back when we had music. And the twin moons, how they danced on the horizon, threading the coming of the dawn…"

Brass scraped into his palm.

"We were isolated, here. Secret. Autonomous. Safe, truly safe—to live without the specter of extinction haunting us. To escape the war, to rest, to start anew. Another year is all we needed. Just one. One year, and it would've been beautiful. It would've, I know it would've, it had to be…"

Beacon lights glowed through the clouds above, descending toward the outpost—dropships. Reinforcements for the Military Orders.

A violet explosion lit the core of the DRC-9. Odune whipped to face it. Arm outstretched, Wil lunged toward Rhiannon, fingers brushing her strap—

An arm hooked him by the neck. Odune hauled him back. Bloody digits slapped steel, fighting for purchase on the hard planes of his helmet. Pressure between his shoulders. A knee.

Odune's breath ran hot against Wil's ear. "You should've taken the draw."

The twist began under his jaw. Up and to the left. Incredible force. The fiberweave ripped. A snap, and an urgent cold followed after.

Wil slapped to the concrete face-first.

Solemn and sorrowful, Odune rose to his full height. He regarded the DRC-9 one last time, softly whispering his goodbyes to Paradise in his glottal Shasvastii tongue, and limped toward the Balena. The cockpit doors hissed open with a simple gesture, and he reached to climb inside.

Wil surged to his knees. Kicked hard. Rhiannon was in his hands. The feed tray wrenched open, splattered with anti-kinetic gel from the cracked interior of his gorget. WILHELM glinted in his fingers. He jammed it into the open slot, breath shaking, and—

There were three Odunes.

They each split and dashed away, each seeking different cover. He'd lost track of him in the draw. Any of them could be the real one under the holoscreen. If he hesitated, they'd disappear. Escape. And Wil would bleed out, sprawled in a rain puddle atop this godforsaken heliport.

Blood cascaded over his left eye, wincing it shut. A startling numbness seized his leg from thigh to toe. Sickening electricity churned through his guts and his lungs, radiating from the knife buried deeper now after his dive.

They all had the same smirk.

No faceplate, no lenses, no geist. No help.

One shot. One guess.

He drew a long, solitary breath. Aimed. And for the length of one trigger, Rhiannon belonged in his arms like he'd been born holding her and just now remembered.

Two holoechoes snapped out of existence. Odune stumbled, spun. He collapsed across the open Balena door with a grunt and a clatter, absent a fist-sized chunk of his skull. His ivory-white dress suit drank up the crimson, then violet, then more, until the fabric swelled and the slurry dripped from the seams.

Odune stared up, mandibles groping without sound. Shock became confusion, became an inquiry. He needed to know what he'd done wrong. How he'd been outsmarted, his tell, the hint—his single fatal error after such a long, smug life.

Wil said, "I was aiming for the other one."

Odune tremored. Bled.

Furious tears raced down his cheeks, and he died.

Steel scraped against the heliport slab. Rhiannon fumbled from his arms. Anti-kinetic gel oozed out of his collar into his hair, mixing among the puddle beneath. Eyelids heavy, he tried to watch the sky, watch the lights descend down toward him, listen to the distant, celebratory voices, but everything was so blurry, so meaningless, so far away.

Until the sound of thunder echoed over the highlands, breaking the surface of Loch Eil.

41

Warmth across his face.

Wil opened his eyes, and a DRC prefab ceiling stared down at him. Laser-diode lights. Domotic smart-cleaned paneling, clean as the day it came out of the Teseum cradle. Milk white linen surrounded him, and his arms were wrapped in gauze.

A medical suite.

Terror threw him upright, one leg dangling from the bedside. His head spun wild on his shoulders, and it took everything in him to focus, to calm. Seeking the source of the warmth, he forced himself to look.

Sunlight shined through a window beside his bed. Beyond the glass, the DRC-9 stretched out before him, brightly lit and bustling. Vehicles circled overhead, both Ariadnan and not. PanOceanian researchers, O-12 peacekeepers, and Caledonian Highlanders mingled up and down the switchback paths. A trio of Kappa patrolled down the road below, accompanied by a handsome Knight of Justice with her helmet tucked under her arm. Out by the pavilion, Fionnlagh perched atop the headless chassis of the Sphinx.

The warmth had been Helios's light. Barely a cloud in sight in every direction.

For an instant, Wil saw red hair.

He leapt to his feet. Instantly regretted it. Agony toppled him back into the bed sheets, teeth clenched, chaining words that would've made Señor Massacre blush. He searched for their source. Steel splints. Tape. Tubes pinched into his arm, his belly, and his chest, opaque fluid trickling from the ports of a sleek, meter-tall medical Palbot in standby at his bedside.

His kneecap was wholly numb, strangled in layers of gauze. No longer sickeningly warm, or swollen. A stent drained pale fluid from inside, and he couldn't wiggle his toes.

The door sighed open. Four heavily armored knights of the Military Orders shadowed the entryway, menacing weapons magnetized to their hips and backs, swords displayed prominently on their archaic cowskin belts. Hospitaller,

Santiago, Teutonic. One by one, the three warriors regarded him before parting. A cloaked young woman strode past them. Among the armored giants, her tall, lithe frame appeared small.

"Privacy, please," Joan of Arc said, voice so much softer than he thought it'd be.

Under her vibrant red hood, the Maid of Orleans' blonde hair was tied back into a lace braided bun, perfectly symmetrical face framed by brow-length bangs and shoulder-length fringes. The black-and-white cross of the Knights Hospitaller displayed prominently along her right pauldron. Her eyes were the most perfect blue Wil had ever seen, the exact color of her Series 3 ORC Mobility Powered Combat Armor.

The door shut. With a single gesture, the glass in the window frosted over until the sunny day beyond blurred into obscurity and they were alone. She strode to his bedside, and Wil's first instinct was to attempt to dismiss the holo-ad.

"Lieutenant." Joan held out her hand. "It's a pleasure to meet you."

Her armored grip was cold. "Likewise," he mumbled, and wished he hadn't. "Apologies, ma'am, I—"

Joan's smile was an interruption all its own. "The local Caledonian forces have been exceptionally concerned for your survival," she said, removing her cloak and sword. "I'll be glad to tell them you're awake and communicating."

Wil sat up, wincing as his dead leg dragged. "The MacArthurs mean well, ma'am. And they're very capable."

"I know."

There was the taste of his foot, again. "Of course."

Joan leaned her blade against the Palbot's chassis, and, straightening her tabard, sat. "I must apologize. If I'd have known that nominating you for security detail on Dawn would've meant all this, I would've waited another month until I could request your presence at Skovorodino itself."

Dots connected. Connections clicked. "You're the one who recommended me to Rajan."

"I only wanted to meet," Joan said. "But God had other plans for us."

"Us—as in, *us*, us," he stammered. "Why?"

"To lend counsel to your soul," she said, as if it was a very normal thing to say. "On Neoterra, any passive observer's unknowing glance might be combed over by a third party and disseminated over Maya. On Dawn, in these far, disconnected reaches? Far more private. If it were only myself I had to worry about, we would have had this conversation soon after Ulveslør, but I suppose late is worth more than never."

He gripped the hem of the bedsheet. "So it's about Svalarheima?"

"In a way," she said. "I've read your doctor's medical brief. You've gone through a terrible ordeal, Wilhelm. Shot down. Taken captive. Tortured."

"I'm sorry, ma'am. Things spiraled out of control."

"The blame is mine," Joan insisted. Her gauntlet laid atop his fist. "I regret the amount of harm this has caused you, Lieutenant, even unintentionally. Your actions last night saved my life, and the lives of countless others. PanOceania owes you a debt of gratitude that can never be repaid."

Wil evened out his breathing. Gave himself a moment and still only came up with, "You're welcome."

"I've spoken to Alastair MacArthur at great length regarding the situation, your sacrifices, and his people's injury," she said. "I believe I've come to a comprehensive understanding of what has transpired here. The only thing missing is your account, and if you'll honor me, I would like very much to hear it."

Now that, he had a lot to say about.

⸙

The crash. Rajan. Odune. Fort Resolute. The Battle for Dun Scaith. Hell, he even dropped in the bar fight and the jog over the highlands, but only because she seemed interested. By the time he was crossing the T on The End, Helios had climbed from one end of the horizon to the other.

Joan eagerly soothed his deepest, most urgent worry: "The Shasvastii under the command of the false Xandros Odune have been purged from the local area, thanks to the intel provided by the MacArthur Volunteer. Most, by their own clan's hand. And not only that, but microbes left on their embedded soldiers' equipment has offered leads toward several coordinates for a possible Shaviish—the nest where the Shasvastii keep their spawn embryos. We've forwarded the details to the relevant authorities on Dawn."

The irony of Odune's reckless desire to remain hidden burning his people's cover planet-wide didn't escape him, and for a single, solitary moment, he almost felt bad for the guy. If he'd never shot him down, if he'd never panicked and pulled that trigger, none of this would've ever happened. Shasvastii were the ultimate survivors, harnessing their paranoia to hone an unparalleled survival instinct. But all Odune's instincts had earned him was an autographed H-12 bullet sent direct from Cailean Rutledge.

"And the DRC-9," Wil said. "What's its fate after all this?"

"A change in personnel, more stringent attention from Bureau Gaea and Ganesh, and a new liaison to handle relations with the local populace," Joan said. "He's a twenty-year veteran, and quite enamored with the idea of connecting with the people here. Apparently, he's part Scottish on his great-great-grandmother's side."

Yeah. Good luck leading with that, pal.

Eideard Carr had surfaced after the battle, attempting to blend in with a gaggle of terrified service personnel. According to him, he was innocent in all of this—a blameless bystander. But unfortunately, a Crosier hacker's rudimentary LAI combed the base-wide surveillance footage and caught a conversation far more incriminating than the one Wil had heard two days ago. Smuggling. Treason. Human trafficking. Until Rodina spared the time to throw him in a cell, he'd remain in O-12 custody at the DRC-9.

Joan adjusted her blonde bangs in an invisible sensorium mirror. "We've sent a small group back to Kildalton via air transport, accompanied by Alastair MacArthur, to assess Mr. Brizuela's physical state. And then, when your recovery here is settled, our business on Dawn will be concluded. Everything else is best left to local government."

His recovery. *Our* business.

Somehow, in the chaos and bloodshed of the last few days, Wil had forgotten why he'd ever come to the DRC to begin with. Leaving Dawn had always been secondary to reclaiming his sullied valor, and finding redemption in the arms of the people who once despised him.

"There is also the matter of this," Joan said. She reached into the pocket of her cloak and retrieved a small brass object and placed it in Wil's hands. Cailean's H-12 round, sans bullet. Besides some residue and stretching, the empty case was pristine.

"I thought that cartridge was a threat. I found it next to your body, along with the AKNovy K—"

"*Rhi*—the machine gun," he blurted. "It's important to me. Is it safe?"

That she still tolerated his shitty manners was incredible. "Private Mc-Dermott was insistent in safeguarding it. He said it was an heirloom. Beautiful engraving."

Wil's breath snagged in his lungs. "Your geist. It translated it."

"Thig crìoch air an t-saoghal, ach mairidh gaol is ceòl," Joan recited, tone far too mechanical to be truly authentic. "It's an old Irish proverb: *The world may one day end, but love and music will last forever*."

Despite the creaking of his battered ribs, Wil failed to suppress his laughter. The old bastard might've been Teseum on the outside, but on the inside, Cailean Rutledge was softer than Svalarheima powder.

The way he would've lost his mind over Joan of Arc bringing 'the ALEPH' out to Dawn—Wil would've given anything to listen in.

Joan sighed. "I hoped a month on an idyllic mountainside far away from the bustle of Neoterra would put your mind at ease. I'd prepared an offer of employment as assistant chief of security at a Skovorodino satellite compound, and was keen to see if you would accept it."

He furrowed his brow, unable to read her intentions. "Why?"

"God doesn't abandon His children," she said. "Neither should PanOceania."

Ultimately, Joan's sole worry was the commercial attaché chosen for the job, Rajan, and his checkered history with women. Her personal query into the redactions in his file likely tipped the simpering nepot off as to the secret of her visit, and like a real, true son of a bitch, he'd kept it hidden from the MacArthurs for one last impotent twist of the knife.

"We'd already had some concerns," Joan said. "Two weeks ago, Rajan Brizuela's Cube broadcast a distress signal for two minutes. His vital signs showed recent injury—and a heavy pressure on the throat. We think he was being choked.

The search party dispatched from our forward base in Capa Blanca entered the distress radius and reported it a systems malfunction due to Teseum interference. I've been told their bodies were found on the outskirts of a nearby settlement."

Something in his Teseum shackle must've interfered with Rajan's comms. Funny that the quickest solution to his problems would've been choking Rajan all along. He told her the search party's fate, but kept his mouth shut about the rest.

As for their tip-off to the danger at the DRC, Joan went into detail: After departing from Neoterra, the *Sword of St. Catherine* arrived in the Helios system via Circular. They'd entered final preparations to disembark the delegation to the DRC-9 when a PanOceanian SOS was intercepted broadcasting from the ruins of Fort Resolute along the AEZ. The signal was indecipherable, carried on an ancient HF radio channel, but led to the discovery of a litany of similar signals warning them of the Shasvastii presence.

The Knights bodyguarding the delegation had planned for ball gowns and black ties. Instead, thanks to Fusilier Glasscock's timely broadcast, they'd arrived sporting MULTI Rifles and broadswords instead.

And as for the hero himself, they'd found Glasscock's corpse fifty meters down the mountainside from where they'd spoken last. Judging by the state of his remains, he'd run headlong into the radius of several antipersonnel mines, assuming its IFF was keyed to PanOceania and not the SEF.

The frosted surface of the bedside window reflected little save for Wil's scowl. "I'm sorry to hear that, ma'am. I wish I could've done more."

"More?"

"Helped him," he said. "Made him come with me, even if it meant kicking his ass and putting him over my shoulder."

His bed frame creaked. Joan had come closer when he wasn't looking, one knee on the mattress. Too close. Her eyes blazed with fanatical light. "You truly believe you could've done more. Remarkable."

Wil shrank back. "Ma'am?"

"Your performance last night intrigued me, Lieutenant. Every moment from don to doff was recorded by the ORC's rudimentary geist. The wounds you sustained? The pain, the suffering? That you're able to talk to me right now is frankly impressive."

"Had a hard time," he said. "Thanks for patching me up."

"You have an inimitable talent, something very few modern PanOceanian soldiers possess. Fortitude. Courage. *Conviction*."

"I mean, I'd prefer to not be tone deaf, but—"

"Your skill, your acumen, your leadership? Phenomenal. You laid low *three* Speculo, a Gwailo, a fireteam of Jayth, and four warrens worth of Taigha. You led a band of Atek warriors into the lion's den—outnumbered, outskilled, outclassed—and seized victory."

"Respectfully, ma'am, I wouldn't be here without the MacArthurs."

Joan drew even closer. The flecks in her irises were perfectly symmetrical on both sides. "This miracle proves my suspicion that God has placed you in this crucible for a reason, Wilhelm. I thought that by coming here, I would offer some small comfort to an abandoned son of PanOceania. Instead, I want to extend to you an offer of commission with the Svalarheima Blizzard-6 Force stationed in Trollhättan."

Wil didn't usually blank.

"The Human Sphere requires men like you to survive what comes next," she said. "God forgives all sin to those who repent. Return to the fold, Wilhelm. Lead. Fight. This service is what He has intended for you."

To go back to Svalarheima, to find a purpose there—it felt right. Good.

But the more Wil considered going back to his old life, the more he couldn't imagine it. After twelve days in Kildalton, a week in the highlands, and two days in Odune's chair, he'd changed. And when he thought of Saoirse sitting alone at her spot in the Croatoan, the more he wanted to get back there and give that rubber-band-flavored whisky a second go.

"When we left Kildalton," Wil said, "it was because I told myself I wanted to save some innocent people. For the good of it, not the gain. But now I know I really did it for this. For this moment."

She took his hands. "Yes. You did."

"But now I'm thinking, why did I care? What was so good about the life I used to have? Why do I need forgiveness for something that wasn't my fault to begin with?"

Her grip slacked. "This is a long preamble to acceptance."

"It's not," he said, and pulled away. "I'm staying here."

Joan of Arc fell back into her chair, betrayal simmering in her perfect eyes. "A PanOceanian soldier defecting to the Ariadnan Army. I've never had such a serious crime confessed to my face."

"Not the Ariadnan Army," Wil said. "The MacArthurs."

"And what difference does that make?"

"I guess that's up to you."

Joan studied his expression for what felt like a full sixty seconds. Then her gaze fell away, and she said, "Existence precedes essence."

Wil furrowed his brow. "Is that... Sartre?"

"Human beings aren't like ashtrays," she said. "For an ashtray, its essence precedes its existence—it is purpose-made, whereas man first exists and is defined after. Sartre used that statement as a way to disprove God."

Philosophy. Okay. He'd play ball. "And how does God feel about that?"

"When God created man, He gave us the free will to choose our own path, even if that meant falling into sin by turning from Him. Forcing you onto a path of my choosing would mean defying God, and would be meaningless besides. Involuntary acts cannot redeem us."

"And that makes me not an ashtray."

"Not by any definition," she said.

He couldn't help himself. "Are you?"

Joan smiled, bright and beatific. "Consider it my rebellion that, in a world of those who refuse their calling, I am the drum on which God beats out His message."

Damn. And without even a pause to consider.

Beam fading, she studied his expression. "Are you sure of this, Wilhelm? You want to give up your entire life on the chance you'll be allowed to stay. This isn't something you return from."

"I'm sure," he said.

After a long exhale, Joan's indignant tension evaporated. "Well. Alright, then."

Wil crooked a brow. "I thought—"

"Forcing you to serve God would, in itself, be a sin. And pointless."

"You're letting me go?"

"Yes."

"Why? What about God's plan, or Blizzard-6?"

She faltered, and the glint in her eye was like fire once again. "One life is all we have, and we must live it as we believe. To sacrifice what you are, and live without belief... that is a fate more terrible than death."

Scáthach's words from the mountainside echoed back to him: *A certain level of controlled rebellion.* Given the choice to believe that Joan was following her convictions over maintaining ALEPH's quota of reasonable resistance, Wil chose the former—if only to make it easier to sleep at night.

Joan rose and collected her things. Her sword magnetized to her hip, and her cloak splayed over one shoulder. Out from its pocket, she produced a widget no larger than her thumb. His Cube, meticulously sanitized.

"Proof of Wilhelm Gotzinger's death," she said. "I'll return with this to the NeoVatican. It's unlikely anyone will petition for your resurrection, so don't concern yourself with pulp-fiction fantasies. Though, perhaps one day, a hundred years from now, you may live again."

Doubt lingered, cold on the back of his neck. The dented primer of Cailean's H-12 round indented in his thumb and brought him a measure of focus.

Joan paused, hand against the doorframe. "One last thing," she said. "When you were facing Odune on the heliport, after he split into three holoechoes. I watched the surveillance footage. You said it was a misfire, but your shot seemed very intentional."

Wil chuckled. "Honestly, I just said that to piss him off."

"How did you know which was the real one?"

"His shoes," he said and slumped against his pillows. "Pressure made the smart fabric turn black. I thought, does his holoprojector know what's going on under his feet until they're raised? I guessed not. So I looked for a dark flicker, and then..."

Joan raced to interrupt. "But a holoecho is a perfect duplicate of its user. The domotics in Odune's clothing seamlessly connect to the holoprojector's control suite. Every detail, including external factors, would be duplicated—including raindrops on a shoe sole."

"Which I know now," Wil said. "But Odune's dumb bullshit didn't count on the rain puddles left by the storm, and only one copy tracked footprints on the concrete."

The Maid of Orleans considered him for a long time, lips turned inward as if she were expecting something else. Divine inspiration. Deific whispers. She gave him the barest of nods. "Of course."

"Ma'am?"

Joan stopped short. Hope sparkled anew in her gentle blue eyes. "Yes?"

"People around here say that PanOceania was a mistake," Wil said. "You're the first person I ever met who made me think it could be fixed."

She smiled—the same as on her poster—and walked out of the room.

Epilogue

Cold. Freezing, actually. Worse. Air iced his naked upper torso. Groggy, he rolled over and lifted to his elbows, bunching up the comforter and the quilt over his shoulder. He reached out for warmth, but Saoirse wasn't in her spot.

A gentle wooden thump urged him awake. It was Saoirse, sat on the edge of her bed, pawing in the nightstand drawer. Morning light bled through the curtains to paint her naked back, heavy shadows drawn across the hills and valleys of her tattooed physique. She slid the drawer shut with a halting creak and turned to face him wearing only a ghost of a smile.

He mustered a sigh. "It's cold, baby. C'mon."

Whispering apologies, she slipped back beneath the covers, drawing him to her side. Despite the snow piled against the windowsills that turned the air to ice, she radiated heat as always. There was no more comfortable pillow.

"Wee shivering blueberry," she said, kissing his forehead between each word. "I'll keep ye warm."

He held her closer. "Merry Christmas, Saoirse Clarke."

Wool scraped along his neck. He propped open one eye, curious, and found a long, dark sock still covered Saoirse's left hand. Carefully, he pried it off her claws, tossed it aside, and interwove his fingers in hers. It was impossible not to kiss her knuckles, the back of her hand, her wrist.

Saoirse tipped his chin up. "Havin' fun?"

Wil kissed her, and then some more. Along the new scar on her nose, tilted left-to-right from temple to cheekbone. Onto her jaw, in the places she liked best. He took her head in his hands and scratched her hard behind the ears, which is where she drew the line.

She climbed atop him. "The hell'd those socks go."

He held in a grunt. Big girl. Kind of heavy. "Wait, wait. I'm still recovering."

"From last night, or the time before?"

"Both," he laughed.

"I'll lick it better," she said, and buried her face in his neck.

He'd missed this, the last three months. Her. Her room, clean as the beach after a Varuna superstorm. The trash metal band posters; the loose kettle bells; the old clothing, piled everywhere and on everything; even the cobwebs up in the rafters. But Saoirse had a duty out in the wilderness, and he had one here in Kildalton.

Three more months, and he'd have her for the summer. He had to focus on that tonight, and what was in the night stand, and a hundred other things all vying for his—

She bit. Hard. And again. After the third nibble, he pried her away. "Hey, no chewing. That's against the Concilium Convention."

Saoirse giggled and grinned. "Just glad yer still here, is all. Gotta keep checking to make sure I'm not dreaming."

"Where else would I be?" Wil kissed the heel of her palm. "If we weren't shacked up in your brother's castle, it'd be a different story. Promise."

"Sounds like *someone* should've cleaned his flat better."

"It's barely a closet," he said. "Your feet would stick out the window."

She laid across his chest. "Mayhaps ye should get a real job, eh?"

"Hey, c'mon. I'm trying. And until then, the gun range is real work."

"Not if Sharlene's still doin' everything herself."

"Yeah, well, when her last kid flies the nest she's heading back to Springfield with her husband," Wil said. "Until then, I'm happy to teach kids firearm safety and inventory the armory until Al needs an escort to the DRC or Rodina."

"Ye better."

"And I wanted to say… thanks. Don't know if I said it enough yesterday, but sixty klicks is a long way to come in the middle of winter for one holiday you don't really care about."

"Hopefully not the last comin' I do," she said, and he shoved her aside to her great disappointment.

With the covers messed, the warmth faded. They bundled back together beneath them. Her hair tickled his face, and his stubble scraped her shoulder. They breathed in the same cadence, in the same way. Eyes closed. Limbs knotted, holding each other.

Saoirse traced his jawline with her claw and asked, "Want your present early?"

He knew by her tone she didn't intend any innuendo. "Surprise me."

"Same," she said, and sat up. "Alright. Christmas time. Got yer knee?"

Wil picked the ugly quantronic sleeve from the puddle of his clothing. It left sleep mode, and lights threaded down the brace. "Yes, ma'am."

"Need help?"

"I'll manage," he said, and hauled his bum leg out from under the comforter. Months on, and his biografted replacement still ached when it was cold. "Do your thing."

Saoirse hurried out of bed and into her bathroom, donning his shirt along the way. Wil admired the view for as long as he was allowed, and when the door shut, he barreled over the bed to the night stand on the other side. Beneath old receipt papers, dog-eared books, and Wil's double-refurbished Detour—a small, dark box, undiscovered despite its awful hiding place.

Wil rotated it in his palm. Popped it open. Admired the white engagement ring inside: Silicone, just like she'd requested. He hoped she'd appreciate the humor, but there was still enough time to consider every reason why she wouldn't, and if he might've missed the perfect opportunity three minutes ago in bed.

The door rattled. Gordon growled from the other side. "Oi. Lovebirds. Y'know what time it is?"

Wil sifted through the laundry piles obscuring the floor, searching for last night's boxers. "Ten minutes!"

"Nora come all the way up from Scone to see you ragged lot. This is how you repay her?" The knob jiggled. "Door's locked, let—"

Wil was about to apologize when Saoirse stretched from the bathroom door, toothbrush clutched like a dagger. "For the love of God, Kicklighter, ye open that door and I'll skelp yer furry arse an' cosplay a bloody Bearpode with it! He said ten minutes!"

He grunted. "Mary and Joseph. Fine. Five, then we're sending in a search party."

She cackled and spoke in Caledonian: "Happy Christmas, Gordon."

"Happy Christmas to both of you," he replied, and thumped on down the hall.

The ring box burned a hole against the small of Wil's back.

Like every morning, slipping on his knee brace iced him to the bone. Antiquated servos tightened to his skin, supporting his weight as he groaned to his feet. Nothing popped up on his comlog screen requiring immediate attention, and like clockwork, his default geist pushed its daily reminder: IT'S BEEN 245 DAYS SINCE YOU ENABLED SILENT MODE. SHOULD I REMAIN IN SILENT MODE?

Yes.

Wallet, check. Keys, check. Brace, on. Clothes, worn. Keys and jacket, done. Dog tags, on, though he hated the chill of the steel on his skin.

Something was missing.

Wil ran his fingers over the mess of the nightstand, in the pockets of his old jeans, in Saoirse's leather jacket. No dice. Worry spurred him. His comlog's flashlight revealed nothing under the chairs, under the bed, and he limped in circles hoping to find—

There, on the vanity below the cabinet. A scratched brass H-12 case engraved with the name WILHELM, balanced precariously atop Saoirse's comlog. She'd sniffed out the gunpowder residue from the floor and put it there for him to find.

Wil ran his thumb over the etching, but didn't touch the primer.

No reason to.

The vanity cabinet had been shut when they'd arrived, but in the chaos and motion of their two-month reunion, it'd unlatched. The morning light reflected from a thin streak within. There was a mirror inside.

He pushed the cabinet shut.

Saoirse lumbered out of the bathroom wearing Wil's Santa hat and asked if he'd seen her 'good trainers' as if that meant anything to him at all. When he failed to understand, she kissed him on the forehead and lovingly called him useless.

Downstairs, the halls bustled with soldiers and citizenry. Any thought of security or secrecy had been erased in the Yule tide, and in the DFAC, an enormous Ariadnan pine stood swirled with tinsel and shotgunned with orbs and ornaments. Its tallest point was topped with an ancient fire safety hazard wrought in the shape of a star.

A colossal blade laid mounted upon the stone wall beneath the scorched wings of the Sphinx who'd carried it.

Food and music and laughter sped the morning along. Every passing moment meant new arrivals, sending cheers and calls echoing up the halls. Soon, the crowd had grown so vast that the only seat available was on the foyer stairs. There, he listened to Nora gripe about how the city kids from Scone mocked her for 'ken like,' and how concerned they became whenever she brought up her Volunteer service in class.

"My roommate asked me if I killed people," Nora said. "How am I s'posed to answer that?"

"Personally, I alternate between 'today?' and 'with what.'"

"Unreal," she sighed. "I might never bring up Volunteering again. Makes everyone look at me different. Gonna just say I was in the motorpool, like my mum does."

Wil clinked his glass atop hers. "Congratulations, Eleanor McDermott. You're officially a veteran."

Conversation leaned toward the other members of the task force, and if they'd be attending. According to Nora, mostly no. She shared a video Kelsie had sent from Xanadu Station, detailing her training in zero-g as a preamble to joining the Scots Guards and earning her azure bandanna. Next stop: Kosmoflot, where Fionn had gone to join the Varangians after Dunne's mercenary group dissolved. And as for Pellehan, his near-lethal brush with an alien Spitfire was enough to convince him to turn himself in and retire.

"Nicest jail cell I've ever seen in my life," Nora admitted. "Bunk's bigger than anywhere I've ever lived. And his telly's bigger, too."

"Dunne ever make it to Varuna?" Wil asked.

"Sends me pictures, sometimes. Beaches and sunsets."

He tipped back his whisky. "And Neil. Is he not coming, or what?"

"Sent him a comlog message. No reply. Last I heard, there was some big test for the 3rd Grey Rifles, and that he'd know if he was one or not by the time he hit Kildalton. If we ask Alastair, you think he'll ken more?"

Saoirse draped over their shoulders, cheeks glowing like roses beneath her freckles. "With all the work to be done buildin' the joint outpost, meetin' with the galactics, playin' envoy with O-12—and the business with Eideard? I'd be surprised if my brother remembered it was Christmas today."

After the DRC-9, Eideard trotted out a hundred different excuses. Medicine; security; diplomacy. None mattered—his negligence and greed had gotten Ariadnan citizens killed. By autumn, Rodina had begun a search and rescue operation for Kildalton citizens sold to the mines on Tanit, and Eideard had been extradited to a more permanent prison in Marp. Sentencing was in a few weeks, and things weren't looking great.

"He's still my uncle," Alastair said. "He deserves what happens next, but I'll be there beside him until the end—whether that's in a cell or an execution chamber."

Gentle ruthlessness.

After a few weeks, the situation at the DRC-9 wormed its way onto every comlog screen in the township. Firsthand accounts, exposés, and hard home truths cycled on Maya, on Arachne, on the local cluster. In the end, Cecilia Reese—better known by her moniker as Hmph—proved the straw upon the proverbial camel's back. Her great-uncle's hired Cube Jäger ducked the Winter Dancers to retrieve her body from the cairn in Achadh nan Darach, and she'd been resurrected before the end of summer. Her testimony as to Rajan's own personal failings, complete with audio logs and bank account statements, led to an inquiry by O-12's Section Statera, by Rodina, by basically everybody, and Rajan's daddy had gone bankrupt in the bribing. After seven months in limbo, locked down in a threadbare DRC domicile, Rajan was finally discharged and shoved aboard the Circular home.

Wilhelm Gotzinger III's death was barely a footnote.

Willem Arturo Díaz Ortega preferred it that way.

It wasn't long until the next big thing wiped the Battle for the DRC-9 from the collective consciousness. Calls for peace and unity in the face of the inevitable march of the Combined Army petered out, replaced by ads for Eco Cars, Myrmidon Wars reruns, and The Go-Go Marlene! Show, ONLY ON OXYD!

Evening fell, and with it, the entire township lit up in a riot of winter color. Children from the village shrieked and raced among the banks out on the castle lawn, bundled in new winter wear delivered via DRC drones from parts unknown. On the eastern mountainside, the Teseum mine glimmered. Maybe operational again. Maybe soon. Only time would tell.

After Alastair had been coaxed from his upstairs office—or dragged, if his complaints weren't exaggerated—the five of them settled outside by a fire pit, crowding a bottle of whisky. They passed it around. Sang songs. Told stories until the ground felt malleable and the winter sky trailed with burning green aurorae. And when their *aqua vitae* ran dry, Wil volunteered to fetch another.

"Bring a shot for Cailean," Alastair said. "Still need to visit him and Rhiannon."

"And Robert," Nora added.

Saoirse pulled Gordon into a headlock. "And one for me, for courage!"

"Hey," Gordon laughed. "Don't be so obvious."

Wil slipped through the kitchen door, down the hall to the main foyer. In the corridor, a pair of fresh Volunteers home from mandatory military service cast a withering glare his way, mumbling Caledonian into their cups.

Galactic. Traitor. Coward. But it didn't bother him. He'd been called worse by people who meant it more.

Within seconds of sneaking into Saoirse's bedroom, he kicked a kettle bell and cursed his way over to the nightstand drawer. The ring box was still there, but when he popped it open, the engagement ring inside had turned silver.

This wasn't right. It was silicone—he was so sure—but how had—

Oh. So that's what she'd been doing in the morning. Saoirse had used the same hiding place and taken the wrong box.

This ring was meant for him.

Like two ships in the storm, rudderless and careening, masts hooked together yet somehow still sailing on when any other vessels would've sunk—what were the odds of two total disasters like them finding each other in an ocean of a hundred-billion stars?

The world may one day end, but love and music will last forever.

Wil stayed in the room until the nervous laughter had faded, along with his fear. Alone, he lingered in front of the vanity cabinet for much longer than he should have.

And hooked it open.

A stranger he hadn't seen in a long, long time stared back at him from the mirror there. Big guy. Tall, but not impressive. Olive skin, a shade lighter than his mother. Hair dark, short-cut. Muscular once, out of practice now. Prominent crow's feet stretched beneath brown eyes, face weathered from years spent baking under the Paradiso sun. Handsome, but not if you looked closely: Three different jags along the bridge of his nose told the story of how few fistfights he'd been on the winning side of. Thin, pale scars dotted his forehead, his neck, his temple, each from a different near-miss: chain shrapnel, Taigha bite, bolt wrench. One corner of his lips was darker than the other from a split that didn't heal right, and fading brands laddered up his forearms in jagged intervals like the stripes on a tiger's back.

Nothing special. The kind of guy you meet every day and never remember.

Cheers echoed from the main rooms. Applause. No doubt Neil, fashionably late and bringing good news. Best to hurry back, to bring Saoirse his ring and receive hers in kind. Shouldn't keep the party waiting.

Wil chanced a glance back to the stranger in the mirror, to the man he'd become since Ulveslør, since Kildalton, since Dun Scaith, past the limp and the scars and the thrice-broken nose.

He looked happy.

And he deserved it.

Acknowledgements

There's quite a few people I need to thank for helping in the making of this book. First off, Brandon and Vince Rospond, for taking a chance on a total unknown based off 1500 words. Secondly, Gutier Lusquiños, for creating the world of Infinity.

The writers and readers who have inspired and supported me: Madason McCombs, Ben Kovac, Mark Barber, Ryan Patrick, Robert McKinney, Sill Bahagia, Tom Schadle, and so, so many more who vetted a line or let me bald-faced steal their words. Thank you so much for your insight, your expertise, everything. Without you all, this wouldn't be half the book it's become—most of the good parts were your ideas.

Christopher Willett made sure this book had a cover, and to that I'm eternally grateful. To the many people who made sure that happened—Dave Peterson, Jackson Probst, Steven Schmidt, Jon Tse, Obadiah Hampton, Jo Tucker, Timothy Teats, Dylan Peters, Edwin Perez, Brian Solomon, Bill Faint, Dan Barnaby, Clay Lundy, Aaron Fortner, Scott Tipsword, Allen Emlet, Keith Sutton, Randy Johnson, Damond Crump, David Seley, Hilco van 't Hof, Wojciech Pukrop, Matt Sproats, the inimitable Lee, Tim Toolen, and the amazing Jeff Rossiter at Shiv Games—thank you, forever thank you.

For all my Caledonian brothers and sisters who I've met, played against, lost and won with, I tried to mention all of you by name in the text. Thanks for keeping our little discontinued army alive.

Dawn is Ours.

Find out more about Infinity and Corvus Belli at:
https://www.infinitytheuniverse.com
and
https://www.corvusbelli.com

Look for more books from Winged Hussar Publishing, LLC – E-books, paperbacks, and Limited Edition hardcovers. The best in history, science-fiction and fantasy at:

https://whpsupplyroom.com
https://www.wingedhussarpublishing.com

or follow us on Facebook at

Winged Hussar Publishing LLC

Or on Twitter at:

WingHusPubLLC

for more information on upcoming publications.

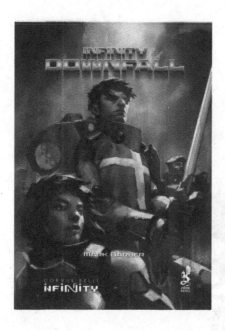

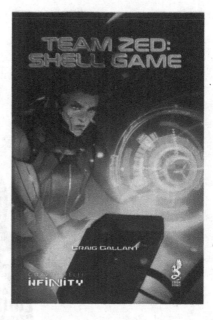